# BLACK WITCH DEATH MAGE

## SISTER SEEKERS BOOK 5

BY
### A.S. ETASKI

Published by Corpus Nexus Press
ISBN: 978-1-949552-09-6

etaski.com
patreon.com/etaski
goodreads.com/etaski
bookbub.com/authors/a-s-etaski
facebook.com/asetaski
twitter.com/asetaski

Cover Design by Eris Adderly
Book design by Guido Henkel

*Dedicated to those who protect others*

*and can feed the soul from afar.*

# CHAPTER 1

GAVIN'S ANSWER TO ONE OF MY FIRST QUESTIONS ON THE SURFACE, the usefulness of horses, was proven upon the Midway.

After scrambling out of the rocky canyon where I'd left him overnight, the Ma'ab Hellhound had been hostile claiming the lead of our group in his unsettled state. Castis, who'd been unconscious and tied to his mount, soon woke being so jostled by the pace. His mood was as foul as his Ma'ab brother's.

"Release me!" the mage demanded.

At the indignant voice, Kurn pulled hard on his black stallion's reins, slowing up and turning to circle us. He growled at the Dwarf, "Do it."

Wordless and wary, Rithal moved his stout pony closer and cut Castis's ropes so the Ma'ab mage could right himself. The two pale men glared at me, as if it had been my idea to tie the Noble down and leave the camp that moment, rather than Kurn's.

I returned their twin scowls with an insolent smile. "Odd. Do we run from something?"

"Silence, witch," Kurn said, turning again and kicking his war stallion, pushing our mounts to a fast gallop, more tiring than I thought wise with the rising Sun.

Yet, even with this familiar tension between us, I witnessed the horses become at ease. With the steady rolling of equine backs and the rumble of hooves, the beasts stretched out their legs and long necks, herding together on instinct and sustaining speed long past when I wished they would slow down.

It was as Gavin had claimed while we picked our way cautiously through the steep mountain paths. Horses were born for exposed terrain like this. All the care invested in these beasts proved its value as we had ridden what I'd grown accustomed to as a full day's travel before the middle of the afternoon. It was far too soon to see the second chain of mountains I'd been told lay ahead, and there was a river to cross before then, yet it was easy to imagine how fast we'd leave behind anyone on foot.

*Or how fast we may overtake them?*

I doubted I would see when the men and Dwarf spotted the mountains on the horizon; my headache increased with the brightness and complete lack of shade. I'd covered my eyes before the time I had yesterday, securing my hood to my hair with small clamps as the wind kept snatching it down to expose my ears.

Little blocked the wind channeled from the South. I could not hear well, and scent was barely useable past the sweat of beasts and riders wafting back. My clothing was dark, absorbing heat and making me stand out on the yellow-green plains. My cloak felt constantly tugged by invisible hands, and my eyes became dry, catching bits of dust while they continued to ache.

Despite the astonishing speed, this was my least favorite part of the journey. I hid my discomfort with tenacity, however, and spoke not at all as I worked to adjust whenever Gavin's mare pitched into a canter or a full gallop to keep up with the others. This was harder for her with her age and two riders; she consistently fell behind.

Mathias and Rithal would continue to look back, however, checking on us and hailing Kurn to slow down while they did the same. The Hellhound would do so only grudgingly, maintaining distance enough from me that he must shout if he were to speak at all.

Fortunately for my ears and patience, he did neither, but even so, the refusal was strange. The Hellhound tried to use a will-bending ruby pendant on me last night, and I still had it in my pouch. He hadn't asked about it or seemed to notice it missing. Not yet. He seemed paranoid to a state beyond reason, fearful of shadows at midday.

What had happened in the canyon after I left him wrapped in webs? It could have been nothing, just a night of scourging dreams. Had the sedative inside my capsule provoked a toxic response in the Surface man's body? Had the surge of my reawakened psionic defense damaged his mind? Had my interrogation somehow left him with a crumbling will after our struggle? It was too soon to tell how he may or may not recover.

Upon further recollection, I realized I must also consider that stone which had dropped from somewhere up high, scaring me out of my skin and preventing me from killing the man. I must weigh that feeling of dread which had overtaken me the moment before I jammed Kurn's own dagger in the hollow of his throat.

How well-timed, and how it *urged* me to run and escape while I could.

*I would have killed the Ma'ab then. Something stopped me.*

Not an hour later, Gavin was tending my wounds and told me he had sensed a magical aura near the camp. It concerned the dour man enough to tell me, when often I must extract words from him like they were teeth.

I could not pretend it had been me and Kurn alone in that canyon; something else had been there. The Ma'ab survived but was in this volatile state, and there nowhere out here could I leave him behind where he could not track me. So here, I followed his lead.

*Keep the wild dog in sight, I suppose.*

My usual hunger returned despite all this; my endurance tested as Kurn pushed the herd harder. We went longer without stopping than any day thus far. I had some provisions on me to eat atop Gavin's mare. He had more in the saddlebags, but I needed time to forage. I thought wistfully how most of the antlered beast dragged to the canyon yesterday had been wasted, plenty of drying meat left behind in the hastiness of our departure.

No one seemed to have much appetite except me. I chewed and swallowed what was in my pouch whenever we would slow to a walk; I was deliberate and slow so I dropped none of it in our jaunting travel. This pattern went on long enough that Gavin looked over his shoulder at me as if to note it; he may have commented had he not confirmed the reason last night.

*A death mage knows I'm pregnant.*

In having to balance this concern with everything else, I envied my Sisters, Gaelan and Jael, if they traveled their missions alone. If they had joined a group, I couldn't imagine what it would look like.

*Not as disparate and petty as this one.*

I had been sure of my benefit from their experience and knowledge, however, especially Gavin and Rithal. I had been able to make a way into a closed group as a foreigner among outsiders. I should expect it came with these difficulties; there were some things which couldn't be kept from mages who read auras.

Gavin promised he would say nothing.

When we at last stopped to water the horses, it was at a smaller "branch" of the big river coming. We were also in the full heat of the day, the Sun a couple hours past its zenith. Without shade, the break couldn't be a restful one. I longed to travel at night. Perhaps I could walk the Midway while they slept, and they could catch me up when the Sun rose?

Indeed, and then what? Would I slump into Reverie on the back of a moving animal, tying myself to the death mage like unconscious Castis?

*The monk would be thrilled.*

I'd long ago given up trying to see; my eyes were closed behind my mask when I slid off the mare and stepped away to test the water and refill my skin. My ears and nose were keen enough to sense the males and their beasts around me and get the task done without stumbling in their way. Meanwhile, Mathias and Rithal quickly worked together on some task.

My ears twitched when I heard the word *shade*.

I peeked one watering eye open, watching through the slit in my mask as the Dwarf pulled out two metal rods tucked between his pony's saddle and blanket. He gave them a brisk twist, somehow unlocking them, and extended them into useable tent poles before locking them into place.

Mathias had a lightweight canvas he'd been carrying for his lean-to at night, using the trees and branches for structure. They combined the two, raising the fluttering shade and beating the poles into the soft, rich soil, creating a decent spot out of the relentless Sun in the middle of the Midway.

Intensely envious, I anticipated squeezing into the tiny patch of shadow afforded by Gavin's mare when she was finished drinking. Then, while Rithal tended both his pony and Mathias's gelding, the skin hunter looked my way and wordlessly beckoned me with his arm, patting a shaded spot in the long grass.

I glanced at Gavin, who was tending his horse, and Kurn and Castis, who were grumbling to each other farther upstream. I decided to accept a seat in the open half-tent next to the bearded Noble. At last, I could take down my hood and enjoy some of the breeze. I sighed deeply, eyes shut again, and heard Mathias chuckle softly.

"Take a nap," he suggested. "We'll be here for a while."

"Not likely," I murmured, thinking of the fresh bandages on my back, covering cuts from my fall upon the rocks and which Shyntre's pellets were helping to close. "Is it possible we will travel more at night?"

"Not in full dark, we'll break our horses' legs. But we'll start early, break during the heat of the day, and continue in late afternoon, as far as we can into the evening. Farther if there's an early, full moon."

My mouth tightened. "Seems we missed midday."

"Yes, we pushed harder than we can sustain. Don't worry, it'll catch up to him. Everyone will need a nap, even Kurn."

I hadn't appreciated the inevitability of this moment until I sat here. There was no hidden cave or tree to rest apart from camp; for the first time, I may have to lay in Reverie with the men. In answer to my rising nerves, my spiders became restless in their pouch.

"Kurn! Castis!" Rithal barked, and I peeked again, his stout arm waving them toward us. "We gotta talk."

The Ma'ab upstream were two blurry, pale faces with black spots for eyes. They looked creepy from this distance. The redbeard faced them, standing straight with his fists on his sides.

"Gonna talk!" said the Dwarf again. "C'mere. We need a plan."

Gavin led his mare closer to the shade to graze while he remained standing to my left, resilient in the wind and sun as if it didn't bother him. But then, he had traveled out this way once, beginning somewhere near Manalar and alone for many days.

At least the apprentice appeared to be making a statement to the other mage approaching. Castis had tried to roast me with his fire spell as he blamed me for Kurn missing from camp, and the death mage had cancelled his spell with one of his own. I remembered the off chill which had spilled out as the magic collapsed.

Leaving their horses to graze by the stream, Kurn and Castis approached Rithal, facing the Sunlight with brows furrowed, eyes squinting in the glare. They had each tied a grey cloth around their head to deflect the light from above, but I wondered if their pale cheeks would burn berry-red or brown without trees? Mathias, Rithal, and Gavin had taken varying tans to their skin.

*Skin turns darker in the Desert, Rithal told me, and hair turns white with age.*

Sighing, I closed my eyes to rest them as the Dwarf remained planted like a stout tree between us. I listened as he spoke, frankly.

"Are we still on the mission tah take down the Bishops an' Witch Hunners?"

"For certain," Castis said in monotone.

"Good. Can ye leave the Elf alone from now on?"

Kurn inhaled to argue, and Rithal roared before the large man could speak.

*"I'm not guidin' ye this far to play power games with a fey lass and lose sight o' the goal!"*

There was a long, silent pause broken only by rustling grass. Neither man nor bearded Dwarf shifted when Rithal addressed the Hellhound again.

"Ye attacked her last night."

"She has been flaunting her arrogance since the Tower!" Kurn barked.

"Look inna mirror," said the Dwarf. "Ye attacked her, an' she got away. She didn't kill ye, though she could've. Figure yerself lucky an' give it up. It ain't gonna end well."

I peeked again. The Ma'ab glared dangerously at him, then at me, but Rithal continued.

"Sirana was right, I shoulda said more before now. I'm sick o' this, Kurn. Ye two are *kids* tah me. I promise if ye don't get yer cocks under control, we're partin' ways at Troshin Bend, an' I'm takin' Mathias, Sirana, an' Gavin with me tah Manalar. The sorcerer will back me up. Meet yer army earlier than planned. Tell 'em what ye will."

"Fine by me," said the skin hunter. "I'm here for the pay and the challenge. Got no loyalty for either side."

Gavin grunted; we assumed it was agreement. I waited in silence for the response without stirring their tension, though I really wanted to laugh.

"That dark creature will stab us in our sleep," Castis hissed.

"Only if Kurn tries to fuck me again," I said loudly. "I don't want his filthy staff, and unruly cocks like him have their shit-puckers churned raw where I come from, *well* before they try to mount a Red Sister!"

Affronted rage boiled out of both Ma'ab even as they laughed.

"Do try, black witch, do try!" Castis crowed.

"You will run again," Kurn snarled. *"Coward* Sister."

I ground my teeth. I should have killed him; damn whatever made me hesitate! My spiders scrambled inside my pouch as if to promise to rectify that, and I subtly touched the laces, waiting for the slightest sound of threat coming toward me.

Then Mathias barked a laugh into the tense air, making me jump.

"Unruly cocks get shit-puckers what?" the bearded Noble remarked, leaning casually on his hands. "'Churned raw'? Poetic! So in plain Trade, you'll shove something up his ass if he touches you again?"

"Yes," I promised. "And if he spurts, it's by accident."

*"Hahaha!* Have you done it before?"

"Absolutely."

*Well, with my fingers. Usually to* make *him spurt.*

Mathias fell onto his back with another howl of laughter, and Rithal shook his head with a reluctant chortle. The larger Ma'ab sounded like he wore a mean smile when he next spoke.

"You do not know the Hellhounds, witch. We take such threats from foreign women as an invitation to try *harder.*"

"For Blaine's sake, put it up," Rithal rumbled. "Yer not part o' the pack, Kurn, yer a loner onna fuckin' *espionage* mission and pulling at yer leash like an untrained mongrel at the first whiff of a bitch."

"How dare—" Castis began.

"Shut it!" the Dwarf barked, and Mathias stopped chuckling. "Why am I havin' tah remind ye both? Who's yer officer who sent ye? Or are ye not with yer pack because they were tryin' tah get ye out of their beards?"

That was a good question, and an excellent turn of offense met with only silence. Then Kurn turned on his heel and tromped through the grass toward his horse, Castis soon following.

*"Hoi!"* Rithal called. "Gonna keep it in yer pants, or what?"

"I'll not touch her venomous hide!" shouted the Hellhound with petulance. "Let us cross the Midway, yes?"

"Fine by me," Mathias said again, no doubt smiling again.

Rithal exhaled, and his stout frame finally shifted in the grass. He turned and said to me, "Keep yer guard up, Elf, but tis a start."

"Thank you, Rithal," I said. "I would rather speak for myself, but he will not listen to me."

"I know the type. I gotcher back now. I changed my mind what I said in the canyon, I'm tired o' this shit."

"I'll not start the fight, Rithal. I didn't before."

"Yeah. I believe ye." He exhaled, lowering his voice below the breeze. "Still got the ruby?"

I nodded affirmative.

"Keep it quiet fer now. All o' you. No taunts. I gotta figure this out."

Rithal returned to his pony, probably searching for something to do, when Mathias turned to me again.

"What sort of tool does a Red Sister use on 'unruly' assholes, if it's a regular act?"

"It's not males alone," I answered coldly. "Any Davrin of age with an 'asshole' may fear it from the Sisterhood."

"Red Sisters don't target children?"

"No. There are other ways."

"Does that count for, say, Human kids?"

I realized I hadn't seen one yet, but... No, I couldn't.

"It counts."

"So firm. Hmm," the man hummed curiously. "You didn't answer my question."

I smirked. "What do you imagine we use? A false phallus, usually larger than natural."

"A hand tool?"

13

"No, attached to us." I motioned toward my crotch. "By magic."

Mathias was dead silent.

*Uh-oh, what have I done?*

He blew out a breath. "Wow. I speak truth, Sirana, I *want* to see that sometime. If not mounting Kurn, maybe another grown man who deserves it."

I grimaced at not having the option more than his surprising interest. "I do not have that tool with me. It was not... issued as a necessity."

"Ah. Pity. Really." The skin hunter hummed to himself again. "Well. I could find a 'false phallus' easily at Troshin Bend, and I can think of a type we'll run into sooner or later. Not even Rithal would protest you lodging something in his ass if, you know, you wanted to work out some frustration."

*Still nudging?* I made a face behind my mask at this unexpected turn in conversation. This was also the point when Gavin moved away. The apprentice grabbed a small blanket from his saddle to drape over his head and shoulders while he sat in the grass, pulling out the small book which he always had with him.

Mathias glanced his way but wasn't finished with me. "Is it a 'duty,' Red Sister? One you don't really enjoy?"

*It depends,* I didn't say.

I certainly knew how it felt at both ends. I could be aroused either way.

*I'm a bit aroused now. Damn it.*

I grumbled inside; I was also hot and hungry, sitting exposed upon the Midway. I'd been threatened by a dog gripping his bone, my blood was flowing, and yet I'd held my actions yet again as I studied the men altering their positions between each other with me as the point of contention. As they had at the tower.

I didn't know *what* to do with this sudden encouragement from another in our party. How had I touched on this taste I couldn't know the nobleman had with so simple a threat? Wasn't it the same as Kurn's?

"You want to 'watch,' Mathias?" My lips widening as I thought to test his resolve. "What if *you* were in the straps, having your netherhole spread open as I taunt you? Would you still want to see me do it?"

Mathias paused again, and then I wondered if I'd gone too far.

"Interesting proposal. I guess it depends if there's something new you can teach me, Red Sister. Is there? If you can't show me anything new, it's only fair I'd get my turn to show you."

He astonished me with the utter lack of insult in his reply, sliding with ease to a rogue humor which was vaguely familiar. I kept my mouth closed rather than let it fall open, but my mean smile collapsed as I sought a reply to that challenge next. I stamped down any tinge of insult, as he had.

"Hm," I grunted. "Is this why you are called a 'skin hunter' instead of bounty seeker? You force sex before collecting the bounty?"

I heard the broad smile in his voice. "Close enough. You could say I'm an interrogator not afraid to get my hands dirty. Why Sarilis called me, in truth. The other reasons were presented as not to tempt Kurn's stubbornness against taking me on."

"An interrogator," I repeated.

"Yes. We might need to 'persuade' Witch Hunters to part with some information the closer we get to Manalar."

I pursed my lips and thought that over. I decided to ask. "And you say Rithal would not protest this?"

Mathias leaned closer, lowering his voice. "Witch Hunters are the *sole* reason Rithal is putting up with these Ma'ab jesters. We both want to get our hands on some if it's all crashing down soon, anyway."

"Revenge?"

"The Dwarf, definitely." The man chuckled. "Me, I want the *challenge*. I have some new tricks to try. I'm also listening for tips if you'll share."

Curious to think about. *Was* there anything I'd seen in Sivaraus that he hadn't in his travels? It depended what "challenges" he'd taken in his short life. This was not what I'd expected from the young lord's brother who had told me to go home lest something "terrible" happen to a young girl.

The moment stretched, and Mathias's tone was jovial as he added, "I bet you didn't blink behind that mask, Sirana."

*Huh?*

"Why should I have blinked, Mathias?"

"Witch Hunters are men only. No chance of interrogating a woman."

I shrugged. "So?"

I heard his lips draw back from his teeth in a broad grin. "Heh. Never quite believed one who thought like you could exist, but here you are."

I arched a brow though he couldn't see it. "You're being obtuse, skin hunter."

"You didn't flinch at my saying I wanted to catch a Witch Hunter and learn some new tricks from you 'churning him raw.' Did you think I was going to use a lacquered prick in my hand when I've got one of my own?"

*Oh.* Well, he was right about not flinching. Such enjoyment was no different from Jaunda's tastes, really.

"Is there something…" I grasped for the word. "Forbidden in what you say?"

"Men mounting men?" Mathias shrugged. "Depends where you are. I *know* it's forbidden at Manalar, and every Witch Hunter be- lieves it a sin."

"A sin," I repeated.

"Do you know what that is?"

"No."

*"Ha!* I think I like you more than before, Red Sister."

My tone was dry. "Thank you."

Mathias maintained a genuine smile with a predator's tilt. He *was* having fun; and I believed him when he continued. "I've never seen a woman force sex on a man *and* make him take it up the ass. Yet, I believe *you* could, even being so small. All you must do is side-step the strength advantage, like you've done already."

He leaned in again, his voice for certain encouraging. "You left Kurn in the canyon when you could have punished him, I'm sure. I'd like to understand why. Tell me. Was it because you didn't *have* the 'tool' issued for that purpose? Would you have used it on him if you had it?"

I lowered my head in thought, pulling a thick thread of grass, and decided quickly not to speak of the mysterious presence which had frightened me away. Nor could I admit that my unborn concerned me far more than engaging in spiteful fights or dominating couplings.

However, this did not change that Mathias *was* seeking an ally, or at least approval in his desires against the Witch Hunters. I knew what he wanted to hear, but did I want to get involved in this? What cause had I to offer ways to torment a Witch Hunter when one could just kill him? Then again, having cause may only be a matter of time. Mathias Briar had spoken so at Sarilis's tower.

*One glimpse at her, and the Witch Hunters won't let it go.*

What did that mean? How dangerous were they to one like me? And why?

"Even if I'd had the magic cock," I muttered in answer, "I imagined it would be difficult working with you and Rithal if I did more to Kurn. Castis would prove dangerous enough to kill as well."

"I love that. 'Magic cock.'" The skin hunter's grin didn't falter. "*I* wouldn't have cared, but you couldn't know that. The other two? Yes, nothing but problems. Makes sense. That's smart. But you're saying the struggle *didn't* arouse you?"

I chose not to lie to him. "No, it did not. But that is Kurn himself who doesn't arouse me."

"Oh? You *do* get aroused in contested ruts?"

I nodded readily. "I have before. Female and males, both."

Mathias exhaled slowly. "What about race? Other kinds turn you on, or is it only other Davrin?"

Good question. Except for my... curiosity about Tamuril, I hadn't longed for any of the few Surfacers I'd met, but that was only a handful. I had many times lamented the idea of no hands but my own between my legs for the rest of the year, so... would I relent at some point? Say, with a Human or a Dwarf? It was an odd match in my mind.

"I do not know," I answered. "I've not been on the Surface long enough to say."

"Honest answer. I appreciate that." He lifted a curious brow. "You like sex overall? Or only the Red Sister kind?"

His tone made me smile despite myself. "Are you proposing I try sex with *you*?"

The man chuckled. "Actually, no. I want men, but I *do* enjoy comparing sketches with smart women who like to fuck as well."

*Comparing sketches.*

Trading information, he meant, and sex greased that squeaky hinge here when it had been difficult to begin that trade with Gavin. This was closer to what Rausery had said might happen with Humans, yet it had *not* arisen in the manner I might have expected.

I smiled. "I understand. Yes, Mathias, I like to fuck as I like to fight."

"Hear, hear," he said, grinning, his own curiosity satisfied for the moment.

I remained awake through our midday break and the long ride far into the evening which brought us in sight of the biggest river we had to cross. Choosing a place to camp wasn't difficult; we chose a slight incline that wasn't soggy from snowmelt. I was tired, my back sore, dirty, and itchy, and my middle stabbed me such hunger pangs, that I wished to forage with someone my first night on the plains rather than deduce what I could alone. I thought Gavin could be discreet and understand my urgency.

"Rithal would be the expert," murmured the death mage as he checked his mare's legs following the lengthy run. "Mathias, as well. Both are hunters, I am not. I made do with what I brought and was lucky to spot any nests for eggs. I spent many nights hungry."

There was no embarrassment in admitting the lack of skill; it was a statement only. He didn't know the Midway as well as the mountains.

"A'right," Rithal announced in a loud voice before we'd done more than build a firepit and a lean-to. "Who all can see in th' dark to scrounge something to eat?"

Silence, and I figured he must be half-jesting as the Ma'ab rolled their eyes.

"We shall wait until moonrise," Castis said, "as before."

"Fine. Gonna weigh it with the watch order. Decide when we get back." Rithal looked at me. "Sirana?"

"I can see," I said. "I can hunt now."

The redbeard grinned as he sucked a finger and tested the air. Turning South, he waved his hand. "Great. Come with me. Mathias, Gavin, okay stayin'?"

The customary grunt overlapped with, "Yup."

Hoping a fireball wouldn't erupt in camp while we were away, I walked in long strides alongside Rithal away from camp, descending slightly and heading upwind. Soon, we were out of earshot, if not out of view.

"You can see in the dark?" I asked.

"Better than them," replied the Dwarf. "What about you? You see colors or just grey?"

"In starlight and moonlight, I see colors," I said. "Deep in a cave, I see shades of..." I paused, not knowing if a Trade word existed for Radiants. "Grey. I see in grey. Well enough to read expressions in detail if close."

"Good. I lose a bit o' color at night, replaced with grey farther out I look. But it don' go black for me like it does Humans. They ain't lying, they *really* can't see without moons or fire, unless some mage worked out a spell for temporary dark sight."

I made note. "Can you see deep inside a cave without fire or magical light?"

"A little," he admitted. "I didn' grow up in the mines or under-city of Taiding. More familiar with pastures and rolling hills, so some o' my far-kin are better at it than me."

"Taiding," I asked with interest. "A Dwarven underground city?"

"Half of it. Other half is up top. Has city streets an' shops, tombs and gardens, everything."

*Hmm.*

Abruptly, my stomach growled, and a shooting stab of pain reminded me why we were out here. Rithal chuckled as I grimaced.

"Right. Lemme show ya how to find stuff we can eat." He glanced my way with humorous eyes. "Gotta say, ye have the healthiest appetite o' any skinny girl I met."

"I'm not skinny," I protested. "I'm a fighter. I burn food quickly despite my size."

"Fair point, Elf. Let's take advantage o' that color vision at night."

Rithal and I returned with a heavy sack of wide roots, eggs, some edible plants, and a handful of small ground rodents. We were expected to share, and it didn't stretch far with Kurn's massive bulk to feed, but the small meal gave me a second wind and more time. I would have to go out again later tonight and apply what I'd learned.

"Sleeping alone again?" the Hellhound asked, addressing me with neither name nor slur.

"No," I said. "Sleeping in camp."

He grunted, curling his nostril. "We do same watch order."

Indeed, the order which interrupted Gavin's rest the most in the hours before dawn and gave me time for Reverie until I woke and stayed awake through the last three watches. I'd have plenty of time to forage.

I waited through the near-silent meal and settling for sleep for Kurn to ask about his ruby. I no longer had it; during our foraging, Rithal had convinced me to pass it to him.

*"Castis will be able tah see it on ye if he tries. Surprised he hasn't already."*

We had agreed it must be that Kurn hadn't told Castis it was missing, yet.

*"Better the Ma'ab don' find it on ye at all, Elf. Give it tah me. I don't know how tah use it, but I will keep it in neutral ground."*

Wordlessly, I had handed it over to him. I still had the blue saphgar around my neck beneath my leather armor. It had heated up during Kurn's mental attack with the ruby, as it had not since I'd left Sivaraus.

With plenty of time to think on the back of Gavin's mare today, I had a good guess what had happened. As Shyntre's pendant had blocked the mind-reading or will-bending magic from Elder D'Shea and Priestess Wilsira down below, so, too, had it helped block the Ma'ab's enslaving stone.

I had planned to keep both in the hope that the saphgar would lessen the ruby's potency, as Headmaster Phaelous noted in its properties. It wouldn't have worked by now; a single day wasn't enough or Callitro's ring and all magic-touched tools on my belt would be useless.

Rithal was right, I'd decided. Castis seeing the aura of the ruby on me was an inevitable and volatile confrontation if I kept it. At least, now, I could use my spider guardians at any time; my little ones would not receive such mixed signals, bite or don't. The Queen's geas was satisfied, I knew of the missing Sathoet, if not his Mother.

*Kurn saw the half-blood among the Ma'ab army, used for training purposes.*

To discover more, I needed someone who knew about the Ma'ab without having any loyalty. Rithal or—

"You can lie by me," Mathias said with a yawn. "I'll share space with you."

"Thank you, Mathias."

I noted Kurn's beetling brow hearing this; he looked suspicious of the other man. I refrained from suggesting to the Ma'ab that Mathias wanted nothing which lay between my legs because Mathias hadn't volunteered that since he arrived at the tower. He had mentioned Kurn refusing to take him on if he knew Mathias's real desires with the Witch Hunters.

I agreed with the discretion, for I'd seen the reaction when I suggested Castis was the bigger man's "stress reliever" on the road. Kurn's indignant response had been telling: *"Enough, witch, you'll speak no more of such disgusting things!"*

*Disgusting, hm?* Men seeking release on each other; this consideration with how I interacted was fairly new to me. Buas caught playing in secret made Sivaraus females intensely jealous that they were ignored, and the retaliation could be severe, but talk of disgust *hadn't* been the first response.

The Davrin caits and their Mothers hated the audacity of rejection, as if the buas had that power over us. I could imagine the feeling if Shyntre and Auslan tried to draw that line, pushing me away as they embraced each other. It was a defiant taunt set to boil any cait's blood.

Putting my homeland aside, however, I kept turning this thought over where it came to Humans, where the male was larger and aggressive. Was this close to the "sin" that the nobleman skin hunter had mentioned? Were the Ma'ab and the Manalari similar in this expectation among their male enforcers? Or was Kurn an out-lier, sent far from his fellow soldiers with only a Noble mage for company?

This pairing for espionage seemed strange in hindsight. What if, for example, I had been sent on a long trek with Curgia of House Itlaun? What purpose did that have unless there was some other goal? I wondered if all was as it seemed then kicked myself.

*Would you need to ask such a question in Sivaraus to know the answer, Sirana?*

Before long I convinced Gavin to sleep under the open-side tent as well; there was enough space for four with the canvas stretched tight and at a lower angle to the ground than it had been earlier. There wasn't room to sit up without forehead meeting the fabric, but it had been staked lower to extend over a greater foot-print for dew protection instead of tall shade from the Sun.

The body scents were thick under the cloth, and I wasn't used to the sound of a Dwarf rumbling as he breathed. There wasn't an easy way to run out into the grass if I needed to, either, but Kurn and Castis made their own tent, and once the men around me drifted off, my spiders were calm when I let them out. I slipped another of Shyntre's mud-pellets beneath my tongue to help my itching back and lay on my side, my arm beneath my head.

*~Keep watch. We'll get food later.~*

I could swear I heard my guardians' chimes of acknowledge-ment before my eyes closed.

Gavin sat upright in the grass when I finished Reverie, sharpening and polishing his cloth-rolls of small tools. Many a traveling companion would have criticized that he couldn't see far from that vantage point; given his talent to see living creatures like floating, mystical lanterns if they crept close enough, his being alert was good enough for me.

I stretched, felt only a small twinge and my spiders untroubled at my nape; I gathered them to return them to their pouch. The other four males were oblivious to the world, and I crept to sit next to Gavin. He leaned away out of lifelong habit but didn't shift his bottom, and I waited for him to return to a tolerant posture.

"Do my guardians speak truth?" I murmured to him. "No trouble."

Gavin shrugged and continued working his scalpel carefully against a whetstone. "The Ma'ab seem to have worn themselves out this night. I'm sure they will be livelier in future nights."

Nodding agreement, I asked, "What is a 'sin' among Manalari?"

I sensed a chill arise around the death mage as he paused. *Uh-oh...what?*

He said, "A sin is a deliberate transgression against a divine order."

*Tidy.*

I pondered that, and my elder sisters at House Thalluen came to mind. Put this way, I did see a type of "sin" among my own, but it was simple as denouncing Braqth or the Priestesses. Of course, they wouldn't like such rebellion. Punishment ensued to dissuade further defiance to their power.

"Who decides what is divine order at Manalar?" I asked.

"The Bishops, though that is a much-debated question to me. I see mortal men arguing like children without parents. They have little choice but to set some boundaries without confirmation from the higher being they invoke. It becomes a self-serving method for a few to bully the masses into compliance."

I frowned. "What if a people received confirmation from that higher being? And it amounted to the same actions in the clerics' claims?"

Gavin arched a dark brow as his blade caught moonlight. "That sounds rather terrifying."

I smirked. *Says one who can see the dead.* "I suppose it is. Your main complaint is there is no confirmation from, um…"

"Musanlo."

"What?"

"The Sun God."

"Oh. Right."

"And you are correct. There is no confirmation which convinces me at Manalar. I see a band of powerful mages calling themselves 'bishops,' putting on a show while servile monks and enforcers babble the same prayers over and over like they, too, can control the weather." I grunted, and Gavin turned to study me. "Do you suggest *you* have confirmation of the code of your…?"

"Spider queen." I hesitated. "Although, the 'code' changes as needed. Her clerics revel in causing fear and do not deny this appetite."

Gavin shook his head. "How have you any structure to your society? Is it all backstabbing and sleeping with one eye open?"

I was about to confirm what my childhood and years at Court had been like but paused. "There is… some structure. There are some who protect each other from spontaneous feedings."

"Interesting way to put it. It gives the impression you are all clambering along threads in a web." I made a face for how accurate that was, and the death mage squinted at me in the dark. "You have confirmed clerical connection to a higher being, yet you're skeptical toward those clerics as I am. Why?"

As if I'd had time to think that through?

"It's not… higher," I tried, failing to grasp that idea. "The Abyss is another plane. We *know* it exists. The spider queen grants genuine power, and there are known rituals to obtain it. There is another qu…"

I choked, my throat closing painfully on itself. I clutched at my neck, my eyes wide in shock. Gavin's eyes widened as well, but he made no sound until I'd caught my breath and calmed down.

"Your supreme being is a demon from another plane," he murmured. "You know this, and your superiors accept the power granted on this plane. And that is all."

I nodded.

"Yet you have no concept of ghosts," he continued, "or of 'sin' on account of this certainty. It sounds less a concept of gods and more the use of power. Would you say your worship is secular?"

"Secular?" I shook my head.

"Wholly of this world and its consequences during life." Gavin paused, adding, "Rather than your behavior being dictated and consumed with what happens when this life is ended."

I blinked, admittedly confused. "I have never thought about what happens when this life is ended. It's nothing, unless we are forced into becoming a…"

*A Drider.*

"Becoming what?" Gavin asked.

"A mindless spider-beast," I said. "A punishment from the clerics. A Davrin is alive but not as they were born. The body is monstrous and diseased. It is unclear when the torment might end, if ever. It is a powerful threat."

Gavin's dark eyebrows lifted. "Hm. We have similar threats and fears, but there is no proof of eternal punishment I could attribute to Musanlo without doubt. There is only punishment from other men or, perhaps in ways I do not understand, from devils and demons manipulating them. As they are you, you're merely aware of it."

I fell quiet to ponder that while he wiped oil off one small blade and selected another. Mathias had told me it was not "comforting" to know that demons were true and real on this world. Was it, in reverse, comforting to have that plausible deniability of the

Sun God when a man desires other men? At least such as had been decided by someone else to be against a divine order.

*He seemed to only care because they have Witch Hunters to enforce it.*

I said, "You say the Bishops have no proof of their God that you would believe in the same way I can witness the existence of Abyssal magic."

Gavin grunted. "I have heard the argument that the more powerful the god, the less they show themselves in any direct way, for our sake. Be it to allow unguided growth and change or because interfering would cause unimaginable destruction. A 'god' that must always dance in front of followers to convince them he is real is either a trickster or is still gaining strength."

I stared at the uncomely scholar as I allowed it to sink in, this shift in how I'd always viewed Braqth. That was a fascinating idea. The Spider Queen a dancing trickster gaining power? That worked for her, but what of Musanlo?

I smirked. *One problem for this to fit him.*

"As one unaccustomed to the Sun," I said, "I might suggest Musanlo's presence is quite constant and direct, so much that you are blind to it. Look around you. The plants grow because of the daylight, yes? You have all this abundance I do not *because* of that burning ball above. You can't help but worship it, though you do not know why it is there."

Gavin blinked and looked around, able to see by moonlight. He scowled in thought. "It is not the proof that the Bishops claim governs them. Nor is it the proof they would *want*, I think."

"So, they ignore it?" I chuckled. "Since when do they get to choose the proof that they would want from a Sun god they claim not to see?"

"An interesting idea, I will grant you. Perhaps this god exists only in what is before us and does not favor taking advantage of 'divine order' governing small men. Not such as a devil or demon might among mortals."

*Wow.* I'd grown up being told they arrived together, and I'd believed it. Would I think like this man after a mere quarter century, if the threat of damnation weren't so real that it could eat me like a bug in a web?

*Does this separate a deity from a demon, then? And what of ghosts, how does this fit in?*

I waited a few instants. "Gavin?"

His wandering gaze turned my way.

"We know you are half-Ma'ab, but you don't speak the language. Kurn and Sarilis assume Ma'ab soldiers fell upon a Manalari woman to make her catch, and her male child was given to an all-male monastery to raise. Is this true?"

Gavin frowned and cleaned a flaying tool. "The simplest answer is often the correct one. Can you imagine a pious man of Musanlo coupling with an enemy Ma'ab witch?"

I smiled; oddly, a hostile D'Shea and a cloistered Phaelous crossed my mind. "Maybe. The unlikelihood doesn't disprove it. You could simply deny it."

He didn't. Not immediately.

"Is that how you learned there were other planes before I mentioned them?" I asked. "Why you resist the prayers and life of the monks given your care. Your mother gifted you with your death magic?"

"I might not call it a gift," he muttered. "More that her heritage is something I cannot escape having drawn my first breath. A boy seeing ghosts and always able to predict if someone will or won't recover from illness may as well learn about death."

"From her?" I prodded.

Gavin shook his head, his lank hair falling into his eyes. "She died in childbirth. Her Vis left this plane without a trace. Nothing lingered, not even around her unmarked grave."

I frowned. "Wait. She was buried near the monastery? So a Ma'ab 'witch' gave birth there?"

The moody apprentice turned dark eyes to me, his lips pursed tight. "I've wondered why she was never discovered by the Bishops' Hunters, who came by often for our hospitality. I assure you; my father was too fanatical to offer any facts about this glaring incongruency in upholding his own faith."

"Ah. Your father was a monk? Disallowed a companion and children, wasn't he? For 'purity'?"

Gavin shrugged like he didn't care; it wasn't convincing. He tested the sharpness of his scalpel's edge. "I looked enough like my mother, not him, that he never claimed me as anything but a bastard she squeezed out while in their care. They assumed she must have rutted with a vagrant before they found her. Somehow, as the monastery's archimandrite, my father proclaimed it was his duty to raise a righteous man out of her foul issue."

I smirked. "And everyone believed that?"

"It seemed so. I was treated by all as a foundling with no lineage."

"Hm? But you have a lineage. Hers."

"She doesn't count. Nor would she if she had been Manalari."

I sneered. "And I suppose your magic doesn't count, either."

"Just more proof to them that she was cursed, and it was passed on with tainted blood which needed cleansing."

Yes, I remembered the hot iron he'd mentioned, pain intended to drive the devil out of the boy who saw ghosts. "Why go to the trouble, if he pretended you weren't his?"

"An excellent question. As good as why he laid with the witch to begin with, and then hid her and her swelling belly from Witch Hunters."

Gavin paused in pressing his tool to his skin. I wasn't sure if the small cut had been an accidental slip or not. Either way, he was bleeding.

"He never confessed before he died," the death mage murmured, smearing his thumb and forefinger together. "And what he said afterward was nonsense."

A chill ran up my spine. To think I'd laughed in Kurn's face when Gavin claimed he'd poisoned all the monks at the monastery before he left. I believed him now.

"You can interrogate the dead?" I asked quietly.

"I haven't a lot of practice. Sometimes I can hear what the Vis *wants* to say. Other times," Gavin scowled, "they deny making any sense of my questions."

*Like the monk-sire he clearly loathes.*

I began to wonder. Was this his basis for negotiating with me, a "black witch," without ever once calling me that? His mother was a witch, a Ma'ab one; he did not get his blood from some hound-soldier. The woman harbored the death magic while simultaneously bearing him his life. For some reason, the monks let her live long enough to achieve this.

*But he never knew her. Not even as a ghost.*

"Rethinking being so at ease with a murderer?" Gavin said as though he expected the affirmative but didn't care either way.

*Is he jesting?*

I chuckled lowly. "I think you're in like company, apprentice. You bore torture when you were too small to defend yourself. When you were larger and knowledgeable, you denied their reasoning for why you must suffer at their hands. You ended their opportunity to continue their enjoyment in using you or anyone else to justify their existence. I approve."

Gavin turned to look at me with suspicion. "You'll pardon my saying this is exactly the sort of reassurance I would expect to hear from a devil or a demon."

I rolled my eyes. "I am interested if you discovered a taste for it. Like Sarilis."

*Or Mathias.*

When he didn't answer, I asked, "Have you continued poisoning others? Or explored other methods to hasten your learning about death?"

His scowl grew quite ugly, but he answered. "No. Though I did not let opportunity to observe pass me by. I drifted among violent, fearful men and among many graves. They were what I knew."

"Until came the day you decided to cross the Midway." I looked around at the open sky and vast grassland. "Where there seem far fewer of those."

"Indeed," he remarked dryly.

"And came upon a tower, tolerating more of the same until you were again unable to stay. And were forced out for reasons unknown."

Gavin held up a long, pale finger, picking up his kit and book with his other hand. "We may cease this discussion here. I am lying down."

I grinned. "Very well." As he stood up, I added, "There is no judgment from me, mage. I am familiar with such stories among my own."

"A sure relief to hear," he said without inflection.

"I am glad. Sleep well."

# CHAPTER 2

AT DAWN, BEFORE I NEEDED A SUN MASK, WE PREPARED TO CROSS an exceptionally large river. It looked slow and ponderous from the bank, yet I knew how deceptive this could be though I'd never seen something of this size.

*A lot of our supplies are about to get wet.*

As if in response to this thought, Castis spread a square of treated leather over some stomped-down grass and motioned to it. "Place anything vulnerable to water here. This bundle will float and repel water. You shall receive it on the other bank."

*Arrgh.*

I should not be surprised that the mage had a solution, and a good one at that. However, it would reveal things about my tools that I would rather these men not know. I would have to change pouches, switch up the knots and varying shades of leather assuming either Ma'ab was that observant—a caster certainly could be— and this was potentially catastrophic for my reflexes, as I had memorized these details in training.

The wax-sealed vials I'd checked were strong and would survive the swim. My spiders were hidden in my hair, and my head *must* remain above water; there was no option, there. Various pastes and poisons were made to resist moisture for several years and remain potent. I wasn't worried about them.

Shyntre's healing pellets, the sleep powder, and the remaining tranquilizer capsules I'd used on Kurn in the canyon were vulnerable to this lengthy submersion, as they worked by dissolution or dispersion. Despite being in water-repellant pouches proven effective against heavy rain, I couldn't be sure they would stay sealed or if they would leak.

While I deliberated, Rithal stepped closer to set his fire kit and a few closed and knotted pouches upon the leather, alongside Castis's entire belt plus a small wooden box from his saddlebag. They'd done this before. Kurn added nothing to the collection as he stood guard with his arms crossed. His face was set between a smirk and a sneer. He had skipped his swordplay exercise this morning.

Castis looked at Mathias expectantly.

"I'm good," said the nobleman, smiling through his beard. "I've done this plenty."

An accepting nod, then the dark-eyed mage looked at Gavin and me, his black eyebrows lifting in silent question.

"Nothing, thank you," said the death mage.

"Not even your grimoire and ink?" Castis challenged.

"I am not inexperienced."

My questioning glance saw Gavin look away from me; he didn't have a solution for me, as well.

*Alright,* I sighed inside.

I removed the hand crossbow, quiver of bolts, short sword, and dagger they knew about, placing those temporarily in the grass. Then I released my entire belt of tools, bringing it forward.

"That's unnecessary weight," Castis said.

"Not much more than yours."

"My spell protects only so much mass. It must be essential."

I shrugged. "All is vulnerable."

The Ma'ab shook his head between disbelief and derision. "That seems foolish planning."

"There aren't such large rivers in my lands. I have never seen this before. It is greater than you described."

"Perhaps return the ruby you stole," his eyes flicked to Rithal, "and I will spend the extra components to carry this weight."

Day two. That didn't take long.

"She don't have it," Rithal interceded. "I grabbed it after finding Kurn in the canyon. She described it tah me in the attack."

The Hellhound snarled, "So, give it *back*, old one."

"Not when I know it bends wills," the Dwarf rebuffed. "'Tis a threat to anyone in this party, includin' me."

Castis oozed Noble warning. "You shall not keep that gem, Rithal."

"Ye get it back when we part ways." The redbeard shrugged. "Soon as Troshin Bend, if ye like."

"We are going to Manalar!" barked Kurn.

"Then go, but I'm not guidin' ye."

"What?"

The redbeard made large gestures, ticking off his points. "Ye threatened me with siccin' Hunners on me along the way, yet didn't tell me about this ruby before ye tried it on the Elf, and yer not willin' tah compromise on a piece that breaks all trust now we know about it. I keep it so none ye use it, or we fight for it *now*."

The Ma'ab laughed in derisive disbelief, though they noticed when I smiled with genuine interest and my hands moved. A fight here on this bank would end the same as it had with Tamuril, even without Gavin and Mathias preparing something behind my back.

"Stubborn Dwarf," Castis spoke like a curse.

"Yeah, we're famous fer that," Rithal sneered in return, looking at the larger pale man. "What did ye think was gonna happen soon as ye used it an' lost?"

Kurn's face reddened, and he resembled any number of caits I'd known below who loathed such reasonableness being spoken aloud. Castis rubbed his jaw, wanting to talk with the big man in private again but all he could manage was a brief exchange. While I didn't understand the words, Rithal seemed to glean the gist as he nodded.

"Perhaps we can negotiate further with the sorcerer," said the Ma'ab Noble, "if you wish to take up with the dark one instead."

"Certain ye can," Rithal agreed, folding his arms. "I gave it a shot, Castis, like ye convinced me at th' tower. This ain't gonna work how we planned. Not gonna get myself killed 'cause of it."

"So, why choose this unknown creature over your contract?" asked the Noble Ma'ab. "She's clearly not a mage, or the *maknuut* wouldn't have needed to defend her from me. And how will you explain her at Troshin Bend?"

"Now yer thinkin'," Rithal replied. "We have some way to go. Gonna think about it. Pretty sure the sorcerer knows more, anyway. Maybe we renegotiate then, 'less ye wanna fight over a ruby here in the grass, instead?"

Kurn ground his teeth; I could hear it from where I stood. Castis weighed the situation as the Hellhound let the mage do the thinking at this moment. Mathias, Gavin, and I waited curiously, prepared for conflict but none overturning the narrow balance Rithal walked to determine how we were crossing the river.

Castis's dark eyes flicked to me. "Well. She seems to be obeying you for the moment, Dwarf."

Mathias emitted a quiet snort. I smirked.

Rithal exhaled. "She's listening tah me, yeah."

"With ears that large…" Kurn muttered without finishing.

*Larger than what's between yours.*

Oddly, I was growing used to being talked about like a mysterious thing to be afraid of and hostile toward. I was unaccustomed to this attention among my own; I wasn't worth it, I was a toy or pawn, but they didn't know that. Still, arguing for myself hadn't worked too well at the tower. Rithal seemed to be doing better, and the less I said, the more I saw. I was concerned what the two had said about the midway point.

*How will you explain her?*

In my experience, the older mages tended to ask the most cutting questions.

"Very well," Castis spoke decisively, adding with imperious command, "Sirana, add your belt to my wrap to stay dry. No metal. It shall be undamaged on the other side."

I bit the inside of my cheek and nodded.

It was a tense, soggy crossing, especially handling the beasts as well—mine much smaller than theirs. We made it, though, and I regained my belongings with nothing missing. After we sorted out the food which was river-soaked despite our efforts, preparing to eat that first, Mathias pointed out a blob of what I thought was debris caught in the reeds on the other side.

"Heh, that's a good idea," he said. "Weaving grass and reeds for a floater raft to drag along while you swim."

I squinted through my sun mask at the partly submerged clump and, oddly, it did seem like someone with hands might have crafted it in haste.

*That is a good idea.*

"*Now* you mention," I teased, and the skin hunter grinned through his short beard.

"Wasn't going to miss someone swallowing the sour pie," he said, mounting up on a squishing saddle and blanket.

It would take the rest of the day to dry out in full, and we were caked by flying dirt-gusts before that happened. I sighed, my head mostly dry with three sets of tickling, arachnid feet settling in for another rolling lope.

I wondered who had made that little raft Mathias had spotted on the bank, and whether we might catch up to them? Were that possible, I also wondered how we could be traveling so fast while the days of bickering dragged on like this?

Only two days after conflict finally erupted in the canyon did I truly feel how much at a disadvantage I was in this foreign land, despite any boldness I'd presented or any risk I'd taken to attempt to blend my Valsharess's geas with seeking either of my Sisters' trails. The energy I spent on this day-to-day touch-and-go with the Ma'ab men meant I'd had far less to prepare for Troshin Bend. I had wasted a lot of time and distance.

These insurgents needed to stop at this place regardless for supplies, and their "contract" was in question because of me. They may part ways and claimed to need the sorcerer as mediator. They still hadn't spoken his name.

*How will you explain her?*

This wasn't good. I worried while inexorably traveling forward if my nerves would hold long enough to spot any advantage at all, or what solution either Rithal or I would come up with.

There followed some days of relative peace, our horses allowed to walk more than gallop; my injuries fully healed in that time. Gavin's mare needed the rest for certain, though my perception of time in the saddle crawled on the flats compared to the fast-changing scenery of the mountains.

I tended to talk to Gavin during the day while we were front-to-back, and with Rithal and Mathias as we bedded down at night. The next time we forded a smaller river, I made my own little raft. Castis sneered but seemed glad not to have to negotiate with Rithal about my tools again.

*You and me, both.*

The worst Kurn had done was grab his crotch and show me the outline of his erection one night while he stayed up for his watch. I also heard him throttling it later, my ears detecting that whether I wished or not. Same as the first time I had spied on his self-pleasure, it did have some effect on me.

I thought about my Lead Jaunda and the times I'd seen the outline of her Feldeu under her reds as she eagerly approached me in the Cloister. I was always wet by the time she won her position and pulled my leathers down. I didn't want any male here to fuck me like she did, but I missed something about that play while watching a stupid, frustrated bull trying crudely to do the same.

I drifted into Reverie reliving the sheer, enthralled anticipation of my companion penetrating me, though who it was seemed to blur as I called out in my dream.

*Want you in my cunt... I can't catch again, so don't pull out...*

It may have been my rough and fun-loving Lead who obliged me so well, or it may have been my angry, obstinate wizard releasing some much-needed pressure. Either way, the cock fucked me hard and didn't withdraw too early; my slit was stretched and loaded up with so much cream by the end, it drained like a river and soaked into the dirt ground when that welcome prick finally left to make room for the next one.

A second cock went deep, used my slovenly sex only long enough to grease the way for what we both *really* wanted.

*~Yes...~*

Kneeling on all fours, I tossed my head back, mouth open but silent to feel a broad, slick phallus burrowing without hesitation into my netherhole. Whoever wielded the cock also had hands free to reach and rub my skin, caressing my flanks and lower belly as they reamed the tight ring between my cheeks. Wet fingers circled the nub hidden between my soggy netherlips. It didn't take long. I climaxed with a roar, my rectum rippling and squeezing in greedy delight around their pole.

*~Yes!!~*

Several others answered me in deep, urgent groans.

My eyes snapped open, my entire body tense and lips pursed tight as I listened to the insects of the night from beneath our shelter on the Midway. Had I made any sound? Did I awaken anyone?

*Who's on watch now?*

I remained in position, unmoving, long enough to determine it was Gavin's watch, as both Mathias and Rithal were on either side of me asleep, short blankets askew. I exhaled in silent relief, until both moaned in a telling way, shifting so that I noticed they also had night-poles in their own trousers.

And a wet spot growing.

*Hm. Uh-oh.*

I reached for my saphgar, confirming it was around my neck and beneath my leathers. This wasn't necessarily a comfort. What had I done? Had I done *anything* in my sleep, like it had been in the Cloister sharing Reverie with Reishel? Or Gaelan?

I swallowed, waiting.

Gavin made no shift from whatever task occupied his mind. Rithal and Mathias remained unconscious and unknowingly damp. I listened underneath the night breeze for anything from the Ma'ab shelter, and I heard…something. Shuffling in grass, a soft moan muffled, like teeth biting down on cloth, then one harsh gasp from a mouth uncovered. Several grunts, then they settled down.

I waited, and the camp quieted in time. When I crawled out, Gavin lifted his dark eyes to watch me approach.

"Ready for some sleep?" I whispered.

He arched a brow. "One question, first."

"Yes?"

"Was Castis wrong about you not being a mage?"

My heart hadn't slowed to normal after that dream, and the usual hunger-nausea returned. "What do you mean?"

The monk narrowed his eyes. "Very well. I will simply ask you not to play with my dreams. You may regret it. This is a warning, not a threat."

I stared at him, and the memory of that night at the tower returned from when I'd been spying on him having a nightmare and talking in his sleep. I remembered that chilling, grinning shadow lingering above him on his too-short cot. I forced a smirk at the memory of his large, pale feet hanging off.

"I imagine I would regret bearing witness to *your* dreams, Gavin. Especially uninvited."

He maintained that studious stare. "Is this what it was? You were doing something just now. Feeding on rutting dreams, perhaps? I have heard of devils who do such to strengthen their magic. A succubus."

I'd never heard that word and shook my head, trying to think how to explain, especially having never considered this idea before. I realized some in Sivaraus may be able to do this, with or without a devil's name, but I could not do this. Or, if I could, then I didn't feel much "fed." It was only me dreaming of Jaunda. And maybe Shyntre.

*It was a normal, horny dream of missing home. Nothing more.*

"Well?" he asked.

I weighed that Gavin was possibly the only one who might not recoil at this new wrinkle in the black witch. I began slowly. "Fighting off the...effects of Kurn's ruby uncovered something which had been sleeping before. I once had a growing talent to know deeper feelings, hear thoughts, or see memories in another mind. It was... exploited by a demon such that, ever since the attack, I have hurt to use it."

The lanky man's dark eyebrows lifted slowly. I couldn't read his face or hear any thoughts, for that matter. I waited.

He said, "Except now. You were not in pain. Go on."

Now he said this, I noticed a mild headache growing. "Mm. I saw no memories or dreams but my own, Gavin. I dreamt of mates at home. Intense pleasure, as I do sometimes, but that is all."

"If nothing was intended," Gavin informed me, "then you should know it affected the others sleeping. All at the same moment. I bore witness, though its reach did not touch me."

*Huh, shit...*

"Noted," I grumbled.

After another moment, the scholar murmured, "You have some natural defense against attacks upon the mind, as well as ways to influence them. That is how you won over Kurn's gem."

I made a face and wondered if he would call it natural if he knew the full tale of how it came to be? "That wasn't *all* it took."

"But the defense exists."

"Injured and short practiced," I muttered back, wary of letting him expect too much of me now that the mystique was gone. "Recall, apprentice, I am young for my race."

"Indeed, I remember, though it is curious to consider century-old Davrin having nocturnal emissions."

I squinted. "Having what?"

He twisted his mouth in distaste having to explain. "Mating dreams that come to…completion."

"Ah. Well, remember, *you* brought that up. It is not unusual among mine." I paused. "Less usual to affect others, however. That requires magic and intent."

"Indeed. Neither of which you claim to have." His eyes rested on a dark horizon of waving grasses. "I have also seen mage abilities 'injured,' as you say. Become less controlled by conscious choice. Sometimes slipping into madness."

*Comforting.* I refused to consider that further. After a few moments of quiet, I said, "Perhaps I should stay outside the coming town. Meet you farther down the road."

Gavin considered but shook his head. "I would not advise giving the Ma'ab complete control of what the sorcerer hears about you, nor depend on Rithal or myself to sway more than your mere presence would. I can agree with Mathias, all tales of the place are of neutral ground. I think your rarity would count for much to any who studied magic."

*As it did for you.* I exhaled. "Do you know this governing innkeeper's name?"

"Unfortunately, no. Best ask Rithal or the skin hunter when they wake."

"Why haven't you asked them already?"

"I plan to suppress my aura and sleep in a barn. With luck, he will take no notice of me."

I rolled my eyes to hear this. "Castis is still sore your mage's punch overcame his. He'll mention you, for certain. I can't stop him."

Now Gavin looked as irritated as I was with him. At least I wasn't the only one unprepared. I suggested, "We can share a room at the inn."

That scowl did not let up. "I am glad you have the silver to pay."

"I do not have silver."

"Neither do I. Some old copper is all I had collecting my things in such haste."

I exhaled again. "I shall ask Rithal, then."

Gavin in turn lay down to sleep. He maintained greater than his normal distance from the others sleeping, and I kept my watch without caressing further memories of Jaunda.

*Just in case.*

While it was amusing to watch four males, each having spurted in his braies, tend themselves where there was no convenient river or pond. I hid any smile or suggestion of my notice to avoid further accusations of manipulative witchery. This time, it held a whiff of truth which I wasn't sure I could keep off my face.

Mathias shrugged it off easily, perhaps as welcoming of such dreams as me, and readily prepared for his watch while I went hunting. Later, Rithal grumbled something about being too old for this dung, whatever that meant. If either of them had dreamt of a black-skinned fighter with tight breasts and white, close-cropped hair using a magic prick to plow them up their ass, they didn't look too disturbed by this.

*Maybe they dreamed their own versions of their lusts.*

Close to sunrise, on the other hand, Castis seemed subdued, spoke nothing, and went farther out where no one could observe his morning rituals. This was not unheard of, but I wondered because Kurn went straight to his waterskin, shoved down his breeches, and used half of his drinking water to scrub his crotch with pants around his knees. We all received a plain view of his pale ass and hairy thighs.

I picked that moment to ask Rithal, "What is the innkeeper's name? Will you introduce me?"

The Dwarf attempted to look away. "Uh, yeah, he's—"

Kurn spun around, his reddened prick flapping out. "He is Master Brom Troshin. We shall tell him about you before we can bring you in."

Rithal palmed his face. "Fer Pung's sake, Kurn, pull yer pants up!"

The big Ma'ab crossed his arms and wagged his black-bush genitals at us. Mathias fell over laughing, and I joined him though without the falling.

"How old are ye again?" Rithal grumbled.

Kurn snorted. "Merely a 'kid' to you, yes?"

"At least ye admit it."

The Hellhound seemed somehow *pleased* with the response, finished patting his crotch dry before securing his trousers and beginning to dress methodically and in full. "As I say, Sirana and the *maknuut* will wait outside while we discuss change to our plans."

"Mm, no," I said. "I want to be introduced to Master Brom directly."

"That is foolish," Kurn said. "Do you intend to strut into the hearth room and throw down your hood as well? Without taking stock if there might be Witch Hunters or worse?"

"She can be introduced behind a closed door in his office," Rithal groused. "An' that's how it's gonna be."

*"Bah!"*

Kurn flipped a hand in dismissal but didn't argue further. We had a few more days' ride. Being honest with myself, however, I didn't like Rithal's suggestion much over Gavin's or Kurn's.

"How would you go about this, Mathias?" I asked.

The skin hunter perked up and scratched his beard in thought. "Well. He'll have some measure of this group before we enter town, unless there's something big going on that's distracting. It's possible he'll come find us."

"In body?" I asked with interest.

"Maybe. Or sending a messenger." Mathias shrugged and smirked at me. "It depends how dangerous he thinks you are."

"As if he could be frightened of *her* to come out himself?" Kurn asked with derision.

Mathias shook his head. "Not frightened, Hellhound. Interested. The lone, dangerous ones always get a closer look. I know."

Kurn took the obvious, "She is not alone."

Mathias shrugged, refusing to debate, and I glanced at Gavin to make sure he was listening. He was.

"Say Master Brom doesn't come out or send anyone," I said to Mathias. "How else might you handle this, if you were me?"

I saw the glint in his eye as the Noble seemed to promise he'd get some questions answered in return. "Walk up to his inn and get a room. He'll find you eventually if it's necessary. Trying to avoid his notice sends the wrong message. It puts you at a disadvantage when he finds you regardless. Don't want his attention? Don't go to Troshin Bend."

I exchanged another look with Gavin, then looked at Rithal. "Have you silver for one room for Gavin and me?"

"Was planning on it," grumbled the Dwarf as he was finished packing and ready to leave. "Knew Gavin was poor, and ye haven't made one mention of knowing what a coin looks like, much less what it's worth."

Kurn chortled as if that was a measure of my intelligence as, at last, Castis wandered into camp looking refreshed and properly imperious. I said nothing as we got mounted up for the day. I knew about coins, of course, but the Dwarf was right about understanding their relative worth. I would be paying attention, for certain.

Yet how would I get out of Troshin Bend if events turned downward? What was my goal now? I hadn't felt much twinge of the Queen's geas since leaving the canyon alive. It was there, for certain, but without any pull to return to the Ley tower and end Sarilis. This must connect with the other part of my mission.

*Listen to all half-blood stories of Elven origin.*

I had one lead, the Priestess's Sathoet, enslaved in the Ma'ab army. These men had also said in Sarilis's tower that this Master Brom had a Ma'ab daughter and that he was older than half a century, by far, but did not look so old. If he was anything like Gavin in his studies, then this sorcerer could have *many* useful stories of Elves than Kurn did.

*Walk in and get a room. He'll find you eventually.*

This seemed like sound advice, oddly. I resolved not to worry the problem to the bone. The details I would need to plan a retreat or escape, I would not have until after I was inside.

Each day seemed to grow hotter as we traveled across the Midway until, at last, the hazy mountains were visible ahead of us; I could barely see them at night and not at all in the day. They were not as tall as those we had exited to the West, but they broke the monotony of the grasslands.

What we estimated was the final day upon the Midway began bright and steamy, the air becoming thick with vapor and strange to breathe; I sweated without any hope of cooling. The insects in the grass were loud and active; the tromp of many hooves did not obscure their noise. I noted each man and Dwarf in turn looking to the South horizon more than once, as if they expected to see something I couldn't. I did not deny the heightened heat and energy within the very air, however.

"What comes?" I asked Gavin on the back of his mare. I had a guess.

"It is likely we will see heavy rain and winds," he said. "It is only a question of if we will reach the mountains, first."

The horses seemed to sense this as well, as they pulled at their reins, allowed to cantor or lope as they answered the push of the coming storm. Kurn and Castis said nothing at all until after the midday break, when Gavin's mare was once again lagging.

"We will scout ahead," said the Hellhound to Gavin and me with a grin. "You meet us there."

"Wait a fuckin' moment!" Rithal barked. "Best we go in as one."

"The old nag needs rest and holds us back," Castis replied. "No point to us all being caught in the weather."

"You can stay, Rithal," Kurn invited. "Or Mathias."

Dwarvish spilled from that red beard alongside the rain. "Sirana. Want tah give Gavin's mare a rest and ride behind Mathias?"

"Indeed, I suppose the *maknuut* can make his way there alone," the Ma'ab mage remarked. "He seems to prefer solitude."

I didn't like the tone of Castis's voice, nor my glimpse of the look on Kurn's face; my spiders reacted at my nape, chiming a warning. "No, I will stay with the apprentice."

"Sirana," Rithal cajoled, but both Ma'ab made puffs of noise and turned their horses to launch at a gallop, forcing his hand.

"One of us stays with the mare carrying two," Mathias suggested to the Dwarf, "and one rides ahead with the Ma'ab."

More grumbling, then, "Fine. I'll ride with th' Ma'ab tah the inn."

The skin hunter lifted his thumb. "I'll stay. Nothing like a good storm."

Rithal's stout pony sprinted at the kick of his boot heels; the shaggy beast may not have long legs like Kurn's stallion, but I had noticed the Dwarvish mount always took longer to reach exhaustion. He would catch up.

Meanwhile, we let Gavin's mare rest and walk leisurely alongside Mathias's gelding, before she began limping. It would have been easy enough to follow the trail even without Mathias knowing the way.

Sadly, the glare grew such that I could only watch the ground below for familiar hoof prints. With the growing, hot gusts and restlessness of the grass, I was vulnerable and blind to a level I hadn't been since first riding out upon the plains. How easy it would be for Kurn and Castis to launch an attack if they intended to ambush Gavin regardless.

Assuming my gut feeling was correct.

"Is there any reason the Ma'ab might want you dead *before* meeting Master Brom?" I asked. "If given opportunity?"

Gavin turned his round ear toward me. "None I can think beyond being mixed blood and an affront to their caste."

"That cannot be it. The sorcerer has a mixed blood daughter. Kurn was not insulted by this."

"I do not know, then."

"Might have to do with you not acknowledging their Ascended," Mathias suggested. "While Master Brom and his daughter do."

Gavin frowned at him. "I know nothing of any ascended."

"Exactly. You are more Manalari and, worse, you've not spoken one word of either respect or fear. You dismiss them as unimportant."

The tension in Gavin's back suggested to me that he disliked being considered Manalari as much as Ma'ab, but he said nothing and kept riding. I recalled that he had also not spoken a word of who or what it was that he *did* respect.

*Whatever is truly leading him, like my Queen's vision pushed me to the Surface in the first place.*

The conversation faded in the increasing heat, leaving me quiet and cranky and keeping my thoughts. We rationed our water and were able to eat from the saddle most of the way as Gavin and Mathias often allowed their mounts to pull tufts of grass to chew as we moved along. I grunted in discomfort, wiping my moist forehead with my glove. The air became thicker, not with dust alone but moisture. I coughed and felt queasy if I was too close to hunger.

"So different to breathe this air than in the mountains," I muttered, and Gavin and Mathias turned an ear toward me as I slapped at a bug.

"Only in summer," said the skin hunter. "It's early for a storm like this. Maybe they had a warm winter down South."

Gavin made a salty remark. "It's not weather-devils causing it?"

The Nobleman paused and surely understood the jab, though I picked up the thought.

"How far South should it be warm to cause a sky like *that*?" I motioned toward a darkening cloud on the horizon, blurry as it was.

"Oh…" Mathias glanced that way. "Two fortnight's hard journey on horse? Or longer? There is an ocean that way, and the twin trade cities, Break Water and Salton Deeps. I hear it is very hot and the people there have darker skin, like yours."

Twin cities, an ocean, and dark skin? Similar to Rithal spoke of stories of Dark Elves in a Desert, but what was an ocean? How broad *was* the Surface?

I closed my mouth to keep a fly from landing on my lip; I puffed it away. "And who taught you to think of weather this far away affecting you?"

"It's not unknown to traveling merchants," replied the other man with a laughing defense. "The sorcerer is free with this knowledge to those who will listen. The winds on the Midway between the Great Lake and the ocean are infamous for how suddenly they change, and his town lies between them. He watches the patterns every year."

"You seem to have notable history with this innkeeper at Troshin Bend," Gavin said.

"I do at that, apprentice," Mathias admitted. "Exactly why your master called me to the tower."

"You didn't speak of all this 'free knowledge' at first."

"I always observe a new band or caravan before doing so, see if I'm wasting words on the deaf." Mathias's leather creaked and stretched as he shrugged. "Though Sarilis is correct I am not as proficient at traversing the Manalari leg of this road as you might be, monk. This is where my lack of faith could get us in trouble."

Gavin grunted irritably as we were struck by a concerning gust of wind; it abruptly turned cold before the heat swept in on us again. The rustle of grass both green and gold was another constant as we followed the trail of the Ma'ab and Rithal.

"If we push a little harder, we can reach the mountains by sundown," Mathias said. "Come!"

With the beating Sun far past its zenith, something passed overhead, and it became less bright for a moment. I lifted my head and tried to look through my blind, as difficult as that was at the speed we traveled. I could make out a half-blue and half-grey sky.

Within another league and Mathias pulling ahead to lead the way, the heat dropped noticeably, and the light's intensity faded further. At first it felt pleasant, like the cool night coming early and a relief to all of us, yet it heralded something of which I should rightly be concerned. I took advantage of a brief slow-down to put my spiders in their pouch, cinching it up tight as the wind eased.

I inhaled deeply and detected that unique scent of sundered air being carried toward us. I had no trouble keeping my hood up for once; the wind came from behind and kept it in place. My cloak felt pasted to my back. I did not like the feeling of warning which crept up my spine.

With the Sun fully covered, I removed my blind and lowered my hood, blinking away tears for a complete view. The clouds on the Southern horizon were astoundingly dark, the deepest grey I had ever witnessed while the Sun was in the sky. I could barely imagine how thick and tall the cloud build must be that so little sunlight could reach through to the ground.

Then my aching eyes caught movement within their depths, and an odd light. Or a trick of the light? Pieces of this churning expanse changed color before me.

"Gavin."

"Hm?"

"Grey clouds turning green is worrisome, yes?"

He grunted. "It means we may get pummeled with bits of ice."

*Ice?!*

"Ice upon dry ground in such heat?" I cried.

"Yes. I recall it clearly. Please loosen your hold, Sirana, I would like to breathe."

I did so without a quip in exchange. Something imperceptible bothered me as well, like a dull edge worried a scar. That low, buzzing whine such as when I had followed a Ley Line to Tamuril's hovel, yet the birds and insects which had been the secondary source of Surface noise beneath the wind had vanished. Something else had taken their place.

"May we speed up?"

"We can't outrun a storm, Sirana."

"But the closer to the mountains before dark, the better. At least catch Mathias."

He expelled a breath at the tone of my voice but kicked and encouraged his mare to pick up the pace. She seemed to catch my urgency or sensed something herself, and we maintained it for some time, coming up alongside the skin hunter, who smiled through his beard, eyes twinkling in excitement.

The storm did not seem to be charging down upon us yet; unfortunately, the wind slowed and the energy in the air seemed to be building. I had the time to consider further what an evening and possibly a night taken over by a lightning storm meant for me.

It was woefully regretful. I could not hunt for food, and I would be vulnerable to the pain of my battered senses beneath continuous wind, thunder, and lightning, never mind being pummeled with ice! If I remained out here until dawn, I would not eat or rest; I would be hungry and physically exhausted coming before the sorcerer.

*I must think of a different plan for tonight.*

I would have little chance of that, either. The first flash of white light and the swell of sound that rolled along the ground to overtake me made me groan, though I could barely hear myself. Fat drops of water struck the ground a few moments later, and wind began to direct some of those drops at my rear flank and the mare's rump.

The Sun would be near to setting by now, but the last daylight for the horses and men was lost to the storm clouds as it became too dark, too soon. Worse, I chanced to risk another look at the densest part of the storm that had not yet reached us, and a bolt of light cut across my vision, soon to be followed by a crack and a boom.

*Aiieee!*

In agony and ignoring the unctuous smell, I buried my face in Gavin's robes, covering my ears with my hands. The mare jerked in fright once, whinnying and nearly throwing me off, but Gavin spun her around and got her under control again.

We were running blind and had no place to stop.

"Keep going!" Mathias shouted as if underwater. "Foothills ahead!"

Gavin's mare changed her gait, and we leaned such as to suggest a slow rise and descent. My eyes and ears were numbed from exposure and my head pounded such I couldn't hear much of the splash and squelch of hooves in the mud as we meandered through the lowest areas between mounds instead of trying to crest each one.

The rain strengthened, beating down upon us, and the thunder became louder each time it pealed across the swollen sky. The darkness may have once been my advantage, but I couldn't begin to see as the lightning blinded me repeatedly, sending my head to splitting each time. Much to my ever-increasing anxiety, I also took longer after each thunderclap to recover any hearing at all.

My senses taken away, numbed by too much light, too much sound, I grew desperate enough to bind my eyes and ears with dark strips of cloth reserved for bleeding injuries. This helped reduce the pain enough to make it worth it.

I had experienced sensory deprivation before in the Deepearth, but that had been in complete silence, leaving only the sound of my heart and blood running in my veins. This was quite the opposite. Given that I hadn't heard of it being used for torture, I imagined not even our enemies could well-tolerate something like this.

*Nothing could be this grand down below,* I thought.

Though over-stimulated, I could still feel when we were pelted by those sharp, icy bits Gavin warned about. Our respective armor protected our torso, but the hard, cold pebbles stung our heads, hands, and thighs. Were my hood not up, it would be striking my ears intolerably. The mare suffered as well, whickering and whinnying in protest as she danced and slopped in the growing mud. I began to hear constant splashes beneath and beside us.

"We must get out of the furrows!" Gavin shouted over the rain, and I whimpered. "The water could wash us away!"

"Agreed!" Mathias bellowed. "This way!"

The horse heaved her way up a slope, hooves sucking and sinking in the muddy grass, or clipping the occasional stone. The rise was larger than I might have guessed and wondered how high the hills had grown as we approached the mountains? Eventually, we levelled out and abruptly worried for my spiders.

All the pouches on my belt were well-made and treated to repel water, and my cloak and clothing had resisted for a while into the storm, yet I felt the wet chill seeping into unusual places on my skin. Would the same happen to my babies or my tools? I doubted Rausery had ever tested for this amount of rain; I might as well have stepped beneath the waterfall back at the canyon.

I touched the pouch and "thought" to them. *~Guardians? Are you there?~*

I *did* feel them, as I was slowly learning to do, and they were well enough for the time being. The pouch was not filling with liquid to drown them yet.

Beneath the rain and the hard hail, amid the heavy and uneven steps of the mare, I thought I heard a shout. There was another flash, and I winced behind my blindfold and waited for the next assault to my ears. When it came, I tensed, swallowed my cry, and pressed harder against the cloth held to my ears.

As the roar started to fade, I doubted I could take more without going screaming mad. How could I determine where to hide from the storm? How could I stumble into a forest so near a Human settlement detecting nothing? It was too late to escape the weather, yet I didn't know how much longer the storm would last. Gavin wouldn't be able to see at all in a few moments, and his mare might stumble and break a leg—

"...Elf...!"

I turned my head suddenly to one side; I had no idea how it related to the mountains, but I thought it came from my left. *Rithal.*

"There!" Mathias shouted. "He's got a lantern! Follow him!"

Thank goddess *they* could see it. The lack of sensitively in their vision made sense if the Surface could be like *this* every summer.

Gavin kicked the mare forward and I clutched him as Mathias guided us down the hill to make the next one. Fortunately, no sudden flush of rushing water blocked our path. The Dwarf met us halfway atop the second hill, and I could make out his voice well enough as I remained ready to flinch at the next crash and boom.

"Goin' the wrong way!" Rithal said.

"How could that be?" Gavin growled with bitter irony. "I am known for tracking through thunderstorms."

Such a burst of spirit surprised each of us, enough to draw a smile and a laugh from me.

"Easy, Gavin, we found the inn," replied the Dwarf. "I'll take yah there."

"Your mare is worn, Gavin," Mathias said. "Let Sirana ride on my horse the rest of the way."

My first impulse was to refuse. "No. We're nearly there, aren't we?"

"There are steep climbs from here," argued the skin hunter. "You'll make her lame, then she can't continue. I can see the signs. The poor beast is exhausted."

Gavin didn't reply at all, and I took that to mean he agreed with the assessment.

"Gavin?" I asked.

"He has a point."

Mathias pulled up alongside. "Come on, climb over, Red Sister. Take my hand."

Clenching my jaw, I reached out toward his voice, and he clasped my forearm. Gripping him and holding Gavin's shoulder with my other hand, I used the balance to climb stiffly to a crouch and transfer myself over to Mathias's slightly taller gelding in one smooth leap. As I settled in behind, noting how his leathers felt and the hilt or two I could touch, Mathias chuckled.

"Such confidence doing that blindfolded, Davrin. Can you walk tightropes, too?"

I made no reply as I flinched sharply beneath another lightning and thunder duet. A murky rumble from Rithal followed, "Le's move."

I smelled conifers and deciduous trees and we leaned with the changing lay of the land. The steep climbs they mentioned arrived quickly, and the horses would slip unexpectedly, making me flinch and want to leap off. Then they were over, and we entered a forested mountain again. I thought we must be on a path or road to be so steady, but the rain drummed out all other details until the wind shifted. Once I smelled it, I could not mistake it for anything else.

A Human settlement. *Troshin Bend.*

"Just keep your hood up," Mathias murmured, "and don't let the few too stupid to go in out of the rain see your face."

"And suppress your aura," Gavin added.

It was then I realized my spiders had grown agitated; water was slowly entering into their pouch as they crowded near the top, warning me of their risk. I could do nothing yet, but...

~Soon. Soon.~

How many other tools of mine were threatened or already ruined by this weather? As exhausted as I was, ill-prepared to meet a sorcerer-governor-innkeeper on his own turf, I could not stay out here all night. As for the thought of stealing into a barn somewhere instead, well, Gavin wasn't making a break to execute that idea, either.

I exhaled, breath shaking. One choice at a time. *Hood up. Suppress aura.*

The horses were as eager to reach the town as we were. Even sodden, the scents increased until I could identify greater numbers of horses and men, much manure, mud, and wood—both wet and smoking. Thunder and lightning kept me from trying to hear or see much, although I at least confirmed that, yes, we were on a road and the going would be easier.

With structures soon looming on either side of us, I huddled down against Mathias, unmoving until we reached wherever we were doing. He went directly into a large, wooden structure; a stable, I recognized instantly as the horses' hooves clopped on a strong wooden floor. The scent of horse and manure concentrated in the closed space, as did the noise of the beasts. It was warm and dry; I could hear the drops falling from our bodies onto the ground and someone smaller than Mathias closing the door behind us.

Then a Human bua who sounded much younger than either Gavin or Mathias said something I could barely understand, and the skin hunter replied.

"Well, now you can sleep, Neal," Mathias said, turning his mount around to put himself between me and the young Human. "We'll take care of our own steeds, thank you."

I heard a metallic *ching*, probably a coin that left the bounty hunter's hand; the 'young man' missed the catch and had to scrabble on the floor for it as it went bouncing. The bua mumbled something like an appreciation and backed away deeper into the stable; he began to climb a ladder.

Other than the boy bedding down somewhere up there, it sounded like we were alone. As luck would have it, I hadn't heard another thunderclap in a while, and the intensity of the rain on the stable roof had eased off as if the storm were passing.

*Of course.*

Slowly as I could, and with no one hissing a warning at me, I removed the blindfold and earmuffs to look around. My aching eyes saw a few dim lamps and a score of stalls, each containing two horses. There were no windows, and I was protected for the moment from an errant lightning flash.

"Dismount," Rithal said.

"How much to board them here?" Gavin asked as we did.

"Already paid, like I said."

"You spoke of private rooms."

Rithal nodded. "Those, too."

With an answering grunt from Gavin that I thought sounded uncertain, we took to giving all the mounts a brush down after removing their tackle; meanwhile they munched hungrily on mounds of dried grasses in a trough. In the interest of steadying my nerves and trying to think what came next, I helped Gavin with his mare and stayed out of easy sight of any who might walk in.

I also took the time when the horse was between us to let my spiders out so I could pour the excess water in the pouch onto the floor. My clothing was no drier on the outside, so they reluctantly crawled in at my urging. I would need time and safety to check over everything else. It remained to be seen if I would get that.

"So, what are the arrangements?" Gavin asked quietly as we finished up.

"Three private rooms above th' tavern, two per room," Rithal said.

"Can't really go for the common area, hm?" Gavin said with that touch of irony.

"Course not. Pairs make the most sense. Includes two meals per day, one evening, and morning."

"How many days?"

"We'll have tah see how it goes."

I'd noticed they weren't using names, assuming "Neal" might be listening in. At least they were experienced in some basics of stealth, though I might not be surprised if Kurn had used our names inside the inn.

With horses resting and secure, we took our packs and belongings and were required to sprint through the rain up a muddy incline they called a road to a large wooden structure, well-built albeit temporary, as it may not last a century. Still, a quick glancing about suggested this to be the grandest building in the settlement; everything else was smaller and less apt to last.

The "tavern" possessed an upper level as well as the main one, with light seeping through wooden trappings which secured the windows against the storm. There was a drone of noise telling me Humans were awake inside, and I moved behind Mathias and to the side of Gavin, double-checking that my hood was secure.

*Walk in and get a room,* Mathias had said with such casualness.

Was this really going to work? My hands were shaking a little, though I chalked it up to exhaustion.

*Evading him sends the wrong message. He'll find you eventually.*

The nausea was a subtle threat against spinning around to run, and if Mathias was being truthful, it was too late to leave unnoticed anyway. My boots kept moving, one in front of the other, toward the inn.

Be this what I sought or no, the Ma'ab had led me here, and I must seek stories for my Queen from the sorcerer of Troshin Bend.

# CHAPTER 3

It was early evening in the tavern, and it was warm and heavy with the scents of Human bodies, hearty cooking, and burning wood. The large, open room upon entry was filled with wooden tables and benches, some unoccupied but others clustered with bodies hunched over food and drink. No fewer than twenty separate voices blended together, wooden chairs and tables shifting beneath their weight, metal plates, cups, and utensils being used adding to the din. Swells of deep-voiced words and laughter occasionally lifted above the constant drone.

The Humans supping were all male from what I glimpsed by size, except for the smaller, softer, straw-haired Humans in simple gowns. Those were women, I realized, bringing platters and pitchers to the larger men so they didn't have to stand up and clutter the long banquet counter any further. This waist-high platform visually sectioned off the mess hall from the rest of the room, and only the women confidently moved behind it.

I recognized them as servants, of course, and this was a practical parallel to a gathering at the Palace, but the unhesitating flip in the roles before my eyes was more disorienting than anything Kurn and the others had tried to describe before now. Bearded Dwarves were present as well, though if any were female, I couldn't be sure in my fast glance.

Motivated to check my suppressed my aura, I looked down and tugged my hood farther forward as well so none would see my face, or worse my skin, as none here were near as dark as I was. A pity my journey hadn't begun to the South, much as I disliked the heat. From the sound of it, I would blend in better should one glimpse my chin or the flesh of my neck.

I kept my traveling companions' bodies between me and the rest of the room as we entered and bypassed the dining, staying closer to Gavin and attempting to make us appear an obvious pair, short of looping my arm around his. He turned to give me a strange look but quickly brought his attention where it belonged when a tanned, brown-haired man came around a long, high counter, drying his hands on a rough, white towel.

"Ah, ye made it, good sirs," he said, his voice rough from much use but speaking the common trade language better than that stable bua. "Yer rooms're ready. Hot meal wit' yer keys?"

Mathias chuckled, and Rithal rumble his reply with a still-dripping beard. "Please, Master Lihgan. Thank ye."

The counter-tender craned his neck around. "Cheri! Got the last ones! Extra towels!"

"Coming, Lih!"

This woman had darker hair than the two others I'd seen, with flower-blush cheeks that stood out the moment she began a smile. She wore a pale apron sullied by the day while protecting her dark blue gown of sturdy weave. She clutched quite a stack of small blankets that looked like they could be used to dry and clean equipment, faces, and limbs.

"This way, masters," she said, moving at an efficient clip up the wooden stairs that the rest of us had to act on keeping up. She didn't look back and hadn't looked at us that closely.

I noted the layout as we walked a straight hallway lined with doors and leading to the rear of the building; the only way to turn was left when one reached the end. Having seen the second set of stairs on the other side of the front room, I guessed that these rooms lined the inn on both sides and formed a rectangle to fit as many travelers as possible. In about half of them, I heard someone inside.

Cheri approached the door in the corner and reached one hand into a pocket of her apron, withdrawing a small, metal key to unlock the door and open it. Inside, I saw a corner room lit with a low oil lantern, with more than one way out available through the shuttered windows. I could hear the rain outside; the protection from any lightning would be better than from the thunder. Still, it was welcomingly dry, with no leaks in the ceiling.

There were two wooden bed frames with what smelled like hay-stuffed mattresses lying atop a tight lattice of rope. The room included a small table and chair, a set of shelves, and a pitcher and basin resting atop the table. A glossy, white pot sat beneath each bed. The next thing I thought was how everything here was vulnerable to fire.

Cheri turned around and held out the key to Rithal, who accepted and handed it over to Gavin. The servant bobbed her head and grasped three towels with one hand and handed them out to the apprentice without looking the tall, ugly man in the face; he accepted as wordlessly. She handed out the rest to the Dwarf and skin hunter with at least a small smile as if she remembered them and bowed her head again.

"Half hour enough before I bring dinner here?" she asked, glancing at me then quickly looking at Gavin, then down again.

"Yes," agreed the death mage, sounding as uncomfortable. "Knock first."

"Of course, sir."

She bounced in a way that must have been an acknowledgement and disappeared to the left, returning to the downstairs where I could hear her feet speed up. Then Rithal drew in a deep breath, exhaling as he motioned to the open room.

"Lay o' the land fer t'night," he said. "a lot o' rooms claimed. Me an' him," he indicated Mathias, "are between ye an' our 'first-comers'."

"Not a bad thing," Gavin said.

"Yeh, but not perfect. Distant enough we won't hear trouble outside yer door. We jus' make it till tomorrow. We can ask 'bout changing fer any vacancies."

"I'll not cause trouble," Gavin said, looking and smelling miserable enough as it was. "I only want to rest."

I didn't speak but made a hand motion and bowed my head. *I agree.*

"Right, good," said the redbeard, looking between us and reluctant to leave us alone.

Mathias clapped him on the shoulder. "Come on, they can lock it. Let's dry off before the meals come."

The Dwarf finally wandered away, and Gavin and I entered our room to close the door and let out a breath we'd been holding. I slid and set the small, metal bar above the handle and held my ear to the wood, listened to everything of interest right after.

"I take it he's busy?" Mathias murmured as they rounded the corner.

"Which one?" Rithal grumbled.

"The innkeeper, of course."

"Aye. None o' us spoke to 'im yet…"

Voices faded and another door opened and closed. There were other bootsteps I didn't recognize leaving another room and heading down the stairs. It was quiet after that. I leaned back with a sigh, thinking how I would be listening to heavy feet tromping through this place all night.

"Good soundproofing," Gavin commented, "compared to many places I've stayed."

I turned and stared in horror. "It gets worse?"

The homely apprentice paused in loosening the knot of his belt, studying me for a few moments and one corner of his mouth twitched. "Do you hear our neighbors, then? Not who moves past the door."

I focused on that, instead, underneath the constant patter of rain. I had to shake my head. "Not at the moment."

"The place is well-built."

I glanced at the oil lamp on the precarious stand. "But flammable."

"Fire would not get far after this downpour, for tonight at least."

Maybe. There were too many smells, and my head ached fiercely after the torment of the storm. Pangs of hunger drove me to think of the servant woman soon to return with "dinner." A warm meal sounded like a perfect remedy to end this arduous crossing of the Midway, though I did not like that I couldn't watch it being prepared. I must watch Gavin eat first, though it would be difficult to refuse unless I simply knew at once it was unsafe.

Gavin hung his robe, and I, my cloak, upon the wall hooks provided, then we each took a bed to use as a working area. I stripped out of all my wet clothes and began to sort through my things. I did my best to dry them with the towels and set out what could be aired out. There was not a lot of furniture, but there was a rod with hooks spanning a man's height across in one corner, as if it were meant for hanging most belongings off the floor. We used that to its fullest.

Although I simply removed everything and tended to it all naked while my spiders explored one corner wall of the room, Gavin took far greater lengths not to strip entirely and at once or look at me working. Instead, he focused on tending to one article at a time. In removing his boots to dry, I saw again his rather large feet, ghostly pale with a few purple veins standing up. Next, he wrung out his shabby, grey robe into the bed pot and hung it to dry, then removed the leather torso piece I'd long since known was there and wiped it down to hang along with his tool belt.

Beneath the robe and armor, he wore a long, linen shirt that reached his knees and a baggy pair of longer pants. His tall, gaunt frame was covered by the shirt when he removed his braies, laid them flat atop a towel, and rolled them up to draw out moisture.

Still damp, he put them back on; only then would he remove the long shirt and do his best to remove the water from it as well.

As he was leaning over the mattress, I studied the many, silvery lines of scars on his white, hairless back, trying to decide what had made them. Hot iron, as he had mentioned? Although most looked like the marks of a lash or a whip, strangely shaped to my eye, as if they had stretched with his growing skin. One of them created a deliberate shape: a circle with four narrow triangles pointed out. *A brand.*

Gavin had been resolute not looking my way—perhaps he'd forgotten he had seen me naked at the waterfall—that I did not expect him to catch me staring at him and returning my gaze with such a glower.

"What?" he asked, essentially a demand.

I shrugged, grasping for the words. "Your body speaks truth of your story."

"And yours seems to erase yours. I cannot see the marks from the canyon. They are gone."

I grinned. "You were looking for them?"

Gavin grunted in annoyance and replaced his long shirt soon as possible; apparently it was enough, and he removed his braies to dry completely. Then he claimed the small table, chair, and lamp to meticulously check over his surgery kits and grimoire, securely wrapped in oil cloth but having suffered for the weather.

I returned to my clothing and tools, sitting naked and comfortable on the bed. Rausery would be proud of the quality of our leatherwork and weather proofing, if not my diligence. Only one of my powders was a ruined, soggy clump—an ingestible tranquilizer I'd not used for putting a man to deep sleep yet—and only because I had not checked the closure recently enough; like that of my oft-used spider pouch, it had become loose.

I sighed and set it aside to dry apart from the rest, though I would be taking it with me; I dared not toss it outside for some foolish Human to find. Otherwise, all my vials, jars, and wraps were fine after being wiped off. My blades were good, as were my hand crossbow and bolts; the latter not being made of wood meant their aim would be true even if I dunked them in a river. My spare shirt, stockings, and cloths washed in the last river were soaked and would need to dry again, but that was nothing.

Gavin wiped down a scalpel before adding it to his kit, glancing at me. "You carry a small armory and apothecary on you."

"Tools of the trade, apprentice," I said. "You carry a hand saw, needles of multiple sizes, thread and meat twine, a cooking pot, and a few bitter solvents. If I did not know your area of interest, I would wonder about the combination."

"Even did you wonder I doubt it would faze you."

"Not at all."

Gavin proved adept at inspecting the meal once it arrived without me asking. He was familiar with many local sleeping drugs—I only mildly wondered why—and some of the obvious poisons. I cross examined with what I knew, and neither of us detected anything off.

"You eat first," I said.

"Should we switch?"

"The *cait* did not indicate one was intended for you or me."

"True. It likely doesn't matter." He blinked. "Wait, the what? The maid?"

"No, the *cait*. A young female."

"Hm."

I shrugged. "'Very well, the maid if you say. Sup first. I am hungry."

"Then why don't you sup first?"

"I risk more than myself. Eat."

Gavin's expression alone was worth that exchange. I smiled and relaxed as he sampled the stew. It smelled wonderful from where I sat, and I waited with thinning patience.

"I taste nothing odd," he said. "Simple enough fare."

I nodded but waited as Gavin ate swallowed several bites. He seemed fine and, with his paranoid caution, I believed him when he said he did not feel drowsy.

"Not beyond fatigue from the trip, that is."

Good enough. I dove in, consuming the stew and bread in short order while it still had a bit of warmth to it. I could have used a larger portion. Going for seconds, however, seemed impossible, unless I could convince Gavin to go on my behalf.

"No," he said. "I've as much reason as you not to draw undue attention to myself. At least one group was Manalari in that room."

"They were?"

"I must sleep," he said stubbornly, leaving me to weigh my near-equal problems of either resting or obtaining food.

*Reverie now. Sneak down to the kitchen after the Humans are asleep.*

The apprentice set a simple warning ward on the door and windows before we lay down and doused the light. My spiders would watch over us whether he knew of them or not. We bedded down—me in the nude and Gavin wearing his threadbare shirt and thin underpants that reached from waist to ankle—and I reflected that while this straw-stuffed mattress was much better than a muddy cave or a wind-blown tree, it also made a lot of noise. I would have preferred the simplicity of a cot or a floor pallet.

Still, I was glad to be dry and have some food in my stomach to rest, even with the constant rustles and steps abounding, the pungent scent of Humans, and the stink of the streets outside. I quickly fell into Reverie with the occasional, distant rolls of thunder outside.

This had been one of the most exhausting days of the journey so far.

Worn down and daring to let down my guard a little, it should not surprise me that a dream of the red sands returned. The setting Sun became the darkest red I had yet seen on the Surface, shimmering to look like bloody water wavering on the horizon.

I was alone. Without thinking, I turned away from the crimson light and headed toward the deepening purple of the approaching night sky. My feet dragged through shifting sand as heavily as the hooves of Gavin's mare had in the sloshing mud of the plains, and I crested three dunes before I spotted a canyon ahead which might offer shelter for the night.

This canyon wasn't like the one in which Kurn and I had fought; it split and curved many times through a plateau that sank into the ground rather than jutting up defiantly in the air. I must keep to the lowest trails to see the banded walls of colors rise above me and protect me from the scouring wind.

It grew dark and cooler. One by one, the stars appeared in the night sky directly overhead, though the Moons were rising fast. The sound of water burbling drew me deeper into the dusty, colorful stone, but so did a hiss and a scuttle. I froze in place.

*Come all this way, traveler,* said a chilling, feminine voice. *Be aware, then. Stay awake. This is no place to rest.*

Something drew my eye down. Near my boot was something that looked like a flattened crawfish, with pinchers and a long tail, arched up in a threatening manner. A venomous, eight-legged hunter.

But not a spider. A scorpion.

It was a bright amber color, bordering on the orange of an open flame, but the sand around it was night blue. I stepped back warily from the Desert arachnid, and when it did not move, I remained staring as a small, hooded snake appeared out from the long shadows. Each were about the same size and color, each attempting to reach behind the other creature for some invisible prize.

The scorpion attacked with aggression, holding the snake's head with its claws, and slamming the pointed tail down into the flesh, then releasing and backing away. The snake thrashed about, hissing, contorting as if it might bite and swallow its own tail. Soon, it dissolved straight into the red sand, vanishing. The scorpion spun to me, tail up and ready, but did not attack.

*What are you?*

I did not expect an answer, but the creature fled into its hidden burrow when feathers flapped from above and a brief shower of ashes fell upon me. Looking up, I spotted a black bird. A crow, I thought, except it glowed like it carried the red coals of a campfire in its breast.

It called hoarsely, crying harshly its warning or its passing. Again and again as its inner fire grew until it was a bird aflame. It took to the night sky, looked like a lantern in a storm, a spotlight along the ground showing me a path to take.

I ran after it, as fast as I could, the colorful walls blurring as I weaved right and left and around. In time or distance, the sheer cliffs closed around me, squeezing off the stars above as the colors vanished.

It grew dark, then it fell to black, as I sought the end of that canyon, scrambling up the rubble like I danced toward the terminal point of a needle, seeking, wanting to find...

I found nothing. My blue-gloved hand pressed flat to a solid rock wall, when I had been *certain* I would find something here. Or maybe someone.

The stone was cold. And hollow.

*What happened here?*

I craned my neck back the way I'd come. When I looked back, the barest sliver of Moonlight had pierced the darkness, laying atop my fingers as it pointed toward the sigils I couldn't read without light. I couldn't read them now, but someone could. Someone else who sought this place.

The meaning turned my blood to ice. *No...No, no. What have you done?*

Small segments of stone softened like clay beneath my fingers, beginning to melt and drip like Human candlewax. Gaps opened up in the cliff's face, revealing the void beyond, while iron bars remained fixed in place so nothing of size could leap out.

Two quivering, black arms reached out through the bars and seized my forearms. Eyes like shining gold stared out at me.

*"Help me, Uncle!"* he screamed. *"Please!"*

I stared in shock at the prisoner behind the bars, my mouth wide open.

*Auslan?* Maybe. Not quite. Not with those eyes. Where had I seen them before?

The Davrin's grip on my arms grew hard as stone, piercingly desperate. "Don't leave!" he demanded. "Don't leave me here! Take me with you!"

He didn't sound like the Consort. He sounded like Shyntre.

"I can't stay," My voice was equally strange to me. "I-I have discovered you by accident. I must return later with aid. I know who can help you."

*"No!* You won't find me again! She'll know!"

"She'll know what? What are her plans?"

"Free me, Uncle, and I'll tell you!"

So desperate. Was this real? Was he telling the truth?

"How do you claim I am your Uncle?" I asked. "I...I never knew you existed."

The shimmer in those unreal, golden eyes faded as blackness overtook them. Wisps of giggling shadow reached up to wrap lovingly around the bua's arms, drawing them back behind the iron bars.

*"Help me!"*

"I must... I will seek help," I stammered. "My... for my family... "

The wail of despair which soared up out of that dark pit echoed all around me, sending me fleeing for the nearest star lest the void drag me in screaming as well.

I bolted upright in a dim, wooden room upon a rough, straw mattress, listening to the soft patter of rain. Despite my racing heart and the tears on my cheeks, there were no warnings from my spiders as they hunted for their meals, though they greeted me in their way.

It was the darkest of night, and my stomach growled upon waking. I glared at my middle. *You were just lying in wait, weren't you?*

No matter. I must find food, somehow. Could I sneak into the kitchen? All was still and well; Humans breathed noisily but otherwise the inn was quiet. I needed no light to move about, and although magic wards protecting the pantry seemed possible, I wasn't without my skills to circumvent them.

Still, I waited. Another quarter hour passed until I was certain every Human on this floor must be asleep; only body shifts and snores. I got up and began dressing, even though not all was dry. I donned my belt, collected my spiders into their drier pouch, and my cloak as well. I would leave my pack and larger weapons here.

Gavin began to mutter in his sleep, limbs twitching, his breath shuddering a few times as if he were in pain. I stopped and watched him as he rolled from his back to his side and curled up. I was not the only one with troubling dreams tonight.

I saw him as I might in the Deepearth. The way his heat surged, and his body scent shifted to one of terror, he may have drawn a predator to him quickly. He might be able to suppress his magical aura to other mages on the Surface, but he had little control over his somatic responses, particularly when asleep.

I listened for a moment to the few words he uttered; the underlying tone was unsettling, but I didn't know them. They weren't in the Trade tongue. Before things got too boisterous or a shadow appeared above him again, I moved to the door and touched his ward.

Gavin partially awoke, groggily rising and bracing himself upright. "Wh—"

"*Shh,*" I hushed. "It's me. Secure the door behind me."

"Where…?"

"Food. I will tap the door twice short then twice long. You will know it's me."

He took several moments to absorb that. "Is this a good idea?"

"I cannot hunt. I need food. Unless you want to give me your spares."

He sighed. "I shall get the door."

Gavin waited until I was out in the darkened hall before getting out of bed to replace the metal lock, then he muttered another ward and shuffled to his bed. I moved carefully along the wood, learning quickly when it tended to squeak or shift, and after only one tell, managed to find the quieter spots closer to the doors.

The stairs weren't as bad; sturdy, of quality, they absorbed the tender fall of my boot quite well. They led me down to the main eating area where all the chairs rested atop the tables and the floor had been swept clean from what it had been earlier. My nose led me toward the kitchen, though I discovered what Gavin had meant by the "common area."

On the opposite side I had come down and one door over from the mess hall, there was a large room with long benches and many bodies lying either atop them or along the walls. This was no doubt the least expensive of the rooms at the inn, tonight with about twenty men, most smelling of lumber and sweat.

I considered the silence and lack of sentries to be fortune in my favor and focused on suppressing my aura and gliding into the kitchen to feed. There was a low-lit oil lamp illuminating the entry, which I snuffed with a twist of the small knob which lowered the wick.

Inside, I spotted two young Humans sleeping near the warm coals. They did not stir as I opened a store to pilfer bread and discovered a lidded, clay pot which contained a vegetable-packed paste that smelled quite savory. Breaking off a piece of dense bread, I scooped out a generous helping and started eating. I did not want to carry it back to my room, and the sooner I consumed as much as I could, the better.

There were a few wrapped leathers with five strips of leftover, cooked meat inside, and I ripped my teeth into one of those as well while I replaced everything as it was, though there was no hiding the missing paste from the pot. I finished the meat and felt content enough to return to my room.

"Was the host's stew not enough, my lady?"

I fell still, thankful I had kept my hood up to cover my ears and white hair, giving moments to gather any wits which hadn't been sent skyward. I withdrew my hand from the dagger my belt.

*Lady?* How long was he watching?

I turned slowly, careful of showing my face. My greeter had dark brown hair and beard; his skin was deeply tan, not so pale as a Ma'ab. He wore a long-sleeved, off-white cloth shirt with a lattice of leather ties to adjust the fit to the chest; they were loosened for comfort. His trousers were dark brown with no belt; he was barefoot and seemed to possess no weapon on him.

*The sorcerer, perhaps?*

The man leaned against the door frame with the confidence of knowing the place well despite his partial dress. He certainly didn't seem to need much light.

"Forgiveness," I murmured, glancing at the sleeping children. "I was hungry and would not disturb others so late."

His mouth formed a mild smirk. "Stealing to eat, hm? So urgent it could not wait to morning?"

I was uncertain of his tone. "Yes, master. I will ask Rithal to spare another piece of silver for my appetite. I am reliant on him for such things."

He tilted his head in curiosity, listening to me. "Hm. Where did they find you? I'd have thought Kurn would sooner slash his gut open than take on a woman fighter."

Again, I glanced at the youths near the hearth. His lips drew back in a smile.

"They will not stir," he said above a whisper. "They sleep like the dead. A moment, then. I am hungry, too."

The man came into the kitchen and, quietly and with great familiarity, collected some orange-flesh fruit, deep purple roots, bread, and cheese, piling it onto a plate. He picked up a sealed bottle of liquid with his other hand.

"Will you come with me to my office, or were you returning to sleep?"

I stared. It sounded as if I had a choice though I would be sleeping no more this night.

The man paused in his exit when I only watched him in silence. "Do I not warrant an answer, my lady?"

"I know not to whom I would answer."

He huffed a laugh through his nose. "Forgiveness. My name is Brom. And yours?"

The innkeeper whose reputation preceded him. "I am Sirana."

"Lovely," he remarked. "If you will, Sirana, come with me to my office."

"Why, Master Brom?"

"It would please me to share a conversation before your travel companions wake up. I am certain I'd prefer your tale over theirs."

"Hm." I took a step forward. "May we trade tales, Master Brom?"

"If you need help returning to sleep," he said dryly, stepping out into the hallway. "Fifty years in the same tavern isn't much of a bard's tale."

"You don't appear that old."

"Such is my blessing."

He led me on the main floor, farther away from both kitchen and common area, to the rear of the tavern. He turned left into a short hallway and came to a thick, wooden door broader than those upstairs, with iron bands reinforcing it and a decorated handle he grasped to pull it open. There was a place for a key, but he did not use it this time.

Firelight spilled out into the hallway with a warm wave of air, scents of exotic spices and surprising cleanliness. Brom motioned that I enter first with a wave of the hand holding the bottle. Against my usual practice, I accepted, keeping my back to him as he had not seen my face.

If he were as old as Sarilis then I could hope curiosity might win out over fear for those first, crucial moments, depending what he may know of Davrin. If it was a terribly bad response, well, I had my guardians with me.

This room was lit by a hearth that burned cleanly. I thought it must hold the greatest of riches and comforts in the whole inn, possibly all Troshin Bend. It was not like the highly decorated Palace or Sanctuary of Sivaraus, or some of the favored Noble Houses, but there was a familiar elegance to it.

*The place is named after him. He may collect tribute for the stability and protection if his magic is strong enough.*

There was a table with three seats farther in, as well as several standing shelves displaying various items of worth: stones and metals set in fine statues, delicately carved boxes, and odder, fantastical pieces that looked to have been collected from far away. He possessed artwork evenly spaced around the walls, all Surface landscapes, nothing abstract. There were a few brass bowls in discrete places that held the scented herbs I smelled, and there were no windows or exits to the outside, changing the room from a mere place to sleep into a marked, protected den.

My next object of note was a well-crafted standing mirror. I did not see my reflection from this angle, but I could see there was another semi-private living space behind a partial wall which blocked a guest's view when standing before a large, heavy wooden desk. Reflected in the mirror were a wardrobe and a fine bed, wider and more comfortable than the guest rooms. I paused to realize this "office" was also his personal quarters.

*He should move that mirror.*

Yet there was a velvet, red curtain partly drawn which would normally provide privacy. The bedding was disturbed like he'd just left them.

*He got up in the middle of the night and came to the kitchen.*

Discovering me.

I drew another breath of the air; the lingering scent was pleasant but not seeming to affect my head. Brom stepped in and pulled the door shut, throwing the metal bolt as well, securing it from the inside. He did not place a ward as far as I could tell. He walked into his quarters, not attempting to see into my hood, and placed his plate of food on the larger table. Then he turned to take down two small goblets from a shelf.

"Would you care for some wine?"

"No, thank you, Master Brom."

Even able to watch him uncork the bottle and pour in my presence, I would ingest nothing that impeded my senses. Given these fermented drinks were low-grade poison, I did not think it safe for my unborn, either.

Silence lingered, and I added, "I would drink water, if you have some."

The sorcerer looked amused but lifted a pitcher on a stand, next to a basin and a thick, soft-looking cloth. He poured the clear liquid into one of the goblets, added a deep red wine to his, keeping his hands in plain sight, and set it on the table next to a second chair. He took his own seat farther away but so that he could reach his wine and foodstuffs on the table. The two chairs would be facing each other with plenty of leg room in between.

"You are invited to sit, Sirana," he said without great inflection, "and I hope you will. My days are usually long running this place, and I admit fatigue."

I stepped forward cautiously. "You've not asked to see who would be sitting with you."

He exhaled slowly. "So be it. Please, take down your hood. That I may see you."

Like Sarilis, I knew he had some idea, but damn me to the Pit if I could read what this was. My stomach tense and preparing for the worst, I lowered my hood at last. My braid was frayed, but the face, hair, and ears would be clear enough. Brom looked up and stared at me, his face placid but with a truer response roiling underneath. I tried but I could not hold his gaze for long.

He huffed as if in disbelief. "Blue eyes."

I lifted an eyebrow. "Is that unusual, Master Brom?"

His mouth twisted dryly. "I don't know."

*Yes, you do.*

"You know what I am?" I asked.

He shook his head. "A disturbed grave or a mirage. An impossible chance." He smirked. "Or a destiny chained to a pillar. No, I do not know *what* you are, Sirana. Not truly. You could be any of this and more."

I didn't know where to begin with an answer like that.

"I must ask again," he said, looking away to reach for a scrap of cheese and fruit on his plate. "Where in all the continent did the Ma'ab find you? And why, for devil's sake, are you traveling with them from the West?"

He put the food in his mouth, chewed, and took a sip of wine, though he was not enjoying it. He may have felt a little ill. Meanwhile, my mouth went dry; I opted to sit facing him at last, reaching to sip the water from the goblet. He never looked away.

"A century ago, the Ma'ab took two of ours," I said. "I seek to learn what happened to them, if not get them back."

"Impossible."

"That I seek them at all or that I can recover after this much time?"

"That the Ma'ab took two of yours to begin with," he said gruffly.

I smiled placidly, though I thought this boded ill for his having knowledge of the Sathoet more useful than Kurn. "Then I must ask again, Master Brom. What am I, that this should be impossible?"

The sorcerer appeared as the tired innkeeper at the end of a laborious day as he rubbed his eyes, pressing a rough palm to his temple like a sharp pain pressed outward. With his eyes closed, he lifted his first finger up but didn't point it at me.

"A moment, Ss… Sirana," he said, sipping his wine then following it up with a larger gulp.

While he wasn't looking, I took a drink of water and loosened my guardians' pouch. The man was acting strange and spoke stranger, like he was half in Reverie. By comparison Sarilis had been direct upon seeing my face, although the necromancer also wanted to show off his knowledge earned over his life. Brom didn't seem to care about convincing or impressing me with that. Somehow, it felt dangerous.

"Here," sighed the sorcerer, placing both hands on the arms of his chair to push himself up. "I want to show you something."

I stood up with him. "Do answer my question, first, Master Brom. So I know where we stand."

The man laughed dryly, and I noticed wrinkles that hadn't been there before, some silver hairs upon his scalp above his round ears. "Mm. You are…or were an Elf of the Davrin Queendom. Mankind has not seen your kind for…" He paused. "A long time."

An Elf of the Davrin Queendom? He wasn't wrong, but it was vague.

*No, he knows Davrin. That's sure.*

"Come," he motioned toward one of his decorative shelves. "I must show you something."

"Show me what?"

He shook his head, refusing an answer, I glanced at the locked door. The nausea of the geas touched my middle with my first thought to leave. I grimaced. *Damn.*

Brom saw my face and chuckled. "Ah. So we are both under some strain? Such are the bonds we forge which won't let us go."

"How many centuries are you?" I asked.

He tilted his head back and just laughed, lightly touching my shoulder to guide me where he wanted me to go. Reluctantly, I went over to the decorations, uncertain which piece I was supposed to look at. Did he want to show me all of it?

"Meditate on these for a time," he said, his light touch settling heavier on my shoulder. "Tell me what you see, and perhaps we can attempt truth between us before we see another dawn, hm?"

A trickle of ice slid down my spine as my gaze drifted without guidance over the array of crafted boxes, ornamental daggers, and jewelry sitting in a brass bowl in front of me. My eye settled on the shape of the bird set as a crest upon a gold ring.

"What do you see, Sirana?" he murmured, a small shudder in his voice. "You recognize something. Show me what… *ahhh*. This?"

He reached with thick, callused fingers to pluck up the firebird ring and set it by itself on the shelf. It was simple and lovely, well-made in the details of a bird rising on wings of fire. I did not know what it meant, but it *was* the bird who lit the way to that Davrin prison at the end of the canyon.

"I dreamed of this bird," Brom murmured. "This night that you arrived. You know its power?"

I swallowed. Another pause, and then he sighed as his heavy hand slid from my shoulder to the back of my neck where he squeezed firmly, holding me in place. He would have run afoul my guardians if they had been hiding in their usual place. For the moment, I couldn't give them the command, and they stayed in their pouch.

"Do you know who I am, Sirana?" he asked.

I swallowed and couldn't answer. I knew, and yet I did not know…

*Anything.*

He could feel me tremble as my body demanded action, from me, from my spiders. Yet I could not move; neither could they. Was that him, or the geas? Was it me? I dared not run, *could* not leave this place knowing nothing. Where would I go that I would not be pursued by someone more powerful than me?

The sorcerer's aura had begun to pulse, hurting my head. He no longer suppressed it so fully, yet it was enough to remind me of Elder D'Shea. Neither fight nor flight was a viable choice for me. I must think of something else or die soon. Me and my babies.

Gripping me with one hand, Brom picked up the firebird ring and slid it onto his third finger with one hand; it was a little loose. "Does your Queen remember me, Sirana? She should. The Abyssal whore murdered my wife and all our children and cost us a terrible war. I would know where she's gone. Where *all* of you fled the Sun's justice."

# CHAPTER 4

My short time as the youngest Red Sister had taught me many new things and reinforced lessons learned from my family. One of those lessons was that lying out of fear, with far less knowledge of a situation than the one to whom I am lying, never worked in my favor. At the same time, I could not cave and begin babbling to this man, to give him anything he asked.

No one on the Surface had gotten this close to me without force, which he was using. It wasn't physical force; the saphgar beneath my armor was warming quickly. Despite the unmooring chill which swept me, I would *not* panic. I wasn't unfamiliar being in such states, unfortunately, and I knew better than to volunteer information. Choosing the firebird ring out of a pile of metal did not mean we'd had the same dream, and I'd proven before I could withstand probing from a Daughter of Braqth.

While I could speak my will, I had a chance. First, I had to prove that I could.

"I do not know who you are, Brom."

"Oh? Maybe you only say that now," he murmured, "because your hubris to walk into my quarters and assassinate me served you so poorly?"

I purse my lips. "I did not walk in here to assassinate you."

He may have had a point about the hubris, though at the time, I'd believed the folly would be greater to leave and wait for his next move.

*Don't want his attention? Don't go to Troshin Bend.*

Wise words, Mathias.

"You are a sorcerer of some repute," I continued. "Your name stretches far sitting at a crossroads. I wanted to speak with a man better educated in magic and possibilities, not mired in ignorance like those I've met."

"Now you try flattery. Predictable."

"You said you wanted truth between us by dawn. Are simple truths never predictable, Master Brom?"

My words tugged a reluctant, cautious chuckle out of him. "Hm. Why does the lilt of your speech have a hint of Manalari, Sirana?"

I continued to "meditate" on his shelves of treasures instead of looking at his face. Nothing else stood out to me, though I considered lifting the lid on a box or two. I braced against the familiar pressure of a mage trying to bend my will, rebounding after that first shock. The force did not increase but stayed constant and did not progress.

I said, "One of my traveling companions has been teaching me Trade. In his dialect."

"In these times, a man from Manalar would *not* teach one like you," he replied with flat skepticism.

"He is from the surrounding area and an outcast. A death mage. They tortured him as a child until he killed them and escaped."

This gave Brom pause. "Very well, that sounds more likely."

I smiled showing my teeth. The sorcerer could have continued his inquiry, and I'd have told him about Gavin, but instead he seemed to become distracted by my... Well, by my existence. Given the accusation he'd laid at the feet of the Valsharess, I hadn't expected him to forget for long.

Brom massaged my neck as if testing the solidity of my flesh; he reached with his other hand to trace the shape of my left ear, making me shiver. Then he took firm hold of my chin and turned my face toward him.

I caught him inhaling my scent, his nostrils flaring, and I recognized an odd, "elder" scent I'd not found among Humans before, not even Sarilis. I tried not to worry about my guardians and their lack of action on my behalf; I didn't know if this was his will, the Queen's, or my own which prevented it.

"Look up," he commanded.

This close, I'd been focused on his beard, noting all the silver and white which had come in since I'd first seen him in the kitchen. His tanned skin seemed darker than before.

"My eyes, Sirana."

I refused. "Not while you touch me, Brom."

"That distasteful, am I?"

"That dangerous to both of us."

He chuckled again. "How old are you? You can't be far into your second century."

I smothered a grimace; he sounded like any number of elder females below. Yet, I couldn't change my youth. "I am that."

"Why were you sent knowing so little?"

Tamuril had asked the same thing.

*"Because* I know little, it seems," I answered dryly.

"You must have a mission or an objective. Your uniform is somewhat different than I once knew, but I recognize a recruit when I see one."

"I stated why I would follow you in here."

He chuffed. "Your objective is to trade tales?"

"I did not lie in this, Master Brom."

"Though you can."

"Without qualm."

81

Another chuckle. I took it to mean he was feeling better, in better control than he'd been upon first sitting when it appeared his head would split from pain.

"If I release you," he offered, "you will look me in the eyes. And we shall talk without attempting to murder each other."

It struck me that Gavin had used that word, murder.

*Reconsidering being so at ease with a murderer?*

How was this different from killing?

"I doubt I would succeed in the attempt," I said with outward calm. "Again, it is not my goal."

"And you are too valuable for me to kill," he said, his grip on my neck loosening. "You know this from my own foolish slip."

Indeed, I had felt the hatred which must have pushed those words out in his first, intimidating reveal. He would not kill me, but I didn't know what he would do to get what he wanted. Knowledge as invaluable as it was terrifying.

I focused on the ring upon his finger. "Did we *both* dream of a Desert firebird this night, Master Brom?"

He removed his hand from my neck.

"You are not from the Desert," he replied in rejection, and I staggered, not realizing how much pressure I'd been resisting until then.

Straightening up, I watched him motion me toward the chairs facing each other, his expression set in a deep frown of concentration or discomfort as he sat and waited for me. I resisted looking at the locked office door and came forward to join him. My eyes flicked to the fresh fruit and cheese sitting uneaten on the plate; he noticed, smirked, and pushed it toward me with one finger so it was within my reach.

"If you want it, Sirana," he said, favoring the wine, now, "my appetite is gone."

Mine hadn't quite returned but nor was my stomach full; I found it difficult to resist the opportunity despite the circumstances.

There had been a time when both our backs had been turned from it, however, so I tugged the plate closer to lift it and bring it beneath my nose. The sorcerer smirked in amusement, drinking his wine as he watched me.

As with the stew, it wasn't complicated enough to hide an obvious additive, but I wondered about refined poisons or sedative a sorcerer at a trade crossroads like this might have access to. I wondered—

"Here," he said, leaning forward to pluck a slice of orange fruit from the plate and pop it in his mouth, where he chewed the bare minimum to swallow it. "You watched me gather it in the kitchen and eat it when we first came in. I haven't tampered with it since. That is truth."

That must be good enough. I ate while I waited for him to get his fill of looking at me. I heard a soft grunt, barely a laugh.

"You remind me of my wife," he said. "She could eat all the way through an argument if necessary, while I could not touch anything solid for some time after."

I slowed my chewing, unsettled to hear the comparison.

He saw my expression and shrugged, sipping the fermented red again. "She was pregnant much of that time. We had…" He paused as if trying to recall something. "We had eleven…? No, almost twelve children together."

I frowned in confusion but kept chewing, and adding another piece of cheese and bread to stay silent. Given the knowledge his "wife" and children had all died violently and possibly at the order of my Valsharess, my probing this topic while he drank wine on an empty stomach was as hazardous as placing my bare feet upon shattered glass.

Twelve children. An impressive troop if all by the same womb as he suggested. Humans bred quickly, for certain. It would take a Davrin five hundred years of constantly trying to bear that many without Priestess assistance. To have the same within thirty or forty years, before she became old?

"Will you look at me now, or would you rather finish eating?" he asked with an edge.

I would rather finish eating but I did speed it up, cramming two bites' worth in at a time and chewing faster. Brom laughed.

"*Are* you pregnant, I wonder?" he mused, his eyes dropping to my middle with a look like he could see straight into my womb. "I knew many fighters who would hide it for as long as they could before I had to pull them off the front lines."

My head and spine chilled to think I could not be less obvious or perhaps he only knew the signs too well, unlike those with whom I travelled. The sorcerer had also intrigued me with that remark.

I swallowed the food. "Do you mean Davrin fighters? You were... leading some?"

Brom's gaze turned inward while he spoke. "For a time. An insane, barking mass of men and Elves, now I look back. Challenging to make work together. Only a small part of it was finding the pregnant fighters before they got themselves killed."

He was toying with me. Wasn't he? Then again, he'd only laughed when I asked how many centuries he'd seen.

...*she cost us a terrible war.*

Humans and Dark Elves, fighting as one in the Desert? Against what threat?

In the silence, I watched the sorcerer's illusion finally melt away. I'd never seen the face before, but it looked like an older, venerable version of what he had been at the start of the evening. The bone structure remained the same, different from the pale men in the tavern, either Ma'ab or not, though it was difficult for me to say why.

His eyes were an intense, slate grey, and he possessed creases around those eyes and the corners of his mouth much like my Queen. He had not lost any breadth or apparent strength; he was a big man, though not as large as Kurn.

Striking to me was how his head hair had become pure white, like mine, and the beard became sparse and trim, yet stark white. His skin was much darker brown than it had been before, darker than anyone I'd seen thus far except for myself. His coloring was so close to a Davrin that it combatted the age lines in my view; he looked mature and experienced but not decrepit.

His aura throbbed with a power I could feel, and he possessed an unnamed presence such that I could believe he had once been a leader. Though he was the governing innkeeper of a small settlement resting at a neutral crossroad for Dwarf to Ma'ab to Manalari, I had a hint how he might enforce such a thing.

*No wonder Sarilis was envious.*

It remained to be seen if Brom would tolerate Dark Elves, though, if one of us was responsible for his family's death so long ago. But how long? And was it indeed my Valsharess who had done it, or whoever came before her? This was the first time I had thought to wonder about a succession. Had there been a Queen before our present one?

*Why wouldn't there have been, if there is someone alive who claims to remember leading us in the Desert...?*

"Did your Desert people have a name?" I asked.

He lifted his gaze and it narrowed. I couldn't tell if the pause was to recollect or to judge me. He murmured, "Zauyrian. The Realms and their Kings are...no more."

"Were you one of those Kings?"

He huffed a bitter laugh. "No. I was their General."

"Why were you fighting beside Davrin?"

Something terrifying flashed in his eyes as we at last locked gazes, not a deliberate attempt to capture my will but a striking blow, lashing out like an angry fist. I flinched. My head felt bruised and muzzy, and I only wanted to leave.

*Go. Leave now.*

I set down the empty plate and stood up, heading to the office door in long strides. Reaching for my cloak, I did not have time to fear how far I'd get before the geas might bring me to my knees.

"Wait," he said, shifting in his chair. "Don't go."

"That hurt, sorcerer, whatever you did," I said, my voice shaking with the effort of donning my cloak. "I know nothing of what murder occurred before. I'll not stay if you only want a target for your regrets."

Dizzy and with my spiders at last coming out of their pouch, I reached for the lock on the door. Brom moved in my periphery, unnaturally so, appearing beside me to catch the door half-opened in his hand and slam it shut again, the handle yanked from my grasp.

*Shit!*

The elder man stared at me with the intensity of a rabid hunter, and I drew a dagger and braced myself to meet him as my three guardians scrabbled onto my shoulders and upper arms. His eyes left mine to count them; the black arachnids twitched in anticipation of a long leap, waiting for my command, which I withheld until he moved first.

Whatever his grey eyes saw, the ancient sorcerer reconsidered.

"Still in the clutches of the Spider Queen," he murmured.

*He knows of her, too…*

"Was it not always so?" I asked bluntly.

Brom's focus drifted downward from blade and fang, staring at my middle like his next thought seeped gradually through a dense barrier. "You have no past. You are ignorant as those you call the same, recruit."

"I shall accept this as 'no,' then," I replied in wry tension, to which my spiders reacted with a skitter while my dagger seemed no threat at all. "Do tell what came before, General?"

He knew better than to give me what I wanted when it was I who could not help but ask.

*"What of a dry-rock valley of many colors?"* I blurted in my native tongue. *"Or a bua with gold eyes trapped behind iron, the way to him lit by that firebird you wear on your finger?"*

If the sorcerer had lashed out at me in frustration at an ignorant question, the language of my dream may have shattered his jaw had it been a fist. The elder man took a step back, stunned as if he could not have expected those words from my lips.

Then he rallied like any fighter.

*"Who sent you?"* he returned in Davrin words. They were strangely spoken on his tongue, as someone who learned far away from the city where the Dark Elves dwelled.

*"My Queen sent me,"* I replied as stubbornly as my spiders remained with me.

*"I deny that,"* he barked. *"You don't know my name! A cutting insult worse than any blade, but this makes no sense unless you have a new Queen since Ishuna."*

I hesitated, lowering an apparently impotent metal dagger.

*"Do you?"* he demanded, his face contorted with rage.

*"I don't know,"* I admitted. *"I do not know this name, either. My Queen is the Valsharess. And I'll not tell you where we dwell."*

We met eyes, staring hard, and I recognized a familiar pressure again when the saphgar became like a burning coal between my breasts. I thought only of Kurn squashing me, attempting to make me bend down to him. As I did then, trapped in my own webbing, I dug my heels in now.

Abruptly, Brom broke our engagement, exhaling a rancorous laugh as he threw up his hands and stepped away. I watched him head for his disheveled bed and collapse upon his back, one hand covering his eyes like they ached from too much light. It was something to which I related as my head began to pound with delayed tears of shock in my eyes.

*"And someone placed upon you an extraordinary mind-shield,"* he murmured, *"for I cannot see her face in your thoughts to confirm for you."*

*"You didn't ask,"* I replied, ignoring the oblique, tempting offer.

A dry chuckle drifted from the ancient sorcerer lying on rumpled bedding.

Tense as a deer ready to run, I stood alone with my guardians a moment, easily choosing not to enlighten him about the source of my protection or its cost. Perhaps psionics only existed below and he didn't know of this, as much as he claimed *me* to be ignorant. Perhaps he had never seen the firebird in my mind in a vulnerable moment, as I'd assumed, but was merely skilled at reading guided, physical tells. It was not an uncommon talent among Davrin.

Reaching for the door, I prepared for a ward of warning; there was none, and I opened it a crack.

"I will find you," he said in Trade without sitting up or uncovering his eyes. "Go where you dare to be seen but don't leave Troshin Bend."

I paused with my hand on the handle then opened it wide to let myself out of his quarters, softly closing it behind me. In the hallway, I lightened my step since we were deep in the Human sleep time.

The sorcerer had resources to track me or sic men on my tail, that I did not doubt. I could not leave without knowing who he was, anyway, never mind I had no certain way to escape this place when need arose.

Truly foolish I'd been coming here with too few questions and forethought. Whomever I had expected to meet upon first hearing of this governor-innkeeper at Sarilis's tower, it was *not* this tired, vengeful revenant purportedly from the red sands of my dreams. A survivor of a war involving the Davrin; a Human who should have been long dead and buried.

I wondered how I could have been unerringly led here while he demanded to know who had sent me. I had no answer. I didn't know. If this had come to be by a royal Vision, I could not yet guess if his Queen and mine were one and the same.

I had more to fear if they were.

*Go where you dare to be seen, he said. Hmm.*

Or go where I was less likely to be seen at all.

In simply attempting to leave the inn via the front door, however, what I'd thought was an unguarded exit turned out to have three dozing guardsmen on the outside; their breathing warned me an instant before I gave myself away.

*Another way out?*

The kitchen was the most obvious; there would be a way out from there, as at any Noble House back home and at Sarilis's tower. I retraced my steps, warily watching the hallway leading to Brom's room. He did not step out before I slipped down the short stairs to the sunken room.

The two children still slept by the hearth, and I spotted three doors at the far end. One of them was the pantry from which I had pilfered, the other led to another tight hall with a few doors which smelled of sleeping workers. The third door smelled of night air drifting in through the gaps. I tested the handle.

*Locked.*

More irritated than I should have been, I kneeled and removed two thin tools, inserting them in the keylock to explore by feel. Ironically, I was better trained at opening the magically sealed doors of important Davrin, but the base obstacles provided by servants' quarters had to be overcome at times.

When I finally sprang the mechanism, I winced at the noise it made, and one of the children stirred. A boy, I thought. He sat up quickly, wide-eyed to recognize the worry of someone at the outside door. His heartbeat kicked into a gallop.

From the empty focus in his gaze, he couldn't see any details, I didn't think. Much as I disliked having a witness of my departure, I opened the door and slipped out quietly without speaking a word. Let the boy try to describe what he'd seen.

At last I was outside the inn and could breathe deeply of fresh air. The rain was soft and constant, the shadows deep with fog or haze absent, and the thunder and lightning long swept itself North. The ground would be soft and slippery in a wider expanse from the rocky slopes where I'd first trained in the rain, but Rausery hadn't been lax in her details of that nature, either.

*Don't leave Troshin Bend.*

Very well. I'd take its measure, instead.

It took me over an hour before dawn to walk the perimeter of a settlement of four score, closely built shelters along curving, winding mud-paths all leading in some way to a modest river on the East side. Only a few extra shelters were built on the far bank and it looked to be a work area. From the lack of grass and shrubs, the deep gouges on the banks, and from the multitude of carts, tools, and half-sectioned lumber, I wagered a main resource for this place were the trees themselves, out of which they build every one of their shelters. Did they cut trees for trade?

*Floating logs along the water.*

My cloak shed the light rain with little threat to my belt tools, and I looked to the North and South, wondering which direction they might try to move the wood. The current drained South, but what lay in that direction but for Manalar?

*Gavin might know more detail.*

My pace was slow and cautious, with several moments waiting in stillness for a chance to cross an open area unseen. There were a few restless minds who were awake inside their huts or sitting outside staring into the night. All of them were men. I had seen children, though, so there must be women somewhere to have borne them.

There was something which I'd thought to be missing from a place purported as a popular stopping point for goods and weather knowledge along trade routes heading in all four directions, but I soon discovered what I sought once I'd circled three quarters the town and was heading toward the inn. It had always been there; I'd simply been unable to see it arriving within the storm as I had.

I passed a wide area at the Southern edge of the town which carried all the signs of a flexible market for traders to meet. There were some shops which stood as permanent houses on raised, wooden platforms resting on vertical logs driven deep into the ground. There were some reinforced tents intended only for a few seasons at best, moving in the gusts. There were many empty spaces suggesting sellers who came and went quickly in the best seasons.

Aside from dealing with inclement weather, this wasn't terribly different from the commoner's market in Sivaraus. The permanence of the merchant's shop merely showed their level of investment, with all pros and cons attached. It was eerily quiet now, but I was curious if I might get a glimpse during the day while people moved about. Further, I wondered if it would get busier the deeper into "summer" we went.

*Early for a storm like this,* Mathias said. *Maybe they had a warm winter to the South.*

More Humans could arrive with fairer weather, seeking to stay at the inn or set up shop here. Greater density meant difficulty staying unnoticed, and I didn't imagine Kurn or Castis wanted to be much observed for long. When might they want to leave and continue to Manalar? Would the sorcerer allow it if they had me in their company? Rithal and Kurn had been discussing renegotiation of their contract with Brom as mediator, but...

*What if he is not a neutral arbiter? What then?*

Assuming they would try, I was curious what argument Rithal or the Ma'ab may try to sway Brom if he had spent centuries without knowing where the Dark Elves had gone after a war. When might I be physically able to walk away, either by my will or his, and not be followed? Or would they leave me here, and I must make my way on the Surface against a sorcerer who said he would find me.

It was too early to say for all these worrisome thoughts, too many unknowns before the next dawn. I must wait and see.

Other than the barn where the horses were boarded, I found no more advantageous place to be caught by the dawn than the inn, and it returned to me that I should check on Gavin. He was my ally, and he may be finished with his restless sleep by now.

Upon approaching by way of the trees rather than the road, however, I spotted a small, female figure out front. Ignoring the guards, she stood at the border of the porch and the wooden over-hang which protected her from the light rain. Her coloring was so Ma'ab, ghostly pale with black hair and eyes, and her posture with men at her back was much like any Noble I'd known—proud and stubborn—that I thought this must be Brom's daughter, mentioned with some delight by Kurn.

Beyond the meek serving girls I'd seen upon arrival, this would be the first woman I'd seen with anything at all familiar about her. Only by taking after her mother's appearance over her sire would the Hellhound to be interested. What was she doing outside in the dark of night? What was she looking for?

Crouching down slowly, I watched her for I had some time left before I must sneak into the kitchens.

She wasn't a patient one. Soon, she paced the porch, always looking out at the town or checking around the corners to either side of the building. The guards standing needed to shake their heads and reassure her many times that they hadn't seen what she sought, either. I listened to her high-pitched voice well enough to recognize it again, but the words were accented and muffled such that I wasn't sure if she spoke Trade.

Impatient and irritable, she let herself inside again. She was quiet enough but not concerned about waking anyone or being caught.

*Hmm.*

With activity this early before dawn, I decided I should return to Gavin sooner rather than later and sneaked toward the kitchen door. Locked, of course, and the barest light from a candle leaking through the door.

The children were probably awake, but aside from attempting to climb and enter Gavin's room by means of the second-story win-dow—risky without warning, to be aware, as I'd told him I'd knock on the door—I had no other means of entry that would not take even longer to case and potentially risk running afoul a different adult man.

I grumbled, removing the same tools to try to spring the lock again, using what method had worked before, albeit like imagining its reflection in a mirror. It was difficult and took longer, but I got it. I opened it and peeked in.

"*Eep!*" squeaked a small animal.

"*Shhhh!*" someone shushed, spraying spittle before a harsh whisper. "*You give us up!*"

Were they trying to be quiet?

I waited, heard no one else larger than them, and slipped in to close the door behind me, keeping my hood low over my face. The two youths were gone from the hearth, but it took only a moment to locate them hiding in a low cupboard with the door closed. Some pots had been removed and placed beneath the table in hopes I wouldn't recall they hadn't been there the first time.

I smiled in humor and headed to the kitchen door without tormenting them further. Tempting if this had been a Davrin House and I was in my reds; far less so with an ancient sorcerer and his daughter about and a whole mess of sleeping Humans that would not know what it was they saw beyond a devil.

I listened to the Ma'ab daughter in the hall; she was outside Brom's quarters.

"*Fadhi, afta shiab,*" she said, sounding concerned and prepared to act. "*Malka ha, malka hadatha?*"

I could not hear his response, but I could be sure she spoke the language of the Northern Empire. That said something for her up-bringing; perhaps she hadn't been born here. Then she said something else, low, conspiratorial, and pleading with her mouth close to the frame. Again, I detected no voice through his door; no muffled command or reassurance, but her response was as though she'd received a reply she did not enjoy much.

Magical protection to prevent anything spoken inside the room from getting out made the most sense, though it was interesting that the daughter was not using something similar. The Davrin had methods for sending a message only to the intended ears on the other side of a barrier.

She exhaled, seemed to agree to something, and stalked briskly past the kitchen door toward the front room, missing me. She went up the stairs which would lead first to Kurn and Rithal's rooms. I opted to slip out of the kitchen and glide around the bar to the other set of stairs which would lead directly to Gavin's.

I would tap twice short and twice long when I returned, I'd told him. I didn't know how quick he'd take to answer or trust who was on the other side, but regardless, I was running out of time not to be caught among the early risers. I was sure it was the innkeeper's daughter whispering with Kurn around the corner by the time I reached Gavin's door.

I tapped, twice short, twice long. I waited, tapped again, tempted to whisper his name but refrained. He shuffled inside and, at last, the apprentice opened the door a crack. Something was braced to catch the door if it was shoved inward.

Impatiently, glancing to my left, I held his eyes and hand signed, *Let me in!*

Gavin looked more curious than confused at the rock and tilt of my hand but grasped the basic imperative. He mostly shut the door, removed the brace, and opened enough to let me inside. I could breathe in full once he'd closed and secured the door. The gaunt, tall man turned around and appraised me, remarking first on the mud covering my boots and the dampness of my cloak.

"Where have you been?"

"Memorizing the layout of the town," I said, removing my cloak and grabbing a still-damp towel to roll it up and try to suck further rainwater out. In the meantime, I noticed Gavin had been up for a while, sitting at the desk and writing. He had ink marks on his fingers and his tools lay in the open.

"Practical," he agreed. "Risky, if you were seen."

"I was careful."

Apart from leaving a trail of flaking mud from the kitchen and leading up the fresh-swept stairs and down the hall to this door. I could hope that the sign would be readily trampled soon as men got up to begin their day.

"Did anything happen here?" I asked as I sat on the bed and worked on removing as much of the mud from my boots as possible, collecting it in a cloth for shaking out later.

"Nothing of note," he said. "I woke and found you still gone. I take it you found your food and left to wander the sleeping streets?"

*If only.*

My pause was intended to be telling; Gavin tilted his head and took his seat at the rickety desk, watching me. Unlike the innkeeper's daughter, he was patient waiting for me to show my hand.

"I met the tavern owner, Brom Troshin," I said. "He discovered me in the kitchen. I believe he sensed me and came out to investigate. We...spoke."

"And? You seem disconcerted."

"Yes. He is most certainly a *strong* mage, and much older than Sarilis may believe. Perhaps centuries, Gavin, though he appears Human."

Gavin grunted, picking up his stylus to dip. "Indeed. That is reason to be unsettled. What does he look like?"

I shook my head. "He showed me two faces. One of them I believe was genuine, if only because he *appeared* old. White hair. Wrinkled, brown skin. The younger one is simply dark brown hair and younger, lighter skin, nothing unusual, except..."

Gavin waited, making a note.

"His eyes are grey in both forms," I said.

"Grey?" he asked. "Hazel, mixed with blue or green?"

I shook my head. "Grey. Like shale on a crumbling mountain."

"Hm. That is notable." His stylus scratched the page of his book; he didn't look at me as he added, "It may be difficult to leave here."

I opened my mouth, closed it again before I could laugh at the irony. "Why do you say, Gavin? Difficult for whom?"

He glanced up only briefly. "For you. And me. Probably the rest unless they cooperate. Or sell what they know of us."

I glanced at the door.

"What are you thinking now?" he probed with a sigh.

With a shrug, I said, "Could be what Kurn was doing with the Ma'ab daughter. She went to her sire's door first but was speaking Ma'ab and I did not understand. Then she went to Kurn's door, and I quickly returned here."

Gavin exhaled, long and slow. "Any plan I should be aware?"

"Not yet," I admitted. "Brom has seen me. He remembers Davrin."

"Oh, does he?"

"Not altogether pleasant memories."

"Unfortunate but not surprising."

His stylus made *scritch-scritch* noises, and a chill rose in my belly. Any one of these men could—and would, eventually—tell Brom that the Davrin dwelled deep below the ground and never saw the Sun. To deny him this knowledge was merely a delay. Yet the more he found out, the harder he would prevent me from leaving.

Should I run? Steal a horse and ride? Ride where? And who better than those dwelling here would know how to track me? Any Red Sister could track someone fleeing on a stolen mount out of Sivaraus.

*Fuck.*

"Why do you think it may be difficult for you to leave?" I decided to ask, having no solution to my problem. "What interest may he have in you?"

"It is not direct interest from the innkeeper but what has been drawn here. Had I known, I would have deserted this trek days ago."

I straightened up. "What do you mean? What has been drawn here besides you and me?"

His homely face made a deep scowl as he stared at his page for a while then began tidying up to return these to his pack. Gavin tried several times to speak, I could tell, trying to choose his words. I grew impatient with him, given how readily I had spoken, but I bit my tongue and let the silence roll on.

"I have a...patroness," he murmured, "who sometimes shows me knowledge beyond mortal ken."

*Patroness?* I did not grasp the structure of the word itself—the translation conflicted with itself—but that was the least important part of what he was trying to say. I pursed my lips closed and motioned for him to continue.

"I have heard whispers from the beyond since boyhood, some of them hers. Portents terrifying in their reach and complexity. This is always a cost to opening one's eyes among such whispers, whether one understands the dangers or not."

Lank strands of Gavin's black hair fell in front of his face as he tucked his book away. He avoided my gaze as he folded his pale, long-fingered hands back atop the table. "I must seek knowledge. She knows this. I always open my eyes eventually to the whispers. Yet, every time, I have regretted doing so even as I thirst for more. That is an inextricable thread of the cost."

Hearing him speak like this made my skin prickle. It was not what I might have expected. As harshly as he judged the Bishops of Manalar with delusions to know the divine order; in openly discussing with an odd, cool awareness of the manipulations of demons or devil; in seeking insight in corpses, in scrolls and books, and having the core strength to release himself from a childhood which would have broken many...

Now he spoke like a power-hungry Priestess caught in the clutches of a dream-figure who may be consuming him in many little bites. Like the terrified buas in the Drider Pit, they said, some part of him enjoyed it.

I sat on the bed and kept my breath steady. I didn't know what to make of this from the man I'd ridden with for weeks, but he still hadn't addressed his real concern.

"What is drawn here which will make it difficult for you to leave?" I asked again. "That you would rather have avoided."

His nostril twitched; his mouth tightened in distaste. "World-eaters. The sort no soul escapes until they've corrupted and consumed its essence beyond rebirth. Those dying near here experience the transition disrupted, and you and I sit at this crossroad, two of many whom the world-eaters may trap with our having little power to do anything about it."

My white brows were arched with concern as I tried to puzzle this out. *World-eaters? Those dying near here...corrupted and consumed...*

I realized then I had never asked the apprentice. I'd only asked Sarilis.

"Warp rot?" I asked with care. "Near here?"

Gavin lifted his eyes, inquisitive and curious before they drifted to the side, then returned. "Yes. As described in the old goat's journals?"

"My leader helped him cleanse it when it was drawn near the Ley tower."

"Ah." Gavin sat back in his chair like he wished to spin his dream to look at it from all angles. "I had not...made the connection."

While it had struck me like a blow.

*Gaelan.*

If this was where she had been heading, she may have only been a few days ahead of me, at most. My stomach tried to squeeze itself into a knot. Was she near?

"Where is the...center of the warp rot?" I asked.

The apprentice shook his head. "I do not know exactly. Perhaps I will recall something later."

"But you say we are two who can do nothing about it? Before, my leader only needed enough mages, and they could do plenty. The sorcerer certainly is one who would care about such a threat, I would think. He may know more."

Gavin frowned. "No. No, if it were only what your leader dealt with, I would not tell you what I dreamed. I would not bother."

"Why? Is it larger? Festering longer? What?"

"More the things *drawn* here, as I said."

"I don't understand. What—?"

A heavy fist knocked dead center on the door. "Oi, ye two up?"

"For some time," Gavin replied sourly.

"Good," Rithal said. "Brom's givin' us a private audience first thing over breakfast. Time to head down before it gets too busy. Hoods up. I'll wait."

Gavin and I looked at each other and wordlessly stood to collect all our things and the key.

Thrown from one enormous concern to another, I resolved to worry less for Gavin's seemingly obsessive hunger for any portents his "patroness." If she had shown him a warning of the world-eaters —of warp rot—and given me my first confirmation that I may be that close on my Sister's track, then I could give him any delusion or desire to worship a goddess.

Perhaps, in time, he would tell me her name.

For now, there awaited an ancient General whose Desert name I did not know, who could be my Queen's oldest living enemy.

# CHAPTER 5

RITHAL AND KURN COULD BOTH LEAD THE WAY. WHEN IT CAME time to squeeze the big Ma'ab and the broad Dwarf into the hall beneath the stairs opposite the kitchen and common room, the redbeard halted first before they would have collided.

Rithal rolled his eyes as Kurn's big boots thudded ahead. "After you, Duchra."

"What you say?" He turned around with a scowl.

"Yeh heard me."

The Hellhound took one step our way, but it was Castis who stepped between him and the Dwarf, murmuring some advice. Without much resistance, Kurn turned to lead the way to a room midway down the hall on the left. It required us to pass two guards, who scrutinized us, peering at me as I withdrew deep inside my hood with Gavin eventually drawing their derision and discomfort.

One of the men knocked on the door. "Governor?"

I heard nothing, but the man twisted the knob and pushed the door open, jerking his chin that we should enter.

The room inside was spacious enough to fit twenty or so men with one long table and chairs. There was another door on the opposite side and closer to the front of the inn that I bet opened closer to the kitchen. Windowless and with no wall touching the outside, it was lit by a series of lanterns bolted around the perimeter of the room. There was no hearth, which was odd at first, though I imagined it must get stuffy and hot in here with too many bodies during the warmest season. Getting fresh air in here would be a chore. For now, it was cool and comfortable enough.

Brom wore the younger face I'd first seen, as I'd expected, and stood up from his seat at the narrow end of the table. Coming around to meet us after we were inside and the guard had shut the door, he didn't appear the least bit confused or distracted as he had last night. His smile was vibrant, eyes focused and confident, and his strong body displayed a swagger I imagined Kurn would respond to.

"Welcome. It's good to see you made it and late winter didn't catch you." His grey eyes swept over us equally without stopping. "And with more than you expected, I see."

With a dull slap of gloves, Brom clasped his right hand with the Hellhound's; the two men tugged and flexed, a gesture I thought crude and overt, but I knew Human men depended greatly on their strength. Like two Matrons meeting at the Palace, these two *would* take each other's measure behind fake smiles. Brom placed a fist over his heart and nodded to Castis rather than reach to jerk the mage's arm, to which the Noble responded in kind.

Brom met Rithal's eyes next, and the Dwarf hadn't need for show as he simply bowed and said, "As always, I'm glad fer th' hospitality, Master Brom. Ain't much out that way until ye hit the coast."

"Oh, there's quite a lot, Rithal," said the innkeeper with an engaging charm. "It's wild and secretive still, without as many Dwarvish crafters as there could be."

Rithal grunted agreement, and Brom glanced at me but looked quickly to Mathias. The sorcerer extended a hand to the skin hunter, who accepted with a smile and not as rough a clasp; instead, they pumped their hands together once and released without obvious contest.

"Welcome back, Mathias," he said simply. "I take it Sarilis is still alive."

The man grinned. "Cranky and eager, as always."

"Mm-hm. I figured he would accept the Ma'ab challenge. I'm pleased he sought to include you, however."

"He wants to know what happens," replied the Nobleman. "I'm enough like him in mind but young enough to make the journey. He knows I'll be wandering my way back."

Brom chuckled. "Agreed. Keen eye, Mathias. I envy your freedom at times, sir."

Mathias smiled and bowed, saying nothing else.

Four different greetings for four men he knew before today, conveying the relative status between them across cultures; I would bear it in mind. Then came the new introductions as Brom waved his hand to Gavin and me.

"And who else have you brought with you? From the West mountains?"

Kurn opened his mouth, lips curled in a sneer, and Rithal hissed at him, "No! I'll do it."

Brom's dark brows lifted with cool interest. He waited; in the others, I could detect some elevated heart rates and body heat as a subtle preparation took place. They didn't know Brom had already seen me.

Rithal started with the easier one. "The tall, thin one is Gavin. Sarilis's apprentice."

"Apprentice?" said the innkeeper with interest.

"Yeah, he was there when we arrived," Rithal continued. "Turns out he's fluent in Manalari, knows the rituals and greetings an' such. Grew up in one o' their monasteries."

"Ah, I see why the old man would have sent him along," remarked our host with curious appraisal. "A death mage as well, or a servant?"

Gavin grunted, looking elsewhere.

"If he was teaching you," said Brom, "you're suppressing your aura, squire."

"As is my habit," muttered my ally, studying a spot on the wall. "Though he's not much of a teacher."

"I don't imagine he is. Quite the hoarder of secrets, that one."

Brom smiled at him though Gavin wouldn't see it. He showed no reaction the man's ugliness compared to the others. If he noticed the likeness to the Ma'ab in coloring, he drew no attention to it. Ultimately, his gaze left Gavin to focus on me.

"And the short, dark one next to the tall, pale one?" he asked Rithal with good-natured amusement.

Kurn muttered something in Ma'ab, crossing his arms, though Brom and Rithal ignored him rather than be distracted away from me.

"Ye mentioned the wild and secretive out West, sorcerer, an' yer right." Rithal motioned to me to take down my hood. "Um."

The Dwarf paused, waited until my hands came up to show cooperation and continued. "This is Sirana, Master Brom. She's a Davrin Elf, a dark magic race o' the likes I've only heard in our hearth tales. She arrived out o' nowhere. Sarilis pretended he knew she was coming, and she backed him, but I didn' buy it. He still insisted she join us."

"What?" Castis said, annoyed. "You could have said."

Rithal shrugged. "'Twas enough the necromancer has seen others before her."

"He has, hm?" Brom murmured.

I winced inside as Rithal addressed me directly. "Still not sure what you want in bein' this far from home, Elf, but I ain't good at dancin' lies around our host, so I'm not gonna try."

"I appreciate that, Rithal," said Master Brom.

*Yes, thanks for the warning, Dwarf.*

The sorcerer's smile had disappeared a while ago as he stared at me. "She is…quite extraordinary."

"You know of her kind, sorcerer?" Kurn asked directly.

"The Dark Elves? Yes, I do. I would say foremost, if she appeared unexpectedly and hasn't left, then you have something she wants."

Kurn sneered. "Is she a demon?"

"What?" Brom was surprised enough to laugh. "No. *She* is not. She is one of the wild magic races, much older than Mankind." A shrug. "She may consort with them, I suppose. There are..." He glanced at me again. "Connections."

I exchanged a glance with Gavin, chewing on why the innkeeper avoided speaking to me directly as if I had no tongue. It was mildly annoying but as he laid groundwork to dispel some of Kurn's stubborn ideas about me, I was not inclined to interrupt. Besides, he was pretending as much as Sarilis had been, except about having *less* knowledge about me than more.

*Interesting what he leaves out versus what he says.*

"Are these Elves a 'wild' race that has their women doing the fighting?" the Hellhound continued bulling forward. "Or is she lying and running from her men-kin?"

That was a new one.

Brom looked at him, equally confused, then at me. "The 'women' do fight, Kurn, and they are dangerous as any man trained. In this, Sirana is not unusual among her own. It is her birthright to learn from her elders."

Kurn snorted in annoyance to hear this from the sorcerer he admired.

"Yeah, about that, Brom," Rithal cut in. "We're havin' difficulty in our group balancin' a woman fighter."

"Just those two," Mathias slipped in with amusement, leaning his head toward the pale Northerners.

Rithal raised a red eyebrow at him but continued. "Need yer advice. We need tah go to Manalar, but—"

"Convince me the black one *must* go," challenged the Hellhound directly. "I have considered her uses over again, and she is no help. Like now, a distraction and point to argue."

"Because ye let her be, an' won't let her show us what she can do!" the Dwarf retorted. "I wouldn't be showin' much o' *my* hand if I was in her place an' still dealin' with you."

I sighed, and Brom smiled at me; it was almost friendly.

"Let us sit," he invited. "I have some questions, first."

There was a selection of food and drink on the long table, which I was glad to see, but also needed to wait for someone else to take from it, first. Brom sat at the head of the table with Rithal, Kurn, and Castis on one side, Mathias, me, and Gavin on the other. Gavin was as close as he could get to the door, and he and I set down our packs; we were the only two who brought them.

"First, why do you go to Manalar, Sirana?" Brom asked. "It is a long journey to make alone even with other mercenaries."

I eschewed my strongest reason from my thoughts, in case he was "watching," and tried to make the rest sound compelling.

"It is as I said at the tower and has not changed," I said coolly, looking about my traveling group. "My mothers wish to see the sacred heart of the temple wrested from the Bishops' hands, as the Captain Isboern shifts their power."

"Interesting," said the sorcerer, his tone thoughtful. "A man important enough to a Queen's Vision to follow him, hm?"

As he spoke, Mathias's earlier remark struck me anew and with greater significance. *That is a strange name among Manalari. Sounds like a Western mountain man.*

"Do you know where he came from?" I asked, smirking like I knew.

Brom huffed a laugh. "Yes. The Western mountains. He stopped here as part of a pilgrimage moving through several years ago." The sorcerer chuckled. "He never left the City of the Sun and is making quite a name for himself if the Dark Queen is aware of him."

Mathias agreed, and both he and Rithal studied me anew.

"Ain't yer mission tah assassinate him, is it?" asked the Dwarf.

*You will find and kill him, Aurenthietti.*

"No," I said, flatly telling the truth. "It is not."

"Tha's good." Rithal sounded relieved. "He's the only one who openly opposes th'Witch Hunners' terror tactics against anyone not Manalari."

"Indeed," Brom said. "Curious to imagine how a foreigner like him became Captain of their guard in five short years."

"He's a mage, simple enough," Mathias said with a shrug. "Using some pressure or charm tactics."

"That somehow the Bishops are overlooking," Brom remarked.

"If he is," Rithal said, "he's far from the worst that ever did such."

"Give him time." The sorcerer chuckled. "In any case, you have your answer, gentlemen, why she travels with you. Dark Elves have some aptitude for prophecy among their own, adding to their own larger strategies. Sirana was sent because it aligns with what you are doing." Brom looked at Kurn directly. "In a sense, you could see this Davrin as a sign some of the wilds support the coming Ma'ab siege on Manalar. As Rithal has suggested, she could be a great help to you if you would accept this."

The Hellhound scowled. "I am not convinced she *must* continue on."

Brom seemed both amused and baffled. "And you expect she will return home if you push her out? Leave the battlefield because you would not accept the aid of her Queen?" A shake of his head. "Oh, she will continue. You will only have no sight of her as you've been granted now."

*Indeed. Keep your adversaries close.* A saying Sivaraus practiced rather well.

I smirked. "He would rather keep me in sight, Master Brom, but that I attend him as a slave to show off to his superiors, like another Ma'ab who must've been lucky. He is chafing that this is not the case as his challenge failed so utterly and the only option is to grant me freedom to be involved."

Brom narrowed his eyes at me, looked at Kurn, and asked, "Is this so? What happened, Kurn?"

"Well-timed," Castis interjected, holding out his hand to Rithal. "The ruby if you please? I'll not renegotiate our agreement until it's returned."

"Fer Luf's sake," growled the Dwarf.

"He keeps something not his," Kurn said to Brom.

"So we could make it here without foolish fuckery from you!"

"You distract on purpose, Castis," stated the sorcerer. "The ruby will wait. What is Sirana saying? Do you recognize her kind from another you've seen before in the Ma'ab Empire? Thus you and Kurn tried to capture her before you arrived here?"

Both Ma'ab were tense and reluctant to answer. In silence I watched their faces. *Say something about the Priestess...*

"No, I don't recognize her kind," Castis denied, "but you said she consorts with demons, Master Brom, and our Fourth, the Divine Enslaver, is a mistress of such matters. The ruby belongs to Her and was intended to provide defense against demons on our trek. The fact that it nearly worked on her is proof she was a threat from the start."

*Crystalline spider piss.*

The pale mage shifted to Rithal without waiting for a reaction. "We *must* bring it back. Make no mistake, you'll not leave this town with it in your pocket. We've tolerated the insult to our Ascended long enough."

"Threatenin' me?" the Dwarf asked quietly, his blue eyes intense.

"You do not realize the depth of your action if that is all you take from your theft."

"As if insults ain't nursed on a teat to justify acting like a toad."

Mathias's shoulders shook in silent laughter, and I started to smile. Brom's presence—his bored expression, in particular—offered an opportunity to shake the bush a little harder.

"Rithal didn't steal it, I did," I said. "Kurn had his head wrapped in delusions at the time, it was easy to take. The Dwarf convinced me to give it to him so I wouldn't use it against you. He was protecting *you* from *me* as you slept on the flats."

"Lass," Rithal grumbled, irked such that the Ma'ab mouths went slack, and Brom perked up.

"What?" I asked, turning my smile to Kurn. "Some curious words spilled from your lips while holding that ruby. It worked quite well on you."

"I have no demonblood."

"A mask to its real power."

"You bluff!"

My brows climbed high. "Oh? But you said you saw a black demon with yellow eyes and a white mane, being used to train Hellhounds, yes? He can shift to be unseen and attack from ambush?"

*"Shaytin alkab!"* Kurn hissed at me, looking shaken.

"Enough," Brom said with a stern frown. "Not at my table."

The Ma'ab swung on him. "She has no claim to that ruby!"

"She doesn't have it. She gave it up at Rithal's suggestion."

The sorcerer straightened in his chair and held out his hand. Wordlessly and without hesitation, Rithal retrieved the red pendant and put it in the sorcerer's palm.

*"Hai!"* Castis objected. "That is not yours!"

"I am aware." Brom peered at the gem a few moments, turning it between his fingers then scanned the table. "What was happening at the time she took it?"

Rithal, Mathias, and Gavin looked expectantly at the Northerners, but when they only wrinkled their nostrils in defiance, the Dwarf spoke.

"Kurn attacked her first while the rest of us were sleeping," Rithal said. "As Sirana said, he wanted a bound servant and used the ruby in a contest of wills."

Brom glanced inquisitively at the Dwarf then to a red-faced warrior. "If she won this contest and had you at her mercy, Kurn, I'm surprised she didn't kill you."

"I should have," I said. "Castis, too."

"Well, too late for this," the mage hissed with oily challenge.

"Your worst mistake, witch," agreed the Hellhound.

No, my worst was hamstringing myself on my Queen's geas when I realized he knew something about Sathoet when we'd first met at the tower. Yet, he did not know as much as I'd hoped.

"You two are forgetting this is my town," Brom said. "No matter what you call her, ignoring my counsel despite asking, I notice, Sirana has my protection if you attack her again while you're in Troshin Bend. Listening to you talk, I see why Rithal doubts you can make the trek to Manalar in this state. I think another deal must be struck and the old one dissolved."

I watched the Hill Dwarf exhale in subtle relief, and while the other two wanted to protest, Kurn and Castis exchanged looks then narrowed them on the sorcerer.

"What new deal, Master Brom?" Castis asked.

"I shall have to think on it," Brom replied readily. "The same as you, I was not expecting a Davrin Elf to join your mission. But in my experience, Castis, her presence means your goals weigh more than your Ma'ab brothers, and your efforts to reach me for advice will advance the outcome at Manalar."

The air of import soothed their pride, transparent and inaccurate as it was to me, but their reconsideration and the following moment of quiet was worth it.

"We can stay only a few days at most," said the Ma'ab mage.

Brom smiled. "Enough time to plan, I think. It's not too busy here yet."

*So, not as neutral as all that,* I thought.

The sorcerer had some skin in this coming siege to the South, and unless he was also helping Witch Hunters to this degree, Brom favored the Ma'ab. I didn't know what to make of that.

Gavin cleared his throat. All at the table looked at him, our various expressions turning to surprise when he spoke.

"Sarilis created two vials of unknown stability," he said. "Two chances to corrupt the heart of the temple. Sirana and Castis each have one."

"*Qarfa'mayit!*" Kurn snarled at him.

"*Maknuut,*" Castis added for good measure.

Brom's eyebrows lifted—I dared think he knew what a *maknuut* was—and he observed the gaunt death mage with interest. "An important part of renegotiation, for certain. Anything else I should know, Gavin?"

My ally shrugged, going silent again.

"Are *you* willing to go to Manalar?"

Gavin mumbled, "I wasn't willing at the start."

"You haven't a choice," Castis told him, but Brom lifted his hand to stay further words.

"What about now?" the innkeeper pressed. "Have you any reason at all to take such a risk?"

Even being familiar with Gavin's low and sour moods, I couldn't read him well at the table. The answer could have been yes or no as the apprentice rubbed his chin and glanced at me.

"No reason independent from the Dark Elf. I am homeless again, and I have always gone where I can learn. She is the rarer source of knowledge to follow."

I quirked an eyebrow—if that was so, it had never felt like he was following me—and Brom smiled with amusement

"She is that I'll grant you. Is her knowledge enough to die for?"

"Of course," Gavin said without a flicker of inflection. It felt like all of us considered if he might be jesting.

"Unusual motive," Mathias remarked.

"No more than yours," the apprentice replied.

The skin hunter chuckled. "Fair."

Brom turned his head toward the opposite door we'd entered as if he heard something and hummed. We did the same, but whatever it was, it was only meant for his ears.

"Alright, this is good information," he said, pushing back his chair to stand, and the rest of us did the same. "I will think of a different proposal which is balanced for your goals, and we may reconvene."

"Master Brom, the ruby," Castis persisted.

"You will be able to return it to your Ascended, Noble," said the sorcerer, though I caught skepticism in his tone, as if he doubted this was the ultimate fate of the stone. "But not until another deal is struck. It is too powerful a temptation, and you hid it the first time you were here."

"It was not necessary to confess. We are not required to expose all our resources, you agreed. It compromises our mission."

"True." Brom's smile was white but not jovial. "This piece is exposed now, however, I don't want it drifting about my town while you're here. I will keep it until you're ready to leave."

I thought Castis might have preferred Rithal stay in possession of it, from the way he swallowed. "You'll *not* change it, sorcerer. My Ascended will flay us for that as much as it not being returned at all."

Brom lifted a hand, palm out. "I swear, Castis, I will keep the ruby safe and unchanged, and I shall return it to you once we both know the rest of your journey."

The Ma'ab Nobleman had little choice but to accept these terms if he wasn't going to challenge the sorcerer outright. He bowed stiffly, and Brom bowed in return, then motioned toward the door where something had caught his attention earlier. Something snapped—a silence ward, I thought—and the door opened to reveal the small, Ma'ab woman I'd seen waiting on the pre-dawn porch.

*"Fadhi?"* she asked, lifting her chin, glancing at me before she refocused on the innkeeper. "How may I assist?"

Her Trade tongue was accented like Kurn and Castis.

"Amelda." Brom waved his hand toward the Ma'ab men. "See our guests are comfortable. I have some meetings to attend in town, but I'll be back by early afternoon."

She frowned, indicating me. "I do not know how to make *that* one comfortable."

"'That one' is Sirana, a Western mountain race," the sorcerer chuckled, winking at me, "and she can take care of herself."

Amelda nodded, looking at Gavin beside me; her nose wrinkled in distaste. At the same time, Mathias straightened his long shirt beneath his leather armor.

"I've a few contacts to check in with around town," he said. "I'm open, just let me know when we reconvene."

"Aye," Rithal said, although he came to stand next to Gavin and me. "I got a thing 'er two to do while I'm here. These two can come with me. We'll stay out o' trouble."

Amelda looked annoyed and relieved at once.

"Good to hear," Brom said, and Mathias chuckled.

"Oh, *everyone* knows there are consequences to drawing you away from your duties, Master Brom. Right, Kurn?"

The large man grunted, restraining an eye roll.

"Indeed, do bear it in mind. I hate to be the adversary to my guests." Moving up to Amelda, Brom placed both hands on her shoulders which drew a smile to her face. He kissed her forehead and bid her a good morning. "The inn is yours, hostess."

"Thank you, *Fahdi*," she said, though how much she looked forward to the task was difficult to say. She motioned to the Ma'ab men. "Come."

The rest of us gestured farewells before making our way out of the negotiation hall, hoods up, and Mathias led the way to a side exit I hadn't discovered yet. We left the inn without passing through the front dining room, which had grown much louder since we'd arrived. I smelled the food and was instantly hungry again, regretting that no one had sampled the food left on the table.

"Rithal," I said. "How can I break my fast?"

He looked behind us as if he remembered the food on the table as well. "Well." He considered. "I know a lass might help us out this early. Her crew makes meals fer the bachelor woodcutters."

That sounded right. I smiled. "Need coin, I presume?"

"Yeah, but I gotcha covered." He looked at Gavin and Mathias. "And ye two?"

Gavin nodded, but the latter said, "Not me, thanks."

"Suit yerself."

The skin hunter went his own way into town with the confidence of one who did not need to hide his face, while the Dwarf led us along the less-traveled paths in the direction of the river I'd investigated in the predawn. Noise rose with axes, voices, horses, and carts. I slowed before I could be casually spotted atop a rise. I didn't have to speak my concern.

"Hm," Rithal pondered, looking about before indicating a thick copse of vegetation. "Wait there? Won't be long. We'll get enough fer three."

*Four.*

I smirked, entering the cover without protest. The air was much cooler than this time yesterday on the Midway, and damp; as the Sun climbed, I did not know if that strange thickness would return. There were too many birds flitting and calling overhead and too many Humans close by to relax, but I put my pack lightly against a tree to think through all this.

From here I might track Gaelan to the North, where "world-eaters" dwelled, and I might track Jael to the South with a siege coming. I was certain of the physical tells when we'd all been with Rausery at the cave; I guessed their directions and the most likely disturbances, but there was so much land to cover.

Gavin claimed to receive a warning about staying here, of not having the ability to stand against it. Any guess what that meant and an understatement if it Brom was the threat, whose measure I still did not have. His younger persona at the negotiating table was comfortable as a well-worn coat. This was his base from which he ruled and listened to the stories traveling through.

Brom had even met Captain Isboern before the Western man ever reached Manalar, just five years ago. Gavin had been seeking the tower in which Sarilis dwelled—*Another dream hint from his "patroness"?*—while I had been on the verge of collection by the Sisterhood.

How was all this happening so fast? Something about how I learned the Surface made my head spin. It was bad enough with Rausery dragging us out into the light. Introduce more Humans and Dwarves? Somehow events didn't seem to hurl themselves forward this way in Sivaraus. I was accustomed to life slowing while plotters waited to act.

I glanced up at the sky, where there might be the crucial difference living beneath the dome of a protected cavern versus existing ever exposed to the weather.

*One must be less choosey what they wish to focus upon.*

Brom going out to attend "meetings," for example. How might that be giving the sorcerer time to recover from the surges of the far past which had assailed him last night? How long before I might see again his darker face with stark white hair? And would that herald the closing of a trap from which I could not escape?

Again, the fear swept me. *Run. While you can.*

"I will find you," he had said.

*Go where I dare but don't leave Troshin Bend.*

Doing so would provoke that unknown measure as sure and powerful as the storm that drove me here, no doubt.

The breeze shifted, and I sniffed something mouth-watering; my thoughts evaporated, my focus needle fine on what cloth-wrapped goods Rithal and Gavin carried toward me in their hands.

*Give it to me…*

They at least glanced around for passersby before entering my copse; with white and red hair covered by hoods, we wouldn't be too easy to spot should anyone wander this way. It did not appear that they had begun eating yet.

"A bit much, but Gavin insisted," Rithal remarked.

"If it is, then they will keep to midday," said my apprentice reasonably.

"Right. Got pasties, hash, bread, an' day-cheese."

I unwrapped the cloth to feast standing up. I tried not to moan. The pasties were hand pies filled with seasoned vegetables and thick sauce; they were still warm. The hash was a scoopable collection of roots, an undefined meat, chopped greens, and something binding it before cooking, eggs, maybe. The bread was coarse and rustic, the white cheese pungent and flavorful.

I kept eating at a steady pace; Rithal watched me the whole time, eating his share as well, which were about equal.

"Mm," I offered between my first and second pasties. "My best meal since the tower, Rithal. My gratitude."

"Heh. Welcome, Elf."

"If we are to stay a few days," I continued, "how might I earn the silver you are spending on me?"

Rithal shrugged. "Don' worry 'bout it. The silver is Master Brom's. He pays my expenses while I'm here."

"You are here often?"

"Two, three times a year, maybe." He smirked. "Not fully independent, since my Hill folk are gone an' I blow around like a leaf."

My eyes met his. "The Witch Hunters."

Rithal contemplated whether to take another bite of his pasty, and I weighed my next question. "I've noticed Brom is not all that… neutral where it comes to Manalar. He colludes with you and the Ma'ab. Yet you claimed he has hosted them in 'his town' before."

The Dwarf grunted. "More to learn what he can, I think. He wants all news to come through, not just th' ones he has an opinion on."

"Do you run tasks for him, then, to help with this? Does Mathias?"

Rithal smirked. "Keen enough. Aye, contact enough to earn some keep. Looser bonds, though. I don' know what agreements the skin hunter has with the innkeeper. It ain't that formal nor of confidence which might require fealty."

"As you said before," Gavin muttered, "an information merchant."

"Aye. An' tends not tah make strong enemies."

Yet. Or one simply not widely known, such as my Queen? Or was it possible for one to actively prod pieces around in a conflict, yet also remain in the shadows for always?

*He is old but acts in the 'now.' The Valsharess carries more time upon her shoulders.*

It had taken an insidious treason from a breeding-obsessed Priestess letting demonblood seep into our Noble lines to awaken Her to show Her true strength.

*Perhaps that ancient part of him had been sleeping as well.*

And I'd awakened it.

"Lots passing behind yer eyes, Elf," Rithal said, resuming his meal. "Does Brom worry ye? He said ye have his protection from the Ma'ab."

I smiled. "I'm sure I shall need it."

Rithal didn't know how to take that, so he let it drop. In the end, we consumed all food purchased with nothing left for later; even the Dwarf had more appetite than he expected and did not continue his comments about how much I was eating. Good. If he created a habit, I would question his intake at every meal as well.

I could believe, however, that Gavin ignored my state unless it was relevant, such as the quantity of this breakfast's purchase. At least there was nothing furtive or secretive in the way he looked at me while eating, assuming he did at all. He was accomplished at minding his own thoughts.

The forest floor was thickly dappled with shade as the day became brighter and my familiar Surface headache resumed. It was far better than the Midway had been day after day, but the vibrant greens and yellows were their own glare to my eyes as the days grew measurably longer since I'd first stepped out of the Deepearth.

Now with hunger sated, I sat wondering what was to come next. With this first day in months where neither training nor travel pressed upon me, what would I do? *What is there to do? Hide in the darkness of the inn room?*

With others plotting during the day, it was foolish to sit and wait for them to act upon me. Wandering during the day in a town held great risk, but the night certainly hadn't held much interest with nearly all Humans bedding down at once; another difference from Sivaraus.

*I must be alert during the day with them.*

"So, whatcha gonna do today?" Rithal asked Gavin and me, and I looked at the death mage first.

Gavin grunted. "I could use a few minor supplies. I will visit a shop or two."

"I ken help barter," the Dwarf offered. "They know me, won't try tah cheat ye with me there."

The apprentice looked suspicious. "If you have no concerns for items I might request."

"Example?"

"Animal corpses or fat."

"Nothin' unusual 'bout those."

"Chalk and water repellant powder."

A shrug. "They might think yer a mage, sure."

Gavin paused. "I could use a spade like yours."

"Eh? Why?" Rithal chuckled. "Not gonna dig up *Human* corpses, I hope."

The deadpan expression and silence in answer stopped the Dwarf's laugh and started my own.

"Not here," Gavin said after that beat. "But I did not have time to retrieve mine from the garden at the tower."

Rithal pinched his nose. "Wait, wait... yer serious? A garden spade?"

"You all insisted I knew the rituals from here to Manalar. I know the death ones quite well and can find the graves."

"Why th' Hells would we need you to do that?"

Gavin smiled without showing his crooked teeth. "Extra arms and watchers."

Rithal's eyebrows went as bushy as an agitated squirrel. "An' ye wanna buy a spade for that."

"It also makes a useful weapon."

"Riiight." The Dwarf paused to think. "I s'ppose it does, at that."

"You're curiously easy to convince in this matter, Rithal."

The redbeard shrugged again. "The way we're goin', guess I don' feel much against the idea o' Witch Hunter victims gettin' back up and resistin' a little longer."

Gavin's smirk was unsettling. "As good a justification as any."

"When ye wanna go?"

"How about now?"

"'Kay."

Shifting their weight, they looked at me, and I shrugged. "I will spend the day out of sight and observing the town. I need nothing specific."

"Hm." Rithal scanned the way behind him; we heard but did not see the horses clopping by with their riders. "Midday meal is at the inn. I still wan' tah ask 'bout a closer room fer you two."

"I rather like the corner one," Gavin said. "Fewer neighbors."

"Closer to Kurn and Castis seems provocative," I added coyly, and the Dwarf sighed.

"Fine," he grunted, "I'll move."

"Why?" I asked.

"You two appear more vulnerable than the Ma'ab," he said, pointing up with a stout finger, "an' I don' care if it's true or not. Appearance is all that matters while we're here, that's what'll draw attention first."

"Very well," I agreed.

"Come on, Gavin. Le's go tah the shops." The Dwarf looked at me. "Be ready tah come back inside at midday."

"Shall be." I winked at Gavin. "May you find the sharpest of spades, apprentice."

I received a familiar grunt as reply.

Moving about was doable but not as easy as it had been at night, even with less slippery mud about. I climbed trees capable of hiding me within their branches, though my view was similarly obstructed unless Humans passed close enough to me to hear any words. Like the stable boy, some of their accents were garbled and unintelligible as they drifted by.

I received some insight into a general quiet day; most were working or trading, maintaining anything from garden plots grow-ing food, animal coops and corrals, or tool-making shelters. I spot-ted women and children; the latter were loud and thoughtless scur-rying around in blatant view without heed for potential damage or interference with others' work. The former was louder in their ex-asperation if interrupted in said work, though some preferred to ignore it until someone was injured.

*Not wholly unfamiliar, except for the noise.* Quite the luxury, that.

There were more men in town by what I could count, most with deeper voices and larger sizes than their females, consistent with my broad expectations. However, only a couple pushed their weight around where I could see them, as Kurn did me. Most men working appeared neutral and focused, rather like Gavin, while some took observable effort to enjoy the other's company on occasion, women *and* children.

I probably missed many subtle cues in a race I'd never witnessed before, and this could be the "commoner" version in any case. I knew how privilege and self-importance altered one's idea of what was achievable around one's peers and less. Regardless, no one here was crushed beneath truly miserable conditions or torment. The work seemed self-directed and cooperative.

Close to midday, a cluster of fifteen men rode into town from the South and East. Such a large group, riding light with mostly arms and armor, told me they had only been out since the morning and hadn't ridden far.

*Scouts. Is there threat?*

I was too far to hear clearly, and the men's return caused enough of a ripple and ruckus through Troshin Bend, drawing shouting children and inquiring adults, that I could not safely move closer. Their gestures were broad and crude, but enough to guess they had been looking for something but hadn't found it.

*Or they simply have some stories to tell in the tavern tonight.*

Anticipating at least some of them might bring their horses to the same stable where we boarded ours, I slipped a long way around to approach it from the rear. There was a smaller rear entrance, too small for horses, that I could slip into and listen within the dim shadows.

Chance would see me do one better as the stable boy, Neal, was opening the front double-doors wide. Having a reasonable guess for it to be clear up top, I took the ladder to the hayloft before they arrived, settling in and remaining still.

"So, what next, Dar?" said one man intelligibly.

"Dunno," he replied. "Like I said, tell Master Brom. Keep lookout North."

"Why would they head that way again? 'Specially without rein-forcements."

"Dunno," said Dar again as he and three other men took care of their tackle and steeds. "Tryina force his hand t'get involved?"

"Governor's not gonna like that."

"Never does, any who try."

"Think it's true? It's gettin' bigger?"

"If it was, I think Master Brom would be doin' something about it." Dar's tone changed, becoming lighter and reassuring. "You know Hunters and their scare tactics. Everything's an urgent insult to Musanlo which *must* be dealt with, hop to, and one don't have time tah put their prick back if caught passing water!"

The men laughed, and some skin slapped together. They saw themselves out and toward the tavern for the midday meal.

*And to talk to Brom, of course.*

I doubted I would be privy to this report but, oh, how I wanted to be! Witch Hunters had been here recently and headed North after making some demand of the governor of Troshin Bend, a demand which he refused. Later and likely at Brom's order, these men had ridden out to check their trail and determined a direction.

*Toward Gaelan.* There might be Witch Hunters between me and her.

I slid swiftly down the ladder and let myself out in enough of a hurry that Neal called out, "*Oi, who goes?*"

The door closed on his question, but rather than draw daylight eyes with a full sprint, I mimicked the walk of the men I'd been watching. If Neal poked his head outside, he would see my dark, dappled cloak and cowl and little else. He chose not to call out again.

Calmly, I made my way to the side door where Mathias had taken us out earlier that morning, doubly relieved to find it unlocked, and let myself in. I could make out Dar's voice with the others at the front; apparently, they waited their turn for an audience with Brom. I moved forward far enough to take the stairs, stubbornly holding on to the slower, clunkier gait. Somehow, making noise helped them ignore me so I could reach the top and disappear out of sight down the hall.

Gavin had the key to the room; I wasn't sure if he'd returned yet, but I could pick the lock if needed. I knocked first, two short and twice long.

"One moment," he said inside.

When he was on the other side, I whispered, "Yes, it's me."

He opened the door and let me in. "You're in time for lunch. It'll be brought here."

"Excellent news," I said, meaning it. "I have some as well. Fifteen scouts just rode in. What four were saying in the stable, a troop of Witch Hunters stopped here recently then went North." I paused. "Perhaps a second time. They were heading 'back' that way without reinforcements, presumably requested here."

Gavin stared at me for long moments. "This is… not excellent news."

I laughed. "No. But interesting, wouldn't you agree?"

"There is a maxim about living in interesting times."

"What you do mean?"

"It's usually used for wishing ill-will."

I lifted my finger to reply then paused. "Hm. Perhaps I've always lived in 'interesting times,' I cannot tell the difference."

The apprentice made a crude face, his opinion on my quip elegantly expressed before he added, "Chasing after Witch Hunters chasing after world-eaters *would* suggest a poor understanding of what 'interesting' times should be avoided."

The urge to laugh returned, as did the impulse to banter. "Your avoidance of conflict is charming on you, homeless one, but not useful if you expect to obtain 'rarer' knowledge by following me around."

The pale man exhaled in mild exasperation and chose not to share his next thought. I was mildly disappointed, but then Cheri arrived with our midday meal to distract me.

"Please bring a second bowl," Gavin said at the door, accepting the tray while I hid behind the door.

"Wha—? You haven't started."

"Last night wasn't enough."

"Um. Very good, master, apologies…"

He closed the door, and I shook my head to hear how meek she'd been. Still, I grinned. "Thank you."

He grunted, and I allowed my patient guardians out to roam around at last and dragged the table closer to my bed where I could sit while he took the chair. We dug into another thick stew, bread, and a shared bowl of red berries.

"Did you find your spade?" I asked.

"I did."

"Are you jesting about finding graves with it for 'extra arms'?"

"Not at all."

"You *can* make servants like Cullen?"

His dark, red-rimmed eyes glanced up at me as he took a moment to recall the name of the walking corpse at Sarilis's tower. He grunted another affirmative.

"How many can you make walk?"

"Depends on time and bodies available to raise."

"All at once, or one at a time?"

"One at a time is safer." He held up his long-fingered hand. "No more. Let me eat."

I sighed, showing my annoyance but ate as well. I listened to general noise of the inn. No urgent noise as if the news brought by Dar had ruffled feathers. I knew not if Mathias had returned or if

Kurn and Castis were being "entertained" by Amelda, but I figured Rithal had returned with Gavin. I could hope the Dwarf might hear of this news and be involved, given his hatred for Witch Hunters.

I felt eyes watching me and looked to the death mage. "You scowl enough to scare children."

"My experience, yes." His black eyes blinked once. "Why would you head North to follow the Witch Hunters?"

I paused with the wooden spoon in my mouth. Was my desire that obvious? I finished chewing to answer; there was little dignity in denying it.

Fortunately, no compulsive nausea arose as I said, "My Queen has sent Red Sisters before to deal with these 'world-eaters,' and Witch Hunters far from their home base seems a good opportunity to test their mettle. Mathias and Rithal would take the opportunity, I'm sure of it."

Gavin narrowed his eyes. "You need mages to cleanse this. You want Brom's help, too?"

I played at confidence, pointing my wooden spoon at him. "And yours."

He sneered. "Still too slim to be sure it will work."

"What about Castis?"

"Would *you* want him at your back? I wouldn't."

I sighed.

Unblinking, Gavin continued. "You weren't sent to deal with this festering forest. It is no obligation of yours."

True. Not mine.

"And we don't have the time to detour in the wrong direction," he added. "It is still a long way to Manalar, and summer has begun."

Summer, yes, the season of wars on the Surface. I shifted in my chair, frowning at my empty bowl. *Not enough time in the season. Must I choose between my Sisters?*

"What was your dream?" I asked, reaching for a handful of red berries to pop in my mouth. "You said 'it' was drawn here, and we stand in the crossroad. I deny there is 'little' we can do."

Gavin fell silent and refused to answer me despite further prodding.

"You tease me as much as Kurn accuses that I do him," I said.

The man wrinkled his nose as if *I* were the ugly one. "I earnestly hope not."

I snorted a laugh, and we finished our meal each within our own thoughts. Much as I hoped against likelihood, neither of us were invited to any private meeting after Brom must have heard what his scouts had to say, and I didn't know where any of the others were.

Later, I peeked out the window, through shutters Gavin preferred to have closed even when it wasn't storming. The town's business—what little I could see of it from this North-facing vantage point—continued as it had in the morning.

I sighed a growl, bored and frustrated, and returned to cleaning and checking over all my equipment again. My spiders kept me a little better company than the dour death mage during this time, for he had scooted the table to the center of the room. With his back facing me, he worked on…whatever it was; I leaned to look.

Instead of writing in a book, he tinkered with a black bird's corpse, using the same surgical tools he'd used on my injuries after the scuffle in the canyon.

*Right after lunch. Good that we both have stomachs of iron.*

I spent some time relaxing on the bed without my belt or leather armor, my hand sliding down to my abdomen to check for changes. It always seemed hotter down low, now, and I believed I could feel an organ inside firmer than it had been.

*My womb.*

I slowed my breathing as my stomach flipped, and I was required to retract the thought about it being made of iron. Thinking how this hard knot of a ball had been scarred then healed, scarred and healed *again,* and this day, to be working still?

*Ugh. Move on.*

Without the leather protection bracing my torso, I was aware again how warm and tender my tits always were as well. Knowing better, I squeezed them. And winced. Oddly, my sex answered like it was jealous of the fondling. Given how bored I was, perhaps that was inevitable.

I glanced at Gavin. He would probably ignore me if I worked my slit into a stress-relieving froth this very moment, though he would be aware. His witness wasn't a concern to me but I did weigh the strength of my urge against his inevitable irritation. In time, the mess of heat, arousal, soreness, inside me—a full belly warring with brief moments of pitching the food back out—convinced me to do nothing and lie still. I relaxed, my hand above my womb.

*Five months.*

Out of roughly twenty-four.

*And you want to go test Witch Hunter mettle. Cleanse warp rot. Find Gaelan...*

Then what? Head South and find Jael, too? Return to Sarilis's tower with them beside me and kill him, then we all go home?

*That wasn't anything near the Valsharess's Vision for us.*

Even pushing aside the many opportunities to perish or be captured, how long might that take anyway? I only grew hungrier, and the Surface grew ever larger. What happened if I made it to autumn, or winter again, and I couldn't find enough food for me and my unborn? If I was stuck on the Surface and couldn't return to the Deepearth for a long time, what would I do?

*Try to give birth up here? Alone?*

I glanced at my belt resting on the floor, specifically at D'Shea's expulsion vial still intact. It would be potent at any time, but the longer I waited the greater strain on my body, and the greater chance I would bleed out and die with the unborn I was trying to shed to survive.

*"Past the halfway mark,"* D'Shea warned me, *"it grows dangerous. Choose wisely."*

I had until winter to decide, then. We would see if it were wise or not.

Gavin turned in his chair, the creak and shift drawing my gaze; he studied me for a few moments, dark eyes lingering. I had been absently poking my hot middle again but stopped when I caught him watching.

"Still bright," he said. "Seems well enough."

*Bright?*

I sat up quickly. "Wait, 'bright'? What do you mean bright?"

The death mage quirked a black eyebrow. "Life auras in good health are bright to my eyes when I look for them. Like a candle with a white center. If it is white, it is full of Vitas."

My hands clenched the straw mattress, making unintended noise. "You can *see* it? You did not say that before!"

He looked at me with mild bemusement. "I said you had two distinct life auras, Sirana. I have been using my eyes."

"Well, but I thought… *ergh!*" I put a fist to my brow. "Aside, then. Can any mage see it?"

"No, not any mage. It depends on their affinity." He glanced down again as if to walk back from his casual remark. "It is still small. At this stage, I would think one must know what to look for."

Or share a horse with me for a few weeks while practicing auras.

"You seem curious," he said then, "about the changes. Your first?"

I swallowed, feeling queasy yet it wasn't the geas. The first I was never supposed to have anyway; possibly my only one as a Red Sister, such as Elder Rausery had when she was younger.

*A Daughter. Used up by the Priestesses.*

The death mage waited a moment but grew uncomfortable by my expression. "Forget I asked," he said and turned around to his dead bird.

I would try. This fretting wasn't helping me.

The afternoon waned and the day grew late, though the Sun was still up. I had just grown hungry again when a shout outside the window drew me out of a light doze. I moved, upright and in a crouch, peeking out of the shutters before Gavin had lifted his head from the table to decide what to do.

"What do you see?" he asked me.

I saw men riding in from the Northern road, the metal of their heavy armor and gear clanking clearer than any of Brom's towns-men. Counting eighteen riders and horses, I noted a symbol on the red saddle blanket of one dapple grey mare: a yellow circle with four narrow triangles pointed out in four directions, with four more of half-length between each of those. It looked like the Sun bursting out rays of light.

I blinked. *Like the brand on his right shoulder.*

"Sirana?"

Gavin stood up as if to look for himself, and I glanced up at him from the bottom of the window, my eyes wide. I didn't have to say anything; one of the riders shouted a call to the town at large.

"Brom Troshin! *Ven itris reitriculum, in nomuli sancji Musanlo!*"

The death mage could not really get any paler, but he had un-derstood the words clear as crystal as he jumped in surprise. I didn't know what they said but had heard the cadence when Gavin spoke to prove his origin.

"They returned again," he murmured.

They had. *So soon.*

Eighteen Witch Hunters were outside Brom's Inn.

# CHAPTER 6

GAVIN AND I HAD ONLY BEGUN TO DEBATE OUR OPTIONS IN harsh whispers—sneak outside to get to the stables, or seek Rithal's room, or remain in here out of sight until dark—when heavy, quick bootsteps sounded, coming directly to our door.

The bolt lock might as well not have been there as I watched the metal bar slide to one side as if by an invisible hand, and some mechanism sprang easily within the knob as a key was turned at the same time. The handle turned, my spiders were in position—

And the door stopped against the brace Gavin had set.

Brom sounded exasperated. "Don't make me break my own door."

"You could have knocked," I replied, glancing at my ally. By the look on his face, he wasn't sure Brom ignoring the Witch Hunter summons in favor of us was a good thing for the circumstances, either.

"Open the door," the sorcerer commanded. "I don't have much time to answer before they do something righteously stupid."

"Indeed," Gavin muttered dryly, the tension in his shoulders softening. "What do you intend with us?"

"To help hide you, of course. I must set a disguise on you both, quickly, then I will go outside and talk to them. My men can only keep them engaged so long."

I looked at Gavin again, showed him my ready spiders and motioned with my chin that he should get the brace. The apprentice moved slowly to obey, allowing the innkeeper into his own guest room. Brom stepped in and palmed the door closed behind him.

"Can you disguise me as a man of your town?" I asked first.

The sorcerer blinked but fortunately didn't insult me by asking why. "Yes, I can."

"Good. Are there mages among them who may see through your spell?"

The Desert man smirked. "There are mages present, yes, but they aren't strong enough to see through it. Never have been."

"Good. How long will it last?"

Brom looked in the direction of loud voice outside, becoming angrier. "In the time I have, not long. Four hours, perhaps."

I did not believe that was the range of his ability at all, even on short notice. I believed that was the length of the leash he would give me to make certain other men didn't snatch me out from under him. It had to be enough.

"Then do it," I challenged. "And get outside."

Young Brom grinned at my tone, approaching cautiously. He'd noted the placement of my spiders again, as I noticed his skin was paler since our meeting this morning.

"I hope you do not require touch," Gavin muttered, backing up.

"Not touch, just proximity," answered the other mage. "I must feel your aura and set my magic to align with it. You should know this."

The death mage regretted the logic which convinced him to stand still for the spell to be placed on him. Brom was probably also taking the opportunity to gauge his aura, as he'd remarked Gavin was suppressing earlier. In truth, I didn't know what he'd find.

*As such things go when multiple threats maneuver you into a corner.*

Brom cast his first spell with words I didn't know and gestures which were vaguely familiar if I thought about our wizards back home. Something was pinched between his fingers each time and combusted into a tiny poof of fire and smoke toward the end of the chant.

He disguised Gavin, though I watched only his coloring change to not be so blatantly Northern, instead granting him a darker tan, unremarkable brown hair, and brown-green eyes. Brom did not change the death mage's face, form, or clothes. Gavin inspected his arms, turning over his hands to look at both sides, and glanced inquiringly at me.

I shrugged. "Looks like you, with Mathias's coloring."

"Ah," came the short reply. I could not tell if this was acceptable to him or not.

"Better your mannerisms fit your appearance," Brom said. "Something authentic you do not have to think about." He turned eyes on me. "Unlike you. You must be doubly careful having a man's form. Witch Hunters are paranoid about devils appearing as mortal men. They look for inconsistencies, spotting them sometimes when they are *not* there."

"Understood," I said, crossing my arms. "Do it, sorcerer, we run out of time."

"Please, put your guardians away, first. They may become agitated at the change in your hum and move to attack the source."

*My 'hum,' hm?*

More voices and some horses whinnying urged me swiftly to cooperate, and Brom cast as soon as the pouch was cinched up. I may have heard something strange deep within my ears or jaw, but I did not feel anything insidious enter my body or mind.

Instead, my hands appeared only a bit larger, covered by thick, dark gloves. My clothes had changed some, the illusion mostly obscuring my weapons belt and crisscross ties at various spots to make it drabber. Expectantly, I looked at Gavin.

He had a weird expression on his face.

"What?" I asked.

"Well," Gavin attempted to speak. "You are...a slender man."

Smirking, Brom pulled out a small, reflective circle and handed it to me, saying, "Again, something genuine in case your concentration slips. There is no mistaking your grace, Davrin, and these men fear those their own size swaying their hips in seduction."

I glowered, taking the bit of polished metal to look at my reflection. "What are you—?"

A blue-eyed, red-haired youth with brown speckles draped across blush-touched skin stared back. I wasn't much like the other men but my ears were round, and my eyes were the correct shape. Still...

*Do Human buas come this pretty?*

"I must get outside," said our host as he turned to the door.

I followed him out without speaking, gesturing to Gavin. He reluctantly came with me, locking our basic travel gear and his new spade inside. We each had tools on our belt, though in Gavin's case, I thought the strapped book and deep pouch holding his rolled kit would trigger a response against some divine order.

"Keep men between us and the horsemen," I whispered.

"Always do," he said, pulling up his hood.

*Not a bad idea.*

I covered my fire-head as well, wondering where Rithal was, as I didn't see him among the crowd as Brom strode out of the front door and down the porch steps. I didn't see Mathias, either, for that matter.

*Witch Hunters right here if they want them. They don't have to wait for a war.*

The front man's voice boomed. "Ah, Master Brom, an honor! At last, you finish your tasks of *most* import to speak with us?"

The Witch Hunter had a yellow beard, wearing rattling metal atop a skittish, brown stallion. I couldn't see his hair color as it was covered by a helm. Gavin and I stopped by a few guardsmen and servants who remained on the porch as well. We had a decent view of the new arrivals and the contingency which had met them at first.

"What are you doing back, Warrant Bictrius?" said the innkeeper, standing in front of the small crowd of men who had gathered, looking up at the riders. "I have informed you, there are no volunteers here in this early season. Come back when the trade fair begins."

"The devil's work shall not wait until the trade fair," came the imperious, chin-lifting reply. "We have reconnoitered your forest to the North. The corruption is spreading, it threatens more than you. Villages are destroyed or abandoned, as is part of the main road to the lake, and you do nothing!"

"Those villages are old and have been abandoned for a while," replied the sorcerer like he was repeating himself. "So is the road being overgrown."

"You lie to yourself. It crumbles faster than you can conceive under a green sheen of sickness! We have come to conscript every mage in this town to scourge this threat, including you."

Brom laughed out loud. "There is often *only* me coming through spring, that has not changed since your visit last week. As I said then, I shall not go, I am needed here. I suggest again, why not send word to Augran? They have many mages who would take the risk for the Temple's gold, I assure you."

The blond man spat a glob of mucus on the dirt. "A city of sinners! Any cleansing is fouled by a motive solely of mercenary pay!"

"Not true, magic is magic," Brom contested. "It's far truer than your claim that I care about my people and thus am the only one capable *and* worthy to deal with this. There are *many* worshippers of Musanlo in Augran. You *will* find help there." He shrugged. "Or if not there, Port Fortnight is a common trade stop for the city. You may get lucky without having to go that distance."

"We must cross the full heart of the corruption to reach the lake coast," Bictrius sneered, looking about the thirty or so townsmen standing out in the growing dusk. He lifted his voice another notch. "Are all of you here truly cowards in the face of evil?! You cannot do without your sorcerous governor for a mere week to assure your children are safe?"

"You won't let him come back if he leaves," one man said. "You'll charge him with witchcraft after you get what you want."

"Yeah, ye been wantin' it fer years!"

"We know how you chodes work!"

"Heretics!" growled a dark-eyed man near the blond. "Repent your insult to our Chief Warrant now, or earn the consumption coming for you!"

"At ease, *Thetri* Jacob," Bictrius held up his hand to stay his fellow's rant. "They are afraid and under a petty delusion they are loathe to lose. They cannot yet hear the true divine within which knows the truth."

Gavin snorted softly, and I glanced at him, repressing a smile.

"Listen, all townfolk!" Bictrius shouted. "We were sent here by a sign! You have the protection of the *Dyos Guerrimos!* We will see this holy deed done, but we require the aid of your Master!"

"We need our Master here with us!" returned Dar. "Not alone in the wilderness with you!"

"Then come with us!" challenged the Chief Warrant, motioning grandly with his arm like we were all about to follow him to the road North. "See with your mortal eyes that he returns safely! Know the truth of the threat which would steal your souls and watch it be vanquished so you can reassure your women upon victory!"

A low, mistrustful murmur circled through the crowd of men as Brom stood straight and quiet with a stern, unmoved face. I nudged Gavin; he grunted without taking his eyes from the crowd.

"Which are mages?" I whispered without much voice. "Can you see?"

"They do not hide it."

"Point them out to me. How many?"

"Three. The Chief Warrant, the one he called Jacob, and the one sitting on the white horse with gold chain on its bridle."

"Confirmed."

So, three mages weren't enough for the warp rot; they needed at least a fourth. How had my Queen believed that Gaelan could manage this on her own?

There was a silence which stretched as the Witch Hunters looked about, feeling their leader fail to persuade the crowd. Brom inhaled and exhaled.

"What now, Chief Warrant?" he asked. "Will you drag me from my home and my daughter on the verge of night, against the will of those who follow me for guidance?"

I would have liked to see them try that.

"Or will you consider accepting my hospitality for another night and reconsider in the morning? You've been riding hard and are tired."

There were louder grumbles of discontent and concern from among Brom's own.

"Sir, uh," said one man, "we don't have the empty rooms available."

"Sure we do," the sorcerer replied. "Move all staying in the common area to fill the empty guest rooms, and the *Dyos Guerrimos* may stay together in there." I heard the smile in his voice as he added, "We would not choose to split up their approach to their great work."

Bictrius listened to this exchange with narrow-eyed suspicion but had not yet stated whether they would accept. He turned his horse around—boldly or foolishly showing the crowd and the sorcerer his back—and motioned for Jacob and a couple others to come close so they could speak in their native tongue.

While this happened, I noted the third, unnamed mage on the white horse did not take his eyes from the crowd while his leader's back was turned. He sat unblinking and prepared to act. *Battle mage?*

"What do they say?" I whispered.

"I can't hear them," Gavin admitted.

"Hm."

The murmuring continued.

"Is Di-ohs Geerymoss their words for Witch Hunter?" I whispered.

"Shh," he hushed, furtively glancing around us. "No. It means God Warriors. Call them the other, and you have proclaimed yourself an enemy."

My eyes bugged out. "They don't call themselves this and no one told me?!"

"Shh!"

Bictrius and his men bowed their heads, and he turned his horse around to face a patiently waiting Brom.

"We shall accept your hospitality once again, Master Brom, though I am disappointed in the mettle of your men," said the Chief Warrant.

"They are woodcutters, not knights trained from squires."

"*Cliso.* Perhaps we can speak man-to-man after sleep."

"My answer will still be no."

"Your stubbornness is baffling, Brom." The Warrant looked about. "This makes me wonder if you are hiding something."

"Nothing that would be of interest to God's Warriors," Brom said with appropriate charisma, lying through his teeth. "Unless an extra bottle of rare, *virxe* wine about thirty years old piques such interests."

Bictrius huffed and smiled as if it was a fine jest, but I wondered if that non-offer may be of interest. He addressed his men. "Steeds to the fenced hill, as before, take your tack with you. Meet in the common room of Brom's inn."

"*Obae, Xeorde!*" they responded in a single voice before riding off to the South side of town.

Once the Witch Hunters were out of Human ear range, I expected Brom to be mobbed by hushed, urgent protests from the men closest to him. I was instead witness to something odd enough to make me realize something else was going on under the surface.

The sorcerer exchanged no words, but instead made eye contact with one man after another, holding only for a few seconds; that man would excuse himself to a task or to proclaim to continue with his evening, and another would step up. It was the most peaceful and orderly dispersals of an agitated crowd I'd seen. Even the servants on the porch seemed to lose interest and filed inside, speaking of meals to be "souped up."

I didn't see Brom's daughter here, despite his mention. I didn't see Kurn or Castis—no doubt a good thing. I wondered where Rithal and Mathias were, still.

"Too many things amiss," Gavin murmured. "Tonight will not pass uneventful."

I was glad I did not have to explain the oddness to him. I didn't have the opportunity anyway, as Brom finally turned our way, smiling as he approached us on his porch.

"You might want to go back inside," he suggested, "before they finish settling their horses."

"And do what?" I asked. "Wait for dawn locked in our room?"

I noted my voice was still my own. Brom smirked to see me realize it but didn't stare as intently at this freckled young man's face. He looked around us, waiting a few moments longer for the last of the locals to wander away. We were alone outside.

"You could pass some of that time in my office if you wish," he said. "We have things to discuss, you and I."

"Ah, you expect a quiet eve over wine?" I challenged with a Red Sister smile. "You invited three *units* of 'god warriors' to sleep beneath the same roof giving me a disguise that lasts a quarter that time."

The ancient sorcerer wasn't troubled by this, and I didn't like how he glanced at Gavin then. "What else could I do for the well-being of my people?"

"Do you intend to trade *his* wellbeing for theirs?" I asked outright, indicating my death mage. My Human face showed my displeasure.

"No," Brom answered forthrightly. "That's both a poor host and a waste of an excommunicated mage." Grey eyes swept to Gavin as if to pin him in place. "You do not realize how rare that is, that a male mage escapes the Bishops' indoctrinations."

"I have an idea," said the former monk warily. "I am no man's tool, Master Brom. Nor am I to be used by either of you. I follow my own road."

"Ah. Does this 'road' have a name?" Brom asked with a dry half-smile.

"Still to be discovered," Gavin droned in answer. "And I would leave this place tonight. It is the height of foolishness for me to stay."

"You would be safer here, I promise you. The *Dyos Guerrimos* aren't wrong about strange dangers to the North, especially at night. There are more of the Temple's enforcers riding the roads to the South and East between here and Augran. You came from the West, *that* will not get easier over summer." Brom glanced due South. "Unless you want to try for the ocean. Even that journey could wait until morning."

At low voices and clanking metal, I looked to my left. The Sun was setting, and the first cluster of Witch Hunters returned from the fenced hill where they'd left their mounts. Their saddles and packs were borne on their backs and shoulders, easily twice or thrice what I could carry.

"Inside," Brom urged, offering us the door with arm outstretched. "Stay the night. You shall learn the invaluable in doing so. I promise."

*Invaluable lessons like, listen to one's gut.*

My jaw tight, and my empty stomach aching with tension, I motioned to Gavin to go in. "Let us stop by the kitchen first, so we needn't come out."

Reluctantly, Gavin took a step forward.

Brom smiled approvingly at us, standing in the way of the stairs down to the road with arms loosely crossed. "I will find you later."

That, I did not doubt.

It was quite loud at the front tavern portion of the inn as the staff got all the Witch Hunters fed for the night. I thought there was no way Kurn and Castis weren't aware, and somehow I was surprised the Hellhound hadn't swaggered in challenging them all at once to a fight.

But maybe I expected only the dumbest bull from him.

"How do you say it again?" I asked.

*"Dyos Guerrimos,"* Gavin replied with a taut patience I found fascinating.

I repeated it several times, forming my mouth in unfamiliar ways until he said, "Good enough."

Quite an accomplishment for the night, which wasn't saying much. I was peeking out the window again, able to see quite far in the darkness beyond as long as I blocked Gavin's candle with my hood.

"Where is Rithal?" I muttered.

"Or Mathias?"

"I'm less concerned about him. He vanishes among men. Rithal is the only Dwarf here, I think."

Gavin shrugged. "He has unfortunate experience to know to avoid Witch Hunters."

"So what's he going to do, sleep in a tree?"

Another shrug, and I sighed, looking out at the occasional body walking by. Finally, I recognized one walking toward the inn from the rear end.

"Mathias," I murmured.

"What?" Gavin asked, but I was turning to snuff his candle. "Hey."

"I'll climb out," I said, opening the shutters in the dark room, then unbolting the thick glass to open that on its hinges as well.

"But you're..." Gavin began but ended on a sigh. "Never mind."

He watched with some fascination as I wedged a metal anchor in the corner of the window between two boards and uncoiled my tight, black knotted cord.

"Pull this up once I'm on the ground," I said. "Use it yourself to climb out if you must, or to toss the cord down when I return."

"Very well," he said, sounding interested as he came closer to inspect how the anchor and cord were set.

I exited the second level of the inn and climbed down with practiced familiarity, placing boots with care and relieved that the shutters for the room directly beneath us were closed. I landed on soft dirt half-hidden behind a shrub and gave the cord a tug, waiting until Gavin began pulling it up before looking both ways and slipping out into the night to meet the skin hunter.

Waving my arm so as not to startle him to the point of tossing a dagger, Mathias paused in his tracks. Neither of us spoke, and his weak eyes required me to get close enough that I could have stabbed him before he could make out much by the rising moonlight.

He peered at me and smiled. "Well, *hello*. Who are you?"

I frowned at him then remembered, *Oh, yes, I'm a bua.*

"Mathias, it's me," I said in my natural voice.

Surprise struck his face and he withdrew a step. "Wh...!" He leaned forward again. "Sirana?"

"Yes. An illusion."

He looked me up and down in a way he never had, his face becoming warmer like Tamuril, and abruptly I was trying to count about how long before this spell faded.

"Wow," he breathed. "Striking. I could forget you don't have a phallus under there."

I smirked. "Only because I didn't bring one from the underground."

His face split into a playful grin. "Mmm-hm. *Lots* of ideas crowding in now, Red Sister."

"To use on Witch Hunters? There are eighteen inside the inn now. I came to warn you. Brom invited them."

"Oh, I know. I'm not deaf. Just been setting up a few things."

"Setting up what things?" I asked curiously.

He ignored the question; the man was still smiling at my freckled, male face. "I really like you this way. Are you hard up?"

"What?"

"By my count, you've been going without for, what, a month? Longer?"

*Going without. Heh.*

"Sounds like *your* month," I said.

"Point. Haven't had a wet dream in years."

I opted to appear baffled as he looked up at the stars, scratching his face hair as he took a small step closer. "I could pretend if you could. We could both come."

I chuckled. "You don't know how I 'come,' Mathias."

He shrugged, nonplussed. "So, show me, Sister. Wearing *this* sweet face, I'll be a good study for once." The man adjusted a thick tent pole. "Either hole you want, or both, I'll give 'em a good ride."

His attitude in offering sex reminded me of Jaunda, and he really did have several of her tastes. I could smell his scent as his skin heated up in the cooler air; it grew musky. It was also odd, and oily;

I didn't know whether I liked the change or not. It wasn't distasteful, just—

"What do you think?" he asked, hands down but fingers clenching.

I didn't know what to think, but I noted that I wasn't letting my spiders out of my pouch. I held my ground as Mathias leaned closer to stare at the illusion over my face. His gaze didn't quite meet my eyes; I wondered if it was intentional or due to the magic or the dark?

He tilted his head and slowly closed the distance. His lips lightly brushed mine, soft and dry. His heart pulsed in his chest, jumping in his throat as he leaned back, his eyes assessing any threat response; he was randy but not gone stupid yet.

Why did he remind me of how some of my Sisters looked at me? He wasn't seeing a Dark Elf; he saw another Human man, albeit one younger than him.

*Hm. More like a Red Sister than not, in that case.*

"Come on," he murmured, teasing. "It'll be fun and feel good."

"For me as well?" I arched a brow. My look seemed to make his breath catch.

"If you like fucking like you said."

"I told the truth. I do."

"Glad to hear."

My gut *was* tight with a familiar excitement, and my sex leaned toward becoming slick for this man, this Human whose breath shook with arousal as my gloved hand reached out, hesitated, and cupped firm, hot genitals through his leather trousers. He sucked in a breath, leaning to brush our mouths together again in encouragement. His lips were moister as he panted, reached with one hand to open his pants while the other rested on my shoulder.

I watched, curious to see, and soon he laid out a bare sword for me to explore. A lot of curly fur nesting at the base and spreading down muscular thighs, not so neat and smooth as Jaunda. About the same size pole, though, and Mathias's tool matched his frame.

His fingers dug into my shoulder when I squeezed and stroked him, and I snickered at the sigh and the way he humped his hips. Mathias smirked and the look in his eye was familiar. So much like my Lead before she pushed me to my knees to thrust her Feldeu into my mouth that I expected him to do the same.

*That's probably what he wants. A bua's mouth on him instead using a cait's slit.*

Where would I rather take his cock? Could I be sure this would be safe for my womb? Was he healthy? I hesitated, checking around us. Nothing worrisome.

"Gonna show me yours?" he murmured, mouth twisting like he expected my change of mind.

I gave it a pleasurable tug. "Would you rather I suck your staff instead?"

His eyes widened, and he swallowed. "Don't see how that gets you off."

*That's a yes.*

"Your fingers," I answered, letting mine dance along his rod. "You, first, though. So much blood loaded below isn't any good for lessons."

*"Heh heh."*

I led him by his prick into deeper cover as he went along with it, grinning. His eyes were sharp as they should be with one's parts in a Red Sister's hands. I urged him closer to a tree where he could brace himself, began pulling and caressing his sack and rod in encouragement and reassurance.

"A slow bite is okay," he murmured half-grinning. "You know how?"

Intrigued, I went to a knee. "Yes, I do."

He stared down at me, disbelieving up until the moment I put his broad cock between my lips, wrapped my tongue around it, and sucked. It was covered in that heavy musk but recently washed with water. His eyes drifted closed for several moments as I grew accustomed to the taste and texture.

Then, slowly, I bit down.

"Ohhhh," Mathias moaned too loud. "Yeah… fuck, yes, little jack…"

His hands tightened on the bark, his buttock flexing beneath one of my hands as I picked up a rhythm, sucking and pausing to slowly bite, my hood falling back where he could see my whole head and pretty, male face. Round ears, and all.

His cock upon my tongue wasn't any larger than Jaunda or D'Shea, and as squishy and sensitive around the head. Although I worked his length for many long, luxurious strokes, there was no pretending that Mathias was Jaunda. I couldn't forget he was anything but what he was.

Meanwhile, he kept calling me "little jack."

I wondered about his response for an instant before I pushed him deep, suppressing my gag flex until his mass of brown curls was close to my nose, smothering me in his scent.

"Shit!" Mathias cried. "Talented little fucker…*ungh!*"

*Shhh!*

Wide eyes fixed on me and my illusion, the skin hunter went still as his cock squirted hot and salty across my tongue in several jets as I swallowed. Mathias shuddered, slowly pushing his hips forward and sinking deeper between lips which, in daylight, must look as rosy pink as Tamuril's by now. Both his hands were where I could see them, gripping the trunk of the tree.

*Keen negotiator.*

Though, he was right; that *was* rather fun.

I drew off him, licking my lips. "My turn."

Eyelids half-closed, Mathias nodded and reached down to take my arm and help me up to my feet. My hands froze on my belt as I heard a branch snap and a following chink of metal. Both our heads whipped in that direction, and I saw the two men stop trying to hide and straighten up as they came toward us.

"You!" said a man in a helm and accented Trade. "What you are doing to this boy?!"

"Ah, fuck," Mathias snarled.

"*Antipedi!*" accused the other man, pointing a finger. "Let him go, *felijio!*"

The skin hunter turned toward them, his chest puffing up; he'd closed his leathers impressively fast. "Look, shitholes—"

"Run to the governor, boy," the first Witch Hunter ordered me, his tongue rolling as he drew a rope from his belt. "We arrest this one! Make him confess what he's done."

I'd withdrawn a large pinch of sleep powder. *Time to rediscover its potency.*

I murmured to my ally, "Hold your breath."

The Witch Hunters strode right up to us, and I lifted my hand up, blowing as strong a poof of air as I could. In the still night air, it went into their eyes, nose, and mouths, and they staggered, coughing, while I wordlessly tugged Mathias's arm to run left and around them. I noticed the skin hunter didn't begin breathing until I did farther down the road.

"Can't believe it," he huffed in irony. "Caught poling a woman this time, and it *still* isn't good enough."

I smirked as we circled around the nearest house. "I'm certain demoness mouths are worse than a man's in their eyes."

Mathias laughed out loud. "Well, I can claim they both make a man see stars. I'm happily damned."

"Not on this world," I said, "unless they catch you."

"Let them try. That's why I'm here."

We paused behind a shed listening for sounds of pursuit. There were none. Could they have fallen asleep, though Kurn had not?

Having the quiet moment, I whispered, "Where is Rithal? I haven't seen him since midday."

"Uhm, I haven't seen him."

"I must warn Gavin."

"They're all in the same inn."

"With luck, they won't find the bodies until after…"

I heard others calling out something in Manalari.

"No such luck," Mathias informed me. "Two others would've been waiting as reinforcements if there was resistance. Common tactic. You just moved too fast."

It hadn't seemed *that* fast. I made a face to realize he was saying four had been ready to involve themselves in a tryst in the woods. *God warriors, indeed.*

I pursed my mouth with rising regret that I could reach neither the inn door nor Gavin's window, though glad I'd left him that cord. Choosing the moment to use it was the hardest part, though. I wondered if he saw anything from the window; surely, he'd heard something. More importantly, what would happen next?

Mathias and I sneaked around quietly, getting closer to listen, see, and be aware if the aftermath of the encounter should die down. The chance of this did not appear in my favor. Though I relied on Mathias's understanding of the language, I could see what was happening.

I hissed in disbelief, "Two of the mules *licked* my powder off their fingers and fell over!"

"Yeah, that's what I'm getting," Mathias said, listening but not peering into the night as I was. "*After* giving the alarm. That's some strong shit, Sister."

"It didn't work so well on Kurn at the tower," I grumbled.

Mathias's teeth were white as he grinned. "Oh, he took a few stimulants of his own trying to stay awake after coming back inside. You didn't stay to watch; you hid with Gavin in the kitchen."

"I was not hiding."

"Either way, this is a bigger dose, isn't it?"

I sighed. "It is untested on Humans."

"Not anymore. How long does it last for Elves?"

"Not long." I converted in my head. "An hour? Less? The mushroom's prized quality is swiftness, not longevity."

"Huh. Well, an hour is plenty long enough to get killed if you're caught by it."

"Precisely."

"What about continued exposure? Say if they're breathing what's on their face?"

"Extended sleep."

I was annoyed to see that three Witch Hunters had figured this out, carefully wiping the two men's faces using cloths dampened by the contents of a flask. Then they set the soiled cloth far away and set it on fire using a torch, retreating quickly.

"Some cleverness in that ignorance," I muttered.

"Yeah, dogs can be clever," the skin hunter agreed. "Is it lethal in too large a dose?"

I arched my brow at him. "Taking notes on my tools?"

Without blinking, he said, "Yes, but we also want to be ready if one of them doesn't wake up."

I grunted. Good point. "Not lethal. There are side-sicknesses the longer one breathes it, but they did what was proper to end exposure."

"Okay." Mathias took a slow breath. "So, when they wake up, they will know the 'boy' is a spell-casting demon who was sucking my cock. Until then, they don't know who they're looking for."

I didn't argue that it wasn't a spell; I saw his point as I watched the men milling about, trying to awaken their brothers with slaps to the face. It wasn't working.

"Note," I grumbled, "the 'boy' will fade soon."

"A pity and, forgive me, but that won't improve things."

"No jest, it will not."

"You want to silence the first two, so they don't tell about what they saw?"

A Red Sister would be required to do that in Sivaraus, yes, though commoners and Nobles alike assumed it was our work. It didn't matter because they could do nothing about it. I wasn't truly a Red Sister here; I was a "foreigner" acting without a Queen's writ, and I hadn't the time or understanding to consider the implications of this proposed killing action in Troshin Bend.

Would it end Brom's hospitality toward me, forcing his hand to ensnare me lest his valuable find be struck down by Witch Hunters? Would he instead help cover my tracks? Would we be required to kill all eighteen men to ensure silence? A temporary measure at best when whatever superior expecting to hear from Bictrius never did.

"What would Brom do if I killed them?" I murmured.

Mathias hadn't gotten that far yet. He stood quietly, listening to the voices. "Hm. That would draw the Church here in force. Brom wouldn't be pleased."

*I thought so. Fuck Braqth's Tits, all this trouble for being caught sucking a man's prick?*

Jaunda would have cuffed my ear for being caught, except I wagered we hadn't been seen but rather, it was Mathias's loud moaning. Apparently, Humans couldn't be silent in sex, but I hadn't thought to insist; I assumed he knew its import.

"I won't kill them in their sleep," I murmured.

"Right," Mathias replied, sounding like he agreed but didn't like what he imagined next.

"You are certain they will not let this lie?"

"Nope. Evidence of witchcraft is always enough to justify breaking their way into strangers' homes."

"They are guests of the town governor."

"They don't care when they're in the right."

"In the right what?"

Mathias chortled. "You're a dream, Sister. Especially wearing that face."

"Stop saying that," I muttered, my groin aching while he enjoyed the calm of afterglow. "That's how we got into this."

"Not our fault. If only 'God's warriors' could mind their own business and weren't drawn to the sound of any man with a dick buried somewhere. But you did attack first, that's all it takes."

*"Pah!* Their moves were threatening. No regrets in being the faster one."

"Trust me, I know. They're not gonna change their minds."

Indeed, and I also didn't know any Red Sister who would pass up the opportunity to catch someone rutting, either. We always had other motives for breaking into any room in the city. Choosing to indulge was no intrinsic failing of mine, just an opportunity being exploited.

*The red boot on the other foot, as it were.*

"Can you reach Brom to explain?" I asked.

"Probably not. If he's not aware now, he will be shortly."

Mathias and I moved spots carefully, following the line of men in armor spilling out of the front door and gathering to chatter outside next to their four downed brothers. Their shouts were growing louder and angrier again, a solid barrier to any contact with Gavin or Brom, any preparation beyond what I had on me.

Having taken one defensive action to an overt threat to my companion, I watched as the Witch Hunters whipped themselves up into a fervor along the road beside the inn. Inhabitants of Troshin Bend were coming out of their houses to investigate as well.

Standing back would not deescalate the swiftly organizing response to this perceived threat in the dark, nor would confronting them directly only to expose me to their ire already enflamed. Goddess forbid my Human mask fade away during such a roast; it may be on the verge of doing so now. Others would get involved as all options beyond survival were ripped from my hands.

Gavin had been correct. Tonight would not pass without event.

*Fuck.*

# CHAPTER 7

THE NEED TO *DO* SOMETHING IN THE WAKE OF THE SURGING noise overpowered me, spreading like illness in my limbs.

*Run. Get inside. Return to Gavin's window. Seek Rithal.*

"Wait," Mathias murmured, going still beside me. "Don't."

I breathed, trembling. Slowly, the panic subsided. It had been turns, *years* since I made that mistake, flushed out of hiding at House Thalluen, fleeing my sister like a scared bit of prey. Doing nothing was the only choice which offered any strategy.

"Brom!" called one of the guardsmen. "Where's Master Brom!"

"Someone get him! Hurry!"

Warrant Bictrius and his "Thetri" Jacob were outside, armored how they had arrived in helm, breastplate, shin, and shoulder guards. Maybe they never took them off.

I counted all eighteen, tried to spot the silent battle mage as well, certain he wasn't one of the four men unconscious. Without his white horse, however, I couldn't be sure at this distance. I supposed I'd discover him if or when he cast.

"What are they saying?" I asked.

"Attacked by devils, find them," Mathias murmured. "What else?"

"Next actions?"

The skin hunter listened. "Search the area. Find witnesses."

"There weren't any."

"With a window view."

*Oh, damn. Gavin.*

They clustered in threes and fours; Bictrius led three inside while three more remained to watch over their sleeping fellows. The last two groups began a cursory perimeter search around the inn, eyeing with suspicion every window and the closest wooden structures. Saying nothing, I left Mathias to slip farther into the dark, mostly keeping to trees and sheds until I could see the rear of the inn and Gavin's corner window.

The shutters were closed—*good idea*—but there was no sign of Brom when voices raised, and I realized they were coming from inside. Something metal struck wood with the weight of a man behind it; I imagined someone throwing his shoulder against the locked door.

Then, the shutters opened. And the glass.

And my anchored black cord was tossed out.

*Oh, no, don't.*

I couldn't blame anyone their impulse to escape rather than be cornered in a small room. He merely couldn't see the other Witch Hunters waiting on the ground until it was too late.

Gavin swiftly climbed down clutching pack and spade, his boots reaching the dirt as the door gave way above, and Bictrius ran to the open window shouting orders into the dark. I could tell that his altered coloring had faded; he was white with black hair and eyes once again—obviously Ma'ab, comparing him to the others—and I could only assume my face had reverted to a black Davrin some time while I'd been watching.

"*Bruxto!*" shouted one of the three Witch Hunters on the ground, pointing.

They rushed him, and there was enough distance to cover that Gavin tried running, first. He aimed for the road, in my general direction and perhaps intended to try for the stable and his mare. He didn't get far before he knew he'd be tackled; before they did, he spun around and raised his spade.

Only by direct contrast with these men did I realize how tall Gavin was; he normally slumped or hunched over. Before I'd finished drawing a breath, he used that long reach and height advantage, swinging the edge of the grave tool at the nearest Manalari before he got close. Whether he intended it or not, the apprentice caught the Witch Hunter in the throat. Blood sprayed as the man collapsed.

Everything went to stone for a breath.

*"Asasiro!"* a second man screamed, his voice breaking with rage, drawing his sword as Gavin backed up, brandishing the stained spade.

The Witch Hunter continued making as much noise as possible as Bictrius and his men surged out of the inn's front door, the front man shouting commands. The others had left, checking the perimeter, and converged on my death mage.

There were so many. And where were the others, Brom, Rithal, even Kurn and Castis? Were they holding back, waiting to see if this unimportant, sacrificial male would be enough to satisfy the rising bloodlust?

*Of course. Why not?*

Davrin did the same at any time.

I wagered Gavin's blood wouldn't be enough to slake the Bishops' enforcers when, for no strategic reason I could fathom, two Witch Hunters broke down another door and dragged the man, woman, and child out into the night, bellowing threats and orders as they pitched them to the ground. God's warriors started pounding on doors before eventually breaking them down.

*They want an audience to watch what they do to him.*

As a warning to the commoners. I understood this, too.

Gavin hadn't surrendered, however. Sword clashed with spade in two hard strikes, while Bictrius shouted orders the swordsman was reluctant to follow.

*"Non matjes, non!"* said their Chief Warrant. *"Afrontise xuzito!"*

Reluctantly, the men switched to non-lethal attempts to seize Gavin, but the silent apprentice was desperate and did not allow himself to be surrounded before he simply ran deeper into Troshin Bend. The Manalari took off after him, less agile in heavier armor but no less determined. Some quickly shoved some wad of substance from a pouch into their mouth as they went; it was any guess why.

*Shit.*

I drew my hand crossbow and sprinted after them, keeping to the shadows the best I could while not sacrificing speed. I gained ground faster than I expected, getting ahead of the mob by taking a shortcut as Gavin led them through a tighter cluster of structures.

I loosened my spider pouch the moment before I chose my first target, Callitro's ring heating up on my finger. My three guardians scrambling up to my nape as I squeezed the trigger. The next instant, the bolt protruded from the eye socket of a running Witch Hunter, his arm up to strike Gavin. A second Manalari went down.

My one surprise shot, and a clear declaration of wider resistance. The Chief Warrant was *not* pleased, shouting challenges at the shadows while townsfolk spilled out of their homes, some dressed in night clothes.

I moved from that spot amidst the resurging shouting as they spun in my direction, choosing another, reloading my weapon as I went. Leaving proved wise, for the silent mage who'd sat upon the white horse made himself known. He growled out a spell, fingers twisting, and set the roof of the house behind which I'd been hiding on fire, offering light for their eyes and suffering for my own, unfortunately.

*A pity I didn't take that mage by chance.*

"Stop! Stop!" someone cried.

A woman yelled, "What are you doing?! Sheirgh might be in there!"

In the chaotic moments after this first blast and flare of flames, as more townsfolk were screaming a high pitch, another attacker shot a crossbow at a second target, striking him in the thigh. I took a shot at that one, too, while Gavin defended himself with his spade. By the flinch and stagger, I had hit, but it wasn't an instant kill.

My eyes were blurring and aching from the fire's rising intensity, and the tickle of smoke threatened the back of my throat with a cough to give away my location.

*Maybe use the entire bag of sleep powder from up high?*

Too late for that to be effective, I saw. The Witch Hunters were spreading out to surround the death mage; I would get two of eleven, at best. I couldn't charge in, either; I couldn't take on that many hand-to-hand in armor. I had nothing volatile enough for sweeping attack on my toolbelt except Sarilis's unknown vial, which I dared not open under such circumstances.

I took another shot at the battle mage, watched it deflect off a magical shield of some kind, and moved again with a curse, continuing in a rough circle. I lost sight of Gavin for a few heart-pounding moments as arcane words bellowed out from the fire mage until I found another shadowed building corner to peek around.

The one who had been shot twice had taken a third, full-sized bolt from a crossbow as well and was down. That was good, but...

*Who is shooting besides me? Rithal?*

And where the fuck was Brom? Wasn't this *his* town they were destroying? What about Kurn or Castis, wouldn't they want to fight their sworn enemies, for the sheer thrill of it? Or maybe they were waiting to see what happened with me and Gavin, first. I had to assume we would receive no timely help.

*It isn't over yet.*

My death mage viciously attacked another who got near, swinging his spade with clear action this time to maim or kill. I no longer saw his pack; he must have thrown it somewhere in the chase. He was bleeding from something which had struck him in the forehead but, as with Castis before, proved capable of shielding against another mage's attack.

I flinched to see fire rain down from directly above Gavin, the bright river of flame parting to spill around an upward surge of cold power, like a waterfall splitting on a boulder. I caught a glimpse before looking away from that searing column of light.

More shouting which sounded like tactical orders. Wiping my eyes with the wrist of my glove, I looked again. Six men had bared their blades before departing in pairs at the Chief Warrant's order. None of the five who remained stuck on Gavin had drawn swords, only clubs.

*Goddess damn it.*

They wanted him alive, but they wanted whoever was shooting at them dead. They would keep me and whoever else was attacking on the move, depriving us of time and good angles as they attacked any resident unfortunate enough to get in their way.

I lost sight of my ally again as two charged my way, their voices blaring at the top of their capacity. Meanwhile, another wooden building caught fire thanks to the blast-happy Witch Hunter. By the time I got into any kind of position to witness or act, something flat-out *loud* filled the space between houses, bouncing off the wood and making my ears vibrate.

*Fucking spider guts!!*

I staggered back, crouching small and tight, clutching one ear and my guardians trilled in agony with me. I dared not move out of my shadow for those long, terrifying instants. My inner ear dizzy and numb, I wouldn't have noticed if a Witch Hunter were standing right on top of me.

After too long, my senses were of some use to me again. Blinking back tears, I checked my immediate surroundings, confirmed I hadn't been found, and prepared my crossbow for readiness before seeking to understand what I had missed.

The five men in the street were trying to get off the ground; something had knocked them down, as it had me. In the interim, Gavin had scrambled on all fours and had taken the corpse of the downed Witch Hunter hostage.

Using the fighter's own dagger to open a large gash in the body, blood gushing out as he reached in deep through the gut with his other hand, he clawed and ripped upward beneath the ribcage like he'd lost a valuable gem deep in the middens.

The Witch Hunters' shouts witnessing this were muffled as I exchanged one shadow for another and a better angle. *"Malit brux-to! Asasino!"*

Gavin wasted no gasping breath exchanging threats; he was shaking either from surge and exhaustion. I watched with wide eyes as he finally wrenched the heart out of the torso with brute force, his fist glossy with blood, his arm stained from the elbow down. He climbed to his feet, and the shouting increased, my mouth falling open, as the death mage defiantly took an enormous bite of the bloody organ where Bictrius and every Witch Hunter could see.

*"Uspri cannic ungrulu,"* the black-eyed monk hissed, spewing red blood from his lips as more spilled down his chin and long, pale neck.

In response to his voice, the corpse jerked, the rest of the intestines tumbling out as it got to its feet. Dead eyes stared at his fellow warriors, its hand reaching to unsheathe its sword.

I wouldn't have guessed such large men could scream so high.

*"Dyos carreblo deshantos!"* Bictrius bellowed, backing up and drawing a short, highly polished dagger from his belt. *"Infini ban-tisma!"*

The five surged in together on command, and the undead Witch Hunter lurched in front of Gavin to protect him while he gained distance. The walking corpse took a volley of powders, splashing liquids, and an arrow to the thigh, unaffected by most of it.

For an instant, it felt like the battle turned, pulling a pleased gasp of surprise from me. The constant shrieking and cursing, the fear blended with frustration and dismay, were momentarily amusing despite the circumstances, and I laughed, the sound cut off with a cough as the smoke continued to thicken.

*Damn it.*

I silenced myself, watching Gavin sprint away and leave the undead as further obstacle for his hunters. My ally couldn't know he had drawn them forward at the right time; soon they would be showing me their backs.

Smearing a toxin on a dagger, my spiders ready as I prepared to move, I glanced down the wall to clear the other direction, and scanned the rooftops for what little I could see in the waves of spreading, orange light.

Nothing obvious.

I waited as the battle mage held to the rear while Bictrius and the two others harried the corpse. The Witch Hunters did not hesitate to bring one of their own down, three men grappling the animated body, trying to behead him with a hatchet while screaming either obscenities or prayers.

I picked that moment to sprint straight across the street, flitting behind the mage and confirming his shield was only in the front. My dagger tip scratched the back of his neck beneath the edge of his helm, and he shouted as I vanished behind the next house.

*"Ardic, Warranti, ardic!"* he cried, pointing the way I'd gone.

*"Retirat! Thetri, retirat!"* Bictrius commanded.

Men were running this way from behind me. *Uh-oh.*

Following Gavin, I nearly tripped over a different Witch Hunter body as I came around a corner. Staring in surprise, I barely had time to note his weapons missing and two gashes on either side of his throat. Whoever had been shooting earlier also jumped this one?

*No time.* I must keep moving and leave it behind.

Anticipating that the river would force Gavin to turn South toward the empty marketplace, farther from the inn and stables, I chose another shortcut to try and catch him. I had not any better ideas for where to try to lose them, but I had to find my fugitive scholar regardless. It was clear we couldn't simply outdistance them on foot.

It must be a running battle, taking one at a time, if Gavin could last that long.

Behind me, the screaming villagers were trying to put out the spreading fires in the wake of our conflict. It was then that I finally heard a hint of Brom's voice. So, he was trying to mitigate the damage left behind instead of quickly defeating the source? I didn't understand why, but good for him I'd taken out the pyro-mage.

I didn't have time to think further. I also didn't know where a certain Dwarf and men were. Or weren't. It was more challenging than I expected trying to head off my death mage, who was running full tilt, gripping his spade. No fireballs followed us, at least.

*We have time.*

As though to dispute my thought, Gavin collapsed onto all fours. It didn't look like he'd tripped but that he'd simply met the end of his endurance.

"*No!*" I panted, finally running up to him. "Don't stop now! Get up!"

He couldn't speak for how his body ached for breath; his heart pounded a disturbing, irregular beat compared to mine. The death mage spared a short, annoyed scowl at me, shaking his head once. Dirt caked the fresh blood on his hands, and he still had the drying streak of dark crimson painted from his mouth down to his chest soaking his robes.

"Gavin," I hissed, staring hard without touching him. "Come on!"

"B-best run," he rasped back, shoving his spade toward me. "Take this. I can't…they'll…"

He coughed, and his body was racked with pain as he first vomited then spat an alarming volume of bloody mucous onto the soil. He was quaking, now; something acute was happening to his body. I considered, for an instant, giving him my one strong healing vial.

Then the stamping of boots and shouting men rose again. I counted eight men charging heedlessly through the dark with torches. They were coming. When I looked back, Gavin's glare was most vicious, the white of his eyes were gone, and he looked as corpse-like as the one he had created in instants.

"Take it," he growled, baring bloody teeth like a beast. "For your unborn's sake, *hide*."

I spent two breaths attempting to command one of my guardians to stay with him. They refused, diving closer against my scalp, and I didn't press as I grabbed the spade and ran with that final pinch of regret. Even if one had obeyed blindly, it would be a waste. Two venom bites against too many men.

I had no choice.

*"Bruxto! Agarlit e bruxto!"*

I crossed over a chillingly empty space to dive behind the cover of a wood stack when they charged him. I prepared a poisoned bolt and tried to aim for Gavin before they reached him.

*Too late.*

So many armored men piled on I couldn't see him. The shouts and cursing, the fury escalating as they beat him mercilessly while he lay curled on the ground. I could see why he'd wanted me to take the spade. If Gavin had not displayed unpredictable terrors, the Chief Warrant might have possessed a clear mind, his warriors deliberate in their methods of subduing their catch.

Perhaps that would have been worse than this, what my scholar tried to avoid.

The wild eyes and desperate orders converged on holding the tall, struggling death mage flat on the ground. Heavy men kneeled painfully as possible on the joints of his arms and legs. Gavin gritted blood-stained teeth as Bictrius loomed over him, red-faced.

"Confess!" their leader blared, brandishing that polished blade which caught the moonlight. "Confess your pact, filth, and Name the devil you serve!"

The Warrant brought his leg back, kicking Gavin's ribs with metal-capped boots; the apprentice groaned. I aimed my crossbow at Bictrius, but then he crouched low among his men, shouting behind cover and in my ally's face.

"Name him! *Now!* We shall send your damned soul to him to pay your due but know we shall send our Bishops after *him* next for what you've done!"

Despite his clear pain in trying to breathe, Gavin laughed wetly. "*Heh heh…* Doesn't matter. You'll s-see her in the end, all of you. You will."

"Her?" Bictrius demanded. "What temptress is this? Speak of the witch!"

Gavin refused, and torture followed where I could not get a clear shot of Bictrius. Then, rather than offer a name as if that would make it stop, my scholar started chanting in that same tongue which I'd heard while he slept. A sibilant, threatening sound emerged from his lips, such as he'd spat out after taking a bite of their comrade's heart, making his body dance before their eyes.

"*Ulshrigaass,*" Gavin intoned, "*frin eidolon ang'prei…*"

The rising fear was swift and unshakable. Bictrius raised his shining dagger high, gripped with both trembling hands.

*Now.*

I squeeze the trigger, and my crossbow bolt lodged in the Chief Warrant's armpit. He shouted in surprise and pain, falling over.

"*Non!*" shouted Jacob, lunging for him. "*Warranti!*"

"*Matjes, matjes!*" Bictrius croaked. His arm began to shake uncontrollably from the toxin. "*Puride!*"

Numbed fingers dropped the blade, and Jacob seized it, rushing to bury it in the center Gavin's chest before I could reload. I caught myself with my mouth sagging as the former monk's body convulsed, his spine arching, body quivering.

Then he went lax and still.

Pointless.

*"Atopa, guerrimos, atopa!"* Jacob shouted, apparently the new leader as he threw an order in my direction.

The men scrambled to their feet, wailing in rage.

*Shit.* I shoved the spade beneath a gap in the wood and ran, wondering why I had taken that shot and given my position away?

Because it was there, and I couldn't do nothing *that* time.

I made the tree line but, unfortunately for me, the surviving Witch Hunters had good sight of their leader's assassin as she fled the scene.

Unlike Gavin, I had a second wind.

Having reached the end of town, I turned around toward the inn rather than flee into the wilderness, keeping to the trees rather than the roads. Perhaps I could have picked them off one at a time farther out among the brush, but it would be a long and arduous game in an unknown territory, for which I was quickly realizing I lacked the endurance.

Against all reason, my belly clutched in on itself, on the verge of making me ill. It was not simple hunger but the ultimate loss of my scholar which drained me more than it should. Not flushed from a familiar fight surge, where surviving assured that I did not think of food for half a day; no, I was hungry and saddened before this was finished.

*For your unborn's sake, hide.*

I'd take that advice only after I'd failed, when stopping to eat wasn't an option and the need only a distraction.

*Fuuuck…*

I recalled four Witch Hunters would be unconscious back where Mathias and I had been discovered, kicking this whole night forward. Had they been left unguarded by their fellows entirely? My count as they chased Gavin through Troshin Bend said that they had. If that was where Mathias, Kurn, and Castis were, surely they weren't delayed so long by four sleeping men?

Well. There was also the fire. And the panic.

The relief to my eyes and no doubt many town residents, the fires were mostly out and smoldering. Most of the buildings had been left standing rather than risking a dawn where all this wood was still ablaze and growing larger by the moment, until no one could stay and breathe.

This priority made sense to any militia, and Brom had made his choice. He must have been quite confident of my escape, figuring he would find me later, as he promised. For the others? I had no idea. Who else but me would try to help Gavin? They had no solidarity with my goals.

A pity, for I couldn't succeed alone, as it turned out.

Suddenly, a streak of brilliant light shot into the brush from the road, a white-burning arrow jutting from a tree trunk three paces away. I was blind in an instant and illuminated amid the shadows.

"Alli!" shouted Jacob, as the dogged hunters loudly charged my way. "Ela alli!"

Fuck.

With my eyes closed, I ran deeper into the trees because I didn't know where else to go. If Jacob could make a shot like that from the road because I'd gotten too close, then let him do it again deep inside the forest.

My toe caught on a root twice as I hurried but I was prepared to catch myself and maintain my distance as the men fared worse in the dark. They didn't give up, though, and the memory of them pushing that substance into their mouths returned to me with odd clarity.

Was that from where they drew this endurance? Maybe it helped. They had been fighting and running non-stop for so long, while I was getting tired, my lungs burning from the spread smoke.

*You just killed their leader, Sirana.*

Indeed. How difficult it would be to escape the Red Sisters if someone assassinated Jaunda before our eyes? How much would she suffer at our hands before she died as well? The killer would have to kill us all to prevent it.

*Every one of us.*

I was ill. I needed help against Witch Hunters, or I would end up worse than Gavin. Would Brom shield me or not? He hadn't thus far. What would I have to offer as exchange if I must tempt him under duress? Whatever it was, I knew I wouldn't enjoying paying it.

A branch broke nearby, heavy feet hurling a body too close.

*Damnit.*

I chose a dark spot to hide, waited until the Manalari in front got closer. I took the shot with another poison bolt, and it grazed his arm. It would slow him down, a fever overtaking him eventually. I moved while he was shouting for the others. I didn't have many bolts left, and I still aimed for the inn.

Behind me and startling the piss out of me, a familiar voice bellowed.

"Found the witch bitches! Castis! Here!"

*Kurn, you mother fucking...!*

"Hahaha!" he laughed, charging into the brush, crunching branches and leaves beneath his boots. "Come, Witch Hunters! We've been searching for you!"

*"Ma'ab!"* one shouted.

He hadn't even seen me.

The number of short-range projectiles slung all at once from both directions seemed unreal. Sharp cracks split the air and bursts of light lit up the forest, forcing me to ground. There was more fire, and men's voices rose in volume on both sides, spilling all through the trees. Not only had the mercenaries I'd been traveling with appeared at last—not the Ma'ab alone but Rithal and Mathias as well —but several of the townsmen joined the fight.

The Manalari righteously answered the challenge, sounding as if they had caught a collective third wind, and the threat rolled closer with all the weight of a rockslide.

*Fuck me sideways.*

Heedless, I took off for the inn, ready to leave these Humans to fight each other, the lights and battering of sound making me regret I had ever gotten involved. And all for *nothing*, as I'd lost my scholar!

Ducking down but thrown off balance at a bad moment, my hood caught on a dead branch and was ripped down, exposing my snow-white hair in the dappled moonlight. Of course, someone would aim for it.

A bottle set alight smashed into a tree near me and spilled burning liquid all around. Some splashed onto my cloak, catching it on fire.

*"Brujix!"* someone shouted in guttural fury. *"Asasina!"*

I beat the fire out with dirt before I sprinted again, but a second Witch Hunter with the first had closed enough distance coming from another direction to hit me pointblank with his bow. The silent arrow struck my back, punching through my armor. I could feel it, but I couldn't tell how deep.

I cried out and fell, my back burning, muscles cramping as I tried unsuccessfully to get my feet under me again. The first who'd pitched the fire bottle launched himself and tackled me, tearing the arrow wound further and snapping it in half as we struggled. I wailed in agony, barely comprehending that he fisted a naked dagger.

*"Brujix chupindi demgalo!"*

He stabbed me twice as my overzealous guardians bit him multiple times on the neck. He missed his third thrust when he began convulsing, eyes staring and mouth beginning to froth. Desperately, I pushed him off me, barely able to roll so the arrow wasn't twisting in its hole. There was so much pain, I puked bile.

The archer ran up to witness this, his brother frothing at the mouth and thrashing on the ground, me vomiting and trying to crawl away, pure horror on his face to see what he'd shot. He hid behind a trunk, too far for my spiders to leap at him next, whether they had any venom left or not, and he kept his cover from my hand crossbow, which I shakily prepared.

The first Manalari died quickly from the spider bites, and the archer cried out.

"*Kirso!*"

Nocking another arrow, drawing it back, the man leaned out from behind his tree to aim at me while I aimed at him.

"*Irmvi! Ali!*"

The baritone voice sounded from high overhead, and the Witch Hunter looked up in clear confusion. "*Kirso?*"

A return arrow struck him in the eye. The Witch Hunter dropped his weapon, his weaving body soon collapsing to the side.

*What in the Pit...?*

"Sirana!" Rithal called. "Where are ye? D'ya need help? Say somethin'!"

One never shouted for help in the Deepearth. *Not when bleeding.*

I couldn't answer, could only stare, my eyes watering, blinking against irregular, flickering firelight. My eyes *must* be failing me.

The arrow was matte black, as were the fletches. This slice of shadow also seemed much longer than what was buried in my back. Within moments, the arrow began disintegrating, falling like ash before my eyes.

*No. What's happening?*

More bushes cracked and shook, and Kurn found me first. The Hellhound's sword and armor were bloodied; he looked flush and fuller of joy than I'd ever seen him before.

"Ahh, here you are, Red Sister," he cooed, smirking as he stepped closer.

It was telling that he kept a tree near for cover. Obligingly, I shifted my crossbow to him, and he grinned, sniffing deeply like he could smell the blood.

Looking between the two dead Witch Hunters, he said, "Impressive, but you came out worse for wear. *Heh heh.* Do you need help?"

I didn't blink. "Stay away."

He sneered. "Where is your filthy *maknuut?* You shouldn't have chased after him. Look at you now. You can't even stand."

My spiders were ready, but I knew their defense was a reaction over prevention when the danger got this close. I held still, leaning sideways against a tree, trying to draw calm breath though it became difficult. An involuntary tremor entered my hand keeping the crossbow up, and I was starting to feel faint as blood trickled out to pool beneath me.

There was a chance I could miss him. All he had to do was step behind the trunk, so I waited. The Ma'ab reached for something in his pouch, and I flinched.

*Thunderstone.*

I reached for my pouch as well, though it was a bluff as I had no web pellets left. We paused, sizing each other up. The fighting beyond the crest had died down, and Rithal's low voice rumbled as he spoke to someone.

Then, "Sirana?"

*Call him. Answer.*

"Come on out if ye can!"

*I can't, Rithal. I need help.*

My voice seemed so clear in my head, though I made not one peep. Kurn watched me with eager, dark eyes, his pale grin growing wider. He glanced at my weapon, made no move forward, but enjoyed my silence under threat.

*Help.*

Before I could unseize my vocal cords or finish drawing a painful breath to attempt a shout, a presence behind us made my spiders skitter with alarm. The distinct sound of a chain uncoiling, dropping next to me, chilled me. I froze up.

Simultaneously, the expression on Kurn's face shifted from smug to pure terror, and his heart launched into a panicked sprint.

*"L'hada yukan!"* the Ma'ab said in denial, tossing one broad hand like he would brush an apparition away.

The chain was still there, drawn back like someone with a strong arm intended to use it as a whip or a lash. This didn't happen before Kurn bolted toward Rithal and the others without another word or glance at me.

I sat trembling, my heart pushing blood out faster through my wounds, and my spiders twitched beneath my hair. The forest fell quiet around me.

When I had the courage to glance to my left, grimacing as my injury twinged sharply, my night eyes could see nothing.

"Who are you?" I whispered in Trade. "Were you at the canyon?"

There was no answer. The presence was gone.

Blinking out the last of my tears, I drew a weaker breath than I would have wished. "Rithal…"

Not loud enough. I tried again.

"R-Rithal!"

"Sirana?"

He heard me.

"Help!" I croaked.

It took a second for his feet to choose my direction, and in that moment, tears of a new, piercing fear threatened to spill. Would this shock force my womb to expel its passenger if I bled much longer? What if I passed out, and whatever they did to help me didn't take my baby in account?

*Fuck! Fuck, fuck, fuck…*

Rithal and Brom found me quickly, and I laid down my loaded crossbow. The sorcerer saw this and added, "Put your guardians away so I may evaluate you."

Sensing they were spent anyway, I slowly secured them in their pouch. Brom kneeled to observe my state; the look in his grey eyes was such that it was easy to imagine he had seen many wounds on a battlefield in the past. I looked away before we could meet eyes.

"J-just take the arrow out," I said. "Please, do it quickly. I have a potion to drink."

"You could save it," Brom suggested. "I can heal you at the inn."

"N-no!"

"Why?"

I sucked in a breath, grimacing at the pain. "G-Gavin."

"I'm sorry, Sirana. They killed him. We overheard them."

"Take the arrow out," I repeated stubbornly. "I must return to his body."

"Again, why?"

"Brom," Rithal interjected. "I'd rather claim his body, too, rather than let yer townfolk do somethin' foolish with it."

The younger face of the sorcerer tilted up curiously at the red-bearded Dwarf. "Such as?"

Rithal shifted his weight on strong, squat legs. "Weird stuff happens around Ma'ab death mages, all I'm sayin'. Thought you knew, havin' a daughter an' all."

"Hm. Well, she's not a death mage."

Brom didn't deny anything else and turned his attention to the arrow at last. He murmured a chant in an exotic language, and an intense point of heat arose around the shredded arrow wound. I felt only pressure as he drew on the shaft, heard a subtle sucking of flesh and liquid as he worked it slowly out. I should have been howling in agony, but it was painless.

"There," he said, showing me the metal tip covered in my own gore. "It's out."

I reached for my healing vial, triple-checking the color and stamp in the seal to make certain it was the correct one. I broke the wax cap and drained the bitter stuff in one swallow, determined to keep it down for the moments required to feel that blissful, soothing magic spread out from my middle.

It was the first time that I noticed, along with the tickling itchiness as the wounds in the skin closed, a peculiar buoyancy to my insides, in particular my gut as I imagined a stressed womb becoming welcoming again. Most importantly the bleeding stopped, and my head cleared for the time being.

This boost of strength wouldn't last, I knew. I needed to rest and eat to fully heal, but I had more time now. I wasted none of it returning to my feet, using the tree trunk for balance, and I took what seemed my fullest, most luxurious breath in the entire night.

"Thank you," I murmured.

"Wanna show us where he is?" Rithal suggested.

*Us.*

I glanced at Brom, who watched me expectantly and would clearly come along, nodding in resignation. Gavin's body was my excuse for getting the arrow out of my back here rather than at the inn. Of course I would see it through, baffled and concerned though I was.

"I do not know about 'weird stuff'," I said. "Precautions when approaching?"

Rithal shrugged and looked at the sorcerer. Of course.

"Unless he had time to prepare for his death," Brom said blandly, "it's just a corpse, Sirana."

*Unless.* I wouldn't think any death mage could anticipate dying on account that his roommate sneaked out and was caught in a spontaneous cock-suck by Witch Hunters. For the aftermath, I'd decided to leave his bloodied spade where it was and not draw attention to it, but his pack would be elsewhere in the town, wherever he'd thrown it. It had his grimoire inside it and his surgeon's tools, other things he kept well hidden.

Would I be able to find it before anyone else? I didn't see how. Any laborer could stumble on it and throw it in the river. As usual, I had no idea as to the cost if I asked Brom. Perhaps Castis would find out and try to claim it, instead, while I didn't truly know what I would do with it if I did find it.

I sighed with a strange, unfamiliar dismay as I began the trek, leading the Dwarf and the sorcerer back to the South end of town.

# CHAPTER 8

IT WAS THE DEEPEST OF NIGHT WHEN WE REACHED THE EMPTY marketplace, though the wind had picked up enough to sweep any lingering clouds from the sky and reveal the full blanket of stars. The earlier sister moon had set, but the much later, smaller one had begun her climb into view.

I noted Brom's confident stride the entire way here which revealed no hesitation in the dark. He didn't need a light source to walk without tripping any more than Rithal or I did. Given his extraction of the arrow in my back, this did not surprise me, and I considered the practical aspects of a Human leading a contingent of Davrin. No matter how long ago, it would have remained a useful skill to practice.

Gradually, however, my unspoken fears of him grew with every mark I spent here. These small details which suggested too much truth.

Both Gavin's and Bictrius's bodies were undisturbed since the Witch Hunters had chased after me. The Chief Warrant had crawled or been dragged farther away from the death mage before having collapsed on his front, arms up and blocking his face.

Gavin was on his back, limbs spread out as if they still held him to the ground. His face had been beaten like the rest of him but there hadn't been much time for skin to bruise or swell. His normal, dark eyes were open and appeared to be staring into the deepest space between the stars. His mouth was open as well. The handle of the polished dagger stuck out of the center of his chest; the rest of the blade buried out of sight.

"Hm," Brom said, studying the body. "He pushed for a swift execution."

Rithal was tense, I realized; his gloves creaked as he flexed hands into fists at the innkeeper's remark. I glanced at him; a gradual and silent expression of hatred had overtaken his face as he stared at the body of the Witch Hunter's leader.

"You may search the Chief Warrant, if you wish," Brom offered to the Dwarf.

Tempted, Rithal raised one skeptical eyebrow at him. "Searchin' doesn't mean keepin'."

"Look. You may find something useful for your mission. Or for Mathias to use pulling information from *Thetri* Jacob."

I squinted my eyes at them. "What about the second?"

As one, the sorcerer and Dwarf looked at me; Rithal wasn't smiling but Brom was without showing teeth. "Mathias captured him alive. The rest are dead."

"I had not thought you would be pleased with that outcome," I said.

"I am not. Whether the Ma'ab win their siege or not, Troshin Bend will be in decline as word spreads. It always does, be it by hare or by snail."

No one spoke for a moment, and I was about to make a remark about his pulling up the tent stakes again and starting over somewhere else, but the warning look in Brom's eyes made me think twice.

I looked at Gavin and finally moved toward him. Rithal took that as his cue to begin searching the Warrant's body. Brom chose to kneel beside me, showing little interest in the leader of the *Dyos Guerrimos* or the half-Ma'ab death mage. He was focused on me, though all I did was stare at a dead body, at first.

"This yours?" Rithal asked me, indicating the bolt from a hand crossbow lodged under the man's arm.

"Yes," I answered.

"Want it back?"

*Why not?* "Yes."

After he yanked the bolt out, Rithal cut a piece of Bictrius's jerkin in which to wrap it.

"You tried to stop him?" Brom asked as the Dwarf handed it to me.

"I *did* stop him," I replied tightly. "Jacob picked up the blade before I could shoot again."

The innkeeper watched me thoughtfully, grey eyes shifting to the dagger in Gavin's chest. "Why did you need to come back here?"

His tone soft but like he knew I didn't have a convincing reason. This only made it sink in how much pure knowledge of the Surface I had lost. Like for like, it had been for weeks. Gavin hadn't cared for power games or intrigue, but he was as curious to know about things as I was. More so.

*He didn't have a chance to tell me about the warp rot in his dreams.*

The sightless, open eyes bothered me, like both he and Brom waited for an answer I didn't want to give. I reached out and brushed his lids closed with the fingers of my bloody gloves. They were damp from clutching my wounds, so some light smears remained. Then I pushed against the bottom of his chin, closing his mouth as well. The sorcerer had an odd look on his face, but I ignored it.

I decided to be bold. "Can we bring Gavin back to the inn?"

"To a shed outside, maybe," Brom replied with suspicious amusement. "Depending how long you want to keep him there."

*How long? Isn't that a key-diamond question?*

"It's clear you're at a loss," the sorcerer murmured, cajoling. "Though it was *he* who said he had no purpose to go to Manalar without *you*. We should talk about what you are to do now, Sirana. You may take time to grieve if you need."

While he spoke, my eyes had been eyeing the handle of the dagger in Gavin's chest. When the sorcerer mentioned grieving, my eyes flicked briefly to him in dry denial, though it struck me how he did not speak like he believed I was a demon or mysterious creature of any kind.

"What are Elves to you, Brom?" I murmured. "To suggest we grieve for the dead?"

He half-smiled, sharp eyes sliding toward the listening Dwarf near finishing his search, saying nothing. I pursed my lips, returned my gaze to the dagger which had killed my scholar, and decided I wanted a closer look at what had made it flash so in moonlight. I reached out to grip the handle, putting my other palm flat on Gavin's cooling chest, and began wiggling it loose to work it out of his stilled heart.

*Damnit. Caught in the bone.*

While I concentrated on this, Brom gasped. Suddenly, his hand darted out to cover mine and apply pressure, keeping the guard of the weapon pressed to the small pool of blood soaking the grey robe.

"Wait," he whispered.

Rithal had spun around with a loot bag in his fist. We both saw the wary, distant look on the sorcerer's face.

"What is it?" I asked. "What do you see?"

Now, Brom was as reluctant to speak as I was.

"His ghost?" I tried.

The sorcerer blinked and looked at me, then chuckled. "Ah, no. I don't see ghosts. Just… wait to remove the dagger if you will."

My eyes narrowed. "Wait how long?"

"And why?" Rithal demanded gruffly. "What'll happen if she does?"

"I don't know, Rithal, but it is as you said. There is something odd about this Ma'ab death mage. I am leery how to handle his body in my town. Grant me some time to study and think about it."

He sounded the same as every magic user I knew.

"Can we take him to a shed at the inn," I pressed, "keep him out of sight?"

"Yes. That would be best."

I was shocked when the innkeeper-governor moved to lift Gavin's corpse like all discussion was finished and the time to act was now. Brom's mouth was tightly closed as he lifted what looked to be a heavy and unwieldy weight; Gavin's head craned back, his blood-caked throat exposed, his long arms and legs hanging limply.

"Do you mean tah carry 'im all the way yourself?" Rithal was incredulous.

"No, I would prefer if you get me a horse, master Dwarf," Brom replied through gritted teeth. "I can meet you on the way."

"Right. Ah. I'll go fer 'is mare at the stable."

Watching Rithal leave with his bag of scavenged possessions, I was not only curious what he'd found but smirked to know I would have been the faster sprinter. I said nothing because I wanted to stay with Brom and Gavin, anyway.

"Gavin had a pack with him when he ran," I said once we were alone. "I saw it, but he threw it somewhere before the fires started. Do you know if anyone found it?"

"Not to my knowledge," he grunted as we walked North along the road toward the torchlit, damaged town.

"Can you sense items imbued with magic?" I pressed. "I know he had a knucklebone that emitted blue light to use as a heatless lantern."

"Interesting," came another grunt. "I could probably help. What else do you want out of it?"

"I don't want Castis to find it first," I said. "Or for Kurn to destroy it because he was a *maknuut*."

"Heh. I see that."

I trailed along the sorcerer with my hood up until Rithal returned riding on his pony, leading Gavin's mare. Brom gratefully accepted his help to lay the body with spine bowed across her back to keep the dagger undisturbed. The brown mare remembered me well enough to be led without discourse, but she snorted her nostrils at the smell of blood on my gloves. I also noticed she was still limping from the hard journey here.

"She's accustomed to carrying dead bodies, I would say," Brom remarked with a smirk.

"Sarilis does use quite a lot o 'em," Rithal agreed.

I recalled Tamuril's face as she had described the old man "using up" the animals as sentries. I glanced at the mare quite docile around death. I'd never asked him but wondered if Gavin had brought her with him to the tower.

We took a skirting road, avoiding the center one. I imagined everyone who *could* be awake this night was widely so, with many eyes peeping out of those dark shutters. Fortunately, no one approached Brom to gather reassurance or gossip about who we carried.

I became aware the sorcerer had been searching for any taste of magic on his own, for he left me and Rithal with the body and walked into someone's chicken coop. He returned with Gavin's pack, knotted closed and with only a few white spots which might have been caused by startled hens. Wordless, Brom held it out to me, and I took it with a nod, trying not to think about what I would do next.

"Let us find you a shed with a table on which to lay him," said my host, glancing at Gavin's still, bloodied face. "Ideally, one that locks."

I would discover soon what Mathias had meant by "setting up a few things" when I had first climbed out the window to warn him about the Witch Hunters inside the inn. I must wonder if he had spied them coming from much farther off before they entered town?

*Was he informed, somehow? Or commanded?*

I could not see this much modification happening on pure impulse without the knowledge or approval from the innkeeper. If Mathias had been working alone, it would have taken most of the day that I had been watching the town and relaxing in our room.

The largest storage shed behind the inn was also the one farthest back, with its crates neatly stacked man-high on the outside. This cleared the wooden floor inside and blocked any light which may seep in during the day. It also provided another layer of sound absorption and made breaking in or out much more difficult.

A strong lock had once existed on a thick wooden door enhanced with an upper and lower band of metal, but that had been recently removed, and...

*Reinstalled on the inside.*

"Ah, Master Brom," Mathias greeted, glancing curiously at me as I stepped in as well, though Rithal had stayed outside with Gavin and the horses.

"Hello, Mathias," the sorcerer said, looking around the place with a nod of approval.

I took in as much as I could quickly. There was plenty of space and new metal anchors and hooks useful for rope and chain alike; a couple sawhorses, planks about a man's width, a low bench, a high table long enough for a body, and a short table bearing a lantern, cloths, and wash basin. There was also a large barrel of water, a bucket, and a middens trench had been dug to flush away filth.

I knew what I was looking at. Mathias had created an interrogation space, much like those the Sisterhood kept at the ready around the Great Cavern. A place to keep a prisoner or a new initiate secure and undisturbed for as much time as was needed to appropriately bend the will to compliance.

There were few tools visible besides the restraints and those intended for the comfort of the interrogator; no obvious blades or torture implements. The second-in-command Jacob lay unconscious in a hay pile in the corner. His boots and armor had been removed, his hands and feet bound with rope, and his mouth gagged. He was still clothed for now.

*Hm.*

Brom exhaled slowly, unperturbed and familiar with the set-up; he motioned to the high, long table. "May we use this for a time?"

"What for?" asked the skin hunter. He looked sweaty for the fighting and additional labor he'd been doing.

The sorcerer looked amused. "Jacob's latest victim needs a place to rest."

Mathias glanced at me and back to Brom. "You got his body already?"

A nod. "I would prefer it remains undisturbed and unseen by the townsfolk for the moment. I know I can trust you."

The man grinned, eyes shifting with a malicious amusement toward his prisoner, his nod of acceptance easy and without reluctance. Mathias moved the high table from its place closer to the middle of the room to align it against the wall farthest from Jacob and closest to the door. Brom assisted in getting it into place.

"Put him here," Mathias motioned. "I won't touch him."

I could see the ploys playing behind those devious, brown eyes, however. No touching, but he would use the body against his prisoner's state of mind. I found the vision appropriate repayment enough not to protest; I also felt the impulse and curiosity to watch and learn.

The skin hunter and I allowed Brom and Rithal to move Gavin again, sliding him from his mare and carrying him inside. They hefted the long, gaunt man up and lay him flat along the table, Bictrius's dagger in place. As I expected, Brom made eye contact with Mathias and immediately indicated this weapon.

"Do not remove this," he ordered. "I sense a ritual aura clinging to it, but I'm not sure whose ritual it is. Not yet. I can't speak for what might happen if you disturb it."

Mathias nodded smartly. "Gotcha. Looks fine how it is, Master Brom."

"Good." Brom looked at Rithal. "If you would tend to the horses again then do as you will, master Dwarf."

The other arched one red eyebrow. "Not interested in what I found?"

"I have guesses. We can go over it later. For now, I must speak with your Elven travelling companion alone."

"Aye," Rithal said, slow and unsurprised as he hefted the loot bag on one shoulder.

The Dwarf also excused himself quickly from the interrogation room while I was reluctant to leave it. I believed I would rather have stayed with Mathias and Gavin's corpse than be alone with the sorcerer again.

"Go on," Mathias assured me, smiling with another glance at the body. "He'll be fine for a day or two, especially out of the sun."

I swallowed, forced a small smile in return, and followed Brom to the inn carrying Gavin's pack. My stomach growled audibly, and Brom huffed a laugh.

"I'm hungry, too," he said. "After all this chasing things around in the dark."

I chose not to reply, though he was right about that. There had been a lot of things in the dark tonight that even I couldn't see.

Upon entering the side door, which put us on the opposite side of the kitchen and his quarters, we were found by his daughter who'd been waiting.

"*Fahdi!*" Amelda whispered, stepping up to us and blocking the door to the meeting room.

He exhaled softly as he acknowledged the petite woman. Black, Ma'ab eyes flicked from him to me and back; it was clear she wasn't pleased with my presence. She spoke rapidly in Ma'ab.

"Then *handle* it, daughter," he said in Trade, his voice set like stone. Her brows lifted in shock at his tone. "They have their direction and can wait until daylight. This meeting will not wait any longer."

Amelda tossed another stabbing glance my way. Despite my tension at what he meant and for how much her mannerisms screamed *Noble* to me, I gave the small woman my best bored expression from my time at the Palace Court. Despite Rausery's prediction my blue eyes would calm Surfacers, now I wished I possessed the common red eyes if it would perturb the Ma'ab to meet them.

Brom's daughter lifted her chin defiantly and spoke with a heavy accent. "Where is the *maknuut* who follows her?"

*Too innocent,* I thought. Kurn blabbed about the meeting that morning.

"He was executed by the *Dyos Guerrimos*," said her sire.

She dared to look pleased. "Shall I collect his belongings from the room and bring them to you? We may inspect them."

Brom looked tired. "It can wait, Amelda."

*Hm.* I could believe he had forgotten I carried Gavin's things on my back. If she went into the room anyway, at most she'd find *my* pack, which had only mundane items I could in theory replace. I was convinced I did not want her or Castis anywhere near Gavin's book or tools.

Amelda thought what to say next, clearly wishing to delay him stepping past her. "Let me assist, *Fahdi*. I will keep watch as you question her."

I waited without expression for the sorcerer's response.

He frowned with disapproval. "Absolutely not."

"I am troubled by change I see in your pattern when she is near," Amelda insisted.

"Something I shall handle. This is from long before you were born."

"And I honor your legacy!" she said. "Enough to leave Ennikar. How can I learn from you if—"

"I shall handle this," he repeated slowly and with warning.

She softened both her voice and her eyebrows. "You are troubled by this, *Fahdi*, I know you do not see, but I do. You need an anchor to explore this deep in your past." He hesitated long enough to embolden her; she sent another sharp look my way. "You *do* something to him, dark one. Stop it now."

"I do nothing," I said, knowing she would choose not to believe it. "The truth is I would rather spend the night outside than with you or him."

"Then, go."

"No!" Brom said. "Too many threats if she is seen."

I glanced pointedly at the blood drying around my healed stab wounds. "You waited too long if that was any concern, Brom."

"He was outside when the fires started," Amelda rebuked. "No mere traveler is priority on a regular day, less when the town is burning!"

Brom opted not to argue that point, but I believed it was because he would not argue at all. I could see how Amelda's offer of being an "anchor" wouldn't help his focus or sense of balance.

*She doesn't want me alone with him.*

She and I agreed on this, but it was a pity she was making her jealousy as obvious as Wilsira did with Kerse. I could use a deft distractor but wasn't up for a woman scantly skilled in it when her opening ploy devolved into a bickering back-and-forth. She must have come of age as entitled as Kurn and Castis, and Brom had less to do with this than I guessed at first.

Amelda wasn't here solely for him. She was here for someone else.

"A question, if I may," I began, and her eyes narrowed. "Why would the sound of a chain frighten a Hellhound?"

Brom looked at me with curiosity and confusion, while Amelda's eyes widened.

"It wouldn't," he said. "Why this question, Sirana?"

I shrugged. "Where *are* Kurn and Castis?"

"Collecting all the bodies and possessions into one place."

"No oversight?"

Brom shrugged. "I care not. They are unable to raise the dead and may have what they want if it's useful. It's their mission against Manalar."

The sorcerer had cared about finding and following me, and then about hiding Gavin quickly where he could "trust" Mathias to watch him and keep Jacob contained.

"Did you *see* a chain?" Amelda asked me with suspicion.

"No," I said. "I heard it behind me in the woods. Kurn saw it, but whoever wielded it vanished."

Sire and daughter were each trying to decide how much to believe me; I was sure both accepted it as an obvious distraction.

"I shall... investigate this, *Fahdi*," Amelda offered.

"Please, do," he said, nodding with approval. "I would value your insight. We shall speak again by sunrise. Come to my quarters if I'm not out before then."

This appeased his daughter as she displayed a brief, graceful bow with arms out, flicked one glance at me as if to say, *Believe you are clever, do you?*

I supposed I was tired, too, and becoming light-headed from hunger. Easier to simply offer truth and let it tempt as it would.

At last, Amelda finally left down the hall toward the main tavern room, and Brom unlocked and opened the door to the meeting room to cut across without us being seen.

"Wait by my door," he murmured. "I'll get us food."

I could not think of another path which would serve me better than doing as he suggested.

*Indeed, so clever, am I.*

The sorcerer had removed his gloves in the kitchen to tuck in his belt before handling the tray of food. I only spotted the firebird ring on his finger as he returned and ushered me inside and closed the door. The dream from my first rest here darted behind my eyes when I spotted his shelf of treasures from which he'd retrieved that ring.

*A scorpion and the hooded snake fighting. That bird in the canyon of colors at night, lighting the way and leading me to the prisoner with golden eyes, in the darkest reaches of that place.*

His desperate cries to be let out before "she" knew I'd been there. I'd refused, not possessing the will. I'd muttered some excuse.

Hearing Brom set down the tray harder than necessary, I flinched and tossed the dream aside for the present. He clutched the side of his head like something stabbed him from the inside. I couldn't see his face when his brown hair turned to white, but his left, round ear and a slice of his face was visible as I watched the skin turn much darker brown than it had been before all the towns-folk.

Dropping an illusion, I decided having seen it twice. He was not simply choosing a new face. He'd said it should be something authentic in case one's concentration slips.

Such as now.

"Has Amelda seen this face?" I asked, sticking to Trade for now.

"No," he replied, turning around to face me with his back straightening. "Though some of her superiors have."

*Superiors.* So, he was aware he was being spied upon as well. Not good for me.

"In Ennikar?" I guessed.

The sorcerer smiled dryly. "Yes. Though you need not pretend you know where that is."

"It is North," I said with a shrug.

Brom guffawed a humorous laugh like he welcomed it. "Ah. True enough. And the Desert is as far South from there as one can go from Ennikar."

While before, Rithal had told me it was as far from Sarilis's Tower as one could reach and "still be on land." I reconciled the two in my mind with one of Shyntre's "bird view" maps. If I began in the upper left quadrant of a much bigger map, the Desert would be in the lower right quadrant.

"Such concentration," Brom remarked of my face as he poured wine for himself and water for me. "Do you seek the Desert?"

*Not unless it had to do with half-bloods of Davrin origin.*

I grimaced as nausea arose from my empty middle. "No."

He blinked in surprise. "No? What do you seek to reveal your existence so blatantly, when your people have been hidden so long?"

*Not that long,* I wanted to say. Sarilis recognized us. So did Rithal from hearth tales. *So do you, ancient one.*

If it wasn't that long, however, why did we no longer remember the Sun? Why could we not tolerate it anymore?

I said nothing, and Brom took a large drink and plucked a few bites of cheese to eat from the tray while standing up. I didn't think he was hungry but did this as the "host," to convince me it wasn't contaminated. There were too many ways around this attempt at transparency, so I approached only to eat the pieces of cheese directly beneath the ones he'd taken.

"Eat all of it," he said, sounding tired. "It's just food. I'd rather you were of strong mind and body, Sirana. My word on this."

*My... word?*

I gave him an odd look, and he sighed deeply.

"My promise? Oath?"

"Oh." I took another bite of food.

"Hm." He eyed me. "At least the idea still exists across our language."

"What idea?" I asked to see if frustration or something else was the greater response; I saw melancholy.

"Any kind of oath being true on the weight of one's word alone."

I chuckled, shaking my head once. "Too easy to exploit, and circumstances will always change to make a single, unmoving 'word' impossible to cling to." I pointed to the tray. "A promise for a moment, that I can accept. A word where you claim to *always* want me of strong mind and body? It *will* change, sorcerer."

Sooner rather than later.

"Indeed," he said in agreement and regret. "So I learned with a long-lived race. It's a quality of Humans, not Elves, unless you make it magically binding."

I noted the side-slap in his tone and frowned, insulted despite the cutting truth. "This is not a quality of most Humans, either. As impulsive, greedy, punishing, and conniving as any I've known."

Brom's mouth twisted, deepening the age lines. "Fair. All are young and foolish with little awareness of how far-reaching their actions are, either honorable or dishonorable. Few live to see it."

While this man sounded somewhere in between Human and Elf. Why was he like this? *How* could he be, claiming a legacy both in the Desert with Davrin and Ennikar with Ma'ab. Whose face is this in truth?

Brom let me finish eating while he sipped his wine, taking a few bites as if to fortify his body as well, for where he wanted to take our conversation next. I didn't know enough to choose the direction unless I wanted to return to that dream which had seemed to slap him in the face before.

I could be patient. I had nowhere else to run or fight for the moment, and I was tired after the Witch Hunters' attacks. I still did not understand why they pushed so hard and fast. They could have walked away from Mathias and me; they could have let Gavin run; they could have waited for their sleeping men to awaken and act with deliberation to find the one who'd done it rather than spread out like they intended to take the whole town.

One would think they had abandoned any attempt to convince the sorcerer whom they claimed to *need* to fight the warp rot. Now, they were all dead except the second, Jacob, and our skin hunter had his "challenge" before we left for Manalar and the incoming siege. Where did that leave Rithal, or me? Without Gavin, did I want to head North or South? After Gaelan, or after Jael?

It depended on Brom at this point, whether I liked it or not.

And I didn't.

*"Who were we fighting so long ago, General?"* I asked in Davrin, sounding oddly like my Mother when she was in a meeting.

Brom blinked, returning from thought deeper than mine. Slate-grey eyes narrowed. *"The Naulor. They were also the driving force for others."*

I shook my head, not recognizing the name, and the ancient man grimaced, baring teeth before tilting his head back in a raucous, bitter laugh that hurt my ears. Brom straightened in his chair and leaned forward, glaring at me.

*"You don't remember?!"*

His voice boomed in the closed quarters, and in pure reaction I stood to gain space, reaching for my spider pouch.

He put up his hand. *"No, wait. I…apologize. You are kept ignorant, that is clear."*

Brom drew in a slower breath, looking down at the floor, holding his head like it would split apart. The sense that he may lose his calm at any moment kept me on the balls of my feet. My spiders may not have a venom-full bite yet, but I had powder, poison, dagger… What would kill him quickest? *Could* he be killed?

The sorcerer's voice rumbled in his exotic accent as he stared at the wooden boards between his boots. *"A queen who took power as*

*Ishuna did wouldn't want her story retold through generations. Nor does the Abyss care about heritage unless it does greater harm to many at once…"*

I could not but hold my mind's skeptical shield in place. I was curious what he knew, but why *wouldn't* he want to slant it as harshly against my Valsharess as possible? Yes, She terrified me, and my Sisters and I were on impossible missions on account of Her. But Brom grew as frightening the more I learned of him.

For the simple fact that he shouldn't exist.

*"How do you still live?"* I asked. *"Why should I listen to you in any regard? How can I but think you are simply mad and claiming a mind-fever as your memory?"*

Brom lifted his head, his hands together and fingers intertwined, grey eyes distant but thoughtful. The governor of Troshin Bend stood up, slow and careful, and made his way to his treasure shelves, showing me his back without fear.

*"I live,"* he said, *"because of a promise."*

I watched him place his broad hands on a small, brown chest, unlocking the mechanism without a key though whispers tumbled from his lips. He lifted the lid and stared inside it for many moments. He whispered again, and the small hairs at my nape stood up as a different sound slithered out in reply.

First, a tremor went through me as the sorcerer carefully lifted a black dagger from the plain chest with both hands. He let it lay flat in his palms, a solid black sheath and a glossy black handle etched with clear, red runes. I worked not to wet myself as recognition sliced through my chest.

*He lifted his fisted hand, grains of red and yellow sediment flowing from the point of a dagger blade. Black, with scarlet runes etched along both sides glowing hungrily. I drew breath to scream as it flashed, biting deep into my gut. I doubled over, my mouth wide open, my voice silent. The blade ate me from the inside out, dissolving my life, my strength, like a spider's venom liquified the guts of its prey.*

"Sirana," murmured the sorcerer. *"You know this blade, as you know my sigil ring. But you do not know me, or the Naulor, or the name of your own Queen. Why?"*

I shook my head in denial. *"Wh-where did this come from?"*

*"A joining gift to my qu'eesan,"* he replied in a voice of distant passion. *"One I took back after her death. A relic befitting a Queen-Matron, and a way for me to always remember. No matter how many lives I live."*

I dreaded to take my eyes from the blade even though it was sheathed, but I must see the sorcerer's face. I met his gaze at last, seeking a pinch of a lie. There was none he made apparent.

*"A gift to your qu'eesan,"* I repeated warily, *"befitting a...?"*

The man with dark skin and white hair smiled, gradual but inexorable. He didn't blink. *"One and the same, Sirana. For a time, the Davrin Queendom and the Zauyrian Kings were united through me, Crisri-phon, Second Son of the Third Realm, and my unbreakable oath to serve the new Valsharess Innathi. Her children were mine. A Davrin-Zauyrian blood bond to strengthen our ties beyond treaties and trade."*

I stared at him, witnessing the memory of belonging and purpose on his face before it shifted to lost grief and wrath on his face. I couldn't feel my fingertips; I couldn't move as a rush of realizations kept me rigid.

Elves and Humans could breed? How many did he say his "wife" bore? *Twelve?* Not any common offspring, but that of a Queen. I could think of no end of Houses who would rebel at this.

*"The Naulor didn't accept this union despite our blessings,"* the former General hissed, lifting the black dagger higher in both palms, fingers flat. *"And Ishuna pretended she did."*

I swallowed, my heart throbbing in my ears, his acrid accusation returning from when he'd held me by the neck my first time in this room.

*The Abyssal whore murdered my wife and all our children and cost us a terrible war.*

*"Who are the Naulor?"* I asked.

The man narrowed his eyes in hatred, again wanting to shout at me for this basic lack. Firmly, I tested this older name, which seemed to suite a Desert General better than Brom Troshin.

"Cris-ri-phon. *Who are the Naulor?*"

The sorcerer responded this time. He blinked, drew a deeper breath. *"The pale-skinned Elves from the West."*

This chasm was bottomless.

The man tilted his head. *"Ah. You know of them, if not by name."*

I struggled with my food-laden stomach. I knew one name: *Tamuril.* The timid Druid had never identified her people to me. No surprise, in truth, unless she was a complete fool.

I also knew there was at least one Naulor in Augran. The Druid had given this away, while I had suggested that Jael might be headed to Manalar. Tamuril had wanted to convince me to go with her. I attempted to, taking those first steps before the geas made me collapse.

Perhaps there had been something to that warning. What if Tamuril or her sister remembered this Desert war with my kind? What had I done to Jael's chances of survival if they wished to revive it?

This next thought I could only speak in the trade language. "Are the Naulor sided with Manalar and Augran? Is this why you are sided with the Ma'ab?"

Cris-ri-phon considered but shook his head. "If they are, I've seen no sign. Why, have you?"

*Smooth, Sirana.*

I jerked my chin, repeating, "Why do you stand with the Ma'ab if not in opposing Pale Elves as you did before?"

A muscle jumped in his jaw. "That is too a long story."

The Zauyrian drew our eyes down to the relic in his palms, his fingers beginning to curl around it. "Look at this. *Please.*"

I tensed, waiting for him to draw it. He only continued.

"It began *here*. Tell me how you know this blade. Was it spoken of by your Queen?"

No, it wasn't. Not one glimmer.

The dagger was from long before my Queen had ordered me to watch for signs of Her guidance in my Reverie. That terrifying relic was from my first spans after my trials, when I'd killed Kain and raped my Consort in the attempt to cleanse myself of the Tragar's filth and the Priestess's magic at once.

I'd nearly caught from him then, but it was only a delay.

"*No,*" I whispered in Davrin. "*A fearful Reverie, but not from my Valsharess as far as I know.*"

"*Who warned you?*" he demanded.

"*I do not know.*"

But I suspected. *Auslan.*

Powerful as a Priestess, I'd decided, having foretelling dreams, unknown and unacknowledged. Traded as a toy and a stud among females up until he healed me, and I was forced to leave the underground. He had been in solitary in the Cloister under my Elders' protection months ago. Was he alive? What about his "brother," Shyntre? Was my wizard well? He should be *alive*, at least, as some favorite of the Valsharess.

And was my Valsharess the same Ishuna from this tale?

The ancient sorcerer-General stood tensely, proffering the dagger which I refused to touch. Cris-ri-phon was subtly quivering as I was, though he had not tried to peel his way into my thoughts, as the saphgar pendant beneath my bloody armor was an inert lump. Then, when I did nothing, the Zauyrian exhaled abruptly and took a step away from me, setting the weapon down on the table next to the empty tray. He took hold of the back of his chair as if to stay upright.

"*There is someone who remembers the old ways,*" he said in my tongue. "*Trying to speak out from the Void through you.*"

I didn't see how that could be. Auslan was two and a half centuries old and couldn't even read Phaelous's scrolls. I'd also been lying with Gaelan in her barracks room when I had that dream of the black dagger.

*"That is why you are here,"* Cris-ri-phon continued, *"you were drawn here."*

Perhaps, though Troshin Bend was also a reasonable stopping point in a long travel route. Yet, as I fidgeted, dreams I'd been having on the Surface filtered back. Me wearing that unfamiliar "captain" uniform on a dusty street, watching a tanned Elf like this sorcerer riding a horse with no tackle. The merchant Toushek talking to me, offering food or treasure, and warning me about a scorpion; how the sting could come upon anyone, anywhere. At any time.

*Only for the creature to show up in Reverie my first night here.*

That seemed like the sign of a Valsharess who remembered the Desert.

"What about the canyon of colors?" I asked, my arms crossed, again switching to Trade to stay more easily in the present.

"That is Koorul," the Zauyrian answered, blinking eyes which somehow seemed a lighter shade of grey, now. "Where I met my future wife."

"Valsharess Innathi?"

"She wasn't a Queen yet." Cris-ri-phon's gaze wavered like he was dizzy. "I was only a young man."

*Try again.* "And the Davrin prisoner with gold eyes?"

The sorcerer's eyes darkened like the storm from two days ago. He shook his head. "No. That wasn't in Koorul."

Not what I meant, but he confirmed what I was talking about.

"Who was he?"

Cris-ri-phon stared at me. "I do not know."

*Yes, you do.*

We were both lying.

"I was drawn to the warp rot, Cris-ri-phon, not your past," I said, which was not untrue. "I find it curious you refuse to address it when I know powerful enough mages can cleanse it."

A gradual eyebrow lifted up as he looked at me. "I'd not address it with Witch Hunters."

"Is it true they would have charged you with 'witchcraft'?"

"For certain." Cris-ri-phon shook his head. "They would not have been able to hold me, but I *had* been trying to avoid killing them all, for their own sakes and that of this town."

I bit my lip on a smart reply. He caught it and smirked briefly, but then shook his head in disappointment. "So suddenly did the tone at the sacred mount change. It didn't used to be the breeding ground for men like that."

*The tone?*

"Sacred mount?" I asked instead.

"The pool atop Mount Sonai," he said. "Where Manalar built its Temple."

*Oh, yes, of course.* Now, I wanted a third opinion on the plan, given Gavin's reaction at the tower. "Will Sarilis's vial make it better or worse if either me or Castis were to toss it into this Temple heart?"

More of the Brom persona returned in his dry smile though his skin remained dark. "Neither of you will get the chance to find out, Sirana."

*Uh-oh.*

I remained calm. "Oh? You've decided, hm?"

"The moment Gavin mentioned it at the table."

Had that only been this morning? It seemed longer, and now he was dead.

"A better use for such a thing," the sorcerer continued, motioning toward my belt, "would be against the warp rot to the North."

My brow lifted. "Are you suggesting we do something about it, now?"

Cris-ri-phon shrugged with a nonchalance that seemed odd and dissuaded me from blurting the existence of another of my Sisters, though she haunted my thoughts.

What if Gaelan needed my help, and I was stuck here? I could steal Gavin's mare, but she'd been limping when she carried her master's body to the shed. They would *all* chase me, these men. There was no sure way to escape.

My eyes slid to where the dagger lay on the table. Had it turned some? The hilt aimed toward me; that was different unless I simply missed a natural spin when he set it down. Could I truly leave this inn with no further answers, knowing this dagger and this history was here?

"Castis will be difficult to convince to throw away his vial," Cris-ri-phon said after a long pause, and my eyes snapped forward. "But I'd be curious if he might budge with Gavin gone."

My face held a full scowl before I realized it. "It wasn't Gavin breathing near me which made them talk to me as they have."

Cris-ri-phon pursed his lips in thought. "I'd not be surprised if it made it worse. You were travelling with him, and any of Ma'ab blood who are not pledged to the Ascended receive only hostility and worse from the noble class."

"Castis should return to Ennikar where he won't meet any, then," I grumbled. "Gavin was far more instructive and interesting to speak with such long days on horseback."

"Ah," he replied, as if that answered a question for him.

I glanced again at the runes etched on the hilt of the black dagger, which was pointed toward me. "Mm… what are you worried for if I remove the Witch Hunter dagger from Gavin's body? Will he rise and lurch about trying to bite us?"

The former General didn't respond at first. "I have not had a chance to study it. We came here to talk, instead."

"You must have a guess. You have seen much in your time, haven't you, Zauyrian sorcerer?"

He did not deny this, though stone grey eyes shifted to one side. "At best, nothing happens, and a pathway I sensed when you pulled on it merely closes. At worst, something *else* claims the body, and we have no way of knowing what until it is looking out at us through his eyes."

A chill passed up my spine from the way he said it. "I see."

In the heavy silence following, we both felt the constant tension. Standing here felt surreal. I was grounded while talking about Gavin, the Ma'ab, and the Witch Hunters; I was far less so when speaking in my own language about dreams, portents, and faraway places with hints of an impossible union between Davrin and Za-uyrian.

"We have a few hours until sunrise," Cris-ri-phon said, motioning toward the relic. "If I lock this away, and you place your guardians where you wish, will you take your rest in here with me? So nothing else happens to you."

*And so you don't leave,* I finished in my mind.

Regardless, it was tempting. I was tired, and we didn't have much time before spying daughters and townsfolk would be knocking on the door asking about last night. Before I must decide what to do next. I looked around the office space, seeing only the bed itself as a place to recline off the floor itself.

I accepted, and Cris-ri-phon reached for the relic, returning it to its chest with a few parting whispers that caused bumps to rise beneath my shirt. Once it was safely away, I spoke.

"If I may borrow a blanket, I will take the floor beneath your desk."

"What?" Caught by surprise, he laughed. "No, you take the bed. You have been on horseback sleeping on the ground for weeks."

"I'll not rest in Reverie lying next to you."

Cris-ri-phon shrugged. "Then I shall take the floor."

I rolled my eyes. "Humans need more rest and are heavier. You'll be far sorer than me."

His smile was oddly relaxed. "I am lucky to sleep as long as an Elf these days."

Good to know.

"You're heavier," I insisted, waving at the quality padding. "You'll be covered in bruises, soft as you've been, governor."

*"Heh!* Hm." He wanted to argue further but yawned first. "Very well, fighter. Take the desk, if you insist. I'll get you *three* blankets and a pillow."

His stare dared me to refuse.

"That will do," I agreed.

"And you'll not sleep in your armor," he added, having gained ground. "Remove it. I will clean and mend it."

"No," I refused.

"With magic," he clarified. "Quick and clean. One of the simplest spells."

I scowled at the old mage, silent as the need to rest dragged at me. If I waited any longer, I'd be hungry again and would not be able to sleep until I begged for food. *Damn it.*

"Fine," I said, finally removing my dappled cloak which was bloodier than I realized.

The damage on each piece I took off wasn't any better. The three holes in my torso piece showed the leather had helped lessen the depth of my wounds, but it certainly needed repairing before it would be half as effective as it had been.

Now focused on bedding down, I saw how everything on us was either filthy with mud or blood or smeared with soot. I hadn't realized how much ash had been floating around but the scent was clinging, and the evidence was clear Brom had been fighting the fires and carrying at least one dead body.

I glanced at the Zauyrian's skin as he finally removed his shirt to show me what he intended to do for my armor. *Not one scratch.*

"See?" he said, distracting me after a magical word or two caused black and brown-red stains to dissolve as motes and small tears to mend themselves.

*Hmm. Impressive enough.*

His tongue-tangling word for this spell, I did not know, but I was sure I'd seen it before in Sivaraus. I decided to strip down to get it all cleaned and mended at once, removing my boots while sitting on the floor next to my belt, affording me the chance to slip my pendant off with my shirt and tuck it in a pouch unseen.

When I stood up to loosen the ties at my hips and draw my leathers down my legs, Cris-ri-phon looked me over as I had him. My skin was also without flaw after my healing potion, but I wouldn't know if he had taken similar, had cast a spell, or had simply never been scratched in the first place.

My mouth twisted on a mental shrug as I thought, what did it matter? It wasn't as if I planned to risk stabbing him in his sleep.

"Thank you," I said when my clothes and armor were clean and mended.

"My pleasure."

I took time to sort and fold things on the floor, my hands obscured by his desk where I planned to make my bed. I made sure all was well with my tools and protections, with my spiders riding plainly on my bare shoulders. He watched me for a time from a good distance away, saying nothing.

The prickly feeling reminded me of Kurn at the waterfall, and I looked over my shoulder. "What? Too distracting? Should I don a shirt?"

The Zauyrian smiled, shook his head once and replied in Davrin. *"Not necessary, soldier, I can control myself. I'm admiring. It's been a long time."*

He wore soot-smeared trousers still, having neither removed nor cleaned them. I was not certain what this was supposed to suggest, and I considered dressing for sleep to deny his lingering gaze. I'd done this as a vulnerable Noble around Jilrina and had felt the urge in front of Jaunda in my quarters at the Palace before I knew her.

But I was a Red Sister now and, like in the canyon without any hiding place to seek and defend, it didn't matter whether I was wearing a shirt or not. A single layer of cloth no longer helped my mental state when someone was watching and would not prevent conflict by itself.

*Either sleep naked or in your armor, Sirana.*

The latter had only ever slowed a Sister down in the Cloister anyway, and it wasn't comfortable. My defiance fortified by my three companions, I slipped nude beneath two blankets while lying on a third beneath the large, Human-sized desk.

"Rest well, sorcerer," I said.

He hummed appreciatively. "Rest well, Sirana."

And vanished into his bed's alcove before snuffing out the light.

# CHAPTER 9

HIS BONES HURT, AND HIS BLOOD RAN AS IF IT SHOULD SCALD his skin, to leave a sunburned rash dry and permanent. He saw faces long-dead in his sleep, but they were gone when he was awake. He could tell with a chilling gaze which women would die birthing their children, and he could see with a different set of eyes on a different day which wives were ready to try with their husbands.

He genuinely did not know whether to try to bed them and give them strength or wait until their blood flowed out and ran still, until their breath stopped. To see what happened next.

His mother had died as he had been born, so he'd been told.

*I wish I remembered what happened to her.*

"Leur! Leur, come see your brother immediately! He has been ill again."

His tending *hamashir* felt tired and useless. These fevers had been rising and falling for five years, but as he slowly became a man, they were changing as well. Cris wanted her either to leave him alone so he could release the torturous ache in his cock in privacy or throw herself down for him and not speak as he buried it in her, again and again.

He refused to speak as he sweated out all his water, as these disturbing thoughts passed behind his eyes. The *hamashir* tried to make him drink, to replace what he lost, while ignoring the stark shape of his hours-old rod beneath his sheets and his eyes staring at her breasts covered by simple, yellow linen.

"Cris, I'm here. I am sorry I've been away. Be at peace."

His vision blurred then cleared again as the youth looked toward the doorway. *Help me…*

His elder brother always came to him, never refused if he could be found in the Third Realm. This time, Leur-en-phon, the first-born son of Begir-al-phon, led a woman into his room, holding the dark blue curtain aside for her.

"Who—?" he croaked.

She was much shorter than Leur, small-boned like most women of the Zauyrian Realms, and wore a hooded, grey robe which covered her head to foot. Gloves covered her hands, dusted with the grit of riding in a saddle over a great distance. They came closer, and as Cris trembled with a new wave of icy-hot pain, he saw her calm aura floating about her, appearing like an oasis that may cool his blood.

*Or is she a mirage?*

"Cris, this is Houda," Leur began.

The elder brother stopped when the younger reached out for her arm, reaching underneath the loose sleeve to touch her skin, and pull her closer to the bed. The fire inside *did* lessen in that simple contact, and Cris-ri-phon breathed out with care, quivering, staring up at her to understand what he saw.

Her face was not old; this was a younger woman but homely compared to many wives of Zauyr, with rough, ashen-brown skin and lank, black hair. There were scars on her face and neck, leading down beneath her robe. The marks were clean and straight, darkened with ash to display distinct circular or angular patterns too deliberate to be from accident or abrupt violence. Her eyes were a smooth, silvery grey, her expression curious and calm.

She did not pull away from him as so many had begun to do when he touched them.

"Houda?" he repeated, knowing he sounded delirious.

"Father summoned her from one of the deep tribes to the North," Leur said. "She may possess insights we need for your, um, talents."

*Talents.*

Or punishments. Clearly, this was a curse. Even Begir-al-phon, a Sorcerer-King over a century old, wasn't sure what to do about his youngest son whose life had killed his youngest queen.

Houda offered a small smile, tugging off one glove to reveal a hand aged beyond her face, further scarred by blade and charcoal. Her hand took his, and he gripped her firmly.

"You cling to the cliff, *shazody*," she murmured, quiet enough only Cris and his brother could hear her.

The ill boy's eyes widened. *She knows.*

Somehow, she knew how it felt.

"What cliff?" Leur asked.

Houda turned her strange eyes to the Third Realm's heir. "That border between the sun and the mists, *Kiroshan*. He sees in a haze bright yet muted, hazy like an otherworld, such that it is difficult to find his direction."

His brother accepted without knowing. "What does this mean for us, *yuradi?*"

"It means he will struggle, and you will watch, but this is not something to fear."

*Yuradi.* Cris received a fitting mental image of this woman as a walker, an apparition spotted by many in the night, traveling the entire Desert without becoming lost.

"C-Can you make the pain stop?" he asked.

"No, I cannot," she said without regret. "Pain is life, Cris-ri-phon. But you can heal more than you yet know. If you achieve balance, you may choose your path." Houda smiled at him. "Keep your memory and your soul, *shazody*, and you may become one such as we have never witnessed before."

Knowing words spoken with such hope for the resilience of a Human soul tethered by a young man's desires. Her hope for balance was strong because such wants were transient with age. They always had been for the Zauyrians, even living longer than the pale men.

*Always transient, the young man's desires.*

Until that hot, clear day when he had seen his qu'eesan for the first time. She had been standing naked beneath the waterfall of Koorul before the whole host of them, a royal daughter from which none could take their eyes. Her white hair long and dripping, ebony skin glossy and beaded with precious water. Bright, scarlet eyes exotic, adding to her otherworldly beauty.

She had chosen *him* to come forward, his captain said. Out of all men present, Cris would strip down first and let her look at him, as he did her. He could speak some of her Queendom's language by this point, though he had only met a few Davrin messengers and traders from the Elven cities, all of them female.

He had never seen one naked or so carefree as this; he was equally certain she had never seen a naked man before. Her wide, curious eyes and hungry smile captivated him, and her mage's aura sang to his inner ear with a hypnotic lilt he hadn't heard since grasping Houda's arm in his sick bed.

Often the drive to taste life at its full flower crashed headlong into the death's call inside him. Standing bare and exposed before this sensual Dark Elf in more ways than one, her song strengthened his focus, pushed any hint of decay aside, and blew him a perfumed kiss.

*Yes,* he answered.

In that pool, she had gone to a knee to taste him, and he hadn't lasted before his cock sprayed her dark breasts. Though he grimaced inside, she had only laughed and invited him to taste between virginal, fertile thighs.

He *had* her, reciprocating with his mouth. He drank her heat and nectar until she gripped his hair, crying out in her ecstatic throes. Before he could see straight, the sorcerer's son had buried his cock to the hilt between the Davrin royal's legs, her slit wet and throbbing around him.

There was nothing else in all of Existence then.

"I-Innathi…"

She undulated beneath him. "Cris… Cris-ri-phon! *Ohhh, quarval, xunsin unsa!*"

*Drive into me.*

He drew back. Drove into her.

*"Yi! Xunsin unsa!"*

*Yes, qu'eesan.* He thrust deep to hear her moan again. He clung, mounted on her. She was *life*. Pure life, with death a long way off.

*Innathi.*

Fuck her.

*Fuck her hard. Until our songs combine, God, yes!*

He'd found his path, he knew.

He found *her.*

*"Get off her! Stop!"*

Cold, small, black hands shoved at him, trying to push him away. They didn't belong to his qu'eesan, who clung to him instead. Rolling away was not possible now, but this other Davrin interfered; she made the genuine effort to disrupt their song.

*No!* He drove them harder. *We shall finish this!*

*"Get off her before I blast you off!"*

She tried to shove him off that terrifying cliff to which he'd been clinging his entire life. She couldn't *know* what might happen to him if she succeeded!

"Get back!" he shouted, lashing out with the one talent he wasn't using, forcing her still. "Let us be!"

She fell, and he grabbed her to hold her still.

He stared at Innathi. *Want you. Only you.*

*"No! No! Let me go!"* The second mage fought with her life to escape him. *"Release meee!"*

He was peaking when he heard something *tearing* at the same moment, something he knew wasn't cloth or flesh. Then all was drowned out in the climactic rush and screams of his qu'eesan, as her body beneath him coaxed a release the power of which left him temporarily blind.

He shouted out, and another's unfamiliar scream matched him.

He collapsed atop his future wife and, to the side, someone wept.

*"All gods purge you! Why wouldn't you listen?!"*

The other's angry, powerless voice slipped away.

And surcease followed.

I jerked awake, trembling, and squeezing my thighs together so tightly, it was as if I clutched a thread between them which was all that kept me from falling into a dark pit. I blinked, gradually realized I was settled underneath Brom's desk.

*Arghh, wha…?*

I really had to piss.

Rolling up, I managed not to hit my head on the underside of the desk and get to my knees, reaching for the chamber pot set nearby. My three babies crawled from wherever they had been hunting, on alert as I slid it between my legs, rested my thighs on the edge to squat low as I could, and emptied my demanding bladder into it.

With shallow breath, I listened in case the sound woke the sorcerer. Nothing yet, and as this bodily stress was relieved, the confusing cries and sensations lingered from my Reverie, as did the silent terror of what it might mean.

"If nothing was intended," Gavin had warned me on the Midway, "then you should know it affected the others sleeping."

*I didn't do it again, did I?*

I hadn't seen my distant home this time. I'd seen another's from long ago.

*In Koorul?*

If that fateful meeting beneath a waterfall had *ever* been true, and not some warped outcome from Kurn catching me naked beneath a stream, then it was beyond a horny dream. A mix of great pleasure and pain, this link returning me to a time on my Elder's bed before I had Shyntre's blue pedant.

My Feldeu had been buried in Reishel, both D'Shea and my Sister using me as the fresh will to rejuvenate the worn auras between them. I had seen what the Prime had done to my Sister attacked by mindflayers. I'd felt every moment she had struggled to live. With Reishel and D'Shea, what I'd witnessed had been true and real enough.

*What of Cris-ri-phon?*

The man on the bed shifted, inhaling sharply, filling his broad chest as he sat up. I froze in place, my skin went cold, and I was glad to be finished pissing. The moment I could move, I shifted the chamber pot where it wouldn't be kicked and got to my feet. I turned toward the alcove in time to see an aroused man approaching me in the dark.

I swallowed. "Brom?"

My voice speaking this name made him hesitate; his naked feet paused on the boards. I didn't sound anything like his qu'eesan, though he still reached to cradle a full erection, tugging gently, in need of relief.

He exhaled. "Sirana."

Was it a good sign he spoke the correct name?

He inhaled through his nose, twice, like he could smell either my dream-slick slit or the contents of my bladder. Maybe both. He drew nearer, broad hands out and empty, breathing audible. He and

I noticed my guardians attached to the sides of his desk, alert but not hopping around in aggression.

"Sirana," he repeated, shifting to that foreign Davrin accent. *"I want to rut you. I must. What is your price to take me in?"*

Price? I couldn't smother the fire between my legs enough to think of anything but boundaries.

*"No will-bending,"* I said. *"No spells or compulsions. A natural body's pleasure only."*

He stroked his rod with a twist of his wrist. *"Agreed. And?"*

*"Do not try to press me on my back. I'll kill you."*

Brom huffed a quiet laugh, his night eyes fixed on me. He nodded without posing questions. *"Agreed. You may press me on mine if you like, but do not force a kiss on me or bite my tongue or my cock."*

*"Agreed. Do not bite or torment my tits. I don't enjoy it."*

Not right now, at least. I saw another careful note.

*"Yes, a light touch on your breasts if any at all. Anything else, Sirana?"*

*"Yes, one more. My price."* I switched to Trade. "Help me cleanse the warp rot to the North."

Brom mouth tightened but gave me a solid nod. "We can discuss it."

"That's not a yes."

"It's an opportunity to persuade me where God's Warriors couldn't," he replied gruffly. "For now, I'd rather use my tongue *below* the strategy table, not above it."

I smirked, and it was my turn to massage my nethers in anticipation. "Good idea. I could use some work that low."

His gaze fixed on my fingers; he heard my reply and closed the gap between us. "Then you'll have it."

His scent was thick as he closed in, and there was no mistaking the unctuousness of an aroused male Human. Rough, large hands rested light on my shoulders only to smooth down my back to my buttocks. The Zauyrian tilted his head and leaned past my mouth, lightly running his tongue full length along the edge of my pointed ear. Gently, he bit the tip, and I shuddered.

"Yes," he breathed.

His fingers squeezed my ass before taking a firm hold on my waist to push me backward. My ass hit the edge of his desk; I could sit on it if I were on the balls of my feet. That proved good enough as the naked man kneeled, pushed my thighs wider, and buried his nose and mouth against my white-furred mound. His tongue swiped out and over my folds, and I groaned, aching so intensely that I prayed my pleasure would not be interrupted.

*Again.*

His slow, determined sucking which followed convinced me this innkeeper *had* served a Davrin Queen intimately for some time. Slow and delicious, every muscle in my middle tightened down as I enjoyed the gradual grind and occasional flick or slap that made me jump and twitch.

*Gah! Yes!*

I splayed my legs wider, grabbing one cheek to spread, and Brom—or, Cris-ri-phon—reached to trace the length of my cunt with the tip of his tongue while his middle finger collected some ready moisture before nudging interestedly around my pucker, first in a circle, then pressing in the middle.

"*Yeh!*" I gasped as my netherhole clenched and fluttered at the welcome attention, waves of sensation joining the pressure on my nub up front. "This!"

Eyes closed to feel it, I reached for his wrist and pushed his hand in harder. A thick, unfamiliar digit burrowed in, slipping in past the largest knuckle, and I squealed happily through a tight throat. My slit grew puffy as the man earnestly sucked me, eager for the coming rides. Goddess, had it been so long!

The Zauyrian took the hint and plundered my ass without further guidance, first noting how quickly I adjusted to his size and suddenly adding a second. I gasped, shocked how he stretched me with only two fingers, and swiftly hit my threshold.

*"Oh, yes!"* I cried, falling backward with a *thunk*, writhing, let-ting my legs fall open. I shuddered in one of the longest, most luxu-rious climaxes I remembered as the Zauyrian allowed me to ride it out to its fullest.

Then his fingers pulled out of my ass. His lightly bearded face lifted from the junction of my thighs, and he used the desk to get to his feet. His long and broad cock was bobbing and seeking; I looked down, my cunt only drooling.

Then I lifted my eyes, briefly met his impassioned gaze, felt something—

"Sirana…"

I brought one leg up high and over, flipping myself over with a narrow miss of my heel to his face. Facing away and grabbing the edges of the desk, I shifted so my feet found the floor and I was bent over in front of him. I arched my back, reaching with one hand to part my buttocks again in offering.

"As agreed," I huffed, seeing him only out my periphery. Ironi-cally, it was safer for us both facing away from him.

Where I couldn't meet those ancient eyes.

The sorcerer couldn't resist the sight for long, staring for barest moments before warm, hairy legs lined up along the back of my thighs. The first, hot, real phallus I'd had since Elder Rausery pene-trated my sex in two, rough thrusts.

"God!" he gasped.

I flattened my feet, spreading them wider to help while he pushed a few shorter strokes to get settled and fully slick. Now, looming over my back, his hands took tight hold of my shoulders.

"Clench down," he rumbled.

I did, tightening my pelvic muscles mostly to absorb his pres-ence deep inside. A deep rumble left his chest, and I had one chance to take one full breath before he began riding me like a gal-loping steed. His skin slapped against mine, making me quake. I gritted my teeth and gripped the desk tightly, listened to the wet sounds as he stirred my guts with a brute's focus. My mouth was wide open, eyes squeezed shut.

Whatever had changed in his mood, he fucked like a Red Sister now! *Oh, Goddess!*

"Yes!" he growled, ramming hard and fast.

I wanted to reach for my clit but couldn't let go of the wood and remain stable. He was getting close to the edge, I could tell. He wanted to spew his Human seed inside me so much.

Of course he would want it. He claimed to breed with a Dark Elf.

*Twelve children.*

How often must he have seeded her? Over how long?

My eyes popped open when Cris-ri-phon leaned down, laying his front flush along my back. His thrusting not as deep but faster, his hips churned as he clung to me. His hands tingled where he touched me as well, and an off-putting hum lingered on the edge of my senses, almost like a Ley Line.

Like something was trying to get my attention. Wanting to be closer.

Impossibly close.

*Augh! Stop!*

What was he doing? What was *I* doing?!

He pounded my cunt, his aura a palpable thing trying to bind, and my middle chilled to think of the waterfall. That tearing sound. That scream as she tried to pull away.

Could... could his aura *hurt* someone without his realizing it?

Could he—?

*Oh Goddess, my baby!*

"Cris!" I cried. *"Fuck my ass!"*

"W-wha—?"

I pulled myself far up on the desk with my arms, pulling my slit off his prick. His rhythm thoroughly disrupted, he stopped, and my feet landed on the floor before he could do anything else. I reached back, pushing him lengthwise into the cleft between my cheeks and wiggling side-to-side.

*"Fuck my netherhole,"* I gasped again.

"But…"

*"I will **not** catch from you,"* I insisted. *"You said it can happen with a man, yes?"*

He swallowed. *"I did."*

*"Then ream and cream my pucker, bua!"*

His prick pulsed against me as if he enjoyed that command, and his weight shifted as he took his cock from my hand, pressing the head slow and steady against my pucker. My well-trained back hole spread open, hugging a pole the size of D'Shea's, and this felt *much* better for reasons beyond relief.

*"Oh, fuck, yes!"* I encouraged as he gradually sank in deeper, straining my ring past what his fingers had done. *"Fuck! Ungh, a fine cock, sorcerer. I know you're there."*

The Zauyrian chuckled, running his fingers appreciatively down my spine. *"Thank you, little fighter."*

His mood had returned to the earlier one, far less feral; when he lowered his upper body down again, each of us on our elbows with his outside of mine, he rutted my backside with greater care than he had my cunt, and slower and easier than Jaunda usually did.

*"Tight,"* he grunted near my left ear.

*"Good!"* I gasped, certain that my slit must be drooling on the floor for how sensually he wallowed in my ass. *"Ohh, yes, spurt it here!"*

His breath shuddered. *"I shall!"*

It occurred to me only now, he might never have rutted his Queen's pucker the same way he pounded her slit, and he was treating me the same. A lucky chance I took with intense pleasure, full length and in slow strokes. I held still for every push and pull, sensations drawing me to quieter times in the Cloister.

Then the Human's gasp caught, and he sped up rutting my ass. His voice was too low to be a Sister. "I am close. Are you?"

"I... ache?" I replied, not sure what he wanted to hear.

One of the sorcerer's hands left the desk and reached down, shifting us backward and farther off the edge as he stuffed my asshole deeper by happenstance. Then the pads of his fingers laid across on my netherlips and began rubbing in circles; my asshole clamped down hard, and he chuckled.

"Like that?"

"Uh-huh!"

I drooled, eyes wide and staring at the far wall as the larger man took a rhythmic, constant pace, sawing in and out of my relaxing pucker while he tossed my slippery netherlips back, forth, and around. Our pleasure rose, quick and together, though I strained on the edge when he made it. His prick slammed in thrice harder before pulsing once, and I knew he was cumming.

*Damn.*

His silence broke, a rumbling, unfamiliar groan spreading over my ears as his strong hand clamped down by reflex, squeezing my entire mound. Sudden, delicious pressure spiked through my gut as he crammed those last-moment humps, pushing as deep as possible and opening me even wider around his base. I yelped, writhed, and came, soaring in a second release as the thick, Human prick spilled his milk inside me.

*Yes, oh, yes...!*

All stress of the night unraveled, flowing out as I coasted down.

I needed this.

Panting, my front settled upon the desk, I was coming down as the sorcerer's slimy meat withdrew slowly out of me. My head was pleasantly fuzzy when my hole closed, now empty, and the thought struck me how two men on the Surface had enjoyed my holes which Kurn both resented and wanted at the same time.

*Heh. And all they did was admit their want and ask.*

It helped that both saw me as someone real without the drive to subjugate me first. Not yet anyway.

"That was…" The sorcerer took the deepest breath as he headed for the wash basin. "Very generous, Sirana. Thank you."

"Mm-hm, a mutual pleasure," I agreed, recalling my Reverie and the possible reason he'd woken up in such a rigid state. Lazily, I lifted myself onto my elbows. My neck was bare; I wasn't wearing my pendant.

While the sorcerer poured water from the pitcher, I peeked over the edge of the desk. My spiders were there unharmed, and all my things, including Shyntre's pendant tucked inside a fold of my cloak. I straightened up then, stretching, feeling the slickness and goo between my legs and cheeks.

"I need the wash basin next," I said, kneeling behind the desk first to don my pendant then my shirt while leaving my legs bare. "And a fresh cloth, if you have it?"

"Of course." He faced away from me as he wiped down his crotch. "It's almost dawn."

*Yes, it must be.*

Soon, someone's over-inquisitive daughter would be knocking on the door. It would be a bright, new day in Troshin Bend after the chaos, killing, and burning of last night. There would be much going on, and all our plans had been fucked well before I was.

I wanted to visit Gavin's body, first.

The Zauyrian and I agreed readily, checking on Mathias and the Witch Hunter was first on his list as well. He eyed my expression after he altered his appearance to dark-haired Brom with the lighter skin.

"You seem disappointed," he remarked.

I shrugged as I finished gearing up, taking up Gavin's pack again. "I prefer the white hair, I think."

"Heh. Most Humans don't."

I smoothed a frosty strand missed in my braid and grinned; his younger persona smiled back without showing teeth.

"Do you want another disguise?" he offered, but I shook my head.

"I'd rather see how the Witch Hunter behaves, if he's aware."

"Mm-hm. I hope your ears can tolerate the noise."

"Noted."

I could smell an early cook fire and hear a few Humans working as he opened the door, though the front room was dim enough to need lanterns. We had to get past Amelda first, for there she stood waiting within the small recess out of the hall.

Her black hair was well tended compared to earlier, brushed smooth and collected into a plaited bun at the nape of her neck. I wondered both whether she had slept and how her skin could be so white if Cris-ri-phon really was her sire.

*"Bint sabhalkir,"* he greeted her, locking and warding his door.

Her shoulders softened a little; perhaps she hadn't waited long. Dark eyes flicking to me though she studied him with more care. *"Sabhati fahr."*

"I shall be visiting the prisoner first," he stated. "Has Master Briar eaten?"

A small shake of her head. "Not that I am aware."

"We will stop by the kitchen."

"There is much for you to examine, *Fahdi.*"

"I won't be long."

I followed him, hood up to temper stares from the working women and children as they greeted and assisted their governor, silent and behaving like a guard until we were able to leave the inn through the kitchen door. Carrying enough food for four men, I started in on the cheese as we walked toward the shed.

Brom glanced at me. "Not nervous what we may find, I see."

I darted a look his way. "Should I be? You seemed approving of Mathias last night. You said you 'trusted' him with Gavin's body."

"Hm. Well. He is willing to protect my interests when I protect his. That is nothing new. I wonder if you have any understanding what those are, however."

I rolled my eyes. "Do you recall anything of *Vloszia Dalnanin?*"

His brows drew down. "The Blood Sisters?"

*Close enough.* I waited in silence as he considered.

"Not by that name," he admitted.

So the Sisterhood may not have existed on the Surface? Or not in its current form. The Prime was old, but not *that* old.

"If you knew more of us," I smiled, "I wager we could teach Mathias something of bending wills without magic, be they *caits* or *buas.*"

Brom arched a brow. "You are not disgusted."

"Should I be?" I shrugged. "At least he knows his desires. To suggest he is foul for this, I would be a... hm, the word... hypocrite?"

The sorcerer smiled through his darker, thicker beard. "Ah. I believe I understand. Interesting."

We reached the shed, which for certain had stronger scents of bodies and their functions about it. We needed to knock and wait.

"Mathias," Brom said. "Breakfast."

It occurred to me to wonder what the sorcerer would do if Mathias wouldn't unlock the door from the inside, though that remained untested. During the small time standing in the muted, predawn light, I heard Mathias get to his feet with a muffled groan and move around. He turned up a flame lantern, sending orange light filtering through the top and bottom of the heavy door.

I listened for struggle or protest from Jacob, but there was none. Mathias had slept well after the fire and the fight, followed by the additional work late into the night. At least we weren't interrupting him.

Mathias unlocked the door and peeked out in a way I recognized from Gavin—he had a way of blocking the door if someone he didn't want inside stood outside. That wasn't either of us, as he opened the door wider, and we slipped in without speaking.

The scents had become much thicker in the closed space from the two living men rather than the corpse. Mathias motioned for us to put the food on the table where he placed the lantern; I did but started consuming my share as studied the space.

The Witch Hunter was unconscious, though by what means was unknown. Jacob was still gagged but not bound in the same way he'd been thrown in here. Wrists, ankles, and neck were roped to opposing metal anchors with little slack, which kept the anchors beyond his reach. This also allowed him to rest in a natural pose with minimal strain, and I could spot no new injuries. Mathias evidently wanted them both well rested, and the interrogation hadn't begun. I wondered about his self-restraint, where the discipline had come from or if it had developed from within.

Meanwhile, Gavin's body was where we'd left it, unmoving and with the Chief Warrant's dagger deep in his chest. I chewed faster; I wanted to take a closer look but not while handling food. Brom and Mathias ate as well but seemed amused by my choice of focus. I didn't understand why.

Or maybe I chose not to.

*It is not direct interest from the innkeeper but what has been drawn here,* he'd said. *Had I known, I would have deserted this trek days ago.*

I wished he'd been able to explain that. He had seemed willing at the time.

"Where is Rithal?" I asked in a quiet tone unlikely to wake a Davrin much less an exhausted Human.

Mathias didn't hear me, but Brom did. "He usually stays with another Dwarf he knows while he's here. I believe, after last night, he sees less reason to stay in the inn watching you and Gavin."

I looked at them. "There's another Dwarf here?"

"On the outskirts, yes. Deeper in the woods."

"Why? Do they not live in 'clans'?"

Brom shrugged. "Some don't. They live longer than Humans, and if they are uprooted, as Rithal was, they tend to wander great distances. Some travel in the same caravans for decades. There are closed, settled clans, and then there are the rolling stones."

*Hmm.*

The ancient sorcerer added, "Where you won't see them as much anymore is in armies."

I sounded surprised. "Anymore?"

"You'll find individual mercenaries or a small band of outcast Dwarves. But a whole clan getting involved in a ground war?" Brom shrugged.

Mathias chuckled, finishing his breakfast while nodding in agreement. "They craft weapons and armor, and other things," he said, "highly prized but expensive for most men. That's about as involved as I've heard they get."

I was frowning. "Was that not always the case? Did they have armies once?"

Brom smiled serenely. "Only according to one of their stories I've heard. I've not seen any proof."

I was curious despite this being neither necessary nor of Davrin origin. "What story?"

The sorcerer stared blankly at the wall for a time, until even Mathias waited for an answer. "That the last time Dwarves went to war, they wiped out another race entirely. Ironically, leaving room for Humans to take over more land than this other race ever did."

"Yeah?" the skin hunter asked, sounding as interested as I felt. "Who were they?"

I tilted my head. "Orcs?"

It was Cris-ri-phon, not Brom, who blinked at me in surprise; I was beginning to sort out the subtle mannerisms. "Yes. You know something of them?"

"Nothing until recently," I admitted. "Rithal mentioned them as one of the three 'old races' before Humans rose. He said Orcs were assumed to have 'died out' along with Elves, unable to compete with how fast Humans breed."

Mathias covered his mouth with his hand, both amused and thoughtful as he looked to Brom for a response. The sorcerer was skeptical.

"Oh, I wager it wasn't as simple as that," he said. "Different hearth stories warn of a bloody war between Orc and Dwarf, reason enough for clans not to take sides in Human wars these days. And you are proof enough the Elves did not die out from slower breeding alone. I would say, neither did the Orcs. If they are truly gone, they were purged in mass."

This competition seemed more likely. It was a source of tensions down below between us and the Tragar, us against the Ornilleth.

My eyes landed on the corpse's hand, on those long, rigid fingers caked in dirt and blood. I poked Gavin's upper arm, testing the resilience of the flesh. Stiff as hard leather. Would this make him easier or harder to move again? What would we do with his body?

"He'll relax again in another day or two," Mathias said. "This dead-stiff phase doesn't last, though a lot of folk think it does."

"Hm?" I grunted, inviting him to continue.

"Indeed," Brom took up the thought. "Often the dead are buried quickly, stiff like this. Should there be a reason to exhume the body later, they will find it relaxed again."

"And Witch Hunters *always* take it as proof that something 'unholy' has made it walk around again when no one is looking," Mathias snickered.

Clearly, the two men had spoken to each other before now of Manalar's enforcers and their methods. The skin hunter's earlier skepticism in hearing me talk about the existence of demons and the Abyss made sense. I pursed my lips, admitting to myself I knew as much about dead bodies as I did unborn babies. Both these men knew more, even one being much younger in years.

*You are kept ignorant, that is clear.*

I resented this now that I was aware.

"But Gavin *did* force a corpse to stand up again," I murmured, glancing at them. "Though it was newly dead."

"Oh?" Mathias invited. "When?"

Brom laughed. "Oh, yes, I heard that part of the tale immediately. During the fight, a Witch Hunter was shot down with crossbows. Gavin seized it, ripped out the heart, and took a bite, yes?"

My mouth twitched in a smile to recall the gory sight.

"That is the fastest way to take control of any remaining Vitas in a fresh body," Brom told us.

*Vitas.* So, this sorcerer knew this word, too. "I assumed he was trying to frighten and enrage them."

Both men chuckled, and the governor said, "I have no doubt he succeeded. But eating the heart was practical, as well. There is a mage knowing how to manipulate the essence released upon death, and there are the mundane and ignorant populace mistaking a natural occurrence as proof of someone using that knowledge."

This was more fascinating than was good for me. Still, it showed me that this man probably knew of what he spoke when he'd prevented me from removing the dagger.

*At best, nothing happens, and a pathway merely closes.*

At worst, something else claims the body, looking out through Gavin's eyes.

I pointed at the weapon. "And this? Will you leave it there?"

"For now," Brom said firmly. "I've not had time to study it."

"When shall you?" I pressed. "Before or after the body begins rotting?"

"It depends how this goes," he indicated the Witch Hunter and the interrogation space, "and what is needed in Troshin Bend between now and then. The monk cannot be my priority now, but I'll not leave it unaddressed, I promise."

He spoke in a way much like his refusal to commit to helping me with the warp rot. I thought either of these things were volatile over anyone living in Troshin Bend right now.

*Hmm.*

Brom's presence stood between Mathias and me as I considered questions I wanted to ask or some plan or goals of the next day or two. At the same time, the skin hunter looked to his prisoner in the corner, his focus that he was awake and fed. I didn't know if I was going to Manalar at this point, so what he pulled from Jacob wasn't of urgent interest to me. Not compared to Cris-ri-phon, the warp rot, or the Ma'ab.

*Or that vanishing black arrow and the chain-wielder that chased off Kurn.*

It was only that Gavin's body was here, that something felt unfinished.

*Unaddressed. For now.*

"What of the Witch Hunter bodies from last night?" I asked. "Are they still in the woods?"

"You'd have to ask Kurn," said the town governor tiredly. "I believe he took charge when you insisted on going back for Gavin's body."

I made a face. "I wager a lot of good insight is destroyed."

The sorcerer didn't look to care though he agreed. "Likely, unless Castis stopped him. The man is not one to let things lie before pitching objects in boredom."

Yet both had to sleep some time, even if they stayed up to loot or collect the corpses further. It didn't smell like they had set a bonfire of bodies, at least.

I stepped away from Gavin toward the door. "I want to retrace my path in the woods."

"Alright," Brom said after a brief pause.

He said nothing until we'd left Mathias to lock the door behind us. For the ease of simple walking around in daylight, the sorcerer replaced the handsome young male face I'd been wearing when the Witch Hunters arrived. At least he'd waited until Mathias couldn't see me; I didn't think anyone except us knew what had set off the violence last night.

With the man walking beside me down the empty dirt road, I noticed his heavier step and quieted my own at the same moment Brom remarked on it.

"You're like a ghost walking next to me," he said. "You can make some noise."

"No one is awake to watch," I pointed out.

"That won't last, and they'll be clinging to me the moment I'm spotted. Better practice now."

It was a pride bruiser, but I scuffed the bottoms of my boots a little.

I found where I'd bled next to the tree, the brownish smudges marking the bark and some of the ground; it appeared undisturbed, and I ground my heel into the soil and sprinkled dirt on the bark, rubbing it in with my glove. It may be too late for preventing blood magic, but I still felt the need to disturb what was there.

Brom was watching. "Your blood?"

"Mm-hm," I admitted grudgingly.

"I can assure you no one last night would have that skill but me, and I have learned to regret the times I've used it. You need not worry, Sirana."

I noted his claim but was not comforted, adding nothing as I finished my search before the light became too intense. Once the morning brought the usual intense headache, my eyes could miss a boulder jutting up in my path.

The bodies of the two Witch Hunters who had seen me close up were gone. There were no black ashes from a vanishing arrow, no strange footprints, no marks of a chain I could find. I smelled nothing unusual, but I didn't expect to be lucky enough that whatever had been standing there had also decided to wet the ground with something before leaving.

*Sigh. Too late.*

"For what do you search?" the sorcerer murmured.

I weighed telling him the rest, as I'd hinted at it trying to distract Amelda last night, but it bothered me that he would neither explain his reluctance to hunt the warp rot nor confirm when he would study Gavin's body. I might have to mention the oddities happening since the canyon, too, and I didn't want to. Maybe those oddities had been there before Gavin had spoken up.

*I sensed a powerful aura near the camp tonight, Sirana. It was not one of us... Either we narrowly missed crossing paths with something we'd rather not meet, or we are being followed.*

Was that sound that knocked down the Witch Hunters last night the same one which had stopped me from chasing after Tamuril back at the tower?

*We are being followed.*

And whatever it was didn't want Witch Hunters to get to me first.

*Oh, Goddess.*

"If..." I began hesitantly. "If something was here last night... I do not know what, or if I am certain..."

The sorcerer tilted his head and motioned with his hand, inviting me to continue.

"Would you have any method for sensing a powerful aura *after* it was gone?"

Brom gave it some thought. "Not without preparation and a better idea what we seek."

"Arcane?" I suggested, repeating Gavin's word, but the sorcerer smirked

"Any mage using a written language has some understanding of arcane magic, Sirana. Castis and I both fit that description. Anything specific?"

Illusion, invisibility, enhancement, all qualities I believed I witnessed last night but wouldn't stand out from anything I saw a scroll-reading wizard do down below. All arcane? Really?

*Well, fuck.*

This was a language whose subtleties would streak past me. Gavin would have guided me, but the sorcerer merely stared at me, thoughts turning behind his eyes. I shrugged, giving up in favor of returning to a tangible search.

"I have nothing," I muttered. "I'm not certain it is not the new land tricking my senses again."

Not that they were this dull after all Rausery's training and my efforts; I was finished giving details if the sorcerer wouldn't fill any gaps at all. I shifted the weight of Gavin's pack, wondering if Brom would take Amelda's suggestion and ask to inspect what was inside it.

Not unless he gave me something to work with prior to that, I decided. I could look first, but I probably wouldn't grasp beyond he'd shown me on our trip—shown, but hadn't explained, unless it was something obvious like a light or needle and thread.

I searched the area South of where I'd been chased and shot; it was greatly churned up from the skirmish. We found boot prints, odd metal objects and ceramic shards, broken and charred foliage, and drag marks all through the woods. It was ludicrously easy to follow where they'd taken the bodies. Brom observed me in silence, offering nothing when I asked him nothing.

We reached the open marketspace away from the permanent buildings, and here I discovered that the two Ma'ab had never gone back to the inn for the night. The local man, Dar, who had been leading the riders as they scouted around their town, had stayed as well with a few others from that group. There was a cooking fire heating water and a familiar lean-to with food and tools in the makeshift camp than had ever been on our nights traveling.

Brom made a hand sign, and I fell behind and to his right as we approached the camp. It only occurred to me moments later that the sign had felt like a subtle Davrin motion over the large, crude gesticulations I had learned not to put much effort into studying, as their signals simply weren't nuanced.

Had I just seen a Davrin sign or was it a chance similarity?

"Master Brom!" Dar greeted us first, glancing at me but not recalling the hooded, freckled boy from the porch when the Witch Hunters first arrived. "Glad you're here."

With Kurn and Castis as company, I had little doubt he was.

"All accounted for," the man continued, "except for the *Thetri*."

The governor nodded. "Just checked on him. He's secure and guarded."

Dar looked behind him, where the two Ma'ab were stirring from a nap, and back to Brom. "Can't let him escape tah talk, can we? That mak-noo-uht Rithal brought to yer inn pulled enough dark tricks last night to draw the Church and take us *all* as witches."

I smirked at the Ma'ab slur. *That didn't take long.*

"No, we're not letting him go," Brom replied with confidence, glancing at Kurn and Castis as they approached. "And the Bishops soon will have too many concerns at their front gate to prioritize sending further god warriors to Troshin Bend."

Some nods of agreement, though Castis was peering at me while Kurn blurted with jutted a finger in my direction, "Who is this?"

"The youth who was traveling with the *maknuut*," Brom replied with a low, knowing grin.

Both Ma'ab narrowed their eyes, and Castis peered like he could confirm the glamour being used. Whether he could see through it, I didn't know.

Dar blinked at me then to Brom. "Name?"

"Leur."

I worked *not* to react to that as Dar addressed me. "So, Leur, who was the mak-noo-uht? What did he want in coming here?"

"More importantly, I would think," Castis elbowed in, leveling a suspicious gaze at me. "Where is his body?"

"Is that his pack?" Kurn asked, pointing again.

My mouth twisted with a decisive lack of answers. *Braqth's Blessing for leaving me no doubt in their first two questions.*

Amelda wasn't much better. Were all from Ennikar this transparent about their plans? I arched a brow and mutely looked to Brom.

The innkeeper said, "There is more to be concerned about this morning, I think."

He motioned toward the seventeen bodies laid out in three neat rows, including the Chief Warrant. They were stripped down to shirt and trousers, their boots removed. Their equipment lay in piles.

"Aye. Burn them?" Dar asked. "Or bury them?"

"You'll never get a bonfire hot enough to destroy all evidence," Castis said. "In the meantime, for this many bodies, you send a signal of scent and sight for several days that a fight happened here."

It sounded like he had experience.

Brom agreed. "Burying is better, and we should spread them out. It'll take work. We'll need carts, spades, horses, and men."

"On it, Master Brom."

*Spades.*

I refrained from looking in the direction but recalled the bloody weapon I'd taken and shoved beneath a woodpile so Gavin might not be chopped into chunks in his last moments. It was newly purchased, not something Gavin selected from the tower as he had everything else on my back, and a mundane tool. Still something I should try to collect if I could.

*Preferably at night.*

With Dar gone and the locals soon to be busy with the large task of burial, and with the day becoming brighter and noticeably warmer in this open space, I turned to the sorcerer in a quiet if natural voice.

"Where do I find Rithal?"

"No," Kurn said, crossing his arms and looking down at me. "He has backed out of any deal. You need not speak to him."

"If he's backed out," I replied coolly, "so have I, and Mathias, if Jacob satisfies. *And* you've lost the one who knew the most about the land, who may have gotten you closer on such a fool infiltration mission. You are ill prepared regardless, now you have no chance."

"The *maknuut* was not the keystone in the plan," Castis replied, looking up at me through lowered brows.

"Which *maknuut*?" I asked. "Gavin or Amelda?"

The Noble blinked, and Kurn growled, "How dare you?"

"She's half-blood, isn't she?" I looked at Brom, who was rubbing his eyes. "Or are you merely acting the role of *Fahdi* without the spawn?"

"No, she is my blood," Brom acknowledged.

"This man has long and illustrious standing with the Ascended," Castis spat, his pale face becoming flushed with insult. "And her mother is *Noble*, not from the slum—"

"So, it doesn't count, understood," I finished, sounding bored. "Well. My Queen sends me a message that the warp rot to the North takes precedence."

"What?" Brom said sharply, and I waited to see if he could get that I was lying as I kept speaking.

"I've seen several portents which will not allow me to head South," I said. "What the Witch Hunters failed to do, I shall see done instead."

Somehow.

The Ma'ab burst out laughing, and the sorcerer looked a little angry. I wasn't unaffected either, as my middle and the tips of my ears burned at once. *So tired of this.*

"A follow up question, Master Brom," I said. "Why *shouldn't* a Hellhound be frightened by the sound of a chain? Kurn for certain was."

That shut them both up; they both looked like they'd swallowed a toad. So, Amelda hadn't warned them.

"What?" Brom asked me.

Something wasn't aligning. I kept pushing, glaring at Kurn. "What did you see behind me, pale man? What made you run instead of pursuing further scrap with me?"

*"Kus,"* he hissed. "You conjured that ghost, did you not?"

"What ghost?"

He ignored that with a threatening step forward. "Just as you've been creating the dreams. You are probing our minds with your wanton, Abyssal claws!"

Brom put up his hand and stood between us. "Stop, Kurn. Quiet down. Let us go elsewhere to discuss this."

"Yes, let's."

Castis sounded too willing, motioning toward the Western forest where the fighting had been, and Brom was inclined by the locals bringing horses, carts, and shovels. I didn't want to go, being entirely reliant on Brom's protection after provoking Kurn.

This had gone deep too fast, and I worried that the sorcerer would *relate* to Kurn's accusation of sleep manipulation rather than disbelieve it. The sorcerer had named me *Leur* in front of Dar.

*Leur-en-phon.* Someone I should not know had ever lived. A brother who brought help to a sick and feverish youth.

*You can't word-dance out of this one, Sirana. Pull out.*

"I have heard enough for now," I said, crossing my hands and sweeping them to each side. "I shall find Rithal myself. We will speak later, sorcerer, I promise."

Awaiting no response, I sprinted East across the open meadow, taking a great risk if either mage decided they did not want to let me go, or if they would sic the dog on me.

*I must know now.*

Behind me, there were brief bursts of shouting in Ma'ab, Brom included. The next instant, Kurn must have thrown another thunderstone, for a loud bang struck my back like a club, and I stumbled, blind with my ears ringing. I still ran. Given the stone itself didn't land at my feet at that range, Brom must have interfered.

It also sounded nothing like what had knocked us down last night.

I was not pursued as men came closer, preparing for burial. I ran to the spot where Gavin had been overborne. Stopping by the wood stack, I retrieved the stained spade and sprinted into the Eastern woods toward the river.

Escaping that confrontation with such ease, I only recalled what Cris-ri-phon had said that first night when I did not know his name.

*Go where you dare to be seen but don't leave Troshin Bend.*

*I will find you.*

# CHAPTER 10

EVEN WITH THE ADVANTAGE OF A HUMAN BUA'S FACE FOR A quarter of the day, I did not try to be seen in the woods. There were men working despite the fires last night, or maybe because of them, cutting down trees with axes and doing other things. I avoided them where I could, though the one place I could not was the wooden bridge leading to the other bank.

Barely pausing long enough to scrub dirt over the old blood on the spade, I rested it on my shoulder and pulled down my hood. My eyes watered immediately, the aching growing worse as I left the shade, calmly walking toward the bridge with purpose enough that I hoped I would not be stopped.

*Just a boy and his tool.*

The bridge was sturdy and required about thirty paces to reach the other side. The flowing river underneath caught the Sun and blinded me with its unpredictable reflections. I had to close my eyes to finish crossing. My boots touched soft bank grass when a voice called.

"Oi, kid! Hol' up there!"

*Sigh.*

I turned my head toward him like a sighted Human would, though all my impressions were by his stride, direction, and proximity, with an unhelpful blur of brown among the green. I estimated he was about as tall as Brom and strong enough.

"Whatcha doin' out here?" He paused when I took a step back. "Why're you crying?"

I wiped my cheeks and lowered my voice, guessing how a half-grown male Human might sound. "I stay at the inn. I look for the Dwarf living in the woods. Can you tell the way?"

He turned his head like he pointed an ear at me; he chuckled softly. "Voice cracking, eh?"

"Mm," I grunted, not grasping the meaning, only that my un-practiced attempt had been rough. I focused on the ground but kept his limbs in my periphery; I would see him move and could react quickly if he did.

"Hm," he responded. "Lost someone tah Witch Hunters last night?"

I nodded, eyes watering and not trusting myself to speak too much. "Lost."

"Gotcha. Yeah, maybe she can tell yer fortune."

*She?* Rithal was visiting a female Dwarf?

The axe man turned and pointed East. "The place is about an hour's walk in. Look for a mound wit' a single hawthorn tree up top."

"Ah, I'm city, uhm," I tried.

"Don' recognize a hawthorn?"

"No."

"Huh, yeah, you sound it. Awright, it's got black trunks, more than one twisted around each other, lots of crooked arms spreading out wide. Leaves make a broad canopy up top, an' this time of year might have white flowers." It sounded like he was grinning. "It has thorns, close up. Known for haw berries and thorns. Hawthorn."

*Astonishing.* I got most of that, and a lone tree like that on a mound should be recognizable even with my poor daylight vision. "Does she require a gift?"

"Heard the tales, huh? Eh, Osgrid's a cranky medicine woman, it can't hurt. Tell ya, though, good thing she wasn't visitin' town last night. Witch Hunters been lookin' for her before. Not sure who they woulda wanted more, her or the one they got."

The Surface felt like pure insanity for mages. I sighed. "Suggestion for a gift?"

Broad shoulders shrugged. "Ehhh, she's hard to impress, I hear. Bring something useful she don't have to gather herself, it's good enough for her not to send her crow after you to peck out your hair at night."

As he ran his hand self-consciously through brown hair, my mental image of this Dwarf continued to change. Nodding, I stepped East, motioning with my hand. "Better to go."

"Hey, if you can get a bottle of her mead, somehow," the man said, "that'd be good trade for the help. Name's Kivin. An' if you need a job, city boy, let us know. Could always use the help."

I paused in equal surprise and acknowledgement, putting up my hood to help cut the glare. "Good. Thank you."

I disappeared into the trees as soon as I could, although, if I were him, I would have had someone follow a stranger passing through like this. The moment I was out of sight, I kicked up my pace while dampening my sound; I could maintain this for as long as it took to lose a possible tail, and my dappled cloak would help any time I stopped to crouch and listen to the forest.

There wasn't one sign of another sentient. If anyone had tried to follow me, they had lost the trail quickly.

On the way deeper into the forest, I spotted a dark and damp cave which was an ideal place to gather edible mushrooms and approached with caution lest the den be occupied. I smelled enough to guess there may be bats deeper inside clinging to the ceiling but nothing ten paces in if I crawled.

Inside, I found mushrooms to gather, pausing to recognize one special one, pale with pink and orange speckles. *Genethsa*. The main ingredient in Shyntre's wellness pellets.

I wondered if this Dwarven female would recognize its value, as Tamuril had. Either way, I had more to offer than plain eating fare. I gathered the cluster of three, added them with the others, and backed my way out of the cave to continue my search for the mound with the hawthorn tree.

It wasn't as easy to find Osgrid's home as the woodcutter had made it sound. Head East for an hour, but was it straight as the bird flies? Look for a mound, but was it deep in a hidden hollow or edging a meadow? Was there a creek to follow, or some other landmark?

I hadn't asked because my voice had been "cracking" and drawing his attention. Brom had warned me about inconsistencies and men being paranoid about a demon wearing a Human form, and I was doing exactly this. It returned that I was also affecting male minds in their dreams, arousing them to urgent states alongside mine, and this wasn't within my control. That would only bring trouble.

It was curious how well I matched the stories of some of their least-informed fears. I wondered if I had no choice but to consciously try and use these mindlinks once again instead of denying them? Still, a blatant display of one's abilities hadn't worked well for Gavin, and the only female mage hinted at lived entirely apart from the town.

Despite the typical noise of the day, I strained to catch anything odd, as I wondered if this counted as "leaving." I'd told Brom I would search for Rithal but would return, and he let me go, for now. Perhaps my speaking with these Dwarves wasn't a threat to the Zauyrian.

After I had reached about an hour's travel into the woods, I began to circle with care, lest I lose my direction. Seeing long distance was not possible unless I climbed a tree, something I opted to do from three different vantage points. I wagered my disguise would not last much longer by the time I spotted it through branches halfway up my third tree.

*There.*

A mound with a hawthorn lay on the edge of a meadow, matching the description although it was too simple of a description for a home with well-crafted retainer stones on all sides, a green-hill rooftop, and a proper front door partly hidden behind shrubs and vines. It was well camouflaged, I granted.

I approached directly, keeping my senses open for guardian animals, especially a crow, or for snaring vines or pit traps. I carried only the spade on my shoulder, though I loosened my spider pouch. When I neared shouting distance without anyone exiting the door, I attempted what I was still unaccustomed to doing.

"Hello-o-o! I seek Rithal the Dwarf!"

Nothing yet.

"Hello-o-o! Rithal!"

Now the door opened, and a bright, red beard poked out. "What in Wickervest...?"

"It's me," I called again, stopping on the nearside of the meadow, exposed to the Sun overhead. "I seek your counsel, and that of the medicine woman, Osgrid. I bring a gift and no harm."

Rithal's mouth was sagging open long enough to catch flies while his blue eyes didn't blink. He looked behind him briefly, as if someone unseen had spoken, then waved me closer.

"Come in, then."

Osgrid's dwelling recalled strongly of Tamuril's in scent and structure, though it had been lived in much longer. I did not see how she could *not* be a mage, another Druid, with as many curiosities in various states of drying, grinding, jarring, or bottling as there were. I noted there were animal parts alongside the plants; Tamuril had favored plants in her stores.

No surprise, the crow watched me in silence, perched on a rack of antlers which had been mounted high above the hearth. No doubt a counterpart or companion like Pilla, the annoyingly over-protective falcon. I could enjoy the cool darkness and shelter from the day, though I waited for the crow to make some unpleasant noise.

Meanwhile, Osgrid the Dwarf took her time revealing herself, wearing a full, bulky robe that only hinted at her full shape. She kept a hood pulled down to cover her face, sitting in a pillow-padded chair made of interwoven branches, placed on the edge of her main room and some distance from me. Her hands were bare, rough from woods work, and appeared enough like Rithal's with less hair that I was convinced she could be the same race.

Rithal and I sat across from each other at the table before the hearth; longer than it was wide, closer to the ground than the Human's tables, it had two benches on either side. I just fit with my knees touching the underside. Gavin's pack sat on the ground at my boots, and his spade leaned against the wall by the door.

Osgrid said something in a rolling brogue which I could not tell if it was the common tongue, and Rithal translated. I thought he was strangely tense.

"She says she'll wait to see yer face, first, before ye see hers."

"Very well." I shrugged. "Not in my control when it fades. The sorcerer at Troshin Bend placed the disguise."

Osgrid asked another question.

"He been placing many spells on ye?" Rithal repeated.

"Two of which I am aware, both of this face. First, when the Witch Hunters arrived. Second, when we walked in daytime to see their bodies."

Osgrid nodded; if she was surprised, there was no sign. I looked at Rithal.

"Yeah, I told 'er everythin', Sirana," he confirmed, interlacing his thick fingers with elbows braced on the stout table. "Including yer appearance at Sarilis's tower. She needs tah know what goes on in Troshin Bend."

That was annoying but I didn't know what else I'd expected from him. "Why does she need to know?"

"Well," Rithal snorted, "that a pile o' Witch Hunter bodies is keen news fer anyone livin' in this area."

I glanced at her again. "What does she want living here?"

Osgrid's hand lifted to interrupt, motioning toward a large, empty bowl in the center of her wooden table at which I sat. "*Pithee indae roond achellae.*"

*What?*

"Put your gift in the bowl," Rithal said, pointing.

*Oh.*

I upended my mushroom pouch, letting them tumble in, pale and plump. I reached to carefully set the three *Genethsa* together and apart from the others to one side.

"*Eh,*" Osgrid grunted, "*ichkena thae'ar?*"

Rithal dutifully repeated, "You know what these are?"

"We call them *Genethsa*. Used to resist wound festering or to cleanse fouled breathing."

"*Mm.*"

She sounded pleased.

"Thank ye, dark sprite. 'Tis a first here 'nother brought."

I blinked in surprise that I understood her.

"Why d'ye have sound o' th'Manalari?" she asked, making effort to be understood without Rithal repeating every word.

"That is the sound of my tutor teaching me," I answered.

Rithal confirmed. "Gavin, I mentioned. Former monk at a monastery."

"Ah, *iyss.*" Deep within her hood, Osgrid glanced up at her crow then at me. "He died last night."

My jaw tightened. "Yes. I am curious, what sort of dagger do Witch Hunters carry for putting down 'witches'?"

The medicine woman shrugged. "All kinds."

"One flashing white in moonlight?" I tried. "I know the usual bright metal. This was different."

She gave it some thought. "Silver, maybe."

Rithal agreed, "Aye. Looked it could be so."

"Why silver?" I asked her.

"Manalari think th' tarnish is evidence of it cleansing unseen spirits."

"Ghosts?" I asked.

"Aye. Dwarves observe it as an earthen response tah water and air, not spirits. But a silver dagger kills a man or woman as dead as steel, so they ken claim it works."

We fell to silence as my gaze drifted about the dwelling, and I breathed the scent of too many new and unfamiliar pieces of the forest to know what they all were. The crow clacked its beak but thankfully remained mute.

I met Rithal's eyes across the table. "You weren't near the inn when the attack began."

A stark and resentful frown appeared. "Wasn't sleepin' in th' same place as Hunners. Soon as they rode in an' Brom invited 'em tah stay—"

"You came here," I finished.

"Aye. Saw the light o' the fire hours later. Took me time tah make it back. Was 'fraid I'd see worse, in truth."

Indeed. There were several reasons it hadn't gone worse for the town overall.

"You were looking for me before it was done," I prompted.

Rithal shrugged. "Only one to bother, aside from her." He indicated Osgrid, who hummed again. I watched a hint of ruddiness enter his cheeks as he cleared his throat. "Sorry 'twasn't sooner. Took a bit tah catch up tah it all."

"Kurn and Castis were holding back deliberately," I said. "I think they were watching. Amelda, too."

"Sounds right."

"What if the Witch Hunters had gotten both of us, not just the *'maknuut'*?"

The Dwarf shrugged. "Brom seemed tah have confidence in ye not tah get cornered."

I grimaced. "To a point. Arrows and shattered glass with fire liquid have farther reach than arms."

"Yeah, I know."

Rithal patted one palm atop his fist as if to calm himself as he looked behind me at the hearth of banked coals. We all heard my stomach grumble, but I chose to ignore it in favor of a question to Osgrid.

"Have you been settled here long?"

Her hooded head lifted with interest. "Tell, how is long?"

I shrugged. "Half a century?"

*"Heh!"* She patted the arm of her chair. "Aye."

"About the time the sorcerer settled."

"Correct." She rolled her tongue.

"He is far older than he appears," I added, and Rithal looked at her.

"Ah," she replied. "Clever *essy*."

I paused. "Do you know how old?"

"Depends when ye start countin'."

"How long have you been following him?"

"Only now." She tapped a pointer finger on the wood chair. "This life."

"On your own goal, or for another's?" I asked directly. "And why?"

I wasn't expecting a clear answer, but she didn't even offer a vague one. It was then that the Dwarf's hands lifted to pull down her hood. I saw tight, black curls which I doubted could be natural for how they formed perfect coils that sprang back into shape when pulled.

Her round face had some creases around her eyes, her complexion ruddier in the cheeks but otherwise the same light tan as Rithal. Her eyes were a paler blue than his or mine. I couldn't tell if she was around the same age as him, though it wasn't difficult to imagine they may bundle together when he was moving through.

I looked between the two Dwarves then for some reflective surface. There was none. "Has my boy face faded?"

Osgrid didn't blink. "Yer face matches yer voice, now. You are as Rithal described. 'Tis always astonishin' when tales come t' livin'."

So about four hours had passed since leaving the shed this morning. A lot of time spent, but was it spent well? What would I have to show for it when I went back? Or, had I "left" Troshin Bend, from the sorcerer's view? How long could I stay before he would find me here? I'd told him where I was going and his asking Kivin would confirm.

"Wager ye don't have much time till Master Brom calls on us," she said, as if hearing my thought. "Tell me why ye walked out here. Was it tah find Rithal?"

"No," I said. "I needed to clear my mind. Brom is confusing and the Ma'ab are conniving. Both are a threat."

"That he is, and that they are," said Osgrid, glancing at Rithal, who looked obstinate about something. "Like many stories sought out, yer not quite what I thought tah meet. Ask what ye will."

My thoughts wished to fly in all directions at this open invitation from the first Surface female I'd spoken with since Tamuril. There were so many questions I could ask, so many paths I could trace.

"Are you a Druid?" I asked.

Osgrid's face scrunched briefly in thought. "Not call mehself that."

"Then what do you call it?"

"Not sure ye can say it." She smiled dry. "I share some teachin's o' their woodlore, know enough healin' tah be tolerated by th' town. More curious tah study how things break down over time.

Me kin craft things tah last, an' we can live centuries, so I get insights tah be had 'round Humans."

"Does this study have a name in Trade?"

The Dwarf shrugged. "I dunno. An 'eve witch'?"

*Witch?* That could not be so. I chuckled, looking to Rithal, who opened his palms like he hadn't a better suggestion. *Very well.* What to ask an eve witch watching one life of a sorcerer?

I pulled out Shyntre's pendant from beneath my armor and glanced her way to see if she would recognize it, as a Tragar might.

Osgrid looked curious but offered no strong reaction. "Sapphire?"

"No." My thumb rubbed over the smooth, blue gem and the polished curve of the moon, then gently removed it. "Want to see?"

"Aye."

Rithal stood up first, holding out his hand. "I'll give it."

*Protective. Good to know.* I gave it to him as I had Kurn's ruby, and he stepped away to place the stone in Osgrid's hand. She turned it over in her fingers while Rithal sat down.

"Aye, not sapphire," she agreed. "Not faceted, but odd smooth, even deep center. Fantastic color. 'Tis not charmed." She paused, her dark brows drawing down in concentration. A shake of her head, then a nod, curls bouncing. "All I can tell. Ye can have it back, Elf."

Hiding my surprise, I accepted it from Rithal and looped it around my neck. "It is called saphgar, mined by... deep Dwarves."

Rithal showed his surprise, and Osgrid shared it with him. "Dwarves? How deep?"

"Such that they may not recall the Sun," I said. "They are dangerous and... mean-spirited like Rithal's tales of my kind."

"Are the Dark Elf tales not true?" Osgrid asked.

I had only to think of Wilsira and why I was here. "Oh, there are reasons for the tales."

Rithal scratched his cheek. "Ye don' seem like 'em, Sirana."

I chewed my cheek. "Thralls aware may not act out unless forced."

"Thrall aware?" Osgrid turned that over. "Ye not here fer yerself."

I shook my head.

"Must not have a choice?"

I answered with a wry smirk.

"Hm. I am. My own goal," she finally answered my question. "Though ye could say I look tah Heligana fer inspiration." She could tell that I didn't recognize the name. "An elemental goddess, sister tah life. She is the power which churns the foundation of the earth, breaks it down and transforms, so it rises anew."

"Destruction," Rithal murmured with a nod. "Nothin' built lasts forever."

"As life does not last forever," Osgrid agreed, then shrugged. "Or should not."

Another remark on the sorcerer she watched. I knew the direction to take with the eve witch.

"I must learn of warp rot and death magic," I said. "Gavin was teaching me of death before he died. He also said something of the warp rot was drawn here and, if he had known, he would have avoided this place. I can't know what he meant."

Osgrid glanced up at her black bird again and made a face which appeared concerned. "Aye. Warp rot is a mystical fester which appears at random. 'Tis a literal wound upon Moorig."

"Moorig?" I repeated.

"Our Mother earth, in particular for the Dwarves, as we often live within her bosom. We know not what causes it, though our mystics can tend it."

"Mystics?" I asked. "Different from mages?"

Osgrid made a thoughtful face. "No, more a flavor of mage. One attuned to chaos over some o' the others."

"Chaos."

"Aye. What grows when warp rot is left unchallenged."

"Different from destruction?"

"Say it is a greater form of destruction. One which may cause a foundation to be lost and not rebuild at all."

I frowned. "Why wouldn't an ancient and powerful sorcerer challenge warp rot known to be North of his half-century town?"

"Good question." Osgrid shrugged. "Yer not th' only one curious what he'll do. Or not do."

"What of you? Will you do nothing as well?"

Osgrid's mouth twisted in regret. "Canno' do much alone. Which I have long been. Most times."

She winked at the blushing male Dwarf.

"But are you a mystic?" I asked. "Or a mage?"

"Suppose. I am not powerful compared to some."

"Would you look inside Gavin's pack, and tell me what you see?" I asked. "I only know the Ma'ab are interested what is inside."

Rithal looked expectantly at Osgrid. He wanted her to look as well, but she exhaled, hesitant.

"Have ye looked already?"

"No."

"An' what have they done wit' 'is body?"

"It's…" I paused, inexplicably nervous. "In a shed, lying on a table with the silver dagger in his chest. Or it was at dawn, and Brom still did not want to look at it or remove the dagger."

Rithal vouched for that. "He warned us not to when we first moved the body."

Osgrid hummed, pale blue eyes again rising to her crow, who clacked its beak and made a *tok-tok* sound. Her black curls bounced with a nod. "Aye, I'll look. Take items out one at a time and lay them on the table. Rithal, move me gift 'shrooms, please."

As he did, I pushed my bench backward to make room for the pack on my lap and worked at the knots. They were strong but I got them loosened in time and began unloading. After observing how Gavin had spent his evenings for many days, nothing was new for me. Surgery kit, belt of spices, pouches of what felt like odd bits for components, needles and threads of many sorts, a carefully wrapped stylus and jar of ink, his grimoire, several pieces of bone, most of them carved with symbols but a few were plain.

If I had expected to find some relic of power or valuable secret to explain Brom's hesitancy with Gavin's body, or Amelda's contemptuous plotting, there was nothing Rithal and I hadn't seen before. Wouldn't that be disappointing to the Ma'ab?

Osgrid frowned, leaned forward in her chair, then stood up to get a closer look at the spread on her table. Like any mage I knew, she reached for the book, first, gently touching the chestnut leather, testing with her fingertips before picking it up. She was extraordinarily careful as she untied the leather knot keeping it closed and lifted the cover, turning through a few pages. Now that she was standing, I noticed Rithal's eyes drifting over her, lingering on her broad hips and enormous breasts beneath her robe. I suppressed a smile.

"I cannae read this," she said. "He's used a cypher. Not unusual fer a mage persecuted. Some o' his sketches an' diagrams are...interestin'."

"May I see?" I asked, slowly standing up, and Rithal did as well.

Osgrid motioned us both over. I did wonder how curious Rithal was, or if he was being careful with an armed Elf standing next to his companion. Either way, I peered over her shoulder, able to see well enough in the dim light, and I noticed neither of them needed a brighter source, either.

The first three drawings were anatomical ones, something I fully expected as he made early notes on dissection. There were a few old blood smears on the pages. Other sketches farther in were abstract and without any letters, cypher or not. I didn't know what I was looking at, could not tell if I should feel unsettled.

"Honest, 'tis what I would expect of a Vis-seer," she said. "My guess, he is not fearin' the ghosts anymore at this point. He seein' something like ye or me would painting a lake. It just exists."

Then she turned the page, and I flinched and heard Osgrid gasp.

"Whew. 'K, tha' is creepy," she murmured.

It was. It looked much like the grinning shadow thing which had been floating above him at the tower. A wave of chill prickled across my skin. *He's seen it before.*

"A nightmare?" Rithal asked.

"Maybe."

I didn't enlighten them as Osgrid turned the pages past that one, and we saw continued anatomical drawings and so much text jumbled past the difficulty of my not knowing the language it was based on.

"Purposeful nonsense," Rithal agreed.

"I am somehow reassured," Osgrid murmured, "we're nae seein' trophy entries."

"What?" I asked.

"Bits o' victims preserved against the pages," she explained, "or writing formed wit' blood as the ink. Drawings o' fetishes, symbols o' fear and murder."

I considered my question to him before, after poisoning his father and the monastery: *I am interested if you discovered a taste for it. Like Sarilis.*

Gavin had claimed not but could have lied. Osgrid's interpretation of his book seemed to support he was telling the truth, though I wondered about some comparison to a similar tome made by his former master.

Toward the end, there were only a few abstract drawings of some form which did not seem of this land. There was also a pale, expressionless face with empty, black eyes and a crack along the temple, as if it were brittle.

"Hm," Osgrid said. "A woman's mask."

*Woman.* I considered Gavin's last words before he was stabbed, rubbing my fingers through my gloves.

"What if," I began slowly, "he told the Witch Hunters, as a defiance, that they would 'see her in the end,' all of them? But he refused to name her when they made the demand?"

The dark-haired Dwarf turned her eyes from the book to me. "Oh?"

"Yes. And he *did* claim to have a...patroness before then. He spoke in a strange tongue sometimes, in his sleep or when he did corpse magic. Also right before he died."

Rithal's brows were high. "Mm. Ye been gettin' along better than I realized."

I made a face. "He was helpful."

*And interesting.*

"Ah. Hm. Awright, then."

I could not read her expression well enough to tell if she was worried by this or not.

"Wha'tis th' reason Brom gives fer his warnin', not removin' the dagger?"

"That there is ritual magic clinging to it," I said, "and he does not know whose ritual it is. He said it could be nothing, a pathway closes, or he said something else could come back and claim the body."

Osgrid closed the book and wrapped the leather ties around to knot it closed again. She set it down gently before folding her arms beneath her large breasts. "Well. He's not wrong 'bout that."

"Could it be Gavin's ritual?" I asked.

"Could be, can't promise," she admitted. "Any ritual can go awry."

Didn't I know this too well?

"Whose else could it be?" I pressed. "The Witch Hunters?"

Osgrid looked to Rithal for insight there. He shrugged and said, "Don' know this Bictrius name, an' the stuff was typical enough when I rooted around."

I watched him for any sign of evasion, though the most I saw was a suppression of anger and a lifted nostril of contempt, but he remained focused on the question.

"If he were capable o' soul-spell stuff mid-skirmish," the Dwarf finished, "that rep hasn' followed 'im."

"Ye said Gavin was speaking a tongue before he died," said the eve witch to me. "An' bein' defiant. Did they try a ritual on 'im that ye could tell?"

I shook my head. "I do not know. They were shouting. Bictrius drew and raised the dagger. I shot him with a poisoned bolt. His second, Thetri Jacob, picked it up and stabbed Gavin, instead."

"Thetri is the only prisoner alive," Rithal added.

"Gavin said Jacob has a mage aura," I offered.

"Hm. Curious." Osgrid looked down at Gavin's possessions on her table. "Most likely Gavin did attempt somethin'. Don' know if Jacob disrupted it, but my lil' bird tells me ye should go tah that body an' see what ye can see."

"What do you mean?" I asked. "What am I looking for?"

"I dunno. But yer monk was keen on precision." She poked a thick finger at his book. "An' was a mystic, seein' flickerin's o' chaos at th' same time. If he warned ye 'bout the warp rot here when he usually don' say much, I'd not leave tah chance what others do wit' 'is body."

The foreboding dragged itself up my spine, intense enough to make me shiver. I exhaled in annoyance. "Well done. But what would you *do*?"

"Again, dunno." Osgrid looked at her crow, who looked back. "Also don' worry. Scales are tipped. This place won't last, an' I must think tah leave."

That was what Brom had said, too.

Rithal exhaled morosely as I stepped away to repack Gavin's bag, replacing items in the same order I'd taken them out. The dark-haired female watched me placidly, eyes memorizing my details while she could, though she exhibited no regrets for having me leave.

"Why did you come from however far ye did?" she asked. "Ye don' give a rat's balls about Manalar, though I see the warp rot is of concern. Who are ye lookin' for?"

Who? How did she know? And who was I looking for? My Sisters, but not directly, no matter how I struggled. I searched for the Sathoet with the Ma'ab. The Priestess, her fate unknown.

*What of the bua with gold eyes behind iron bars?*

The compulsion to seek stories of our blood, of Davrin origin, which I feared I'd plunged right into simply sleeping in Brom's quarters, before he plunged into me.

My stomach trembled with nerves. *I can't speak.*

The geas had not gripped me to sickness in some time, not since the canyon and drugging Kurn. I had thought it was because I had no strong leads on the Priestess and her Son, and I'd been too concerned with Brom and his town to think about it.

I shook my head. and Osgrid accepted my silence.

"What o' th' sorcerer, then?" she asked. "Ye knew he was old. Were ye lookin' fer 'im?"

"No," I could say. "It was a surprise. What alliance has he with the Ma'ab? To have a daughter by one of their Nobles."

She answered without pause. "Relic huntin', at least."

"What?"

"He settled here after he an' the Ma'ab dug up somethin' Dwarf kin would keep buried. I'm watchin' fer signs o' it."

Foreboding clung to my back, and I exhaled. "A black dagger?"

"Ah, *shcitze*," she cursed, nodding. "Red runes?" Her voice went a little high as I nodded. "He showed it tah ye? Why?"

I swallowed. "It has history with Dark Elves. He said it helps him remember us."

"Yer kind made it?" She sounded accusatory.

"I don't know," I said. "He said it was a gift *to* one of us, that he reclaimed after she died. I know not where he obtained it if it's true."

Osgrid's mouth was hanging open in shock. "Did he draw it?"

I shook my head. "No."

"Tis worse than death if he does, Sirana. He makes tah unsheathe it, run an' don't stop, nah matter what he says."

She could not sound more dire, and my knees felt weak as I slung Gavin's pack onto my shoulder. "And what will you do if he does, Osgrid, watching alone as you are?"

"I know folk," she said cryptically. "Wasn't sure he kept it here till now."

"Glad for the trade," I said awkwardly. "I should go."

"Aye, Elf. Ye should."

"I'll come along," Rithal offered.

"I plan to run all the way to the shed." I smiled tightly. "Not sure you can keep up."

He grunted, nodding into his beard. "Nay, but I can meetcha there."

"Very well. I'll leave you to your farewell."

I picked up Gavin's spade at the door and let myself out of the eve witch's dwelling.

It was early afternoon as I jogged swiftly through the trees carrying the spade, ignoring my aching, empty belly to the best of my ability. I saw a crow flying above me for a while, but it didn't follow me all the way to the bridge.

*The bridge. Fuck!*

I didn't have a disguise this time to simply walk across, and Kivin could recognize Gavin's pack and spade carried by the red-haired boy to whom he'd given directions and offered a job. My hood was up and pinned in place from the last time I slowed to catch my breath, but the nearer I got to the men's bridge, the sooner I must decide: sprint or swim?

It didn't take long. I couldn't potentially ruin Gavin's book, and I didn't know how deep or swift this river was, so the bridge it must be. If it were too dangerous, I would have to wait for Rithal.

I stopped inside cover to ease forward and observe the bridge before running out onto it. Donning my sun-blind, I scanned and listened around me for sentries or anyone set to wait for me, since they must know where I'd gone. Heart pounding in my ears, I slowed and deepened my breath for greater control.

Men worked farther downstream but might need to use the bridge at any time. There weren't any posted guards, though I did notice one bored horse watcher stepping toward a tree to relieve his bladder. It wasn't Kivin.

*Now.*

I sprinted out into the open on my "ghost" feet, the light pats of my boots barely rising above the burble of flowing water. I made straight for the nearest bush-cover, reaching it before the young man facing away could shake his member and tuck it away.

*Keep going. To the shed.*

I turned North to circle around the town to the inn, knowing I would be exhausted and famished after this final wind. It wasn't any worse than what Rausery had put us through our first night on the Surface. Well, maybe a little worse, as the hunger-nausea happened too quickly, now, and I had left my pack with the travel mix at the inn. I should have asked Osgrid for a bite.

Sighing at the distraction, I slowed to a sustainable jog, stepping light on the firmest ground. I smelled the food being cooked, the residual char of last night's fires, the horse and Human dung. I spotted more animals than I realized had been here, not just chickens but dogs and cats exploring damaged areas for anything interesting or edible. I related to the impulse. There were crows as well, to be expected with carcasses around, though they were mostly making noise in the trees above.

I approached the soundproofed shed from the rear first, listening for anything at all. To my instant displeasure, a feminine voice with a familiar noble quality floated out from an open door.

Then Castis answered.

*Fuuuck.*

I quickly stepped forward, following the wall on the far side from the nearest road, and peeked around the corner. Amelda was entirely inside while Castis was barring the way. A warm man-scent wafted out, thick enough to suggest the door was only recently opened. I looked for either Kurn or Brom but did not see them yet. The next words spoken were as clear as the day.

"Don't touch it, witch!" a man gasped. "You! Tell her not to touch it *pi'domini sancti!*"

"How long will this take?" Mathias sighed in an odd tone of annoyed amusement. "And, yeah, the governor explicitly said, don't pull. Where is he, anyway?"

"Searching for the black witch with Kurn," Amelda said in her heavy accent, sounding distracted and disgusted. I wagered she must be close to Gavin, peering at him.

"We can help you remove the corpse," Castis offered, sniffing the air. "It cannot be helping your concentration."

"On the contrary," Mathias replied with a grin in his voice. "It's very useful."

*"Ma'ab brujix!"* Jacob spewed. *"Teu digos derreteran tocha sancti reliqshe!"*

Amelda laughed. "It's not a 'holy' relic, ignorant fool. Just a dagger. You have not *seen* true relics as I have. I shall touch it if I please."

The Witch Hunter's voice careened higher in threat as I presumed that she moved to do so. Was she touching it to prove her point, or did she intend to pull it out? I didn't wait to find out by listening.

I stepped in silence up to Castis, staring at him until he could wrench his focus from inside the shed to me approaching in his periphery. He recognized me and jumped in surprise. "Sirana!"

I shoved him hard, forcing him fully inside and out of my way to step in and close the door to the shed. Ripping off my sunblind as it went dim, I could tell by all their expressions that they were blind for the moment. I took advantage to step in between Gavin's body and Brom's daughter, shoving her backward using the handle of the spade as a bar.

"You!" Amelda snarled, stumbling to regain her feet. I noted Castis didn't dive to catch her, maybe because he couldn't see.

I brandished the long spade and prepared to draw a pinch of sleep powder for good measure. Neither mage rushed me or lifted their hands.

"Welcome back, Red Sister," Mathias said wryly, as his single lantern on the small table helped the others to see.

Jacob's voice filled the room, making my ears ring. "The demoness! Bleed black guts between your legs!"

My mouth tightened at that curse striking too close to truth, though my blood was red as any other. I watched as the dark-haired man scrambled up to his knees, hands bound behind his back with rope. His deeply tanned body was shirtless and bootless, the rope anchored to the opposite wall where I'd last seen him unconscious.

"You murder my *Warrante!*" he bellowed.

"And you 'murder' my death mage," I replied.

"Yours?" Amelda asked with a small laugh.

"Mm-hm. Ask Castis how Gavin left him impotent and me unscathed."

"You—" the Ma'ab noble began.

Jacob shouted over us. "That Ma'ab heretic was foul! Horrid sins of the darkest magic of the North must be cleansed!"

"He wasn't ours, but yours!" Castis barked back. "Tainted by your god!"

The Witch Hunter laughed and spat again on the hay covering his corner, jerking his chin. "Purified! The black rot seeps out of him even now!"

*What? Black rot?*

"Yeahhh, about that," Mathias began, giving Jacob a kick in the gut to take his wind.

"What is it?" I asked to the man gasping but quiet.

"I was looking to see when you closed the door!" Amelda flung her hand toward the corpse like an untidy mess which irked her.

*Shit. Something changed?*

I turned slowly, my back to the wall and the spade at the ready. Lowering into a partial crouch, I peered at the lethal blow again. Amelda hissed something under her breath in Ma'ab, but if it wasn't a spell, I ignored her.

*Let it not be warp rot, somehow.*

I didn't know what the signs were, or how it spread. Last night, there had been a small amount of blood which had welled up in his chest as we moved him onto this table last night. Today, this had turned from red to black and appeared viscous like tar. The tiny sliver of the dagger's blade I could see in his chest bone was...

*Tarnished.*

How fast did silver tarnish when exposed to air and water? I didn't know, but surely not this fast.

"Clearly, you have no learning in this," Amelda remarked. "This is at least touched by our domain. Let me see."

Her face became a Priestess of Braqth in my mind, hearing her speak. I glanced at the pale woman. "You're not a death mage."

"I am Ma'ab," she said proudly.

*And half-Zauyrian sorcerer.* I did find it interesting that she insisted on studying Gavin rather than running to tell her sire, who was supposedly looking for me. I glanced at Castis, then, and caught him trying to open the door.

If anyone would tell on me, it would be him.

"No!" I barked, swinging the spade at his head. He ducked, and it struck the metal ring on the door, chiming as it kept it closed.

"How dare you?!" he snarled, backing up closer to Mathias as if for protection.

"You'll not run to tell your sleep-rutting hound where I am!"

The skin hunter snickered as Castis's face flushed an odd dark pink, and I wondered about Kurn's accusation before I ran to find Rithal in the woods.

*You probe our minds with your wanton, Abyssal claws.*

The chiming sound continued as Castis watched me warily, settling deep in my ears where it refused to fade. My vision blurred briefly, and I shook my head and blinked, trying to clear it.

The sound wouldn't stop. I planted a palm over one ear. *Argh... Little ones? Guardians?*

They were quivering, agitated inside my pouch, but the chime wasn't theirs. Mathias made the same motion I had, planting a palm to the side of his face, and grimaced. The room abruptly tilted as I stumbled sideways trying not to fall over.

"Witch's spell!" Jacob blared helpfully.

Castis surged in and yanked the spade from my hands as my vision continued to swim with the unceasing ringing in my ears. Rather than wait to see if he would strike me with it, I attempted a sprint and tumble which turned into a fumble as both my palms slapped wood and I hit my head on something.

Amelda laughed.

"Whahz goin' o-on?" Mathias groaned before a heavy weight fell to the wooden floor. "S-Stop it!"

I struggled to stay conscious despite not knowing the direction of the ceiling or trusting which pouch contained my spiders. I couldn't hear them, and the first three pouches I cupped, I wasn't sure. Like a nightmare of falling into the Abyss, I was somehow clinging vertical, my knees stuck to the sheer sides above the Void, gasping for breath.

Someone grabbed my shoulders, everything blurred as I took a shot with my fist. I missed and hit hard wood again. I kicked out, hit nothing but air.

"Get the pack!"

"A moment, will you?"

I struggled harder as my arms were drawn behind me; Castis was pulling off Gavin's pack. I panicked and twisted to slip out quicker, giving it up rather than have my arms bound like the Witch Hunter.

"Bring it here!"

When I fell again, I closed my eyes, trying to still the nausea of a world turned upside down. I sniffed hay and Human sweat, realized I was closer to Jacob than I'd intended. His bare heels were digging into the straw near my head.

*"G-guerrimos forche!"* he moaned, sounding as sick as me before it became a stubborn chant. *"Cansio malvad limbia, guerrimos sollix, en noctri forche sollix!"*

"Here it is!" Amelda said triumphantly. "My father will need this."

I cracked an eye open, able to make out a hazy image of the Ma'ab woman going through Gavin's things. Of course, she had the book. Jacob continued to chant and realized it was *his* doing; he was countering the sound-spell which had upended all our sense of balance. Mathias was too far away to be aided, but I had a few instants to decide what to do.

I chose when Castis picked up the spade again.

Scrambling along the wall, I slid behind Jacob and drew a dagger, cutting the ropes around his wrists.

"Run, god warrior!" I hissed in my most menacing voice. *"Run!!"*

The Manalari scrambled onto his bare feet and threw himself at Amelda while I rolled up and launched myself at an open-mouthed Castis.

"No, get back!" the sorcerer's daughter shrieked.

"Amelda!"

Castis reached desperately for his belt, willing to take us all down with a thunderstone. I grabbed the spade with both hands and wrenched it toward me; he stubbornly held on, his questing hand leaving his belt to secure a two-handed hold on the weapon. We grabbled for control of it.

*Perfect.*

I lifted our arms up and swung my leg, slamming my shin into the soft bits between his legs. Dark, Ma'ab eyes bugged out, a silent mouth opened, and with a twist and sidekick, my boot struck his gut. Finally, he released Gavin's spade and fell to the floor, keening as he curled up. It was only then I absorbed Amelda was screeching in Ma'ab and Jacob braying in Manalari as they—

I looked.

As they fought over the Chief Warrant's dagger in Gavin's chest.

*Fuck.*

Amelda was scratching and clawing at the Witch Hunter's wrists to pull his hands away. Jacob ignored the bleeding and viciously stomped her foot. Even lacking boots he made her jerk and sink in pain as he finally shoved her to the side.

"Hey, wait!" Mathias called, getting up from the floor. "No, Jacob, don't!"

The first pull failed to free the dagger, which was caught on bone as it had been for me, and Mathias tackled his prisoner the next moment. Having the strength to weigh him down, the skin hunter pressed him forward onto the corpse and kept the dagger in place as the Manalari began to shriek in such terror that I winced.

*"Sancre nigra, faimi toc sancre nigra!"* Jacob yelled, pitching his head back and catching the skin hunter in the eye as he turned his head.

"Argh, fuck!"

The second heel-stomp wasn't as effective on Mathias's tough boots as it had been on Amelda's thin summer shoes, but it gave Jacob an opening to throw them both from the corpse table, nearly taking the dagger with them as they toppled onto the floor and wrestled further.

The temperature dropped in the warm, close space. The silver dagger was partway out, and the hairs raised up on my neck as I saw a bluish, sunken eyelid twitch and shift, like an eye was rolling beneath it. More of that viscous fluid appeared out of the wound as if an organ inside had squeezed it out.

*Corpses don't bleed.*

Gasping and shaking with rage, Amelda grasped the edge of the table to pull herself up and beside Gavin's body again, having lost his grimoire somewhere in the struggle. She saw what I did but much closer and gasped in horror, reaching out to push the blade back into place with a firm, pale hand.

The air remained chilled, familiar, like at the canyon when he defended me, and the black flow bubbling up around the silver did not stop.

"Castis!" she cried. "Where is the spade—?"

She turned to see me standing between her and her ally, him useless on the ground rocking his genitals.

"What would you do with it?" I asked neutrally, lifting the weapon as if in offering.

"Cut off the head." Urgently, she reached out to me, beckoned. "A path is open somewhere. Quick, give me the spade!"

Gavin's eyes rolled beneath his lids, and his long fingers twitched, as if something claimed the body. Brom had said we had no way of knowing what this might be until it was here, looking out at us through his eyes.

I stepped closer to the small woman, holding up the spade with sharp edge smeared with blood and dirt.

"Now!" she commanded, dark eyes wide and scared. "Quickly, Sirana, we must take its head!"

*"Citis!"* Jacob cried from beneath Mathias, his face pressed sideways to the floor. *"Citis, profanis limbia!"*

He sounded to agree, though I hesitated, as the cold increased until I could feel it on an inhale. If I obeyed in this, sharing their fear, I'd never know if Gavin had attempted a ritual and succeeded. He and I knew there were other planes. So did Amelda. Either way, it would test Cris-ri-phon. He wouldn't have the option to brush this away.

*A path is open.*

I stepped forward to offer the spade to her, though my arm drifted away from the table. Amelda's eyes followed it. She never saw my other hand reach and grasp the hilt of the Witch Hunter's dagger. The Ma'ab witch tugged on the handle of the spade at the same time I wiggled and stirred the dagger, finally drawing it out of Gavin's heart.

The temperature plunged further.

"Whoa!" Mathias cried. "Sirana, what in the Hells?!"

"What have you done?!" Amelda cried.

After a final effort to claim the spade, she relinquished it the moment I pointed the tarnished blade toward her, covered in thick, black fluid. The Ma'ab noble pitched herself backward until she hit the wall, huge eyes staring.

"Don't," she whispered.

Smiling a little, I sniffed gingerly at it, thinking there would be stronger smell. There was extraordinarily little scent for where it had been.

The shed grew quiet but for Castis's mewling, as we stared at Gavin's unmoving corpse. Waiting. The air grew warmer again. The blackened bleeding had stopped.

Someone banged on the door, and we all jumped.

"Amelda!" Brom shouted. "What's going on?"

*"Fadhi!"* she cried. "Sirana removed the dagger!"

"What?!"

"Squealer," I said.

"Open the door!" Kurn demanded.

My eyes soared skyward. *Even better.*

Mathias had his hands full with wrangling Jacob to his corner, but Castis clambered to his feet to swing it open before I could stop him. Both my hands were taken up with Gavin's coveted spade and a tarnished dagger that might as well be covered in Drider venom for how the Ma'ab daughter avoided me.

I could only put a wall behind me so, spotting Gavin's book partly beneath the table the rest of his pack leaning against a wall, I chased Amelda away and claimed the wall closest to the corpse's head, my boot close to his book.

*Just in case.*

Of what, I didn't know.

Castis opened the door, sunlight streamed in, my eyes watered. It was crowded with the addition of two more men in the shed, and worse that I couldn't see beyond their outline. Heavy boots tromped in then both paused.

*"Fadhi,"* Amelda cried, "drag this *maknuut* body out in the sun this instant and burn it!"

Brom sounded surprised at her vehemence and held up his hand to stay Kurn from doing so. "Why? Nothing happened. If there was a path, it's closed now."

"Something is hiding in it!" she insisted.

"Did not know you were a death mage," I remarked.

"Do not attempt to deny this!" she sneered. "You saw it as I did! You felt it! Look at this!"

"I don't know what I saw," I countered. "Your magic turned all our senses to collapse on each other."

"Hmm," Mathias said as he finished gagging and rebinding his struggling catch. I saw how his erection strained his trousers. "She could be right, Master Brom. I don't know half what happened after Amelda cast—"

"That was to claim the pack!" she griped. "You were lying *atop* the thing, by the gods! It was over by then!"

"Stop."

The voice rasped and gurgled, mostly air but with annoyed force behind it. My guts turned to ice as the tall, laid out corpse turned his head toward me and grimaced to show black-stained teeth. Then slowly—unnaturally slow—he sat up.

Jacob started screaming through his gag and thrashing until Mathias had to knock him out again.

"Thank you," Gavin said, then coughed.

More of the black stuff bubbled up and spilled down his chin, leaking down his pale, blood-stained neck. I'd become stone in place only until Kurn moved to draw his sword. I lifted the Chief Warrant's dagger, prepared to throw it, and he could see this.

The Ma'ab paused and tried nudging the sorcerer instead. "Master Brom, we should do as your daughter says."

Oh, *now* he listened to someone with a *kus*?

"Unwise," Gavin's throat grated, as he swung long legs to hang over the side of the table, rubbing his eyes despite their being covered in dried Witch Hunter blood. "I warn you against touching me to injure. You will regret it."

"Is that a threat?" Kurn rumbled, his hand on the pommel of his sword.

"It is a warning, not a threat."

I stared at solid black eyes as he lowered his hands, amazed to hear those words again verbatim. Despite the quartz-white flesh, grotesque black streaks, and brown-red stains all over him, once he'd cleared his throat, he sounded so much like Gavin.

"Who are you?" Brom asked calmly, his arms crossed. "May we have your name?"

The dead man turned his head with an audible pop and a raised eyebrow. "Gavin. The same as when last we met."

My heart leaped as I suppressed a laugh. *Goddess, that expression.*

It was spot on. Dare I think this could be what it appeared to be? Was my ally returned somehow, not lost to me? Maybe Amelda was right and this was a trickster. A talented one that knew all his quirks, giving me what I wished for.

"Mm-hm," Brom said with skepticism. "And who am I?"

"You are many, sorcerer, but you introduced yourself as Brom Troshin, innkeeper and governor of Troshin Bend."

He paused. "Where did you travel, Gavin?"

The lanky man paused, his filthy black hair falling forward in matted strands. I watched as shining, pale blue appeared in his black eyes, first as a pinprick but soon to spill outward and fill in his irises, confirming that he focused on Brom.

"The Nexus," he answered. "Where else could an eidolon go and be given the choice to attempt the long walk back?"

# CHAPTER 11

"*HARRIK,*" AMELDA WHISPERED, SHIELDED BEHIND BROM AND Kurn. Her face appeared like she was offended by rancid meat. "*Fahdi, mafi shiro—*"

"Shh," urged her sire.

With effort, she quieted as we watched Gavin place his boots on the floor and stand upright. Unlike the rest of us in the shed, his heart was not pounding, nor was he gasping. I was keenly aware of his height looming over me when he turned unreal eyes on me, his robes torn and filthy, his skin smeared with mixed black and red fluids. I suppressed the need to piss again.

"Sirana," he said, nodding acknowledgment, pointing to the weapon which had killed him. "Have care with that dagger until I can clean it."

I unstuck my dry mouth to lick my lips. "I shall. Um. How does my aura appear now?"

Ice blue eyes lowered to my middle and drifted upward. I held my breath on whether my question had been unwise.

"Still bright," he answered in that familiar tone. "Seems well enough."

A small, shuddering breath passed out of me. For him to affirm the sex hadn't harmed my unborn was a relief, but even more so to hear him phrase it exactly as he had last evening before the Witch Hunters arrived.

*This must be the apprentice I knew.*

The pale man pointed toward the floor by my feet. "May I have my belongings returned, Sirana?"

I leaned the spade against the wall and, with one hand, collected his grimoire from where it had landed, slipped it into his pack, and cinched it up. Lifting it by the strap, I held it out to him, and he claimed it without hesitation. Amelda huffed in frustration and alarm, Kurn's heavy weight shifted in response, and Brom again urged them to silence.

In defiance, I also handed Gavin his spade. The corner of his downturned mouth twitched as he accepted.

"You, hm," Brom began, and Gavin craned his neck to look at him. "Were I to provide them, would you accept a wash basin and new clothing before we speak of your journey, Gavin?"

He shrugged. "If that aids your comfort, Deathless. It matters little to me."

Deathless. Brom paled through his illusion to hear that, though the description suited what seemed true about him. Amelda was shocked to hear it as well.

"I will assist," I said. "I want to speak with him alone, first. I must be satisfied it's him."

I met all their eyes, daring them to argue otherwise.

"Not smart, Sirana, being alone with him," Castis said, motioning toward the standing corpse as if that should be convincing enough, and it should have been.

I shrugged, lifting the silver dagger of which all were wary. Mathias made not a peep at the far side of the shed as he watched us from the floor, braced against the wall with his legs arched over the unconscious Witch Hunter.

"So be it," Cris-ri-phon said, staring at me intensely for several moments. He was not pleased, and in my experience with powerful mages, I'd made the noncompliant choice. No doubt he or his daughter would make it messy for me later.

Once Kurn no longer blocked the door with his big frame, we filed out: the Ma'ab and Brom first, then Gavin, and me last. Behind me, Mathias let out a breath he'd been holding and got up to close the door behind us without a word. Meanwhile, I chanced to spot an orange-red blotch to my left and saw Rithal spying from across the road, but he quickly ducked behind a tree. I let him be. There was too much else to worry about.

For example, the reason no one else saw the Dwarf to call him out: they were staring at Gavin.

"Great Ascended," Castis whispered, backing away behind Kurn as crows cawed overhead. "What is this?"

Blinking as we passed into direct sunlight, I squinted, focusing in front of me. The detail to jump out was that Gavin's pale hands were ash grey and darkening further as I watched. I forced my gaze up, taking one step to the side, and saw the same happening to the death mage's face.

"Gavin?" I squeaked.

"Hm?"

He sounded placid and unperturbed, though he lifted his hand to look as I pointed. His skin—his face, neck, and hands—had become as black as mine!

"Does that hurt?" I asked.

"No."

Gavin exhaled in what might have been amusement, tilting his arm straight up to let the sleeve fall back. His arm beyond his wrist had been white as before, but as soon as the sunlight struck it, the dark color of his hand spread toward his elbow, shifting grey to black.

"Mahtka raastre," Brom murmured, unsettled and disbelieving.

He watched the change but also glanced up as crows continued making their racket. The Sun was too bright for me to do the same, but Amelda confirmed by her expression that she hadn't understood her sire's words.

Seeming to ignore it all, Gavin walked toward the inn, forcing us to catch up. As we passed beneath the shade of the trees again, I was astonished to witness his skin reverse its change. Out of the direct Sun, the dark skin lightened from charcoal to ash grey to misty pale. Castis and Kurn were whispering under the curious caws of black birds.

Amelda took her sire's bicep in both her small hands. "*Fadhi?* Is it wise to bring him inside?"

The Ma'ab did not recognize what we saw, despite claiming broader knowledge of death magic. The Zauyrian recognized something, however, and this might have been the only moment I saw something akin to terror in his eyes before he closed them and put a hand to his head. It seemed the stabbing pain from when I'd stood in his office had returned.

"We shall give the grey traveler hospitality," Cris-ri-phon answered, gruff and impatient, his odd silvery eyes a lighter shade in the Sun. "Nothing has changed in this, daughter."

She drew in a deep breath. "Yes, *Fadhi.*"

"If you've decided, then," Gavin said, motioning toward the side door with his spade.

Castis shook his head but said nothing while Kurn's teeth ground; they glanced at each other. I was impressed how hesitant they were to make a remark or poke the apprentice; any jeering contempt for the *maknuut* was buried beneath pure caution for the moment.

I stayed silent as well, sticking to Gavin's side, until we could be alone.

"*Grr*, may *uroan* rut her pucker so loose, she can't hold her shit in."

The gore-covered man paused in his disrobing to turn unnatural eyes at me. "Mm. Creative."

"Amelda went through my pack," I grumbled, searching for the travel mix yet uncertain I dare eat it.

Gavin nodded. "As she went through mine. I shall check to see if anything is missing."

"She did not have much time to pocket items of yours," I told him, "though, yes, do check. She wanted your grimoire most but had no time to open it."

"Unsurprising, and good to hear. What of your items?"

He pulled the torn, filthy, and smelly robe off and over his head, dropping it on the floor. He was as pale as the night we'd arrived in the rain, and just as thin; I could still see his spine and his ribs. He kept on his braies but was again barefoot. While he washed the gore off his hands, first, my eyes lingered on black toenails.

*Those are different.*

"Mm," I began, pulling myself back. "I'm annoyed I can't eat the food. Anything irreplaceable I took with me when I climbed out."

"As did I." Gavin picked up the cloth to dip it in the first of two wash basins. Wringing it out, he briskly scraped the streaks and smears from his arms. "Though I am curious how my pack came to be beside me when I sat up. I recall throwing it away while being chased."

"Into a chicken coop, yes," I said. "Brom found it."

Gavin turned around to look at me, and my breath caught to see the inhuman eyes again. I glanced down at his chest wound; it was a disgusting mess. I chose not to wonder how he could speak so normally.

"Was the sorcerer searching for it?" he asked.

"Only because I asked him to. I got wind Castis and Kurn might want it for Amelda, so I searched first. The sorcerer didn't open it, he gave it to me."

Gavin slowly tilted his head. "Interesting."

I kept in further questions while Gavin scrubbed down his torso and did a cursory washing of his long, stringy hair. I had the chance to see the stab wound itself, which was much smaller than I'd thought, not gaping or ragged, but…shrunken. Like it had been stitched closed without needle and thread.

By this point, the water in the first basin was filthy. He dried off, donned a new long shirt to cover down to his knees, and started using the second basin after removing the braies. Like the first night we were here, Gavin avoided showing me a totally nude body. If this were a trickster claiming Gavin's body, it had taken over every old habit and might as well be the abused monk I'd met at the tower.

"Do you remember how you died?" I asked, my voice soft.

Gavin paused. "Clearly. After the Witch Hunters chased me down and beat me sufficiently, one of your bolts struck and poisoned the Chief Warrant, so the Thetri took his blade and finished the kill for him."

"Yes," I sighed.

"I warned you to hide. That was not hiding."

I pursed my lips. "I survived."

*We survived.*

"And they didn't," I finished.

Gavin grunted, replacing the cloth into the less mucky basin, donning new braies, a drab brown-grey robe, stockings, and his original boots while I considered whether to describe the chase and skirmish that followed. How close it had been, how much help I'd needed, and I didn't know where all of it had come from. Gavin needed to know once I could decide how to describe it.

"How much time has passed?" he asked, picking up the silver dagger which had killed him, placing it in the water, then meticulously searching through his belt which I'd stuffed into his pack.

I blinked. "Not a full day. The attacks were last night."

"Mm. Interesting."

The silence was pregnant as I was as I watched him remove a small jar of powder and add it to both basins, whispering something which sent a shiver up my spine. I stood up to see better. The water wasn't clean as one might expect from dirty bath water, but there was no more black or grey tinge, and the Chief Warrant's dagger shone silver again without tarnish.

Gavin removed the naked blade and wiped it dry, setting it aside as he would any other tool, then went through his pack thoroughly, especially his surgery and writing supplies. As he selected his grimoire, stylus, and ink jar, Osgrid's remark about his focus on precision returned to me.

"How much time passed for you, 'traveler'?" I asked. "And where is the Nexus?"

He sat at the table, and I noticed his clean fingernails were black like his toenails. His teeth hadn't only been stained by the black blood—they *were* black, now. Perhaps it was a good thing he didn't smile often.

Pale blue eyes floating in inky black glanced over at me. "Neither of those can be answered in the same context, but...I traveled the Greylands for longer than a day, though asking 'where' is like asking your Priestess to draw a map to the Abyssal plane."

*Point taken.*

"The Greylands?" I asked.

"The aspect of the Nexus recognized on this plane as the land of the dead. Albeit more complicated than that, I discovered."

*Keen on precision, indeed.* I sighed. "You are Gavin, for certain."

"I am. Be assured." His stylus scratched against the pulpy pages. "I thank you for pulling the dagger free. I take it you did not know what would happen."

"No," I admitted. "What did happen?"

"You removed the most disruptive element obstructing my path back."

"And there were dire warnings against doing that."

He took notes.

"Did you plan it?"

His stylus paused as he frowned in thought. "I had been for a while but delayed following through for some time."

"Why?"

"Fear of the pain before death, I suppose. Though pushed to violence, I thought I failed."

I squinted. "Failed?"

Gavin looked at the Witch Hunter's dagger but said did not elaborate. "We are being listened to. Do you wish to continue this conversation?"

Of course we were. I hadn't said anything truly secret before now, but he was right, this was a good place to stop. The rest wouldn't wait much longer before someone came to the door, though I didn't know what would happen next. So much had gone askew and was yet unexplained, and I'd been anchorless before last night. Most answers I'd sought only led me down a deeper path of unknown questions.

"You said you chose a 'long walk back,'" I murmured. "Have you any purpose for doing so?"

"Of course," he answered. "Many."

"Tell me one," I challenged. "The first."

Gavin laid down the stylus and gave me his full attention. I realized then I had not seen him blink since opening his eyes in the shed.

"The first," he accepted. "I shall help with the warp rot, as a start. Let me finish a few notes, and we shall seek the sorcerer before he calls."

*Bold.* I liked it better than waiting for another fist on the door.

Nodding, I checked to make sure my guardians were awake and well. When Gavin was ready, I stood up. "I'll take you to his office. Maybe he'll show you his other face."

Gavin proved capable enough of stealth and speed as we slipped out of the room and left the door open, taking everything with us. I had to slow myself lest I rush his heavier weight on the wooden boards, but our hoods were up, and the front room of the tavern was empty of guests. Everyone was taking the day outside.

The stairs creaked beneath Gavin's boots before we touched the landing, but I did not stop, turning right and looping to head past the kitchen and deeper into the rear offices. As I anticipated, Amelda was waiting in the small alcove, guarding her sire's door.

*"Harrik,"* she said, straightening up in a rush. She wasn't surprised to see us but taken off guard how abruptly we appeared.

She reached into a pocket. I'd had enough of that.

I seized that reaching wrist and pinned the rest of her to the wall, my forearm jammed roughly into her throat. Her eyes bugged and a squeak escaped her lips; her hand lost its target. I tested a pressure point beneath her arm that would render any unprepared Davrin helpless with pains lancing through their back without cease.

Amelda's face proved it worked on Ma'ab Humans. She began to quiver in my hold, grimacing as I grinned, turning my forearm to grip her throat with my hand. For a few quiet moments, dark eyes stared at me as I constricted new blood from entering her head, then they rolled upward. Her small, quaking form slumped and went limp; I caught her and laid her down.

"Hm," Gavin remarked.

I couldn't tell if he was impressed or pleased at all, but it didn't matter.

"We have a handful of minutes," I murmured, softly rapping my knuckles against Brom's door to see if he responded.

Nothing. I couldn't hear if he were inside. Should I call? I didn't want to in case it drew Kurn and Castis next.

Gavin pointed a long, white finger at a carved inlay on the right at about shoulder height. "Lay your palm on this. It allows a message through a ward."

*Ah. That explains it.*

I removed my glove and pressed skin against it, recognizing a magical sensation enhancing my senses, not unlike the runes I'd touched as a novice under Jaunda's tutelage, and Feldeu, in the Sanctuary's spyways.

*⋆Yes?⋆* answered the tired sorcerer.

Although Amelda had needed to speak aloud to answer, I discovered my focus well prepared to answer in silence. *⋆It's Sirana. I'm with Gavin. Let us in, Cris-ri-phon.⋆*

The long pause suggested hesitation.

*⋆Where is Amelda?⋆*

*⋆Asleep by your door. She will be well.⋆*

I heard a dry chuckle. *⋆Little fighter shows her fangs again?⋆*

*⋆You haven't seen my full effort.⋆*

*⋆Neither have you seen mine.⋆*

No doubt. I swallowed. *⋆You have seen something like Gavin before. You haven't finished with me. Let us in before your daughter wakes unless you want her to bear witness to tell her matrons.⋆*

The sorcerer sighed in acquiescence, suspending the ward. I removed my hand from the sigil, and he opened the door, wearing the younger, paler face still. Wordless, he motioned us in, closing the door and leaving Amelda unconscious in the alcove, though not without a moment's hesitation.

As the sorcerer reset his ward, I watched Gavin and where his unearthly eyes looked within the office. It did not take long for him to pause on the shelves which had held both the firebird ring and the box containing the black dagger. Fortunately, his gaze didn't linger on the desk where I'd invited the sorcerer's pole early this morning.

My death mage said nothing as the "Deathless" joined us in the center space of his office, allowing the illusion to fade without my having to ask. The white-haired, dark-skinned Zauyrian watched Gavin for a reaction, though there was none.

"I take it she's told you?" he asked.

"Told me what?" Gavin responded.

"You're not surprised at what you see."

"On the contrary," he replied, "though I was given warning you possessed a wizened form."

The older man's white eyebrow arched sardonically. "Do you know my name?"

"Beyond that you've offered me directly, no."

Cris-ri-phon glanced suspiciously at me, and I shrugged.

"He's been dead half the time we've been here. There's been no time to gossip about your past."

His smile was a reluctant one. "Heh. Very well." The Zauyrian paused. "Are you hungry?"

I looked elsewhere, thinking about chewing wood.

"I would accept a meal, thank you."

We both stared at Gavin, astonished, but our host followed through. Brom had a fair amount of bread, fruits, greens, cheese, and wine brought from the kitchen earlier, for he carried it out of his sleeping alcove to the table, divvying it into three on separate plates. He poured wine for himself and water for me without asking.

I dug in as I had before, watching Gavin curiously as the pale man chose a small piece of bread to tear off a bit and place it in his mouth. He chewed slowly and did not appear to relish flavor or texture, but he swallowed it and kept it down. Meanwhile, I'd already consumed half my share.

Cris-ri-phon was staring in silence, watching as Gavin next selected a single red berry, chewing and swallowing that slowly, then following that with a crunchy, green vegetable, and finally, a piece of cheese. Neither pleasure nor disgust passed over his face.

*"Hmph,"* the sorcerer grunted, shaking his head. "Wine?"

"No, thank you," Gavin answered, pushing his plate toward me with one finger. "You may have the rest if you want it, Sirana."

I paused for a breath then tugged it closer. "I do, thank you."

Our host narrowed grey eyes at me for a moment but could not neglect Gavin's unblinking gaze for long. My death mage chose not to fill the tense silence, and I could see the Zauyrian struggle with what he might say first, what was rising to the top that he most wanted to know. Given I could not guess, I followed Gavin's lead and kept my mouth full of food.

Then Cris-ri-phon murmured something in a language neither of us knew. *"Tu charavahe vokar, ki vahand ujaale ke rahega, roshanee vahera bihir."*

"Sounds ancient," Gavin observed. "Scripture?"

"It is. Albeit in a dead language." Cris-ri-phon smirked and quipped, "Though not the language of the dead."

*"Risskaara ung'al,"* Gavin said.

"Indeed, there is a difference."

"May I ask the best translation of that scripture?"

The Zauyrian tapped his fingers against the arm of his chair then made his decision. "Fairly easy. 'You shall know the Walker as a light in the dark, but also the darkness in the light.'"

"Ah," Gavin said. "You recognize my calling?"

"I am not certain," said the sorcerer tightly. "I have *never* seen any of Ma'ab descent change in the Sun as you did. That was a quality of mystics of death once found in the Zauyrian Realms of the Sorcerer Kings." A heavy pause. "But they were all exterminated, and you are not from the Desert any more than *she* is."

Gavin's dark brows lifted in surprise. "Why should either of us be from the Desert?"

I paused in chewing as the sorcerer glared at me. Shrugging, I spoke out of one side of my mouth. "Witch Hunters interrupted. Never reached that part."

Cris-ri-phon exhaled slowly, tilting his head and massaging his neck with his eyes closed. "Why have you two come here? You appear to me now as ghosts, as a taunt and a curse in one. Why?"

*Chance?* I guessed, stuffing bread and cheese in at once to chew together.

"Dreams?" Gavin asked. "Visions of the mist?"

Annoyed as my mouth went too dry to swallow, I sipped water to loosen it up, and the Zauyrian laughed bitterly at the suggestion.

"If you want me to swallow that, tell me whom you serve," he commanded. "Who gave you the choice to take the 'long walk back,' eidolon, and is this figure the same both before and after your death?"

"She is the same," Gavin said. "My Lady Death goes by many names. I do not know them all."

"Name her," Cris-ri-phon insisted.

His demand was not unlike the Chief Warrant from Manalar as he and his men beat their captive, although this time, Gavin obliged.

*Sort of.*

"I stand upon the crossroads," he intoned like a riddle. "Past, present, and future are as one to me. My truth is of all time, life and death, real and unreal. I am the Grey Maiden of the Shrouds, I am—"

"The Grave Mother," Cris-ri-phon finished. "Nyx."

Gavin bowed his head without a hint of pleasure that she was recognized by someone other than him. In comparison, the Zauyrian appeared enraged before he shook his head, his expressions passing through confusion and mourning, then settling on satisfaction enough to smile. If I had blinked, I would have missed half of that jumble of emotion caused by so short a name. Like the Court and the Sanctuary for how far I dared relax around the sorcerer.

"Curious that I'd meet someone devout to her at exactly this time," Cris-ri-phon chose to say. "Though I understand why you are going to Manalar. Best not tell the Ma'ab this, however."

"Too early to say if we'll walk that path."

"What? You *are* going to Manalar to see the Ma'ab victorious, aren't you?"

"Perhaps not."

The sorcerer narrowed his eyes then groused, rubbing his face. "*Grrr*, I forgot how aggravating Deathwalkers are."

*Deathwalkers?*

I felt like young Grelio at House Itlaun, staying small and squeezed beneath a table, yet listening to it all with big ears. I also pulled the sorcerer's untouched plate toward me since he didn't want it. He glanced my way, eyebrow raised, though the frown shifted to a chuckle as he waved the food my way.

"Although," Cris-ri-phon sounded to correct himself, "while all Deathwalkers I knew followed the Maiden of Shrouds and changed color in the Sun, *none* of them had eyes like yours, nor did they bleed black, nor have teeth or fingernails like yours. You appear as if an Ascended got hold of your body."

Gavin didn't respond, and after a chilly silence, the Zauyrian shrugged. "Given how Amelda reacted to that dagger today, I will say you have a defense that the ancient Walkers did not possess."

"His blood is poisonous?" I guessed.

"Mm," our host considered. "Nothing so mundane."

My ally grunted, choosing not to elaborate and changed the topic. "Sirana did say you knew the Davrin Elves from before as well. If Deathwalkers were once part of the Zauyrian Realms, then were the Dark Elves as well?"

Cris-ri-phon tossed back his head and laughed. "Oh, no. The Davrin Queendom existed long before the Sorcerer Kings. We had to catch up to them in magic to be worthy of trade or alliance."

I spoke up. "Which was accomplished, you said. You served as the General of a combined army of Dark Elves and Zauyrians."

"Indeed," he acknowledged, the bitterness leaking in.

"A General leading an army implies a war," Gavin observed as I had.

The Deathless briefly smiled at me. "We chose a side, hoping to preserve what we'd built. Elves are their own worst enemies."

I slipped a fruit slice between my lips, and Gavin asked, "What do you mean? The war was Elves versus Elves?"

"Pale and Dark, yes. We discovered through great loss how powerful the Naulor Queen could be, though we *could* have routed them if we hadn't been betrayed on the inside at a crucial time." Cris-ri-phon swallowed more wine. "My first experience of many patterns of war, as it turned out."

"How is it that you are the only survivor of that time?" Gavin asked.

Cris-ri-phon wouldn't answer something so direct with specifics, I could tell, but he turned it over, nonetheless, staring at Gavin's ice-black eyes with defiance.

"I had two paths to walk as one mage born," he said. "I can tell you it is impossible to bear both at once, and swinging wildly between the two also leads to madness. I could have chosen to be a Deathwalker. I almost did."

*Then he saw his qu'eesan naked beneath the waterfall.*

I brought my water cup to my lips to help hide my face as a flash of arousal darted through my gut.

"What was the other calling?" Gavin asked.

Cris-ri-phon smiled without showing teeth; no joy reached his grey eyes. "Life. Fertility. An understanding of such that it was the pinnacle of Zauyrian magical discovery that allowed the alliance with the Davrin Queen to happen. When the time came, and my life was at its end, I took for myself the 'long walk back,' eidolon, confronting death to try again at life."

He paused. "So, you see, I wasn't a survivor. I merely sought and found the impossible, the rent in the border of transition. And the Ma'ab would one day thank me for that."

*What does that mean?*

Oblique as that was, I watched for any sign of displeasure or accusation from Gavin. Neutrally, he said, "Indeed, and your discovery would lead my mother to be born in the North, where one day she found the monastery where my father lived in the South."

The man was surprised to hear that. "Your *mother* was Ma'ab."

"She was. A death mage, and she died giving birth."

"That is not...unusual, though I am sorry to hear."

"I doubt she would have lived long afterward," Gavin said blandly. "That she was pregnant at all may have been his reason for hiding her from Witch Hunters."

The Zauyrian agreed. "You are of two paths, then?"

"No," Gavin said. "One. But it's of interest to me that you observe the mixed heritage in me."

"So it appears," Cris-ri-phon granted, taking a cautious sip of wine.

"Do the Ma'ab call you the Deathless?" I asked, and the sorcerer jumped, apparently tense.

He wiped his mouth with the back of his dark brown hand. "Yes. I'm known in Ennikar within certain circles as the Deathless, by reputation if not by appearance."

"So, you've allied with them, too? As you once did the Davrin?"

His eye twitched like he had another headache. "I suppose I have."

"Have," I pressed, "and do so now. You want the Ma'ab to conquer Manalar."

"I *want* the Temple heart freed of the Bishops," he retorted with a hint of a snarl. "The same as Sarilis. The same as the Ascended. The same as the Guild, and others aware of the change in the Ley Lines since they took over Mount Sonai."

*The Guild?*

Cris-ri-phon motioned to Gavin. "And now the Grey Maiden, whose worship was the first change viciously *eradicated* from the Ley site, touches a Walker on a mission to go there." He looked away from me to my ally. "And you say, 'perhaps not'?"

Gavin still hadn't blinked, as far as I knew. Did his eyes no longer dry out?

"I will go if the warp rot is eradicated, first," he said.

The Zauyrian slumped with a long sigh. "I walked into this. Do what you will, then, Walker."

I jumped on that. "Surely you're powerful enough to help. Are you afraid?"

Cris-ri-phon tilted his head toward me playfully. "I promise you, little fighter, that's not the path to persuading me. But you may try."

I lifted my eyes upward. "Why do you need to be 'persuaded'?"

He took a drink, peering at nothing across the room. I grumbled but consoled myself that Gavin had explicitly said he would go North with me, which was a complete reversal from the night before he'd died.

*Longer than a day in the Nexus.*

Some unknown time spent answering a calling to the Grey Maiden, about whom he was finally willing to speak. Gavin certainly acted like he'd been given more time to gather his wits after he died than I had, and Cris-ri-phon had validated… *everything.*

"Do you care to persuade him, Sirana?" Gavin asked. "We could simply leave to go North, return to meet up with Rithal and Mathias later. And Kurn and Castis may decide their next move without us distracting."

I caught the look in Cris-ri-phon's eyes, though my death mage was focused on me as he spoke. My middle felt deeply chilled though I kept my face straight. Gavin didn't realize neither the Ma'ab nor the Zauyrian would let me go my way so easily.

I smiled. "I care to try, yes. We should stay another day or two, at least."

Cris-ri-phon's shoulders lowered, and Gavin's rose as he shrugged.

"Very well," he said. "I should check on my mare in that time."
He looked to our host. "And I am curious, were all the Witch
Hunters killed?"

"Except Thetri Jacob for Mathias to play with," the sorcerer
answered, "yes."

"Where are the bodies?"

"We began burying them this morning. The men are almost
finished."

"Will you show me where? I'd prefer to see any not yet buried
first."

"Why? They're not all together."

"That is fine."

"They've all been looted as well."

Gavin tilted his head. "You could have been a Deathwalker, and
you ask what value could remain with a corpse besides trinkets?"

"Heh. Well put." Cris-ri-phon looked at me. "Would you like to
come, Sirana? You ran off this morning before we could speak
much. You'll have a chance to... persuade me this evening, I'll see
to it."

I squinted at the pause, and he smiled wider. The memory of his
weight on my back returned, of his penetration. I needed to steady
my breath as next came the intense sensations of his wet cock
sheathed inside me, in my cunt and my ass, for moments both glo-
rious and terrifying.

*Two paths to walk as one mage born, life and death.*

Of course he would want to fuck again.

"Certainly, I will come see the graves," I answered, standing up
having eaten all the food. "I'm curious to hear anything Gavin dis-
covers."

Once again, Cris became Brom in appearance as well as behavior, and he left his quarters first, taking time to reassure, hush, and guide Amelda away from the door while Gavin and I waited out of sight. I could hear the fast speech in Ma'ab, her tone conveying her shock and displeasure at being sent away again.

*"Harrik,"* Gavin murmured.

"Hm?" I prompted. We'd heard it a few times now.

"Against the First. Like a sin, but specific and offensive to the Ebon Flame."

I arched my brow. "You understand her words, now?"

"Castis was correct," Gavin replied. "I decided I should learn Ma'ab. I had time."

"And someone in the Greylands knew the language?"

"The Ma'ab language originated in the Greylands."

I was shocked to silence, and we listened as father and daughter argued farther down the hall.

Finally, I whispered, *"Harrik* doesn't sound negotiable."

"Indeed not. It's an adversary unforgotten."

"What do we do, then? You want her telling her matron in Ennikar you exist?"

"What is your suggestion?" Gavin replied placidly. "Assassinate her in her father's home? What of Kurn and Castis? Should we let them leave to tell tales of you or me outside Troshin Bend?"

That thought had crossed my mind before, especially after the fight in the canyon when Gavin uncovered his knowing of my pregnancy. Yet I knew why the Hellhound and the mage expressed admiration for the "innkeeper" with Sarilis. I could not ignore the threads held by this man, linking dreams of a Davrin Queen in the Desert to the Ma'ab who had stolen our Priestess. I did not see how I could kill Amelda and the aggravating Ma'ab and be assured no worse consequence or retribution would follow me.

"I do not know," I admitted. "I don't know enough of Cris-riphon."

"Who?"

"The deathless sorcerer."

"Ah."

Brom returned to the open door without his daughter but carrying an earthenware jug, tersely tossing his jaw toward the hall. "Come."

Wordlessly and each with our hoods up, Gavin and I followed him out the front door of the inn and down the wide porch steps first to the barn, entering through the rear way I had earlier. Neal was present, rustling around inside of a stall along with the stamping and clopping of random hooves before poking his head out.

"Master Brom!" he exclaimed, semi-articulate for this man's name, at least.

"Neal." The innkeeper motioned toward us. "Where are the mounts of our most recent guests?"

Nervously, the boy avoided making eye contact and glanced at Kurn's black stallion and the others, pointing. "This way."

Leading us to Rithal's shaggy pony, Mathias's and Castis's geldings, and the ornery stallion, Brom shook his head. "The dark brown mare?"

"Ah, she 'cross th' way. Had move her t'th'box."

"Why? What was wrong?"

"She lame," Neal said apologetically, grimy hands out and holding his muck shovel. "Tried walkin' 'er yesterday 'fore the Hunner arrive. Hurts too much. Couldn't get out th' corral. Walks on three legs."

"Ah? Show me."

*Oh, this is bad.*

I glanced at Gavin in concern, but he didn't look at me. Instead, we gathered at the stall where his mount was kept; she was off her feet and lying on her side, breathing heavily in the hay. My ally said nothing but studied her with his death's eyes.

"Don' know what to do," Neal admitted. "Legs 're hot an' puffy."

"Pour deep well water on the hot spots three times a day," Brom said. "Ask Dar for a poultice to wrap around her joints, and make sure she rests. Don't walk her but make sure she eats and drinks."

"Yessir."

Gavin said, "My thanks, Master Brom. We knew she was under strain upon arriving."

"Indeed, it has not been quiet here of late. Unfortunately, it could take days or weeks before she might be travel ready."

*Convenient.*

Yet another obstacle to leaving had arisen. Was Gavin's mare this bad when we arrived, and I hadn't understood? Or has someone harmed her and made it worse since? What would we do now, kill the Ma'ab and claim their horses, instead? Not if I could somehow persuade the Deathless to help with the warp rot.

Even should we also receive other help from Rithal or Mathias, then Brom providing a mount for Gavin and me was yet another dependency on the sorcerer. I didn't like this imbalance or the risks it would take to challenge it.

The governor motioned us out the front of the barn. "Do you want an illusion again before my men?" he asked once we were away from Neal.

"No," Gavin said. "I assume they're aware I was killed last night."

"Well. They got a good look at who was being chased, yes."

"Then I shall be as I am, though my aura remains suppressed and my head covered."

"Good enough."

I watched how the skin on Gavin's hands was changing in the late afternoon as they talked, as we moved in and out of the trees. It wasn't so chaotic as a flickering candle suffering a breeze, but the gradual shifts made him appear as mottled as my cloak. Oh well, what did I care if further men became afraid of—

Then I recognized Brom's motions and muttering and tried to interrupt.

*"Hey!* No, I—"

He finished my disguise then pointed a finger at me. "I'm sorry, little fighter, *you* don't have a choice. Ignorant men do stupid things around small female 'demons' especially. I'm sure Kurn has convinced you of this."

"But you let Gavin walk as he is?" I challenged.

"He's taller than me. That makes a difference."

*"Pfft!"*

"At least if you run off again, someone like Kivin won't think twice to let you by to visit the eve witch again, hm?"

"Eve witch?" Gavin asked, leaving me fuming.

"A lady Dwarf who lives as a hermit around here," Brom told him. "No doubt where Rithal will be until the Witch Hunters are silent and gone from sight." He looked at me. "How is Osgrid? Well, I hope?"

"Her and her crow are fine," I said, noting how Gavin's brow quirked and he looked up at the trees as if expecting to see those black birds. I still heard them.

"Hm," said Brom. "Did she say anything about last night? She must have seen the fire."

"She did, and she was the only mage to suggest removing the dagger from Gavin," I said, a partial truth.

"Reckless counsel without seeing it first," he remarked. "Though Osgrid doesn't tolerate any but her own opinion. Did she tell you why she's here?"

"Watching you," I said, sounding bored and flipping my hand. "What else is there to observe in this place?"

"True enough. I imagine she's another spy for someone, probably the Guild in Taiding."

*Taiding.* The Dwarven city Rithal had been to. I muttered a thoughtless Davrin curse, frowning with the pretty-bua redhead face again, and Brom chuckled.

"Thoughts wrapped up on webs of connections again, hm?" He smiled wider when I darted a scowl at him. "If you're curious why I tolerate her, Osgrid's good at medicine, and the loggers like her brews. So, I leave her alone while she leaves me alone. Though, if you should recall why she suggested waking Gavin, I'd like to hear it."

"As would I," he chimed in.

I sighed. "Very well, she did *not* state that. She only said I shouldn't leave his body in Ma'ab hands and 'see what I see' about the dagger. Obvious, I think."

"That sounds more like her."

We followed the dirt roads through the town and, with Gavin's eerie presence any time we were stopped by a local to ask their governor a question, we weren't delayed too long. Soon enough, we caught up to the ground of four men led by Dar sweating in the warm afternoon as they dug through heavy root systems and rock to bury the Witch Hunters deep. There were only two left, we were told.

"Excellent work," Brom spoke in a loud and confident voice. "May I suggest you all take a short rest?" He offered the jug he'd carried all the way here to Dar. "Wet your throats."

"Much obliged, Master Brom."

"Thanks, govunna."

"Aye, whew! Let's get in th' cups."

I narrowed my eyes suspiciously at Brom as they wandered out of earshot, removing their shirts to wipe down their faces before taking the first drink.

"Not a curious glance at Gavin's walking corpse," I observed.

"Nor at you," he countered.

"Where *is* Kurn's ruby?" I asked curiously. "Would you happen to be using it while you're keeping it safe for him?"

The sorcerer smiled at me. "Only to quiet the hinges."

"Odd wording."

"The last thing I need is burning panic like last night while you both stir up the sandstorm inside me as well. It's for your benefit as well as mine."

I quieted as I ran out of excuses to be contrary, and Gavin ignored us as he stood unperturbed by an open-back cart holding the last two, naked Manalari. All I knew was neither were Bictrius.

"I'd ask you not to make their corpses sit up or walk for amusement," Brom said. "I don't care to watch."

"That won't be necessary," Gavin replied, withdrawing a scalpel he'd had prepared in a nearby pouch and unwrapping it. "I only want to ask some questions, if they can answer."

My ears perked up, and we watched as the Deathwalker pressed the edge along the heel of his right hand and drew a mark as long as one of my fingers. The wound welled with the viscous, black substance which now flowed in his veins, sluggishly, with how Gavin squeezed and manipulated the wound before his long arm reached into the cart.

Briefly, he touched the men's eyelids, mouths, and earlobes to leave black smears behind. Next, he pressed his wound to the chest of one of them, slightly high and on the left, and began murmuring in that "dead tongue" again. I moved to cover his back, since he was leaning over obliviously, and to see down into the cart.

I didn't expect my stomach to become queasy when the Hunter's eyes opened on their own and twitched, but I did. Then hollow air escaped the opened mouth, and my skin erupted in bumps. There flowed a chill I expected by now, but the environment changed no further. Gavin merely spoke in Manalari to the corpse, and if he heard an answer or saw anything, I could not perceive it.

Observing Brom was more insightful while Gavin shifted to the other side of the cart to press his fast-shrinking wound to the chest of the second man. Not only could the sorcerer *see* something happening, could hear and understand it, but Gavin scared him in a way that I did not.

Unlike Gavin's lame mare, this was neither good nor bad. Perhaps an opportunity? What might this fear drive him to do in time? Attempt destruction or alliance? Neither, but only encourage him to leave Troshin Bend as soon as possible? *Would* Gavin leave if it were made clear it would be alone, without me?

*I can't allow that choice to be presented.*

Gavin drew in a deep breath, filling his lungs to chant something in one, long song which caused both sets of eyes to close again. Their corpses hadn't moved otherwise. He straightened up.

"Where is Bictrius and the fire mage?" he asked.

"We'll have to ask Dar. Let me call them back."

Again, I observed that not-quite-natural pressure for the men to act calm and jovial and work hard. Perhaps this was how they behaved when their town wasn't thrashed with violence and the true concerns were only being delayed.

Soon enough, we left them behind to follow the directions to where Bictrius had been buried.

"What did they say?" I asked Gavin, placing him between me and the Zauyrian so I could watch him, too. "Did they answer your questions? I mean, their eyes opened, I assume...something was there?"

"Yes, the Vis was nearby and could still be called to the body as a temporary anchor. Now they know which way to go."

"What?"

"What did you ask them?" Cris-ri-phon interrupted gruffly.

"I asked what they saw to the North which drove them here a second time, where they would perish."

The sorcerer snapped off a thin branch with some irritation, bending it further with one hand. "And what was it they saw?"

"Not what I might have guessed," Gavin said, looking at me with a curious expression. "Why I must speak with Bictrius and his fire mage next."

"Oh? And what wouldn't you have guessed?" the sorcerer growled.

"I'd rather not say now. The dead do not lie but they do not always know what they bear witness to while alive."

I suppressed a snicker to watch Cris-ri-phon chew his patience as much as I did. Oh, but how I wished I could mind-link with Gavin then, with intent while we were both awake, so he could give me some idea where the sorcerer couldn't hear.

Considering that wish, were it to become a skill, I didn't know where to start. The only times it had ever worked that way was with Elder D'Shea or...or with Kerse, or the Ornilleth, *commanding* me.

*Then everything went numb for a while.*

The only time recently I force my will out was with Kurn on top of me. Some psionic defense had returned, as when I had against Wilsira. Cris-ri-phon could not mine my thoughts like a Tragar looking for gems, but I didn't have much else under such stubborn control. Certainly not rutting dreams that resulted in hard cocks sinking into warm holes.

*More than just me, from the sound of it.*

"Here is one," Gavin said with a level certainty which pitched me out of my brooding. He tapped with the handle of his spade a mound of disturbed earth on the edge of the Southern market.

"Bictrius?" Brom asked. "Or the pyro mage?"

"Neither," Gavin said, again drawing blood on a different spot on his right hand; this time, he merely allowed the black blood to land on the dirt with two sentences repeated three times.

"What are you doing?"

The question held a subtle threat.

"Offering direction," the Deathwalker replied.

"Gavin, you're—"

"They do not have to take it. I am finished. Come."

"Are we finding *all* their graves?"

"I think that is best, unless you want to risk the warp rot reweaving the Vis with the corpse later. Such false life will not look right, I assure you."

Cris-ri-phon hissed, and I found myself smiling and holding my peace. The ritual was fascinating on its own, but the irritation and uncertainty of the Deathless was better, though I should be concerned about the imagery Gavin was painting in our heads, of warp rot somehow winding a body and spirt back together.

*Goddess, I hope this isn't a trickster, and we should be stopping this.*

The day was close to dusk when Gavin had located all sixteen graves and performed the same ritual. I could mimic the chant by now, and Brom had calmed down some as if he was convinced this was the better option. Gavin also chose to speak with a few select ghosts, but except for the two dead mages, I didn't know why he chose to speak to one but not the other.

As it turned out, Bictrius had relied on the fire mage's senses to make his decision to return to Troshin Bend to try to conscript the innkeeper's help, so…

"The pyro last," grumbled the governor of Troshin Bend. "So be it."

This grave was the only place where I had a real sense that *something* was there, some essence I couldn't see or smell, touch or hear in the darkening forest. It loomed and spread slowly; it made me afraid, wanting to return to Osgrid's earthen home or find that cave of stone on the way in which to hide.

I'd killed this one. With a poison scrape to his neck, I'd stopped his lungs from breathing, because he set the town on fire and had called a downpour of flames upon Gavin when he'd only been trying to defend himself.

*Trying to escape the pain before death.*

I watched as Gavin continued to speak to this Witch Hunter; his voice was firmer, slower, deliberate. His offer of a "direction" was not taken well; the ghost seemed to fight his will and his voice, drawing more effort out of the Deathwalker lest something go wrong. His repetition in Manalari or the dead tongue—or both— continued as if wearing the roused spirit back down into the ground was the only option.

There seemed to be no further exchange between ghost and Deathwalker, and my death mage cut himself to bleed and help quiet the fire mage again. Cris-ri-phon stepped behind me and put protective arms around me, drawing me against him as the temperature grew colder.

"You must be careful around magic like this," he whispered. "It can harm Elves in particularly tragic ways."

I grunted, annoyed with the attention unasked for, and tried to draw myself out without disrupting Gavin's ritual. Strong, Human arms tightened, and to grapple with him harder would have required disruption.

*Shit.*

I stopped before it became a struggle, waiting tensely in the former General's arms, my hands resting atop his should he dare to reach for my belt. I waited until Gavin's eyes shifted from void-black to show me those ice blue pupils becoming more familiar at each new grave.

Gavin's voice had stopped. He stood still, breathless, studying first the damp and dark soil, then looking North. Toward the inn, toward the prison-shed where he'd woken. Toward the warp rot.

I pulled free in one determined motion, stepping forward. "Gavin, what did you learn? Why did they come here a second time after Brom refused once?"

He hesitated.

"Gavin," Cris-ri-phon insisted. "Enough. We've checked every grave. You've been as thorough as any Deathwalker I've known. Speak what you've learned."

My ally lifted his pale hand, watching the last cut he'd made slowly close again; the flow had stopped. He was still as a standing corpse for a few breaths, then he picked up his pack and spade and walked down the small decline.

"Each story was similar," Gavin said, "with variances based on their position and frame of mind. They were caught in the same storm we were on the Midway when they encountered the warp rot forest where everything was twisted, and the very wind laughed at them."

Neither me nor the sorcerer spoke; we waited.

"Deeper in, they saw…" Gavin's eyes looked into mine. "Something which looked like you. Something followed them from the rotting forest, haunting and tormenting them for two days and two nights through the storm, screaming and casting curses. A black-skinned, blade-eared demon with glowing red eyes and hair gone pure white from fear, until it vanished, only to reappear ahead of them."

I shook my head, pleading clarity.

"After they killed me and targeted you," he said, "after they got close enough to see, some of them recognized you as the same chaos-bringer trying to destroy the town."

*Insanity!*

"B-But…I'm not, I was never…"

I stopped, couldn't speak another word past the ache in my throat.

*Gaelan.*

"Warp rot easily mimics fears," Cris-ri-phon said. "And it would not take much to imagine a demon with Davrin coloring. I've seen it happen before."

"Perhaps," Gavin said amicably.

I didn't hear what they debated next with the force of my next thought. *Jacob is alive in the shed.*

I could talk to him, as I couldn't all these ghosts. Had they seen her? If so, what did they mean she followed them? Was the screaming and haunting because she was fallen to the warp rot, or because she was in pain and seeking help?

Where was she? Could Jacob tell me *anything* of my Sister, no matter what filthy thing he called her? I couldn't miss the chance, regardless how long it took to leave here.

"I must ask Mathias something," I said in the calmest, most intrigued voice I could muster, squashing down pain and terror.

"Sirana—" Cris-ri-phon began.

I spun around, smiling as broadly as the qu'eesan beneath the waterfall. He stopped.

*"I shall meet you soon at your quarters, General,"* I promised in Davrin, *"to 'persuade' you to look into this matter with me. But I must first see how Mathias is doing with his Witch Hunter if I may get one answer out of him. If I do, I shall tell you what it is, why you should help me, and why I'm here."*

"Hm." He looked tempted. *"Do you want an escort?"*

I lifted my hands toward my face. *"No, I will be well, you've seen to it. It would be best if I speak alone appearing like this. I should hurry before the illusion fades."*

Cris-ri-phon accepted without speaking, then I looked to Gavin.

"Will you be well waiting for me?" I asked.

"For certain," replied my death mage. "I have much to do, still. I will be busy."

"Where shall I find you?"

One corner of Gavin's mouth lifted. "The hayloft in the barn, I think. Quiet enough to think and write, a place I'm quite accustomed, and my mare will get some rest."

That might send the boy Neal elsewhere, but I could not be concerned for him. I signed a farewell to them both, causing the sorcerer's eyes to brighten for a moment, and left them there. I ran to the shed to try and catch Jacob in some useful state.

Before Mathias got all the challenge that he could wring from him.

# CHAPTER 12

THE GROWING SHADOWS PROMISED RELIEF FOR MY CONSTANT daytime headache and eased my path in slipping by clumps of men and women settling up their tasks into the evening. I estimated I had been following Gavin around at the graves for over two hours, so I may have an hour at most to use this face for any advantage.

*It should be enough.*

I gave the inn itself a wide berth, wary of spotting any of the Ma'ab waiting, hoping they no longer cared what Mathias was doing since he was not the caretaker of Gavin's corpse. I neither saw them nor did I have reason to believe they saw me skim by. My eyes found no one crouching among the crates forming the perimeter, and I paid special attention to any wards or small, instinctive warnings that anything was wrong.

*Nothing.*

Rithal hadn't shown up where I could see him, either; not since hiding again when we exited the shed with Gavin earlier. I didn't know what he was doing with his time, and I weighed Brom's assertion of the Dwarf's avoidance versus what I knew of his motivations. I wondered if Rithal had returned to Osgrid after following me here, after seeing I was well enough.

*After seeing Gavin walking again.*

Perhaps the deeds of the Witch Hunters made the place truly intolerable for him? Or the Dwarf realized he had gotten farther into this cloak and dagger conflict than he wished. If so, lucky him, as he might extricate himself from the web. I could not; it had been too late from the moment I entered the inn.

Sneaking up to the door, I put my ear to the wood to determine what I might interrupt should I knock. Within moments, a startlingly familiar slap of leather on skin and accompanying gasp sounded, followed by a soft cry and a grunt at once. Two voices in unison; another slap, another gasp of shock followed by a growl expertly manipulated into a cry of uninhibited release.

"I-Inomilu..."

"Such a mess, Jacob. Best penance you ever endured, eh? Tighten up now, my turn—!"

The lash landed again, and a man replied in Manalari, a phrase spat out in astonishment as the tempo of thrusts increased. My heart pounded in my ears to hear the submissive man's warbled denials and voiced challenges mixed with unmistakable gasps of pleasured torture I'd heard before. I might as well have been in the Cloister, spying on my Sisters blowing off tension with each other. I massaged the rising ache between my legs.

That the dominant male enjoyed every strike and lunge was without doubt, but the Witch Hunter forced to submit was aroused as well despite being captive, if only while floating in an altered state. The aftershock would crash in hard after climaxing from something one found disgusting, I knew. But after being caught in the clutches of a psionic Tragar or unable to escape intensely sadistic Sisters, I'd learned it was a viable method of survival.

Would this familiarity make it easier or difficult when I walked in?

"Uhh, yeah!"

*Slap, slap!*

"*Ai, inomilu sancji, Musanlo puriquel!*"

"Louder, so He can hear those wailing prayers at dawn and *not* wonder why you're still on sore knees!"

Jacob shouted obligingly at him, threatening at first but ending on a yelp rising into a squeak as the skin hunter played his prisoner like a flute. Mathias was close enough to his peak that I didn't interrupt the climb. Instead, I checked around me for anyone approaching, saw no one, and waited for what the skin hunter's fulfillment would tell me.

Was Mathias like the Prime or like Jaunda when he got what he sought? The longevity of my interest in this game depended on knowing this now.

"H-here's more heretic's spunk, Jacob," he gasped. "Want it in you, or *on* you?"

Jacob grunted but didn't answer.

"Think its foul filth will burn your back... like it did your asshole?"

I smirked. If Mathias's prick cream burned, then he wasn't Human. But, if Jacob had been initiated this night, I could see how it would seem so the first time. Either way, I could not understand when the Manalari replied at last; I did not know if he'd barked a choice or a curse right up to the edge of that inexorable moment, when Mathias was shuddering and moaning in release, his cock spurting jism *some*where.

I drew in a slow breath, removing my hand from my aching crotch, as their gasping slowed together. Jacob chanted repetitive whispers, and Mathias quickly gagged him before he could finish a third time. I waited longer still, until the skin hunter had wiped down and let out that final breath of satisfaction, letting Jacob rest.

*More like Jaunda, then.* The Prime would have started something else by now.

I knocked softly on the door. "Skin hunter."

After a considered pause, Mathias approached, unbarred, and opened the door a crack. The scent that wafted out hit me full in the face; I took a deeper draw to become accustomed. I'd smelled worse. Mathias was fully dressed and stared at my face, recognizing the youth he'd wanted to see sucking his cock. Fortunately for me, his bearded face was amused rather than instantly lustful as he had been the first time.

"What are you doing here?" he said in a low voice.

I used the non-carrying whisper of my homeland, such that the man had to squat down to my level and turn his ear toward me.

"Gavin can speak to the dead. He told me something the other Witch Hunters knew that I want to ask Jacob if he knows. Will you aid my questioning, interrogator?"

The bearded noble's eyes narrowed in suspicion as he smiled wryly. "First, tell me how long you were listening."

I shrugged and smiled. "Best penance he ever endured. You'd think a Red Sister taught you."

*"Heh heh heh!* Alright, come in."

He opened the door, I stepped inside, and Mathias closed and barred it again. It was dim inside, the low-flame lantern on the table the only source of light with the Sun set. The air was thick, still, and warm, the scent of sex inescapable and arousing even if it wasn't Davrin sex.

The Witch Hunter was trying to look over his shoulder, but I wagered was unable to see more than a blurry figure. I saw the deeply flushed face when I entered, his buttocks flexing as if he could hide what happened. He said something through the gag, sounding like a question.

"You'll see, Jacob," Mathias chuckled, teasing, as he went quiet and let me look around to observe what I would with no explanations, no justification. No apologies.

He was correct that I didn't need them.

Jacob was tied belly-down to the wide and low bench I'd observed before, arms lifted straight forward, his knees spread and bound to the heavy wood. His red, half-erect genitals hung low in front of the wood with a leash wrapped around his testicles; his hairy ass was presented toward me and thoroughly used. His back was also covered in droplets of fresh liquid.

*Well, now I know.*

More interesting to me was that Jacob's skin was heavily marked but I detected no appreciable amount of blood, either in color or as that metallic tang beneath the sweat. My gaze drifted over the handful of leather straps and whips which hadn't been visible when we placed Gavin's body here. The shapes among the set of beating tools matched the red welts decorating Jacob from his shoulders down to his buttocks, as well as on his flanks and thighs.

*Deliberately placed and gradually laid out.* I didn't see a tormentor who lost control in a rage with a resilient rebel. I saw a slow, calm inflictor testing the limits of a pain-drinker responding to the rising intensity. Jacob's skin must be a blanket of sensitive heat by now.

"Training?" I asked.

"He was trained to endure worse," Mathias remarked, dipping a cup in his water barrel, and gulping it down, exhaling then licking his lips. "As I've heard Witch Hunters are. Why I wanted one."

Jacob interrupted with a muffled bark I couldn't make out.

"Right. 'God warriors'. As I was saying," Mathias adjusted his crotch. "These hunting packs whip themselves and each other like this as penance for 'impure' thoughts, except it's common they'll draw blood. See? You can see some old scars. I didn't have time to make those."

I nodded as he pointed. "I see them."

The skin hunter's smile of satisfaction hadn't waned. "Less common that you'll hear they bend over and be the sheath for a ranking officer's sword, though I think a lot of them would offer if it didn't mean, you know, excommunication. Or execution. I forget." He pointed at Jacob's ass. "I got lucky with this one. He 'confessed' why he came the first time just from the strikes. Most of his 'penance' ended with demons plaguing his dreams until he painted his braies with spunk, anyway. Punishing him for impure thoughts made them worse."

"In what way?" I asked with pretend innocence, so he'd continue.

Mathias winked, casually massaging his crotch, and continued after another drink of water. "Well, I've never seen a prick recover so fast after I beat his back, insulted his devotion, *then* fucked him—in that order—I'm betting he's pretending I was the Chief Warrant, to bust his nuts all over my bench legs as he did." The skin hunter lifted his voice. "Isn't that right, Jacob? Do I rut that tight hole as good as your *Warrante* did in your sinful dreams?"

The Witch Hunter spat something vile sounding at him, pulling at ropes and knots which had no slack. The bench didn't so much as lift or rock due to a new iron anchor.

"Yeah, don't lie, sweet cheeks. Just wait. I'll be dipping between them again before we're done, 'cause you're still hungry, you slimy-holed harlot. Bet you wished Bictrius would've punished you by lining up all the lower ranks to take their turn pig-corking you in the stocks, each finishing with a piss in your mouth. Leave you a loose, soggy sow at both ends, eh?"

Jacob erupted into a bellowing tantrum which tested the firmness of the bench bolted to the floor, with such volume that I had to cover my ears. I was glad I didn't understand Manalari. Meanwhile, Mathias laughed and plucked up a strap, stepping forward to slap his prey's belly and phallus which had begun to get full.

"Look! We can see what *speaking* it does to you!" Mathias landed a hard strike on the Witch Hunter's buttocks, making him jerk. "Am I wrong, filthy liar?"

Jacob *was* becoming erect, and I genuinely wondered how these Humans could act so much like my Lead putting my sister Kaltra in her place, and many others. I'd been in a similar position with Jaunda enjoying my struggles against her restraints as she slapped and took my ass.

Regardless of how it came to be so far from the Deepearth, the skin hunter had been right on the Midway. I was excited by the powerplay, but couldn't indulge in the game yet.

*Focus.*

While Mathias was distracted, I released my spiders from their pouch, silently instructing them to wait on the underside of the table. *~Stand guard.~*

Once Jacob had yelled himself hoarse through his gag and further coloring of his skin, his cock hard and bobbing, the skin hunter asked me, "So. Why are you here? You said you had a question."

*Right.* I took a deep breath. My question wasn't as thrilling as this game of pain and pleasure, especially if I didn't like the answer.

I attempted a lower timber to my voice rather than a whisper. "I want to ask about the evil thing that chased the *Dyos Guerrimos* here, to try again to persuade the governor."

Mathias raised his brows in curiosity, and Jacob lifted his head, turning his neck in cautious surprise at my choice of words.

"Intriguing. You'll have to stand at the other end of the bench."

Mathias also pantomimed that I disarm first, and I understood why. Bringing weapons within reach of a prisoner, even a bound one, was a stupid risk. With a small nod, I removed my belt, setting it gently beneath the table where my spiders hid, placing my cloak over it next. The skin hunter approved lightly touching my shoulder.

"Alright. Let him see you, boy."

I wasted no time, positioning to see Jacob's face as I kneeled on the floor near the bench. His wide, bloodshot eyes drifted over my appearance; the pretty Human bua was no threat to him, I could see. He was curious, keeping quiet after Mathias removed the gag with a threat of consequence should he try to cast. Jacob didn't seem to hear him as he stared at me.

"*Dyos Guerrimos,*" I began. "I must ask you a question."

Jacob blinked, his eyelid twitching as several emotions crossed his sweating face. His accent was like Gavin's. "Are you a righteous boy?"

I shook my head. "No. I sin. *Nomuli sancji.*"

The Witch Hunter nodded like he wouldn't have accepted any other answer. He swallowed to wet his throat. "How do you know this... defiler?"

I glanced up at Mathias, who shrugged, indifferent how I answered. I tried the truth. "I sucked his, um, sword for trade."

"He defiled you, too?"

"No, I sin," I repeated. My stomach growled loudly then, distracting us, and I motioned at Mathias. "I was hungry. He bought a meal and room if I sucked him—"

Jacob spat at the skin hunter. "Curse you beyond the Hells for putting a child of the South on his knees before you!"

Mathias grinned rebelliously. "Oh, the boy sucked like we wouldn't see the dawn. I saw God's face with his lips wrapped around me, I'm sure."

Jacob gasped. "Heretic!"

"How sore *is* that pucker, sinner? You want to go again? I'm game."

I waved my hands to get their attention, frowning. "Stop! Warrior, your brethren caught us in the trees! They tried to seize and bind him."

"As they should!" he replied.

"Yes, but Mathias likes it the other way around." The skin hunter snorted; I suppressed a smile, continuing. "He fought to get away, and I ran and hid. That was how it started. *All* this because of me!"

Jacob's mouth went slack, then muttered through clenched teeth, "Then we flushed a real devil from the inn by unseen guidance but... failed to vanquish it. For the demoness that followed us from the twisted forest reversed his banishment."

*Uhh, no?*

"Yes!" I said. "From the North? I fled here before you, I may have seen it! The evil in the twisted forest, if *she* is *here*, then where she began is important. The early signs tell how to get free of the curse on this town!"

"*Sabi chipu*," Jacob murmured, nodding, eyes drifting to the side. "*Truxje es'maliq aci—*"

Mathias brought a strap down on his back, strangling his last word in a yelp. "In common tongue, Jacob! I want to hear how you tumbled into my hands, so I know who to thank in my prayers."

The Witch Hunter snarled at him against at some length but, to my relief, voluntarily returned attention to me. "We brought this evil here when it followed. We thought Brom Troshin could not ignore if it was in his town…But… but it moved too quick for us to persuade him."

"What did you see?" I asked.

Mathias stayed quiet, thankfully, as curiosity won over taunting for now. Jacob seemed to forget his nudity and hot markings as he looked inward, murmuring prayers. Then, "The land North contains a green rot, smelling of magic sickness, making us vomit and unable to sleep. We searched for the source, to cleanse and purify the devil's corruption. She tried to mislead us…"

"What did she look like?" I pressed, willing him to look at my eyes.

He did, and he answered. "Her face even beneath His Bright Eye was black as pitch, eyes red like old blood. Hair as white as an ancient corpse. She could *see* which of us were blessed by God, I am sure. We shone before her, only me, Bictrius, and Fariq she targeted. Only we three she tempted, to lure away from the others. Toward a foul pool of… of…*pesdralo dialva*…"

I resisted looking at Mathias for a translation, so as not to be required to prove more than one prayer phrase to seem Manalari. *Ask later.*

"What happened?" I asked. "You resisted the—"

"*Brujix nigri.*"

"Yes, black witch." I knew that one by now. "Um, but something caused you to flee here. What happened?"

Jacob shuddered. "She...released the hordes of the Nine Hells on us."

I doubted that, taking two or three breaths to tamp down my patience. "What does this mean, *Dyos Guerrimos*?"

Jacob stared at me, his face flushing in anger. "It means screaming, flesh-eating corpses, *chipu*! Corrupted souls trying to escape their eternal torment, like the one she let escape from this shed! We fled upon our mounts when they could not be controlled farther! For all day into the night, only by God's Will did none suffer a broken leg!"

I nodded urgently, beckoning as I tried to see some truth in the spinning threads. "You *saw* her unleash them on you? She was there?"

"We heard her chanting! Like no other words I've heard."

"She was chanting," I checked, "not screaming? Did she throw anything at you?"

"What does it matter? We were pursued by her ghouls and hounds!"

"*Dyos Guerrimos*, you must think!" I barked back. "This is important. When did you last see her before you reached here? Halfway? Less? Closer to this town?"

Jacob blinked, looking resentful, but considered. "Not... at all."

"What?"

"She never appeared to me on the way here," he said grudgingly. "I looked for her foul magic, but...no. It was her hound which harried us, terrified us. The black beast with eyes shining at night, like a mockery of the Sun."

In this stuffy, sweltering shed, a frigid fist clenched my gut.

"She *and* that beast were here the night we found the corpse abuser," Jacob continued. "That's why we are all dead. All of us. The evil followed us out of the forest and will *not* give up our souls. I am the last one marked."

My head spun. *Black beast with yellow eyes? Serving a…black witch with white hair.*

It couldn't be the Sathoet. *Impossible.* Not a hundred years later *and* where Gaelan had been sent? Was she somehow on the same mission as me? I didn't understand, but knew I had no choice.

*I must go North. I* **must** *convince the sorcerer.*

Time in the makeshift dungeon seemed to stop, and I supposed Mathias could sense I had nothing else for Jacob when he crouched down, lightly touching my shoulder.

"So. You…joined us on the road," he murmured, "because you've been looking for another like you? Is she missing?"

My eyes snapped to him, fury flooding me, my mouth open ready to scathe his pride for such a sloppy mistake—

"*B-brujix!*" Jacob hissed, his body beginning to quiver as he stared at me with insane grievance. "You… you trick me, *dialva an-uli!*"

Mathias chuckled. Covering my surprise and panic, I pulled off one glove to confirm. *Black as pitch.*

"Your diseased cunt of maggots had taken the innkeeper's cock before we arrived!"

"Whoa." Mathias sounded impressed.

"You wore this boy's face, deceiver! I recall you on the porch of the inn! What have you done to this town, soul-eater? *Il Warrante* would have begun the cleansing that moment had we known!"

"Cleansing?" I asked, incredulous.

"Don't ask," the skin hunter warned.

The fervor in Jacob's eyes blazed; his smile disturbed me, reminded me of a Priestess in dramatic ritual.

"Do not pretend we don't know your methods, Hells queen. You *fear* us for we do not flinch at what must be done to stop you! You soil the wives and maidens first, always. You lick at their thighs, suck out the womb blood as they shudder in wild joy, leaving it flow and poison holy ground! We find *them* first, slut devil, to steal your power and weaken you by cauterizing your evil out of their cunts with hot iron, a blessed rod overwhelming any witch's touch! A blessed *purging* from infestation!"

*Purging.*

I stared at him, swept by tremors of revulsion. Memories from before I left Sivaraus, of the Sisterhood purging of the tainted Consorts after Wilsira's demonic betrayal, leaped onto my back and clung stubbornly.

*Oh, Goddess…*

I hadn't enjoyed any part of that mass killing like some Sisters, but I knew *why* the Valsharess had commanded it. I'd stared up at Kerse's eyes as he sacrificed me; I'd felt that touch of the tainted Consort in the Sanctuary. The threat was *real*, cultivated over three centuries in secret, revealed beyond any doubt of true demon's blood in some of our Davrin births. We had to cull them, and I tried to make it quick as Elder Rausery advised.

At least we had methods and magic to know who they were. If the Witch Hunters would have swept into all the homes of Troshin Bend on this same fear from spotting Gaelan, *one* Davrin Elf, and not knowing what she was—

If it was not quick, then it was a gruesome fate avoided by the serving women here. For better or worse, Gavin had only been whipped and branded on his shoulder in the monastery.

"Yes." My words slipped out with the contempt boiling up. "I've *seen* how you cherish your hot iron on children, too."

Jacob spat at me, quaking with rage. "Any girl without a husband who succumbs to the devil must be cleansed as well!"

*What?*

Mathias dared me. "Ask him how they know she's not a virgin."

I glanced at him. "What is a virgin?"

Jacob brayed a laugh in my face. "You can't know that blessed state, womb of maggots, reborn in the blood of sin, conceived with your father's feces-covered staff in a goat's cunt!"

I made a face. *Gross.*

"A virgin hasn't taken a cock yet," Mathias added helpfully.

*Oh.*

That was even worse than I meant.

It wasn't necessary to prompt the Witch Hunter; he couldn't stop talking now. "If she doesn't bleed when a holy warrior opens her womb, she is not pure and must be cleansed with hot iron," Jacob stated, staring as if to stab me. "If God wills her to live, she may work and pray for salvation but never marry to bear a tainted soul."

"That makes no sense," I floundered, looking to Mathias. "The ones bleeding are fouled by a devil sucking, but if she *doesn't* bleed when, ah…"

"When a Witch Hunter rapes her, then she is *still* fouled? Yeah, I know." Mathias shrugged. "Sense and reason make no difference to zealots. Damned if you do or you don't. One reason I did."

I understood. Whether I had meant it or not, whatever transgression Jilrina claimed would justify her whims at the time. There was no winning the game with words.

Fortifying myself for the worst, I asked Jacob, "Do you 'test' Dwarven witches in such a way? I know you have destroyed their towns, as well."

*At least one.*

Disgust overtook him as he gagged and retched. "God, never! Beheading is effective and what they deserve. And the power they're so proud of in those beards, we cut them off to see them try to breathe around it!"

A flicker of rage stirred within me to imagine Kain or Rithal choking that way. Jacob saw it with pleasure, his eyes narrowing as we stared defiantly at each other.

"Yes," he rasped, smiling as he goaded me, "you are not afraid, are you, *dialva anuli?* You are a slut queen with heavenly blue eyes shielding your decaying soul from my prayers. As you wished, your minion has *had* me. Yes, he tries to weaken me, but I will resist your corruption to the end and see our blessed Musanlo!"

With an explosive jerk against the ropes, he shouted, "I am not afraid to die! I have earned His blessing. I shall become His warrior beyond, and your reign on our Sun-touched land will *not* last. The *Dyos Gerrimos* shall never cease routing those who listen to the inverted gospel of the First Witch Reborn, wherever it may spread!"

"Inverted gospel, huh," Mathias remarked.

"Tell me that story," I suggested.

Jacob undulated his spine in an odd way, his laugh high and off balance. "Of course, you want to hear of your first failure and how our Chosen tracked you down, prideful queen of sodomy!"

Mathias burst out laughing, and I shushed him with an unintended giggle that seemed to grab Jacob's anger again.

"Yes, I do," I prompted, adding a licentious licking of my lips. "It's been, what is it, a *century* or more for me in the other realms?"

"Three hundred years!" he boasted. "We have been vigilant for your return, each time to try to retake the sacred pool!"

The skin hunter seemed to grasp my direction then and shut his mouth, a wicked playfulness in his brown eyes.

"Yes, *that* Chosen," I sneered. "Who was he?"

"His Holiness Iarmod Tefornin," Jacob said with reverence. "His calling as Archbishop wasn't yet acknowledged, but he unveiled your demonic ties with the Rophan lords through the ages to keep Mount Sonai under your thumb! The sacrifices to the Death Witch that fed black blood into the holy pool and gave birth to Hells' Witch upon our land."

*You speak only of Hells yet punish like the Abyss.* I didn't speak but glared at him.

He continued eagerly. "Tefornin trapped and bound the blackest witch of legend, Halete Ebtryne! The fire-hair woman serving as the vessel for this pact. He revealed how she coupled willingly with *your* black-skinned hounds, spread herself like a bitch in heat to take their corrupting seed in all three holes to keep the Mount desecrated!"

"Filthy," Mathias murmured, aimed at me. "I think he's jealous of that first witch-bitch. He's only got two holes and no black dogs. Could we remedy that?"

*"Corta vu lingas, herex!"* Jacob shouted to make my ears ring.

For a time, Mathias couldn't stop laughing. The Witch Hunter's words spiraled into a mixture of Trade and Manalari that made no sense. I attempted a few times to get him to continue, but he grew hysterical and soon only spoke the Southern language, such that I could question him no farther.

*Thanks, Mathias.*

Still, could this somehow be another story of Davrin origin at Manalar? Did this have any link as to why Jael was sent there? Who was she supposed to kill, in truth?

"What of the Captain Willven Isboern?" I asked after our captive at last ran out of either enough breath or curses.

Gasping, Jacob looked up with wide, astonished eyes. He could barely focus as he sweated and shivered from his self-induced fit. "D-did you send him from the West to protect those who hide among us? You did, *brujix*, didn't you?"

"Apparently, you've done everything, Mistress," Mathias answered, slowly shifting himself closer to me. "All at once. *Everywhere.* Queen of it all."

*Ha.*

"Death Witch," Jacob muttered, his lips frothy with spittle. "Now you call to rise legions from the North to take back the pool, to corrupt it again. You'll never succeed, we are ready!"

A warm palm rested on my thigh and my eyes dropped to it as Mathias leaned close to my ear.

"I'm reminded that I owe you one, Red Sister, for that gods-shattering mouth job. Let me repay you here, now. Show me how to touch this cunt so it all drips down your thighs."

The skin hunter could not have spoken worse to his captive. Jacob wailed so loudly at us, at me, that my ears could take no more. I straightened on my knees and lashed out, striking the bound man with my bare hand. The dull sound of my fist cut off his shrill voice and, at last, silence. I shivered, struggling to hold a morass of feeling as my blood sped through my body.

Mathias kneeled up with me and tried again, tentatively sliding his fingers up my thigh toward the junction of my legs. I did not stop him. When he massaged lightly through the crotch of my leathers, watching the horror grow on Jacob's face, my netherlips tingled. I was receptive to his touch despite, or because of, the gleeful regaling of what happened to witches caught in these hunters' path.

A fate many women of this town had narrowly escaped.

"Teach me something new," Mathias whispered, cupping my crotch firmly. "Let him watch me repay you, pleasure for pleasure."

Jacob wouldn't enjoy watching that, would he?

Drawing in a deep breath, I tugged at the leather ties at my hips.

"No, no, *brujix*," barked the naked prisoner, "do not, *desstrate luxur!*"

I smiled and pushing my leathers down to midthigh, where Jacob's eyes fixed to the white fur of my mound. Mathias was leaning to see, too.

"Wow," he said, with a gentle stroke along my inner thigh before petting my sex like a pelt. "I wondered."

"Demonic slut," Jacob hissed.

I chuckled and didn't argue the point; I'd be lying with no gain. Taking Mathias's broad hand, I led it between my legs, sighing as I guided the pressure on my nub and netherlips slick and sensitive.

"God damn," Mathias murmured. "You're wet." He glanced at Jacob with a grin. "She enjoyed watching, too."

"Watching," I said. "And listening to Jacob moaning as you strapped him and plowed his asshole with your hard cock."

It took several tries for the Witch Hunter to collect enough breath to speak. *"Nomilu sancji herrera puti gahnna!"*

"What I said," his captor laughed. "I saw pure light putting my cock in her mouth, Jacob."

Mathias let his fingers slide deeper inside my cunt, exploring like a careful bua new to caits' slits, and I sighed. Pushing him deeper, I moaned with enjoyment, pressing his palm to me and grinding my hips in slow circles.

"Ohh, there we go," cooed the skin hunter. "He should see this, I think."

Still gripping my crotch, Mathias leaned against a wooden pillar, coaxing me into his lap where I could relax and lift my legs, spreading them as much as leathers around my knees would allow. The man's forearm rested on my belly, and his wet fingers slipped deep into me again, curling and stroking at my direction, and Jacob had that full view of my violet-red netherlips to accompany the sloppy noises of fingers fucking me. The zealot could have looked away, nothing prevented him. He didn't, and I took his continued insults of the appearance my sex as fuel to climb higher.

"Ah! Yes, Mathias, that's right!" I gasped, my hands reaching around my thighs to guide his. "Now slow, but *harder...*"

"Like that?"

"Y-yeah!"

Mathias maintained that stroke, his cock like stone under my buttocks, and his other arm wrapped around the outside of one thigh, his fingers playing in the damp mess which leaked toward my pucker. He took a breath, nudging it once.

"What about... here?"

I chuckled. "You want to dip into my black hole of filth?"

I heard the grin in his voice. "Oh, yeah!"

"Yes, please."

Eagerly, Mathias's fat finger circled the rim to spread my slit juice around before he plunged it in, dead center. My body jolted, my pucker fluttering and squeezing around him, and I grabbed his wrist in front to hold his palm against my clit and his other three fingers inside my slit as I peaked. *Yes, yes!*

I doubted I'd ever infuriated another so much by climaxing before, but Jacob's howls of protest easily overwhelmed my long, low moan of release.

"Fucking God," Mathias exclaimed, squirming heavily under my flexing buttocks to pull his breeches down, soon rubbing his naked erection along the cleft. "Augh, Sirana…?"

"Put it in my ass, Mathias," I challenged. "Fuck my hole but spurt up his!"

"Fuck, yes."

"No, witch-sucking defiler! *Do not dare!*"

Oh, surely Jacob knew the game by now. His captor would dare in order to hear his denial. Mathias was prepared with a small jar of grease nearby which he smeared on his own prick's head and shaft before pressing hard at my netherhole. Jacob didn't look away as the man's broad phallus spread my dirt star open and began burrowing between my ass cheeks.

"Goddess!" I cried, laughing.

"Any goddess is a lie!" Jacob bellowed.

"Auranka wants a word with you," I sneered.

Mathias pulled partway out and thrust in again, and I cried like a bird as he began rutting with uninhibited pleasure.

"She feels real to me!" he cracked.

"You'll pay for every atrocity you commit upon the righteous in her service, Mathias!"

"Yeah, I'm still waiting, Jacob. *Ungh!*"

My ass squeezed him as I touched myself, working fast toward another peak. I'd never truly come down from the first and teetering on the boundary of all reason and control. In a familiar game like this, it felt like… *It feels like the Sisterhood.*

It felt like home.

*Bend. Don't break.*

"*Yes!*" I cried in Davrin, about to fall off that cliff. "*Oh, goddess, yes!*"

Mathias surged up, rolling us forward to plant me on my knees but hook my upper body by my shoulders so my hands didn't leave my crotch. He leveraged for much harder fucking, reaming my ass, his hips slapping my cheeks as hard as Cris-ri-phon had my cunt.

I couldn't think far beyond that. *So good! Yes!*

Then I screamed in release, hearing but slow to recognize the bar drop off the hooks by the door to land with a loud thump. I was quivering when Mathias stopped and cursed softly, panting and holding his staff deep in my backside, as someone stepped in.

"Master Brom."

I stopped breathing. *Oh, shit.*

"You betray God, sorcerer!" Jacob wept. "For what?!"

Cris-ri-phon ignored him, his tone chilly. "Are you finished with him, skin hunter?"

Mathias's response was confident, though he immediately withdrew out of me. "No, sir. We're just warmed up."

"What about her?" Brom spoke while striding closer, barely enough time to yank up my pants but not tie them.

"We're done," Mathias said behind me.

"Good. Carry on."

"Wait!" I protested, drowned out by Jacob's ranting again, neither affecting anything, as Cris-ri-phon lunged at me, pressing something hard to my brow.

Gently, like sinking to the bottom of a warm spring, my mind went dark.

*★I have been waiting long enough, little fighter.★*

# CHAPTER 13

I AWOKE WITH MY HAIR UNBRAIDED AND SPREAD OUT ON A SOFT pillow, my boots and stockings removed. My head was muzzy, but I recognized the bed space where I reclined.

*The sorcerer's quarters.*

I still wore my shirt and leather pants, but nothing else. My chest piece, bracers, and gloves were gone; so was Callitro's ring. I patted my chest in sudden panic for Shyntre' pendant, found it present, which didn't help. This didn't tell me how closely I'd been inspected while blacked out. Maybe Cris-ri-phon had let me keep it, for now. Where were my weapons, belt, and pack?

*I placed them beneath the table in the shed with my cloak.*

Which I also couldn't see nearby.

Then my heart surged in my chest. *~Little ones?~*

My guardian spiders. They weren't nearby, I knew. Were they killed or outside? Would they come find me if they lived, or would they wait for me where I'd left them if I could not be sensed? What had D'Shea told me of that circumstance? I couldn't remember.

Slowly, I sat up, and sucked in air through my teeth. *Oo. Oh, yeah.*

Mathias had been vigorously fucking my asshole not long ago. It burned a little though was slippery with grease. We'd been interrupted, and I'd had no time to clean up; the crotch of my pants felt tacky against my cunt.

The chair at Brom's unseen desk scraped the floor, and I stilled, my eyes flying wide. By the time bare feet and a heavier weight warned me to expect the red curtain about to be drawn back, I held a placid expression for the white-haired sorcerer as he peered in at me.

"That wasn't long," he offered. "I thought you would be out longer."

He stepped into the alcove and let the drape close behind him. Seeing he was about to invite himself onto the bed, I rolled to stand on the other side. He moved quickly, gripped me by the back of my neck before I could land feet on the floor. Then, like the first night here, I couldn't move.

"Don't," he warned. "Stay. I will not hurt you. Especially now."

I felt queasy with foreboding. Or was it hunger?

"Especially now?" I repeated warily, reluctantly lying on my back after a firm tug.

Cris-ri-phon settled next to me, propped on one elbow, grey eyes admiring but distant. His dark hand lifted the hem of my shirt to bare my belly, then his palm smoothed over my abdomen until it rested directly on my womb and full bladder. I tensed for both causes, my breath quickening.

"You *are* pregnant, Sirana," he said. "I know you tried to hide it, but I am sure. It's well settled, not newly begun, though you have far yet to go."

"Uhm." I stared, trying to kick uncooperative words into sensical order before he tugged my loosened leathers down my hips to reveal my mussed pubic thatch. I went rigid. "Uh!"

"Shhh," he hushed quietly, scooting partway down before leaning down to touch the tip of his nose to my stomach, drawing in the scent of my skin as he dragged a light circle below my navel.

He said in accented Davrin, *"Nothing was ever so captivating as my wife with child."*

"Uh, Cris-ri...uh—I-I'm not—"

He pressed warm lips reverently where my baby lay within the cradle of my hips. *"I can barely see it, now I know to look, but all the signs were there."*

"S-Sorcerer—"

He trailed a further string of kisses down before pushing his nose and mouth into my matted fur, humming in pleasure. I gasped at the vibration.

*"Sore breasts you do not like touched,"* he murmured against my crotch before nuzzling at the cleft and my stiffening nub. *"Quick-rising hunger and a large appetite."*

He brushed hot lips and a silver-grey moustache along my thighs.

*"Easily aroused by danger. Boundless spirit."*

"C-Cris-ri-phon—"

His tongue swept once across my swelling netherlips, distracted me as his rough hand pulled down my leathers past my knees in one jerk.

"Ah!"

*"Skittish to accept aid when needed."* The Zauyrian chuckled, rising to pull off my pants completely before unfastening his own trousers, releasing an erection as eager and stiff as the one last night. *"Davrin caits haven't changed."*

I quivered, staring at him from the waist down, at his cock leaking. My nipples tightened, visible underneath my black shirt. My sex ached horribly.

Why couldn't I calm down and stop this? I *wanted* to open my legs and let him mount me, yet I didn't. We *both* knew where he would drive that fat prick in; we *both* wanted to make me scream as the skin hunter had. I *wanted* it.

Yet, I didn't.

Like the first time at the waterfall.

His weight shifted to cover me.

*No!* I surged, rolled away again; he grabbed my shoulder and pressed me back with force. The pendant burned against my chest.

*"Stop!"* I forced out through clenched teeth. *"I hate this, w-whatever you are doing!"*

*"Seducing you?"* he asked, leaning over me braced on one fist by my shoulder.

I couldn't punch him as I had Jacob. *"Using magic to do it!"*

He tried capturing my eyes, but I was searching for pendant shapes beneath his white shirt. His other hand was down between open legs, caressing me pleasantly along my sex. His fingertips tested my wetness; there was plenty. It felt *good* as he eased one in up to the second knuckle.

He said, *"I've told you I won't hurt you or your baby, Sirana. My oath."*

*"So what?"* I growled. It took a mountain's strength to close my legs on his hand and to muster what resistance I could against the darts of sensation when he wiggled it. *"I have a m-mind, so you n-need to use the s-same tricks as the Priestesses of Braqth to lay a cait, General?"*

He stopped, and I saw the insult tighten the deep lines of his mouth. I heaped one more.

*"At least Mathias can ask or use a mundane whip to spread some cheeks!"*

"Sirana."

*"Truth!"*

Voluntarily but with a disappointed sigh, he withdrew his hand from me, using it to stroke his cock instead. He returned to Trade. "Those are… impressive protections, Sirana. What is that blue pendant? It's not magical, yet it glows strong in the presence of it."

"Anti magic," I answered tightly. "I don't know. My leader gave it to me to shield me on the Surface."

"Hm." He continued a light stroke of his cock, spreading his own fluid around. "What happens if you remove it?"

"Then I hobble your ankles with your nut sack."

Cris-ri-phon grinned widely with amusement and challenge, letting go of his staff long enough to pull his shirt over his head and toss it aside. As I'd suspected, he wore Kurn's ruby. He motioned to it, otherwise nude.

"What happens if I remove this?" he asked.

I shrugged. "Then I press you onto your back and ride for both our pleasure, but I do not force a kiss, or bite your tongue or cock."

"Ah. Our agreement."

Despite what I thought was a reasonable counteroffer, he did not look ready to accept. Impatiently, I waited. Goddess, I was horny *and* hungry, and neither would fade on their own!

"You see, Sirana," said the ancient mage, "I'm not sure what you claim is *all* that will happen if we couple again without some protection."

*Protection?* I squinted. "For who?"

"For your unborn," he said. "And for me."

"You?"

He lifted his pointer finger. "No will-bending, the first demand you made. Only natural pleasure. We agreed."

I glanced at the ruby and looked away. "Yes. I'd make no change."

"It was to go both ways."

"What?"

Cris-ri-phon frowned. "Sirana, I have *lost* myself in *ancient* memories I've not lived in centuries three times now, whether sleeping near you or being mounted *on* you."

My face and crotch flushed.

"And something else interesting, Kurn and Castis described something similar to me this morning after you ran away."

*Goddess damn it.*

"On the Midway," the Zauyrian pressed, "trapped in a strange trance up until they had no choice or control, they needed release, *any* release. They did something *neither* thought they would ever do." He paused, tilting his head. "They're blaming you for manipulating them. And you knew they would."

A fearful chill cooled my ardor so that I only felt hungry and queasy again. I said, "I am *not* attacking them. Or you, General."

"But you *are* doing something?"

I clutched the pendant under my shirt. "Protection, like you said. It is dangerous for me up here."

"No argument, but if *that* is protection, it is as reckless as pouring unknown potions in someone's cup and hoping they don't notice. What is it, Sirana, magic you can't control? I may be able to help, but you must tell me more."

*Never.*

I stared at the corner of his bed as he reached out one warm hand to caress my thigh. He was *still* hard.

*No will-bending. As agreed.*

He hadn't used any that first time that I could tell. But had I? And thus, he considered the agreement nulled, opening the use of the ruby?

"What were you doing before when you were mounted in my cunt?" I asked, to which his eyebrows raised. "Before I stopped us to switch holes."

"A...trance, as I said," he answered. "I was trying to help you conceive, believing for that moment alone you were my Davrin Queen long dead. I did *not* know you carried, Sirana. You were right to stop us or it could have been tragic for you, and I could never forgive myself."

My hands covered my belly while I waited for my heart to settle down from its fearful tattoo.

"Do you see how dangerous it is, what you're hiding?" The Zauyrian motioned at my unseen stone. "If you will not remove your stone then I shall not remove mine. But for that one adjustment, I would accept your offer. *You* may mount *me*. No will-bending, either way, and no merging auras. We see what happens."

I squinted at him. *Merging what?*

"And," he added, "you will eat your fill right afterward."

*Spider piss.*

Cris-ri-phon shifted to lie on his back, settling close to the middle of the soft bed, and waited expectantly with his pole ready.

*"I want your slit,"* he made clear in my language. *"Not your netherhole."*

Why, because Mathias was just there? My mouth twisted. *"It sounded like you're less dangerous to my baby up my shitter."*

He huffed a laugh, shaking his head. *"Now I'm aware, I'm no danger wherever we slide it. Though, I'd prefer your wet cunt."*

For certain, it was that.

Sighing, I straddled his hips without further delay, pushing aside any hesitation as I nestled the red, Human glans between my dark lips. We both felt it settle at the mouth of the desired hole, and he *pushed*, gliding halfway in before grabbing my hips to draw me down to sit on him fully.

*"Hey!"* I gasped as he took the full depth available, nudging uncomfortably at my womb. "Cris!"

*"Goddess, yes,"* he exhaled, his grey eyes closed, chin tilted up.

He hadn't heard me. I smacked his cheek. *"Let me move, bua!"*

Grey eyes opened and his grip loosened, rough hands sliding to rest on my thighs as I shifted so he wasn't so deep.

*"Ah,"* I sighed to begin humping him freely, *"that's better."*

*"It is, oh, yes,"* he groaned, his throat tight. He tugged at my shirt. *"Take this off."*

*"My tits hurt."*

*"I want to see them."*

*"Look, don't touch?"*

*"Light touch? I'll be gentle."*

*"You'll spurt without it, I can tell."*

*"Please. I'll do something you like."*

I grinned. *"Worship my ears. Like you started to do the first night."*

*"Done."*

Still riding him, I pulled my shirt over my head and moved Shyntre's pendant to hang down my back, baring my breasts to his gaze and tentative fingers as he reached for them. How hot they were, not only in the open but compared to his hands, and my nipples tingled painfully as he couldn't resist scraping thumbs over them. I squeaked, grimacing in discomfort.

*"Apologies,"* he murmured, sliding his hold to the side, cupping them before rubbing the sides the full length of his hands. My breasts didn't fill a Human-sized grip, but Cris-ri-phon didn't seem to care as he never blinked.

His cock squishing wetly as I never stopped stroking my sex all over him, the sorcerer sat up, wrapping his arms around to brace me, and gently nuzzled and kissed my breasts as reverently as he had my belly.

As he embraced me closer, I tugged the ruby's cord, so it didn't touch my skin, lifting it to toss over his shoulder; it flopped against his back. Cris-ri-phon chuckled, humping his hips in unison with mine, and his voice drifted up from between my tits.

*"You haven't changed."*

Doubting I could climax yet, I explored his round ears and thick, coarse hair while he sniffed at my chest and the scent wafting up from our coupling, his big hands squeezing my ass and massaging into my back muscles with strong fingers. He drew me closer the moment I sighed a little.

*"That's good,"* he murmured as he lifted his face from my chest, kissing my jaw. *"At ease, little mata."*

Slowly, I blinked. He *knew* that word.

A first-time mother.

*We'll see.*

Cris kept his word and began caressing my Davrin ears with his mouth. Lips on one side and fingertips on the other, slow, and luxurious; then he switched sides. I shivered as the sensations rolled over me down to my toes, my nipples tightening further. From his little breaths of awe and the tapered spots where he lingered, he sounded as one who'd known ears like these but didn't have them himself.

*Ohhh, Goddess.*

My sex squeezed around him, and he growled, hips thrusting upward, and he kept touching me from ears to thighs as I swiveled my hips on his lap. This was enjoyable, I did not pretend otherwise, but I was only drifting, waiting for him to finish.

I'd climaxed twice in the shed as intensely as I ever had with my Sisters. Without that loathsome influence from Kurn's ruby, the space between my legs was too roughly worked over for me to come a third time from this slow, sensual build. I could have, but not quickly enough before he was on the edge, fucking me faster.

He moved his mouth from my earlobe to my neck, grunting, "Ah! Innathi…"

I frowned.

Then his hand caught my jaw, holding me steady so his mouth could seize my lips. He kissed me with force, his tongue abruptly in my mouth and tasting of wine. I pulled back, and he followed, rocking his large, heavy body forward until I landed on my back. He collapsed upon me like he lost his strength yet entwined his fingers with mine, gripping so tightly they ached.

"Cris—!" I wheezed.

He settled between my thighs and drove in deeper, his forehead pressed to the bed beside me, his grunts muffled next to my ear. Another handful of thrusts and he stopped, tensing as he groaned open-mouthed. Though in shock, I felt the wide cock flexing as he came inside me. I wriggled to free my hands from his clutches; he made the mistake of letting them go. I snatched hold of the pain point that worked on his daughter.

He jolted, blurting a shout as I yelled, "Get off me!"

The sorcerer rolled off, his cock leaving a slimy trail across my thigh as it pulled out, but grappled me as I tried to slip free. I jabbed my knuckles at the hollow of his throat, watching his eyes go wide with pain and shoved him backward so I could get up. He lunged, our arms blocking and locking, and I stared him down.

"I said *don't*—!" I snarled.

Only to be swept up in those grey eyes. In an ancient, waking dream.

When I rolled over again, every rock, pebble, and grain of sand pressed into my skin, beaten raw. I hissed at the pain, my gut writhing and my limbs losing all strength as the memory of shame rushed in to fill any part of my mind not distracted by the fire on my back. Her proclamation pealed inside my head.

*If you survive, Captain, you may return from exile one day.*

Exile.

What had I done?

More, what *hadn't* I done? Had I failed her?

*Survive.*

I walked naked across the dunes and beneath the stars, alone at first. The Sun scorched what skin wasn't broken and dirty if I couldn't find sufficient shade to hide within during the day. At one point, in the empty sands, I admitted aloud that I hated the Queen-Mother's judgment against me, against her own Daughter. She was wrong.

Ishuna was trying to tell us something.

One early dawn, lying beside a tiny oasis I dared not leave yet, I spotted the Zauyrians riding toward me. Perhaps they hadn't been searching but found me, nonetheless.

"Who are you?" said the Sorcerer's Heir.

"Captain," said the death mage woman beside him. "Your light is fading."

"What under Musai's Eye happened when we left the waterfall?" Cris-ri-phon said, sounding young and angry.

Leur-en-phon looked at his young brother and back at me. "May we help you, Captain? On my word, we'd only see you well. You may leave our hospitality at any time."

I was hesitant to believe him, but… I wasn't ready to die. I accepted water, a potion, a blanket. I left the Queendom to live in the Zauyrian Realms, and in return, taught some men how to fight. Wounds healed though scars remained, and days blurred together. Davrin came to trade sometimes, and I saw among them—I was certain—a trader I had not yet met.

*Toushek.*

The handsome male seemed to sense me watching. He turned to look at me from across the courtyard, his sclera like polished ivory, and smiled in pleasant recognition. He approached; I chose not to flee.

"Captain," he said in the Queen's tongue. "A surprise to find you here."

"Is it?"

"Exiled like your uncle, I take it. A disturbing turn."

"How could you know my uncle?" I demanded.

The trader shrugged, his dark skin perfect, his hair long and blinding white. I saw no sweat upon his brow. "How could any Dark Elf *not* know the House which quickened our two lovely qu'eesans within the womb of our Queen-Mother?"

"That's not what you said."

Toushek smiled. "Isn't it?"

Building noise in the courtyard distracted me, and we both turned to see the Sorcerer King Begir-al-phon preparing to leave for V'Gedra with his two sons.

"Two sons," Toushek murmured, "and two qu'eesans…"

I frowned. "Two Humans, and two Davrin. An alliance passing from Begir to Leur at best, a dalliance at worst."

"Indeed." The trader turned his red gaze toward me again. "Did you meet anyone in the Desert before the Deathwalker sensed your life fading?"

Chill prickled my skin, but I answered. "Meet anyone? Like whom?"

"No mirage, even? No voice promising the rescue which was coming?"

I shook my head. "No. Just me and the lizards. I, um, ate a few."

The trader chuckled and bowed his head. "As you must to anchor your heart, Captain Ja'Prohn. It is a true pleasure to meet you, but I must go."

"Wait, Toushek, who was the—?"

Memories blurred, turned upside-down, and spilled amongst the stars. I was still in the Fort Li-Phon, but Leur and Houda had returned without Cris.

Someone else had traveled from the capital in his place.

"Your grace."

Suddenly, I held the younger qu'eesan in my arms, felt her tremble. My back ached from old injuries.

"I won't tell Mother you're here," she whispered. "I won't."

"As you like, your grace. That is between your Mother and you."

"Mother is wrong about so much," she said fiercely. "I'm a seer! And no one believes me but Houda and Leur." She sniffled against my armor. "Meanwhile, my sister's toy bua says he's *sorry*, but he still doesn't know what he *did*."

"Qu'eesan," I said, waiting until the quaking had eased before leaning back. Lightly, I hooked her chin, so she'd look up at me. "It will get better, your grace. I'm glad you're here. I will guard you better this time. I won't leave you alone again. My oath."

The royal Davrin lifted her head and gazed up at me. Her eyes had always been oddly light for a copper-eyed Elf but, unless my memory had been warped by the Desert nights since, they had since shifted a tawnier shade, like topaz.

"Thank you, Xala," she said. "And here in the Humans' Realm, just... call me by my name."

"Very well. Ishuna."

Cris-ri-phon was howling, gripping his head as he staggered naked through the red curtain into his office space. I scrambled for my shirt and pants, fisting them in one hand as I fled the alcove with the blind hope that I could seize my armor and run.

I couldn't find it before the Zauyrian slammed his body against the only way out, red ruby swinging across his bare chest, his expression like a bear wishing to maul me to pieces. I could feel his cum smearing my thighs, but I couldn't feel the bottoms of my feet. I feared I would collapse if I took a step.

Was I trapped in a trance or a spell? Did he see the same vision I had? Were we awake? Was this *real?*

"Sun scorch the Infernal," he muttered in Trade like a Witch Hunter, shaking his head, and blinking to clear his gaze. He focused on me. "Ishuna is still your Queen. Good. I am grateful to know I am not too late."

"T-too late?" I stuttered, recalling the incredibly young face of my ruler, younger than me. "If you haven't acted, wh-what have you been doing all this time? Where have you been, dabbling with the Ma'ab Nobles?"

The Zauyrian stared at me, his eyes growing cloudy, his face haunted as he lifted his hand to see the firebird ring on his finger. It fit better than the first time. "I either never knew where she fled, or I...haven't much memory in between. So it has been. But with you,

Sirana, it feels like only one life ago." He looked up at me. "Tell me, how are you doing this?"

"How?" I clutched my clothes to my heaving chest, the saphgar covered from sight, and glanced around again for my boots and armor. "I don't know what is happening! You are the 'Deathless' who mounts me from missing your 'wife' and then complains of stirred memories. I *told* you not to press me on my back, but you did. I only felt panic, no pleasure!"

"Hm." He looked chagrinned. "Have you been held down and raped by a man before?"

"What?" I was incredulous. "No! I've been forced onto Braqth's altar, you *khalizi karlick!*"

The Zauyrian closed his mouth, daring to look amused but swallowed it down. "I see. That is a different place. My wife enjoyed sex like this. She knew it was harmless and only showed my passion for her."

"I don't care," I hissed. "I am *not* your wife. I am *not* from the Desert!"

"I shall remember that."

"Best you do."

Cris-ri-phon exhaled, stepping to a wardrobe to open it and withdraw what he'd taken of my belongings. Carrying them to place in the chair nearest the washstand, he stepped away again, waving his hand.

"Please, clean and dress. I will send for food. You must eat, Sirana."

Just him saying this made me lightheaded and queasy. Swallowing down bile, I focused on this task. Not only were my black boots and leather pieces here, but so were my cloak, weapons, and tool belt. But not my spiders.

Were they still in the shed? Had he captured them, or were they dead for trying to bite him?

"My guardians," I said calmly, plaiting my hair and tying off the braid. "Did they not attack you when you seized me and brought all my things here?"

Cris-ri-phon was dressed and groomed, as I was, and briefly combed his silver-white hair back from his creased brow. "Oh, they did. They didn't succeed."

A stone seemed to slam into my gut. "Did you kill them?"

"No." He looked over at his shelf of treasures. "Perhaps I should have. They are extremely venomous and aggressive."

"Protective," I corrected. "And I control them."

"Another gift from your 'leader' to help shield you on the 'Surface'?"

I grimaced to realize I'd slipped, and Cris-ri-phon smiled at me.

*Goddess damn it.*

"Yes," I answered.

"The Spider Queen went underground," he said with pretend blandness, walking over to his shelves to open a different chest from the one containing the dagger. "That explains your night vision."

My teeth clenched. "Where are they, sorcerer?"

"Right here. Have no fear, they are well."

He lifted out what appeared to be a hollow glass or crystal sphere the size of a large fruit. My babies were inside, hopping about madly trying to get at his face until he settled it in his palm, then they focused beneath them, trying to pierce his hand through the clear barrier.

I appreciated their effort but could see by the sorcerer's expression it wasn't going to work. I didn't ask yet how to let them out or when I was getting them back but watched the ball roll around with them inside after he set it on the dining table near a used plate.

*~Calm, my babies, I'm alright.~*

"Can they breathe?" I asked, not hiding my concern.

"Yes, they can," Cris said, craning his neck toward a different thought. "So, your leader knew you were pregnant and still sent you on whatever this mission is supposed to accomplish."

I glanced up from the rocking sphere with no response I cared to give until I saw what else he had in his hand. I blinked in surprise. *D'Shea's expulsion vial.*

"You searched my things?" I began.

"Were you planning to use this?" he asked, setting it down on the table near my spiders.

I frowned. "Not unless survival forced me—"

The sorcerer picked up the metal plate and smashed it down, shattering the vial. I jumped, staring in shock.

*"No!"* I blurted. "What have you done?"

"There is *always* another way!" he thundered. "I won't have this poison in my town, but especially if you might be the one to drink it!"

My stomach boiled. *How dare he?*

*"Any* poison on my belt can cause miscarriage, 'life' mage!" I barked, pointing at the glass shards. "You destroyed the safest one for me!"

"You don't need it, Sirana!"

"No? What will I do should the Ma'ab take me in this state? Like they did the Priestess and her son!"

His eye twitched at the mention, then he denied it again. "I never saw or heard one hint of such a capture."

"Well, I *did*," I snarled, my voice rising. "Ask Kurn when the fool tried and failed to use that ruby against me, as *you* did!"

Cris exhaled. "I will make sure this doesn't happen. I will protect you."

I huffed incredulously. "I refuse your protection, sorcerer. It conflicts with my mission."

"Sirana—"

"I have not asked for your help!"

"I am the *only* one who knows your importance!" he roared. "Not even *you* know it, if you're risking your child to be sodomized by a killer in front of another killer for the thrill! You *need* my help!"

I bristled. "I do not *want* it! You interfered for your own desire! Do not lie to yourself like that fool Witch Hunter!"

Cris-ri-phon and I were heaving to catch our breaths, each of us shaking in anger as we refused to blink. Only when a whisper rose within my ears did the ancient mage blink and wrench his gaze away. Neither of us spoke, and a few moments later, unwelcome tears of frustration climbed into my eyes.

*Goddess, he smashed my vial!*

He had taken what Elder D'Shea had risked so much to be able to give me. It wasn't his mission. It wasn't *his* fate, but *mine!*

"Ah, don't cry, Sirana," Cris-ri-phon said with regret, rubbing his eyes. "I apologize. I did not want to get angry, but I was deeply concerned for you when I heard the shouting in the shed."

I wrapped my arms around myself, one hand covering Shyntre's pendant. He thought my tears were from showing his anger. What did that matter compared to what he'd done? I was cold with the proof that this man wanted to own my fate, wanted to wrest it from the Valsharess, and would use my unborn against me exactly as I feared someone would.

*I must escape this town. I must.*

"It's just…" the Zauyrian continued when I remained silent. "Elven babies were so precious in my time. They take so long to grow compared to Humans, both to birth and to raise where they could fend for themselves. I had men in my army enter training and serve an entire career to retirement before a Davrin infant was independent from his mother." He huffed a laugh. "Even the fighting *caits* who caught, I tried to find them and convince them to wait it out in safety. My coffers would pay for their care!"

I listened, wondering how often that succeeded if we truly "hadn't changed." The Zauyrian would answer that question next while shaking his head.

"I never understood why they were so reluctant. So many ran away or didn't keep their word. It was damnably infuriating."

*I can imagine.*

"My guess, as a *cait*," I said, watching as he lifted his gaze. "She had discussed it with her Elven elders and sisters already. And if she didn't tell you, it wasn't a Human matter."

Cris-ri-phon's eyes narrowed to splinters. "As their *Human* General, yes, it was a matter of *great* importance for my force. You weren't there, little fighter. You can't understand."

My hand deliberately covered my gut. "Neither were *you*, innkeeper."

He glanced down and scoffed, shaking his head. I stared at the shattered vial dampening his table, my stomach roiling and requiring effort to tamp down dry heaves this instant. Somehow, it still protested my lack of food with a loud gurgle.

This gave us both an out.

"Ah, yes," he said. "I promised you could eat your fill. It grows late but I can wake Elana to prepare food for us."

"I won't eat in this room," I stated. "The scent is making me ill."

His face tightened, and the desire to command me was clear for an instant. He took another breath, choosing a different battle.

"So be it," he said. "Your spiders will stay here, but you may eat in the kitchen itself. Fewer will see you there."

I shrugged. "I won't wear another disguise, and I don't want you hovering over my shoulder, making certain I eat what you deem is enough."

I listened to his heartbeat and felt his heat rising. He smiled coolly. "I hear you loud and clear, Sirana. You may go. Elana will meet you there."

There was a subtle sound of air tearing as the ward on the door dissipated. I spared one look for my other babies, locked in their own sorcerer's prison, then turned to head outside where I could breathe. Maybe think.

"Sirana," he said as I grasped the handle. "Should you be unable to resist sneaking out the side door into the night, my first rule applies. Take your time but don't leave town. I will find you."

Without verbal reply, I glanced back, made an ugly face of acknowledgment, and let myself out. His sigh of disappointment followed behind me.

Callitro's ring was missing, D'Shea's potion was spoiled, and my guardians couldn't guard me. What *else* had he taken while I was out?

*Braqth damn him to a metal web!*

I would have gladly thrown him into the Keeper's Pit to become Auranka's permanent child if preserving them was so important to him.

I stopped by the door as cutlery clinked, catching my breath so I wouldn't plunge into the kitchen like a snorting *uroan* and scared this "Elana" to make her eyes roll back. I needed food, but I needed to breathe, too. To think.

Where in the Abyss did I stand now? How could so much in the Surface be turning in on itself, making my head spin, still? Did it slow down up here?

The questions kept coming.

Was Ishuna my Valsharess, then? Was the sorcerer correct? But then who was Captain Xala, and why did I see through *her* eyes after rolling on the bed with *him*? Who was Toushek, for fuck's sake, and was he the source of these goddess-damned tricks in which Desert dreams were playing me?

They skewed my sense of time and self, lifting my feet from anything solid as if I could stand on a bridge of light or sand and somehow *not* fall and plummet into the Void's Chasm. Auslan had warned me of Toushek, but Toushek had warned me of the creature I'd seen in Koorul.

*"Beware the Scorpion's sting. It can come upon anyone, anywhere, at any time."*

Cris-ri-phon wasn't that firebird on his finger guiding the way. He was the scorpion who lunged out of stillness to seize his prey.

I was afraid, standing outside the kitchen, but I could breathe. My hood up, I opened the door and stepped down into the stone room. There was a woman working busily with the two children I'd seen sleeping by the hearth my first night. They were preparing a new fire and at first avoided looking at me.

"M'lady," the woman said, eyes down, bobbing her head.

"You are Elana?"

She blinked. "Aye, I am. We were told to expect you."

"I only want food."

She seemed baffled. "Aye. We're feedin' the fire, now."

Elana looked older than Amelda, her skin weathered, lightly brown, her hair a muted blonde, simply plaited. She wore a sturdy, modest dress of deep green with a well-used linen cloth tied around her somewhat plump waist. Her boots were practical and plain. Compared to the pink, tender hands of the young Humans taking her direction, her own hands were aged and callused.

She asked me, "Any ale wit' yer meal?"

I took a moment to translate, she'd spoken so quickly. "No. Clean water."

"And d'ya care for meat or plant? Bean or grain?"

I smiled a bit. She wasn't remarking on my appearance but nor was she assuming that she knew how to feed me. "Some of all, please. I will try anything."

"An' you'll eat in here?"

"So you may report to my host? Certainly, but I shan't linger."

Elana's freckled face flushed, and she poured water from a large pitcher into two cups, drinking from one and handing me the other. My eyebrows raised as she guzzled her cup, placing the pitcher within my reach. It was a lot of water.

"Serve as ye wish," she said.

"Thank you."

First, she collected a large serving of cheese, fruit, and vegetable, adding a chunk of bread and a savory paste like that I'd pilfered before, though this one contained softer shreds of dried meat and smelled to have different seasonings. She and the two children each took part of it to eat in front of me and slid me the rest.

"'Tis cold but fast," said the woman. "Warm course, next."

I sighed as I dug in, somewhat fascinated that she obeyed and passed on instructions given to her as nervously and diligently as a male cook would his Matron. I wondered if it was her first time as food-tester, as well.

The three kept busy but sneaked looks at me, which I ignored cleaning my plate. In the better light, I could see the boy had hair blonde like honey and was a little taller but as soft-faced as the red-blonde girl. Neither had traits that would suggest they were nearing breeding age yet, but Gavin's interesting talk suggested that could change in as little as five years.

*Astonishing.*

The "kids" wanted to say something to me, many things, given they'd seen me come in at night at least once, but were still afraid. I decided, after they froze in place when we made accidental eye contact, that I would start.

"How many years are those two?" I asked Elana, indicating the children.

Her dull blue eyes blinked, and she glanced warily at them then me, wiping her hands on the cloth around her waist. "Ah. Layne is nine years, m'Lady," she indicated the boy. "And my girl, Imara, is seven."

The impossibility of Davrin birthing children this close together struck me soundly enough that I believed I missed something. "They are your breed?"

Elana blushed a brighter red; at first, I thought she was angered. "I-I'm sorry?"

*Sorry for what?*

"They are your bloodline," I tried again. "You birthed them?"

"Oh, uh. Y-yes, m'lady."

She wasn't angry; she was confused but there was something else. Shame? For what? Bearing two children within two years must have taken a lot of focus and effort.

I noted then that her son seemed to loosen up and frown at me; he was no longer frozen. I focused on him. "What did I say, Layne?"

"Don't lookit her askance just cuz she had us without either man stayin'!" he said. "*They* the bastards, not me an' Imara!"

"Shh, Layne!" Elana scolded him.

I quirked my eyebrow at him and narrowed my focus. The courage fueling the boy's outburst waned, but he fisted his hands, inhaled, and shifted in front of his younger sister, as if by making himself stiff and big enough, he wouldn't run away.

*Interesting.*

"Elana is the mother of the first two Human children I have seen," I said, motioning to him. "You and her. That is all I asked, Layne, and all I care to."

The woman turned around to fuss with the "warm course," but the boy squinted his eyes at me.

"Why?" he asked. "Next question is always, 'where's our Da' or 'where's yer mum's husband'?"

I smirked at how he sneered the questions as if he was tired of hearing them. "I do not care. His prick served to help her conceive, but after that, what *she* does is notable where children are concerned."

As it had been with Tamuril in her hovel, I did not see agreement in their eyes. There was confusion, doubt, even distress. Why would my saying this be upsetting? Layne hadn't wanted me to ask about their sires, so I hadn't. I *didn't* care. At first.

Mentally, I backed up a step. "You... want a husband or 'da' to stay?"

All three faces fell sadly, and the girl nodded first.

"Yeah," Layne admitted. "Jus'...not those dingers who left her. Someone good, who takes care of women an' children, like Master Brom."

Elana sighed, sounding less embarrassed and prouder of her son as she petted his hair. "Aye. I am grateful to the governor, that he lets us remain here to work for him. He does not judge me."

I sucked on my cheek. "Judge you?"

"For having children but not being a wife to anyone."

I did not understand this.

"Well," I nudged my empty plate. "That... desire to see infants born seems to suit him."

"Indeed, it does, M'lady." The blonde woman smiled. "He'll do anythin' to see a woman keep her baby, even when she has nothing. He's a good man."

I frowned, recalling what he'd taken away to be certain of this. "Why does she 'have nothing' in the first place?"

Elana's face dropped. "I don't understand, M'lady."

An awkward pause.

"Ready for more food?"

"Yes, please."

Layne and Imara watched me intently as I first observed Elana prepare the food and then ate a large amount, which was without doubt satisfying. I waited to see if these Humans had the spine to continue our awkward conversation, but I had slowed my pace due to fullness by the time one opened her mouth again.

"You have swords an' arrows," Imara stated, making sure to point to them.

"Long daggers and bolts," I corrected, thinking a cait her age should know better. *But I don't have my spiders, or my ring. Driders fuck the Deathless.*

Layne craned his neck. "Where's the crossbow for the bolts?"

I gave him a look. I shouldn't have been surprised. *Alright, then.*

I moved my cloak to show him the hand crossbow; and the boy peered at it. He knew what it was.

"Do you have a husband?" he asked bluntly.

I began to smile and found I couldn't stop. "No. I do not own a place to keep one. 'Husbands' are expensive to keep."

Three sets of small eyes rounded even further, and I chuckled.

"Ah, m-more than one?" Elana asked.

"Some mothers I know have five children by five husbands. Both take much to feed and protect, but the child is worth more to her rank, so she may trade the husband away. This is why I only asked for the mother, Elana."

Imara was utterly lost by my words, and her mother shook her head as if to forget what I said in an instant.

Layne stared at me; his curiosity was obvious. "So… yer a dark girl who fights an' don't marry cuz husbands are exp… expensive?"

"Correct," I answered, warming up to the young male.

"Don't the husbands earn the coin and own a place, so they're not expensive?"

"No, they can't."

"Why not?"

I glanced at my empty plate, unable to picture buas with that agency. "Because their mothers won't let them."

"Heh!" The boy attempted a laugh. "That only works until he gets big enough."

"Layne." Elana glanced worriedly at me.

"Well, it's what the loggers told me," he added as he hunched. "Then it's *his* turn to pick her up and put her to bed."

"Oh, God!"

*Indeed.* Feeling the Zauyrian's weight on me again, I shook it off.

"Maybe Human males get big enough," I remarked lightly. "Mine do not. They stay smaller, like Imara will be smaller than you."

Layne glanced at his sister, who said nothing. "You mean your husbands are like wives?"

I considered, surprised how clear were the visions of Auslan, Shyntre, even Callitro in my mind's eye. "Maybe. They can be clever and smart, and earn their way without size. But the game is balanced against them."

His smooth brow furrowed. "Game?"

"The rules you follow to live with your kin."

"Rules?"

I shrugged and motioned to his mother. "Why can't *she* own a place without a husband and not be 'judged'? Why must she work as a servant to a man who owns an inn, to shelter and feed you two?"

"It's the way things are," Elana replied stoutly as she fluttered her hands. "No reason to change it. It works best this way."

*Best?* The sudden spirit and resolve in her face only to defend where she stood was dismaying to see on a female, and if Cris-ri-phon was any example of a "husband," I hated the very concept.

Placidly, I shrugged. "Just the way things are."

I couldn't see it changing for my buas when I went back, either. Even if one of them had the will to be independent from us, the torment he'd face every cycle he tried—

*Torment that he's faced before.*

"Wow, I wouldn't like living there at all," Layne said with conviction. "I don't want a woman to take care of me!"

I smiled dryly but said nothing. Shyntre hated it beyond what this little Human could imagine. Yet, I considered him as a consort and doubted the cycles would ever be boring if the Headmaster's son lived with me.

Maybe him *and* Auslan. We could roll in bed, the three of us, and I could see what they were *really* thinking. See the look on their faces when I climaxed, or when one of them did. If my wizard had been seized with passion after learning I'd conceived by that Consort, how might he be when my belly was showing?

*Whew.*

"Layne, apologize," Elana suggested. "You've upset her."

Abruptly, I shook myself out of my heat-dream. "Hm?"

"I'm sorry," Layne said obediently though confused.

*You aren't the only one, bua.*

I asked him, "What do you want when you get 'big enough,' Layne? Learn to fight? Marry and own a place?"

He scratched his head. "Maybe both?"

I shrugged. "Hm. In that case, ask Master Brom how."

"But he don' have a wife."

"He did once. He outlived her."

"Oh?" Layne considered. "Wait. He can fight, too?"

I grinned. "On many levels. He keeps his *secrets*. Else how would he know a fighter like me?"

I winked. Tentatively, Layne smiled back.

"You gonna leave with th' big man soon?" he asked.

"The big man?" I repeated.

"The Ma'ab, Kurn."

*Ugh.*

"Maybe," I said. "Why?"

"Well, Amelda's talking how to get a ruby for him, so—"

Elana wrung her hands in her apron. "Layne, I told you not t'spy!"

I showed my annoyance with her interruption. "I would like to hear him speak, Elana."

She tried nervously to convince me. "He doesn't know what he heard. He thinks he understan's Ma'ab from Amelda."

"She taught me some!" Layne insisted. "I know they were talkin' of the demoness."

"Shh!" his mother scolded.

Indeed, in this case, her caution was right. I turned my ear toward the door to the kitchen. Nothing I could hear. I turned on my stool to look at the boy. "Best to keep your voice quiet when you offer secrets, Layne."

The young Human agreed with amusing seriousness. "I'll be."

Elana rubbed her face, seeming afraid, but waved her hand and shook her head again. "Then tell her, Layne, but no more spyin' whether the governor's daughter teaches ye or not, d'you understand me? The Ma'ab are a cruel people."

"Sorry, Mama."

I waited as the golden-haired boy approached me slowly. His warm brown eyes seemed to want to take in every detail of me that he could up close. Perhaps that was the trade he wanted for gossiping.

"Amelda wants a ruby so the big man an' the mage can leave," he said. "They want to ride fast but need the necklace first. And they want you to go with them."

*Voluntarily, I'm sure.*

"When did you hear this?"

"This afternoon."

"Did they mention a direction?" I asked. "Or a place?"

His face scrunched up to think, and he looked to the side. "I dunno."

"Did you hear 'Manalar'?"

334

Layne shook his head. "Nah."

"Hm," I considered, showing more thought than I was giving it. "What about 'Ennikar.'"

His eyes brightened. "Yeah, that sounds right."

I sighed inside. This wasn't going to end well between the Ma'ab and the innkeeper, and I was the center-web prize in this contest. If it somehow happened that Kurn and Castis dragged me to their superiors, it was worse for me because Cris-ri-phon had smashed my expulsion vial. Goddess *damn* him.

The General would have to prove to them how much he really remembered.

"Thank you, Layne," I said, standing up. "That is good to know."

"You gonna go with him?"

I made a face. "No. Kurn knows he'd have to fight me again. He lost last time."

The boy's eyes grew huge, and he gasped. "I wanna to see you fight!"

"Layne!"

Elana brought her apron to her mouth, aghast, and Imara hid behind her mother when I walked around the table. I smiled at the boy, and it felt good to laugh out loud.

"Maybe you will," I told him, slipping out the side door otherwise unchallenged.

After a big meal like that, I needed to sit somewhere quiet and do my own planning. Somehow, a hayloft in a barn with a dead man seemed far more appealing than any bedroom in Brom's inn.

# CHAPTER 14

I STEPPED IN THROUGH THE BARN'S REAR DOOR, WHICH WASN'T blocked or barred. I wasn't sure if this was smart or not. Should the Ma'ab want to confront Gavin alone, there was nothing to stop them, though I supposed they would have to know he was here. Likewise, if Kurn simply wanted to check on his stallion, having a communal place locked or barricaded would only draw hostility and challenge.

I decided it was smart.

"Gavin?" I whispered.

Long noses blew and snorted, tails swished, and I smelled the thick scent of horse hide and dung. The animals were nervous but not such that I could tell if this was normal or not. It could be me; it could be anything.

I stepped in on silent boots. "Gavin, it's Sirana."

Finally, I heard him. He was not up in the hayloft as I'd expected, but in the "box stall" with his mare. He stood up off the floor, and then a ghastly, pale face leaned out over the chest-high door, his eyes glowing pale blue as he peered at me. I paused from pure fright.

And *this* was the face of my best ally.

I exhaled. "Gavin."

"Yes," he replied.

"May I sit with you?"

"If you like. May I ask why?"

I shrugged. "I'm not safe here anywhere. At least I know the Ma'ab dare not cut you." When he didn't reply, I smirked and spoke honestly. "Yes, I would use you as a shield so I can rest."

The Deathwalker grunted in what might have been agreement and disappeared from my view until I walked up to the stall. Looking in, I saw his aged mare lying down on her side. With a sigh, I opened the latch and let myself in as the death mage had backed up to make room.

"So, she cannot carry us anymore," I said. "Your mare."

"Not yet," he agreed.

"The boy in the kitchen told me he overheard Amelda planning to get the ruby so Kurn and Castis can leave for Ennikar."

Gavin nodded. "To be expected."

"And to take me with them."

"Given their masters, they'd be foolish not to try."

I felt a pinch of annoyance. "Equally foolish to try."

"They seem reluctant to acknowledge that part."

One side of my mouth raised. Wordlessly, I sat down with my back to the wooden wall, opposite of Gavin to give him the space he preferred. I breathed in, noticing it was difficult to make out his scent among the animals. Whatever he was, it was not a rotting body.

I asked, "Are we being listened to?"

"Not this time. I found the spelled object that Brom hastily placed and have set it deep beneath the dung in the corner."

That made me smile. *Good.*

"Cris-ri-phon wants me to stay with him, to 'help' me, and use force," I said. "But he hasn't given me one hint what he would do about you."

Gavin waited, and I spoke my largest concern.

"He knows I'm carrying," I said, unable to keep fear out of my voice. "H-He interrupted my questioning Jacob, put me to sleep and trapped my guardians in a sphere. I woke up in his room, and he only wanted to mate again."

"Again?" Gavin sounded neutral, but the interjection made sense.

I groaned, clutching my head. That had been so stupid when I knew he wanted to find my Valsharess!

"Yes, while you were dead," I said. "I will explain but of greater concern to me is that he went through my things while I slept and destroyed a potion I could have taken if I am captured or am starving and may die."

"What kind of potion?"

I met his eyes. "One my elders gave me to empty my womb, if it becomes unlikely to carry and survive, or if an enemy would seize two prisoners." In a pause, I saw that fate again inside my mind. "If my baby would be born enslaved and used to control me, to force me to reveal where the Davrin are... I..."

The Deathwalker lowered his chin. "Hm. And he destroyed it. Is the Deathless one of those enemies, along with the Ma'ab?"

My throat aching from suppressed tears. "I fear the Zauyrian over the Ma'ab, though they want the same thing. It is more than greed or fear that drives him."

"Perhaps he would reclaim part of a past life with you?"

"Perhaps," I agreed. "Cris-ri-phon is a son of a Sorcerer King from the Desert, and he claims a Davrin Elf was his 'wife' and bore children of his breed, once. Further, he claims that she became Queen, and he was her General."

Gavin tilted his head with a mix of interest and confusion, but I wasn't finished.

"But they were all killed in the war with the Pale Elves he mentioned to you, betrayed by my Valsharess who sent me here." I opened my empty palms helplessly. "I am drawing out these memories from before their deaths just being here, and he is far too interested in seeing that I give birth."

"Ah," said my scholar. "To be expected for a life mage who rejected death."

"There is more," I continued.

"Yes?"

*He needs to know.*

"I would explain why we mated at all."

"I am listening."

"My...dreams have hastened his memory's return or made them clearer. Intensely so. As when you observed me affecting the others in their sleep on the Midway? When you warned me on the grassland?"

Gavin nodded.

"After you were killed, Cris-ri-phon let me sleep in his quarters for simple protection," I explained.

"Practical," he agreed.

"But he dreamed of the first time he mated his Davrin Queen and, *uhm*, I did as well. I saw his dreams, I am sure."

His placid expression didn't change, as if this were not unusual.

I swallowed but continued. "The sensations throttled any good sense I had. We both awoke, and he asked to couple. He...*asked*, and we bargained. I let him mount me because I wanted him to."

Any of my Sisters would have at least smirked, or rolled her eyes and shook her head at my dumb youth. Gavin hardly moved; I only saw his brief motion of pale fingers to continue.

"I-I can't control what is happening in my sleep," I confessed. "It is a... linking of minds I have not done since I was home, after I was injured. But I am *seeing* some of these distant times as dreams and cannot tell what is true." I shook my head. "When I watched him crush that vial... I must escape him, Gavin. I dare not stay to learn more of him or what he will make me do."

Regardless of the many warranted questions or specifics Gavin must have considered while he listened, he didn't ask them but accepted it as spoken.

He said, "I take it you no longer care to persuade him to help with the warp rot to the North."

I shook my head. "No. The cost is too great."

"Which direction would you go next?"

"What do you mean? I thought you said you must see it eradicated."

"So I must. That does not mean you must put your unborn in such danger. You could go another way after you escape."

I clamped down upon a feral fear clawing my chest, my arms wrapped tight around myself. I spoke before something stopped me. "I cannot. Mathias knows why I crossed the Midway with you. He'll tell Brom."

"Oh?"

"I-I seek a... a sister sent to destroy this same magical rot. Thetri Jacob *saw* her. That was what I left to ask him. He didn't know what she was, but she was *alive*. If she is still, I m-must find her first. I must help her. I go North."

"Indeed. I'd begun to wonder at the similar accounts from the dead. Is she a mage?"

"Mm-hm," I murmured, shivering from tension.

"Very well. We will go North and discover what we can of her."

I exhaled in relief. "Please, tell me what you said the eve you were attacked. What was drawn here that you would have avoided this place if you'd known?"

The Deathwalker weighed what to say, I could see in the familiar tics of a mortal monk. It did not take him long to choose. "Many elements are entangled, Sirana, but what I saw in my dreams that night suggested the Deathless is the cause of the warp rot, whether he knows it or not. It spreads toward the crossroads, to consume this new-built town because of what he keeps hidden here."

I huffed. How many things that could be! "What does he keep here?"

"A relic last known to cause great strife far from here, in the lands the Ma'ab Empire overtook when they found their way onto this plane."

*Relic? Fuck.* I dropped my forehead on my knees. "A red-rune dagger?"

Gavin tilted his head. "Yes. Have you seen it?"

*"Sirana,"* murmured the sorcerer in my mind. *"You know this blade, but you do not know me or the name of your Queen. Why? Was it spoken of by your Queen?"*

No.

*"Who warned you? … There is someone who remembers the old ways. Trying to speak out from the Void through you."*

"I have," I said. "In his quarters. He showed it to me, said it had been a gift to his Davrin Queen and he took it back."

My ally fell unnaturally still. "That is… disquieting."

I huffed without looking up. "The eve witch Osgrid agrees. She says the Dwarven folk would have it left buried, and she watches for signs."

"Hm. You mentioned the Deathless has gone through your belongings, and your guardians have been neutralized. Is there anything else missing?"

I blew out a breath, straightening up. "I will look."

I had known I must, and it did not take me long to take stock. I wanted to punch the wall after I'd finished.

"He took Sarilis's vial," I said. "He has my magical ring, my spiders, and he shattered the expulsion vial. The one intended for Manalar's heart is gone, but all else is here. Poisons I might use on him."

"I would guess he only removed that which is a threat to him. It stands to reason this sorcerer is more difficult to kill than it might appear."

I growled softly. "He also told me Sarilis's vial would be effective against the warp rot, not the sacred heart of Manalar. That we would not get the opportunity to try Sarilis's plot."

"Hm."

After one grunt, Gavin was silent for a time. I let him think while it was quiet. He turned his head from me to his mare, reaching out to touch her neck with his fingertips. It was then I noticed that she wasn't breathing.

"Oh, Goddess," I whispered. "Has she died?"

"Yes. Shortly before you entered the barn."

For me to not grasp that much sooner proved how afraid I was. I resisted a worrisome twinge of despair. "We need another mount. We cannot walk, we'd be overtaken within a day."

"Agreed. I have been waiting for the proper time."

"Proper time for what?"

He reached inside a pouch, withdrawing one of the carved bones I'd seen in Osgrid's hawthorn dwelling, and my stomach tightened. Should I tell him I'd gone through his belongings as Cris had gone through mine? I hadn't known my ally would come back. *I didn't take anything.*

"Remove your glove and hold this," he said, leaning forward and stretching out his arm.

I needed to meet him halfway to take it but hesitated.

"No harm to your unborn," he murmured. "I need a focus to attune her to your aura."

My eyes widened. "Her?"

A haunting gaze and cadaverous face watched me and waited, his hand too still in holding out the bone. Tugging at the fingers of my left glove, I slipped it off and got to my knees to take the object. It felt ordinary despite the stained carvings.

*Stained with what, though?* The markings were greyish-brown but hadn't been in Osgrid's place. It felt a little gritty.

"Rubbed with ash and blood," he answered like he could read me.

I was alarmed. "Blood? Yours?"

"No. Hers."

I had to crawl forward to look for it, but I spotted the small, fresh cut on the mare's chest, stitched closed with knotted threads. A shiver swept through me as Gavin began to whisper, and I retreated to my wall again clutching the bone in my palm. Although his un-earthly words remained quiet, I detected two pitches, one his normal voice and another exceptionally low beneath the sibilant chant.

The other horses in the barn began to whicker and neigh, knocking hooves against the stalls, and I worried the stallion would draw Kurn's attention, but then the bone in my palm became like ice while my lower belly grew warm like I had swallowed a small coal a day or two ago.

*What's happening?*

Absurdly, Shyntre's remark about disrupting a mage's concentration on purpose seemed exceptionally relevant. Wanting to gain distance, I held my breath.

"*Ushga'sselinum,*" he whispered. "*Granczikahrel'nosk.*"

My heart pounded while my body became warm all over and my vision blurred. *No harm to my baby, he said.*

How did he know? Or Cris, for that matter? Who could I even ask?

Without fanfare, Gavin stopped and withdrew his white hand from the horse's damp neck, and I waited for something to happen. His gaze held a close study to the body while also skimming the air around it, like D'Shea and Gaelan sometimes did. Then Gavin stood up in the stall and motioned for me to do the same; I was relieved to do so. Without a grunt or a huff, the mare craned her neck and rolled up to her belly, legs curling beneath her to sit.

"*Quarvalsha,*" I whispered.

Gavin glanced at me curiously, as if my Davrin word was more important than his dead mare sitting up. "What does that mean?"

"Uh, 'goddess,'" I muttered, gripping the bone tight in my hand.

"Ah. An exclamation pleading higher understanding in fear of the unknown."

I scrunched my face, my eyes flicking to the dead horse gone statue-still. "Yes. And Humans spout them all the time. No surprise, given their overall understanding of their world."

"Believe me, I know."

Ignoring the look on my face, Gavin returned to his mare, and I noticed how empty her eyes appeared up close, how she wasn't breathing. She did champ her teeth, though, and nuzzle at some of the hay, which was disconcerting.

"Only muscle memory, she won't eat it," said the death mage, next motioning to me. "I would like to test something, if you are willing."

"What?" I invited warily.

"As you would with your ring or any magic which needs your focus, Sirana, do so with the talisman and command her to get to her feet. Try again, if necessary. Take your time."

I grappled with that as my mind returned to Gaelan teaching me to attach her Feldeu to my body, her and Reishel eagerly await-ing my success. It hadn't been as effortless as it appeared when Jaunda did it, and I had *wanted* to focus then.

But here, to command a lame, dead horse to stand up?

*A good thing Gavin isn't looking at me like they did.*

I held the bone in the same, bare hand which lacked Callitro's ring. That helped, somehow. I had been using that hand to focus for months on the Surface. *To hunt and to eat.*

I missed my spiders, worried for them, but also recognized that same inner voice which they evidently understood. Despite this sucking pit of pricks which I'd fallen into, for an instant, I found that small, still place again. It was blessedly quiet.

*~Stand up.~*

Without apparent lameness or hesitation, Gavin's mare heaved her body to stand on four hooves. Gavin and I took another step away as she did, and my scholar appeared surprised.

"First attempt?" he asked.

My lips twisted. "For a dead horse, yes. Not so for magical commands."

"Fortunate." Gavin collected her saddle blanket, bags, and saddle. "Put on her bridle, if you please."

Slipping the bit into place had her champing her teeth again as I cinched the knots and Gavin saddled her. Once she was ready for riding, my ally picked up his pack and spade before he unlatched the box stall door.

"Let us lead her out to the forest to wait."

"Wait for what?"

"We'll speak of that." He hadn't paused, reaching for the barn's front door. "For now, I would rather you practice using my talisman to guide the mare."

I glanced at it, oddly cool but not frigid. "Why? Will she not obey you?"

"She will. You possess the better night vision between us. She no longer sees at all, so that strength at speed lies in the eyes of the rider."

*Better eyesight, hm?*

I followed his thinking. It was best to escape at night when pursuing horses could not see well. They may fight their riders' urgency for speed or risk a stumble and fall.

Gavin opened the barn door partway, peered then stepped outside, leaving it open wide enough for one horse. He waited for us.

I watched the night mare and stepped outside the stall. *~Follow me.~*

She lifted her leg and clopped one clumsy step forward and then another. After all four limbs had moved her forward, that "muscle memory" seemed to take over. While not flawless, her gait became more natural. Nothing about it reflected the injuries to her legs from the night of the storm which had brought her low.

Gavin stepped out of my way as his mare followed a Davrin Elf clenching a bone talisman out of the barn. The living horses whinnied; I imagined it might have been in relief.

"Where's Neal?" I whispered.

"He won't be back until morning."

As I expected. "What happens if I drop the bone?"

"Try it."

Clearing the space around us first, I did. The mare stopped in front of the talisman, and her head drooped down toward the dirt. She did not move. I picked up the bone again, but she didn't lift her head. I tried waving it side to side like a signal torch. Nothing.

"She is not blindly following the talisman but the one attuned to it," Gavin told me. "Have no worry if another seizes it from you. They will not have control of her by holding the bone. She will simply stop obeying you."

"And you could take her reins, magically."

"Correct."

"Could Brom seize her with the bone?"

He considered, shrugging. "We would see how much death magic he remembers, if he ever learned."

Gavin waited for me to mentally push the follow command again, and the three of us began walking toward the North side of town before he continued his trail of thought.

"Regardless, it would take proper time to reattune the talisman to himself," said the death mage, "assuming he could do so contested. There may be other spells he'd prefer instead."

I tested if I could speak and keep the mare walking at the same time. "Contested. Such as the contested spell between you and Castis outside the canyon?"

"Indeed. A contest of concentration and auras. I have no affinity to elemental magic to counter fire with another element but disrupting the Vis with a briefly awakened sense of mortality…" Gavin shrugged.

"Had the same effect," I finished. "His fire spell collapsed."

"Indeed. He believed for an instant he was dying. This was all it took."

I looked over the pale and ghastly man. "I've felt more chill around you since you sat up in the shed. It is not a breeze. Sign of a stronger death aura?"

"It is."

"What is a Deathwalker?"

Gavin was quiet in thought. "I am not sure."

"What? You're not?"

"I am still learning. Some death-touched know or call to the Grey Maiden in her many forms, and they take names for themselves. I believe the context the Zauyrian remembers is, *hm*, specific to a Desert practice I never knew. Perhaps it is only my association with you that he calls me such."

"Not only. Your skin shifts dark as mine in sunlight. You never corrected him, either."

He shrugged. "Part of that is I have no better name. Yet to be discovered."

With a smirk I studied his long, unhurried gait then looked behind us, focusing on his mare. She began to mimic it, as well as a horse could. It was humorous and fitting.

I grinned, turning back. "I like Deathwalker."

"If you say."

We entered thicker brush and trees, and I learned the night mare did not have any sense of space in enacting her duty. She trampled straight through brush when a simple step would have gone around and avoided the gash in her knee. Then she became stuck between two narrow trees when that was the shortest distance to me.

*~Stop.~*

She stood still, unresponsive, ribs and saddle caught by tight-angled trunks like a stone in a sling.

"Hm," Gavin grunted as he turned around, waiting braced on his shovel for me to fix this somehow.

*Fine.*

*~Walk backward.~*

She tore bark off getting free, clambering backward.

*~Stop.~*

The saddle was scuffed, and she clearly did not feel the gouges in her shoulder, but I grimaced and glanced at Gavin apologetically. "If she feels no pain to know to avoid damage, she will eventually tear herself to pieces."

"Indeed, as with a living body, a dead one does require maintaining. I will ponder this."

We located a hidden place for her to stand and, after a few awkward tries, I managed to guide the mare around obstacles without stepping into her direct path. As long as she didn't move, she couldn't be seen—Gavin assured that was no worry—but she could move ahead to the road without running into a tree.

"Very good," he said, observing as I set the talisman in my palm and pulled my glove over it to hold it there. "You have greater intuitive understanding than I realized."

I raised a brow at him, gesturing at him. "As do you. When I first spied the tower, I never imagined the man hunched and muttering snide remarks, with this same horse pulling his cart, would become anything like...you."

*And so abruptly.*

The Deathwalker looked toward the inn and the shed where he'd returned. "Such is how transition and change flow and mingle, sometimes."

*Whatever that meant.*

I sighed. "What next?"

"I am assuming you cannot leave this moment."

"No," I said, annoyance covering the other emotions as I scowled at what I could see of Troshin Bend. "I've not tested his means to find me should I leave town with no intent to return. But even were I ready, he has my guardians and Callitro's ring."

"Does Castis still have the second vial?"

"I assume yes." I considered. "Should we take both if we can? So—"

"So they are sure to chase us North?"

"Why would we want that? I would rather kill them. Poison them. Whatever it takes."

"And the sorcerer? You said you hadn't tested the length and speed of his reach, but we must unless you would somehow kill him, too. And his daughter."

Given how that night had gone, with only five Witch Hunters catching up to me in the forest while injured enough to need one of two healing draughts, I couldn't imagine it going well fighting alone against the Deathless sorcerer, his daughter, and the two Ma'ab who loathed me.

*Hmph. Where is a black-arrow, chain-dangling archer when I need one?*

"There was something else here the night you died," I murmured. "I do not know what, but it...aided me. And you, I think."

"What do you mean?"

"Another shooting arrows as I shot bolts at the Witch Hunters."

He frowned. "Hm. I... do not recall."

"Perhaps not in the smoke and noise," I said. "But I'd have been shot by a Manalari or further injured by Kurn without the second. It killed with a magic arrow—"

"Magic? How?"

"It...dissolved. It was not made of wood."

"Very well. And?"

"And it drove the Ma'ab away with a chain but didn't answer me when I attempted to call it out. It vanished when Brom and Rithal finally caught up."

Gavin lowered his chin and tilted his head. "With a chain?"

I decided to ask. "Kurn was afraid, I saw him. Why would a Hellhound fear something wielding a chain? Brom said that 'he wouldn't,' but Amelda interrupted, then Kurn later accused me of conjuring a ghost but did not explain."

I saw a spark of recognition.

"Hm," Gavin grunted. "Well, I have only heard tales of the Ma'ab raids on their neighbors. It was far from the monastery where I was born, and stories do become exaggerated."

"Go on."

"Some Hellhound stories claim they wield a barbed chain that moves on its own like a serpent. No common man in any Noiri town or village could fight this weapon, and in addition, the chain-bearing Hounds seemed invulnerable, their hide turning blades. Stories say they wrap the chain around one arm when not guiding it and do not bleed."

I recalled the sound again, able to imagine a tall man slowly unwinding a chain from his arm. *Before it whipped back, about to strike.*

And Kurn ran.

"That may have been it," I murmured. "The sound matched perfectly."

"I will trust your hearing on that."

I smiled dryly and considered the morning before I'd sought Osgrid.

*You conjured this ghost,* Kurn had shouted at me, *probing our minds with your wanton, Abyssal claws!*

The big Ma'ab had done something he never thought he would do, him and Castis. I knew Mathias and Rithal climaxed in their sleep as well and might guess what each of them might have been dreaming to bring them over like that.

Later, the dream of Cris-ri-phon and Innathi in the pool by the waterfall was the strongest.

*No will-bending. Pfeh.*

Clearly, that hadn't worked for me since the fight in the canyon. If only it didn't come solely in Reverie.

"How long until dawn?" I asked, attempting to see a telling star through the trees. Most were obscured.

"Five hours," Gavin answered. "Six at most."

I wasn't tired. I'd rested in Brom's bed, despite my waking call.

"Do you need sleep?" I asked him.

"Not tonight."

I made a face. An odd answer, though I could see it being related that tiny amount of food he'd eaten before he passed me the rest. A little food, a little sleep.

*Are you dead or not, Deathwalker?*

The Greylands were more complicated than he'd expected.

I sighed, weighed actions I might take to escape Troshin Bend, and had not found one I liked when a wide, familiar boot crunched a twig to my left. My head turned, and I spotted Rithal's beard beads in a red braid catching a touch of moonlight.

"What do you hear?" Gavin asked.

"Come out, Rithal," I said as reply, raising my voice. "I heard you."

A crow cawed overhead, then another; I thought this was odd at night but wasn't sure. It fit a moment later when the Dwarf cautiously pulled Osgrid into view.

*Ah. Sneaky birds.*

"No danger, we are," Rithal said, his wide palm up and toward me. "Osgrid wanted tah meet Gavin. Er, whoever's in his body."

"He *is* Gavin," I replied firmly as they came closer. "I am certain."

"Certain's good tah hear," said the eve witch in dry humor as they closed ground. "Gettin' along, then?"

I glanced at Gavin. "Yes. We are."

He didn't protest.

"Heh. Mm-hm." Osgrid tilted her curly head up to look at the tall Deathwalker. "Huh-boy, whoof. I see a new bogey tale fer th' woods around here. Pro'bly gonna be blamed on me again."

"You are Osgrid, the 'eve witch'?" Gavin asked.

"Aye. I'll say bluntly 'tis not often I hear of someone's end only for them to stand up recalling where they been. Never a peaceful thing for others."

"Peace is merely when base needs are met with nothing urgent to be addressed," Gavin said. "Disruption usually implies need regardless of motive."

"Oo, a grey thinker." The Dwarven witch smiled, glancing at me. "Not easy on the eyes but I might get why ye missed yer tutor, Elf."

I folded my arms, biting down a reflexive denial. I supposed I had missed him, at least compared to certain others I wished to leave far behind or dead in his place.

Gavin asked Rithal, "I take it there was no renegotiating your aiding the Ma'ab while I was dead?"

"Nae," he grunted. "I'm done with 'em. Brom, too."

"Where do you go next?"

The redbeard shrugged. "Augran, probably. Still ain't done wit' the Bishops."

"Vengeance gonna getcha killed, Rithal," Osgrid said.

"I know, moonlove. M'sorry."

Gavin tilted his head. "What of Jacob Thetri?"

Rithal shrugged. "Gettin' what he's earned under Mathias."

"An' glad you aren't doin' it?" Osgrid asked.

"He'd be dead already, were it me," Rithal growled, then addressed Gavin. "Jacob's the one that killed you, what I heard."

Gavin agreed, "He did, though it easily could have been Bictrius or another. It doesn't matter who made the final blow."

"It doesn't?" repeated the Dwarf, sounding angry and incredulous. "Cause you got t' come back, thanks tah some goddess or other, unlike th' rest of us?"

My ally paused at the tone.

"Not without an exchange," I said, nudging Gavin's arm with my finger. "Tell them. You told Brom, and he knew who she is."

"Aye?" Osgrid asked, interested. "Is this the woman with the pale, cracked mask?"

The Deathwalker narrowed his eyes. "How would you know that detail."

The eve witch held his gaze. "I saw yer grimoire. Sirana came tah me, wanting advice. I'm guessin' from another female."

I swallowed as Gavin showed me his resentment. "I… I thought you were dead and knew Castis and Amelda sought your things. I was curious and did not trust to ask the sorcerer, either."

"She's trying tah learn," Osgrid interjected.

"Sirana went back fer ye on 'Grid's advice," Rithal added, tossing his bearded chin toward his companion. "Got there in time tah stop whatever the Ma'ab were tryin' with yer body. Yer in one piece thanks tah her."

Gavin grunted, reconsidering. "Very well. Perhaps this is…necessary." He looked at Osgrid. "The masked woman is a form the Grey Maiden has taken in my dreams. I am not returned at my pleasure but at hers."

The eve witch's expression brightened in recognition and she glanced upward. "Aye, the Seer for th' Dead! Scrolls back home mention her."

"Is this Heligana?" I asked her. "As the end of things?"

"No, no," Osgrid replied, waving her hand. "They are not the same, Elf. My own Heligana has domain only of this world and its change, the rock below the sky as it breaks and reforms. The Grey Maiden is…" She glanced up through the trees to the stars then to Gavin. "Otherworldly. Of th' spirit, not the rock. More like th' Sun Brother. There's reason both Musanlo and Nyx were once worshipped at Manalar fer centuries 'fore th' Bishops."

"I've begun to see," Gavin replied. "It seems the Dwarves have longer memories than men."

Osgrid's ruddy, round cheeks were pronounced as she grinned. "We always have."

"Why'd ye come back, Gavin?" Rithal interjected. "What service are ye tah perform for her?"

I knew that Gavin was unaccustomed to discussing his plans with anyone, especially concerning his secret Maiden. To be asked an informed question *and* be ready to be believed was something he'd never known while alive.

Belief may not be difficult now. To see the man this way lessened my doubt about how much had been real before. Much like the Driders were proof of Braqth's influence among the Davrin, this Deathwalker was the proof that Gavin said was missing among Manalari while they worshipped an ever-present Sun while seeing only devils everywhere.

*Why have you come back?*

"Oddly, we're brought full circle," Gavin answered the Dwarf.

"Oh?"

"You said you weren't done with the Bishops."

Rithal jerked his head in a nod. "I did. Ye goin' tah Manalar?"

"It lays in my path."

"Go on."

"First, I agree with what Sirana learned from Brom. The vials Sarilis provided are not suitable for their intended use."

Bushy, red eyebrows drew down. "They're not?"

"Not when there is a better option in Jacob Thetri. An opportunity to return the quality of soul they've cultivated to the heart of their temple."

Rithal glanced at Osgrid, who provided no hints in her enigmatic smile. "Not sure I'm followin', death mage."

"I could use your assistance," Gavin said to him, "if Mathias will allow me to see to Jacob's transition, assuming we're not too late."

Rithal glanced at me and back. "Why my assistance an' not hers?"

"Yer driven," Osgrid answered succinctly.

Gavin glanced at her and agreed. "A shadow follows you by invitation, Rithal. The state of Sirana's Vitas is not suitable for this task."

An oblique inference to my pregnancy, maybe? My arms were folded; I kept them so waiting for my ally to close his agreement while I pondered my own.

"'Kay," Rithal said slowly. "When?"

"Tonight, preferably."

"Before dawn," added the eve witch.

Rithal glanced at her with appreciation. "Awright. Whatcha need?"

As I listened to Gavin's answer, it was no different from what the Witch Hunters and Priestesses wanted. *Presence. Focus. Witness.*

"It's a sacrifice ritual, isn't it?" I said.

"Yes," Gavin replied without remorse.

"And it could be dangerous to me," I added.

"It could be."

"You'll be in the shed with Mathias for a while?"

"I will."

"Then I will use the time to retrieve my things from Brom," I said. "And tell him what his daughter's planning with the ruby."

Gavin nodded; Rithal quirked one brow in confusion.

Osgrid asked, "Ye want me t'come with ye?"

I didn't see how she could help and drew breath to refuse, then paused as her answer to my question came back. *How long have you been following him, Osgrid?*

*Only now. This life. Watching for sign.*

If nothing else, she'd be an anchor to this time, and those ancient memories against which I had no defense would not swarm us both. I didn't know precisely what she could do yet, but I hadn't proven to have any advantage being alone with the Zauyrian.

"Yes," I said. "Come with me."

# CHAPTER 15

THE THREE TRAILED BEHIND ME AS QUIETLY AS THEY COULD, though I could only hope any who heard the Deathwalker and two Dwarves might mistake them for a dog or deer rustling through the brush.

*Snap!*

I winced. *Or maybe a boar.*

It was extremely late into the night, at least, and the events of the past few days found no Human with the interest and strength to be out tonight, either making mischief or standing guard.

Perhaps the "governor" using the Ma'ab ruby to keep panic down and men working as if the night had been ordinary required a price to be paid in exhaustion. Not the men alone but the sorcerer as well, given how many headaches he seemed to suffer. I huffed quietly. If that was the average willpower for the mundane man under one mage, I should assume every Human leader was a mage until proven otherwise.

I wondered, what did this make me? Not a leader, but I'd withstood two of three direct attacks from different men with the same red stone. I was not mundane, but how much of this was consequence of encountering Kain and how much was being a Davrin coming of age in Sivaraus?

Approaching the shed from behind, I inhaled, catching the mix of scents I expected by now, including blood. Listening, however, there were no sounds except breathing men. I turned my ear toward it and slowed my step. *Yes, two.*

"What is it?" Gavin asked in a low whisper.

I stopped and turned, waiting until he was beside me. "Mathias and the Witch Hunter are sleeping. There was no blood when I was there earlier, but now there is."

Unperturbed, the Deathwalker nodded as Osgrid and Rithal caught up to us. "Unfortunate we may have to be loud to wake him."

"Maybe not," I said. "Let me check the door."

As I expected, Cris-ri-phon had caused damage to the door when he'd barged in earlier to seize me from the skin hunter. The inside bar was in place, but there was a greater gap between the door and jamb where I could see the bar across the door. It was no longer level and sat loose in its cradle.

*Hm.*

I drew two daggers, slipping one in between the door and jamb to lift the bar high before pushing the bar forward with the other, so it would miss the cradle in its way down. The wood creaked and shifted, my efforts weren't noiseless, but neither man inside stirred regardless.

"Oi," Osgrid whispered to Rithal, "weren't playin' 'bout her dark sight."

I smirked. Most of this was by feel; I could have closed my eyes and accomplished the same.

Grasping the handle, I braced my body and pushed in enough to peek in a crack. As before, the thick scents of two men filled my nose and the recent memories returned in vivid form. I paused, letting every moment pass through and grabbing only one.

*Jacob saw Gaelan.*

I wanted to leave tonight if I could. Staying another day meant only that much time she was alone and greater opportunity for my enemies to become allies against me. I would rather not leave Sar-ilis's vial, since it may be what I needed against the warp rot, but I would if necessary.

Could I leave my guardians with Cris-ri-phon? Or Callitro's ring?

*We'll see.*

Inside, the shed was just short of lightless; the lantern was turned as low as could be without snuffing the flame, and moon-light could not reach into this cave-like dwelling. Nonetheless, the forms of Mathias Briar and Jacob Thetri stood out to me, the for-mer curled up on the floor and the latter strapped to the same table Gavin had once been lying upon.

The table had been moved to the center of the shed and away from the wall; the Witch Hunter lay on his back now, still nude, gagged, and filthy with body fluids and oil which appeared to have been added later. The captive possessed all his limbs and digits that I could see, so either Mathias had become vicious with the whipping and branding, or Jacob had stopped feeling the same intensity he craved and demanded greater punishment.

Desiring harm like that wasn't unheard of back home, usually a bua bent that way by his Matron or mistress. His type didn't last before he was used up, and she would always search for another to train if she wanted to feed her appetites.

I could see why Mathias traveled a lot.

"What d'ye see, Elf?" Rithal whispered.

"Captive and captor sleeping," I replied. "Taking a rest from the games."

"Games?"

Without answer, I opened the door and stepped in. Finally, Mathias shifted, quickly sitting up.

"Mmm? Who's there?"

"It's me, Mathias. Care for some light?"

"Sirana."

The skin hunter fumbled some with the oil lantern on the table nearby, and I watched him do this, ready to catch it if he knocked it over. Squinting as the wick brightened, hurting my eyes, I met Mathias's bleary eyes and saw his smirk.

"Back so soon, 'witch'? What's wrong, is Brom a little bland for your taste?"

"Bland *and* heavy," I answered dryly.

Mathias laughed, and Jacob inhaled at the sound, groaning through his gag. His eyes were closed for the moment; his head lolled. Behind me, Gavin ducked his head and stepped inside before Mathias could ask me anything else, and the interrogator responded by standing full onto his feet. Rithal stepped in next. The nobleman wasn't slow.

"The fun's almost over, isn't it?"

"Aye," the Dwarf answered, staring coldly at the bound Witch Hunter as he came forward. "Here tah kill th' last one so we can move on."

"Aww, pity," Mathias replied, sounding like a Sister who'd pounded herself into exhaustion. "I'm not sure I can catch another *this* good closer to the Temple City, but I can try."

"You don't hafta go," Rithal offered. "Gavin an' Sirana still goin' wit' me, but we're not travelin' wit' the Ma'ab."

"Oh?" I noticed Mathias didn't look Gavin in the eyes. "Why bother with Manalar? You're intimidating now, apprentice. You could head back to Sarilis and take over the place when he died. Maybe sooner. You seem to have, uh, beat him to the dying part."

Gavin didn't acknowledge this. "I want Jacob when you're through with him, skin hunter. His passing will serve a purpose."

Mathias perked up. "Payback?"

"If that matters, yes. Whatever way, I want his death."

"Me, too," Rithal said. "I'm here tah make sure."

"Well," Mathias remarked dryly, glancing at me. "Are you as bloodthirsty tonight, 'devil'?"

I smiled; my lips sealed.

About then, Jacob opened his eyes and recognized each of us—Gavin and me especially. His face flushed deep red as he began spewing muffled Manalari curses at us. He possessed astonishing recovery in his rage and hatred, enhanced by the pain of lashes on his back. I wished I could see that snarl change to a whimper when he realized Gavin wasn't playing games like the skin hunter. Or me.

Mathias looked between us and chuckled. "Well, I'm curious."

"Good," Gavin said. "You wish to stay?"

"Damned right." The skin hunter noticed when I turned toward the door. "Hey, Sirana, you're not staying?"

I paused. "I agreed to seek Brom again soon."

"Heh. He's tightening the leash, is he? He does that. I knew he'd be taken with you."

Squashing my irritation, I smiled and winked at him instead. "We don't want him breaking in *again* to interrupt *this*, do we? Lock the door. I will be back."

*If I can.*

I left with the Witch Hunter becoming rowdier and defiant, and Rithal barred the door behind me. Osgrid stood nowhere near the door when I stepped out; she looked unsettled, like she was glad to get away from the shed. We walked around the rear of the inn to the far side, where we might enter through the kitchen.

"So, what things did Brom take from ye?" she asked along the way.

"Three black spiders trapped in a sphere, a dark vial, and a plain, gold ring."

Her crow fluttered its wings above us, and the eve witch didn't question any part of my answer. "Gonna try tah steal 'em back?"

I shook my head. "I'm not practiced breaking his wards."

"I can dispel a lot o' barriers, Elf."

"You can?"

Osgrid smiled. "Destruction of things, recall? Just show me where they are."

"Hm." I smirked. "We'll see. I'd rather not corner a bear in his own den. We may have to talk but having you there will throw him off from last time. We recall different lives for the Deathless."

"I hearin' ye, Elf. So mote it be."

Touching my finger to my lips, I continued as she fell back with intent, giving me space and time to listen at the kitchen door and test it.

*Locked.*

Would Layne and Imara be there to call through the door? Where did Elana sleep when she wasn't up late serving strange guests for her master? I held still for a long time, ear to the door, drawing breath with care, separating the scents: wood-burning stove, ash and coals, meat and spice, fermented drink, something floral, something bittersweet, a jumbled, vague scent of Humans' dwelling which I was accustomed to in the inn.

It was a nuanced mix I'd find intriguing if I could leave at will.

There was shush of clothing, a body shifting far from the hearth, sitting close to the inside door. Someone sighed, drew breath to speak, and I held up my hand toward Osgrid, signaling her to stay.

*"Fahdi—"*

"Enough, Amelda. I don't care for that suggestion, and better for you this once if you can refrain from plotting behind my back."

"I am concerned for you," she spoke firmly. "I *watch* your back. You are lost in the mists."

"It happens when you've lived as long as I have."

"The black 'Elf' is causing this confusion."

"I never claimed otherwise, though it is far less intentional on her part and desired on mine than you want to believe. I will work through this. She will see, I will convince her."

His daughter exhaled another sigh and changed the topic. "Thank you for giving the ruby and vial to Castis before we leave on the morrow."

The sorcerer harrumphed. "Those *things* Sarilis made won't last to Manalar, Amelda. It's foolish to try. They'd best not ignore my warning."

"They believe as I do." Amelda shifted on her seat. "We shall purge the warp rot for you and return to plan something different."

"We will, yes. I will know more by then. While Sirana stays, the Deathwalker will, too."

A tense silence.

*"Fahdi.* This 'Deathwalker' is *harrik.* He must be brought to the Ascended."

"He is here because of the Dark Elf, and I will find out what it is."

"The Dark Elf is sent here after you!"

"I'm not certain about that. Her Queen is a Seer like the Vermillion Lady and rarely so direct."

The Ma'ab scoffed at the comparison, and her sire didn't answer in kind when she pressed him in her native tongue. Cris-ri-phon let the silence draw out.

*"Fahdi,* he offends me!" she relented.

He growled back. "The purpose of Gavin's kind existed on this plane *long* before the Exodus, Amelda, and were linked to Sirana's people once. They were also linked to Manalar. This is not by chance he has risen."

"He is not a 'kind' of the before-times," she protested. "He is Ma'ab! A *maknuut* with our blood and magic! If he worships a Greylord, then he is a traitor to his gods who gave him birth. It doesn't matter if this Grave Mother was once worshipped in these lands before. Her influence on him is plainly invasion against the Ma'ab! *Harrik!"*

"I've heard you, Amelda, many times. I will sort out my memories and discover where the Davrin are now. Sirana went to a lot of trouble to keep his body undisturbed and ultimately decided to complete the ritual. Either she knows more than she's said or was guessing on something Gavin told her."

"*Fahdi*—"

"Even your mothers would want to know how this came to be. It's difficult to ask if you burn him immediately with no method to capture his Vis, and you know trying to hold or torture his body will go poorly for you. It is wiser to keep Sirana nearby by any means. He is not likely to go far if we have her."

"And if he does?"

The Deathless did not sound concerned. "Then I will reach out to the Vermillion Lady as you ask."

There was another pause, and I glanced toward Osgrid again. The Dwarf had accepted I was listening to a conversation she couldn't hear and had turned her back to the wall of the inn, keeping watch on the forest surrounding us.

Amelda started again. "Are you certain you do not want the gods' help with finding the Davrin Queen? You have only to ask. The Chirurgeon of Souls has been studying all forms of life for centuries—"

"Enough. I can imagine too well what *that one* would do with Elves if she got her claws into them."

A body shifted.

"Amelda," Cris-ri-phon said, sounding suspicious.

"Yes, *Fahdi*?"

"Have you heard whispers of the capture of another Dark Elf, or something that could be Sirana's kin?"

"No, of course not." Her tone was confident and soothing.

"No? Not a hundred years ago, while I was away from Ennikar searching for this?"

No reply, although something metal dragged along the table.

"Uhm—"

"It's odd, thinking on it," the Zauyrian murmured. "The Hell-hounds began around that time. Or at least Divigna did."

My eyes grew wide as my ears grew large. I held my breath, urging him to continue as I tried not to shiver against the door. Osgrid noticed my tension and collected a pouch into her palm, waiting patiently.

The sorcerer said, "Kurn keeps claiming Sirana summoned that image of Divigna to scare him away from her. The sound of the chain as well. Why would Kurn think she had anything to do with the Eternal Hellhound?"

"From her mind tricks, *Fahdi!*" Amelda scolded. "Such as I fear she plays on you! She doesn't truly know anything of the soul dagger, she bluffs. She has made both of you see all manner of phantoms unreal. She is an illusionist."

"I don't think so," he replied. "I know illusions. This is not. I don't see things, I *feel* them, remember them, not my sight but all senses. Touch, smell, taste…"

He drifted off. Metal turned atop the table again.

"She pulls desires from our deepest thoughts, yes," said the Ma'ab woman. "Shakes our control. That is how she tricks, like all those touched by the demonic or infernal."

"Demonic, for certain," her sire agreed. "Though taken by force, from what I've heard. She would leave the Spider Queen, I think."

"She is lying to you, *Fahdi*, you could not be so blind. Stirring those senses to such heights in you is deliberate, part of her resistance to the ruby. The Ascended can help you seek the truth she keeps from us, she cannot stir *their* passions in such a way."

"Noted."

Amelda sighed with exasperation. "Are you certain she will return here?"

"Before dawn, yes."

"We could search for her."

"No. She will evade us out of doors at night, and if we go far enough from the inn, she will attempt to break into my quarters. Kurn and Castis will be up soon. They can search if she doesn't come by dawn."

My mouth tightened with chagrin that he was both precise and correct about what I would do. He had my spiders, Callitro's ring, and the best food. I was beginning to hunger yet again, though the empty feeling hadn't turned to audible gurgling, yet.

He also hadn't set a ward or done anything to muffle sound, I noted. Was he expecting me to listen in? Perhaps he only meant to keep it mundane, not wishing to deter me from entering this door. I wondered about the other two entrances, if they offered any advantage.

*If only for being less predictable.*

Or I could simply step in, pretending to be unaware, pressing a next move from this sire and daughter sitting together in the kitchen after sending Layne and Imara elsewhere to sleep. It wasn't an ambush; they sat out in the open, and the Zauyrian no longer had the ruby. They argued about keeping me and Gavin here while the Ma'ab went North to face the warp rot.

Cris-ri-phon *wanted* to talk before he involved the Ascended. I must use that somehow, because the matrons of the Ma'ab Empire learning about me and Gavin seemed chillingly inevitable unless I somehow killed all who knew about me in Troshin Bend.

*Not possible.*

Kurn and Castis would be up soon to leave Troshin Bend, taking the ruby and both vials. I hadn't the backing of allies for such a short-lived plan. Rithal might side with me but might run; the same for Mathias after he'd had his fill of the Witch Hunter. The nobleman might turn against me; Brom said he trusted him.

Osgrid wasn't powerful, by her own claim, wasn't a fighter, and had her own motives for watching this place. Gavin was a scholar and monk holding a spade, hearing a different voice clearer than mine, and he saw death differently. He could talk to the dead; killing someone didn't necessarily silence them.

*No backing for a coup of any sort.*

Meanwhile, the Ma'ab and this Zauyrian were closely tied, focused on what they wanted even as things changed. When the final line was crossed, would the Queen's geas allow me to leave, much less kill them?

*Maybe Cris-ri-phon won't have to force me to stay.*

I tamped down my fear and breathed out. Above me, a crow began cawing loudly; out of my periphery, Osgrid tensed and looked the way we'd come. I peered that way, sure I saw no one sneaking up, but the hair raised on the nape of my neck.

On the other side of the inn, I thought a man shouted, though it was brief. Inside, Cris-ri-phon inexplicably stood up from his chair.

*"Fahdi?* What is that?"

"Something outside, near the shed."

*Damn it.*

I gripped the door handle as if I didn't know it was locked and pushed. Inside, they fell silent as it stayed closed. Withdrawing a set of picks, I worked quickly to leverage a bulky bolt from the inside, hoping I held their full attention.

*Come on, come on, pesky lock.*

No boots rushed to the door. They waited for me to unlock it, like my Sisters in the Cloister evaluating my competence.

*If only the worst consequence for failing this was Jaunda's Feldeu up my ass.*

My tools coaxed enough give to pull the bolt out of the way, and I opened the door a crack, quietly, ready to run should any object or word be pitched my way.

"Sirana. Thank you for returning."

I paused to mark my surprise then pushed the door wider, leaning in. The Zauyrian wore the younger Brom's face with the dark brown beard.

I said, "I was trying not to awaken Elana's children."

"They're across the hall tonight." He smiled. "How is Gavin?"

I made a face, glancing at the table which was empty. "Walking and talking. Though, less of the latter."

"Ah. Well, please, come in. Have something to eat while we talk."

"About?"

"The warp rot. I've decided to help, as you asked."

It took effort not to frown at that. I lifted my eyebrows instead. "You have?"

"Yes. Step in and close the door."

*Right into the center of the web.*

One shoulder out of sight of those inside, I gestured for Osgrid without looking away, listening for her boots instead. "I presume you want to place a sound ward so we can plan in the kitchen?"

"While you eat, yes," he added with ill-chosen humor.

I scanned the room as cool night air flowed in, spotting Amelda. "Oh, it's you."

The Ma'ab woman stood proudly near the inside exit from the kitchen, her arms folded as she waited with a disapproving look on her face. At the same time, Osgrid tugged once on my cloak, and I had to assume that meant she was ready to enter.

"Amelda is part of the plan," Brom said.

"I see." I stepped in with a stout eve witch following right behind me, closing the door behind us without locking it. "Then so is she."

*"Fahdi!"* Amelda exclaimed with unmistakable irritation.

"Night bless, Master Brom," greeted Osgrid, adding a nod toward his daughter. "Amelda."

"Hm, Osgrid." Brom looked at me. "Well done, Sirana, you surprised me."

I smiled. "I sought mages to deal with the warp rot since you would not commit. Osgrid agreed to help. I did not know you tapped your daughter's shoulder."

"Indeed, we're sorry you wasted your trek from the woods, medicine woman," said Amelda as prickly as Tamuril's thorny vines. "We cover this matter."

"It is as well she's here, Amelda," said Brom, raising his hand in an arcane gesture.

Osgrid glanced behind her as the sorcerer set the sound-dampening ward. She was tense, and although her heartbeat was slower than mine by our different builds, it sped up as she focused on the innkeeper.

"This place be gone inna few years, like it never was," the Dwarf predicted. "Begun with what happened wit' the Witch Hunters here."

"Indeed, sooner," Brom agreed, smiling through his beard. "You won't be able to watch me anymore. A pity for those who rely on your reports, hm?"

Osgrid shrugged. "Not much relyin', jus' interested. None'll keep ye here but yerself, Master Brom. 'Tis not in Heligana's favor tah hold back the ends of things or hasten them."

"Ah, yes. The only reason I let you stay for so long, Osgrid. You're a humble and devout witch, and a skilled omen reader."

He reached behind him on his belt, and I tensed, nearly springing back when he motioned at me, addressing the Dwarf as he seemed to adjust something. "What does Sirana's remarkable appearance tell you?"

"Like a quake o' the earth begun far away," Osgrid said. "Takes time tah feel the first tremors but inescapable when they overlap with waves made elsewhere."

"Inescapable, but possible to ride those waves."

"Aye, but only throws ye farther away from th' cause."

Brom chuckled. "Not if you're part of it."

Osgrid paused; she did not look away from the Deathless while I kept an eye on Amelda. My sleeping powder was ready, and she was aware of it. She narrowed her eyes.

"I'm here tah speak clear, Master Brom," Osgrid continued, showing both hands, stubby fingers straight and together. "Ye should let this quake pass by. Return to Sirana whatcha took. Let her an' Gavin go where they will."

"No!" Amelda blurted, shocked. "The *maknuut* stays with us."

I was as surprised at Osgrid's bluntness as she was at the Ma'ab's reflexive protest. Brom seemed to consider the Dwarf's advice until he touched his belt again and the *want* passed plainly behind his eyes.

*He can't let me go.*

"You've been a wise woman for many decades, Osgrid," he said like they were locals meeting about a pair of disputed chickens. "I appreciate the service you've offered my town, but this is not your concern. For your own sake, return to your hawthorn tree."

Was that a threat?

All three were visibly distracted then, holding still, and turning their heads in the vague direction of the shed.

*Again?*

Looking up at the ceiling, Brom motioned to drop the sound ward, and heavy bootsteps thumped somewhere upstairs just before a door opened and smashed against the wall.

"Brom! Amelda!" called Kurn from the hall and thundering toward the stairs. "Outside! The shed!"

*Braqth damn it.*

A second set of boots followed which I presumed was Castis. The Ma'ab had also disturbed the few guests who hadn't fled the night of the Witch Hunter fires. More frightened voices called out for the innkeeper, and Brom snarled at the interruption, glancing at me. I wasn't sure what to think, either.

Then Osgrid spun around and pulled the handle, throwing open the door and bolting outside.

*"Fahdi!"* Amelda cried, pointing.

"Brom!" shouted Castis. "The *maknuut* tortures the Manalari! We must stop him—"

I had one chance to follow Osgrid, but Gavin wasn't finished. I lunged at the small, pale woman instead, as Amelda took some unfinished action. I struck her jaw and her gut with both fists, hard enough to stagger her and fall on the stone floor.

"Sirana, stop!"

Seizing the Ma'ab noble by her hair, I wrenched her up and threw her down on the floor again. She screamed; her mouth bloodied.

"Amelda?" Kurn shouted, bursting through the inside kitchen door as Cris-ri-phon closed on me. The big Ma'ab and I met eyes, teeth bared, and he was too close for me to use anything except the long dagger I'd drawn from my boot.

Behind me, the Zauyrian reversed course and pushed the outside door shut, blocking the way.

*Shit.*

"Away from her, *kus!*" the Hellhound snarled.

"Kill the Elf," warned the sorcerer coldly, "and I kill you."

"Subdue her, Kurn," Castis agreed, pulling out the ruby like he couldn't wait. "She's worth a hoard alive."

Frigid cold swept me as I backed up, and Kurn seized Amelda to pull her behind him to protect both mages with his large mass. He pulled binding cord from his belt as Castis donned his red pendant.

"Sirana," rumbled the sorcerer as the Hellhound leaned toward me. "This is your one chance to surrender. We'll talk."

*Too late for that.*

I could not focus on one, and I had nowhere to run so threw the entire pouch of sleeping powder against the wall above the kitchen door. The white cloud bloomed, and Kurn charged me as I darted to the side, leaping over the cooking table in the center.

No one dared talk now. We held our breath as both doors to the kitchen banged open simultaneously by an invisible hand. Next, a strong wind blew in from outside, clearing most of my cloud.

*Drider guts!*

My only hope after that waste was hearing Amelda cough and choke up.

Kurn ran around the table instead of clambering over it, which gave me time. My dagger naked, I hastily dug the tip into the paste of fever-inducing poison, fumbling the cork as it bounced on the floor.

This wouldn't work as fast as my spiders' venom; it wouldn't kill the large man before he might be cleansed. It *would* drain his strength and give the mages something else to worry about. With my options fast shrinking, it was better than nothing.

Castis tossed something at the ceiling which burst into a pure, familiar chime. Then, as before inside the shed, Amelda took over the spell. A distressing tilt formed in my vision as an unceasing vibration settled once again deep in my ears, attempting to drive me insane.

*Gragh!*

I ducked beneath the big table to get closer to the ground before I fell, stabbing out at Kurn's legs, failing to graze him but making him leap back. To my pleasure, he stumbled, not fully immune to the Ma'ab spell. Then my stomach heaved as my head whirled with magic, and the stone floor beneath me seemed to quiver and lurch.

*Arrgh...*

I blinked rapidly, but seeing only made it worse. I closed my eyes instead, hearing a rumble and creaking rafters within the magical slosh in my ears. The flat stones tremored beneath my palms. Was this real or a further trick of my senses? Why would Castis or Amelda cause a quake? Was it Brom? Osgrid?

There were too many mages in this fight.

Brom's and Kurn's voices overlapped, shouting in Ma'ab. Amelda coughed again, speaking nothing as Castis threatened me. There were a lot of crows outside the open door, making a racket. The earth still shook, but the dizziness receded as Amelda struggled to stay awake.

*"Ta'lil huna!"* Kurn growled, crawling closer to me, reaching beneath the table.

Fully blind, I struck out with the dagger tip and hit something.

*"Hairenith kus—!"* cried the Ma'ab, boots scuffing and weight landing hard.

I bolted toward the sound of crows, skimming past Kurn as his large hand clipped my boot. I couldn't see, but I could smell the night air. I had a clear path.

So I thought.

My forehead struck something scentless but solid, dead center of the open door. Tumbling back and seeing stars, I moaned then barked in pain as a boot kicked my poisoned dagger from my hand. Cris-ri-phon grasped both my wrists, hauling me to my feet and into his arms.

Of *course* the sorcerer could summon a shield like Shyntre.

*Stupid move.*

I leaned backward on my full weight, attempting to yank my hands free. The Zauyrian braced and held us both, gripping tighter and pulling me close with superior strength. In this struggle, Cris-ri-phon manipulated my aura, shifting me in a desperate and violent rush headfirst toward rutting desire. My fear, anger, and arousal tangled up as one, this time without the ruby.

He was like a Priestess that way, and no better.

"Don't make this worse on yourself, Sirana."

I screamed. *"Let me go!"*

We wrestled standing up, and the sorcerer grappled for a sure hold I couldn't break. I dared not open my eyes to look at him. In my mind's eye, his grey gaze fixed hungrily on me, ready to consume. I tried stomping his foot with my heel, attempted a headbutt despite the swelling on my brow.

With no solid hits, there was time for Kurn to recover as I fought desperately to get free. The inner dizziness had receded, and my senses were clear enough without my eyes to know Amelda was down but Castis and Kurn were closing in on me struggling with Brom.

"Listen to me, Sirana! Submit! Stop fighting now!"

"*No!!*" I roared.

Behind me, the larger, gasping Ma'ab sucked in a deep, deep breath, and bellowed in the close quarters as his fist smashed into my back. Pain exploded to the left of my spine, and I screamed as loud to combat the reverberating yell bombarding my ears. The other men admonished him, but it sounded weak.

"Kurn!"

I'd gone limp in Brom's arms, stunned, struggling to think past the agony in my back. Kurn tossed my cloak to one side and seized my hips in both hands, tugging and fumbling for my belt. I writhed ineffectually to escape his hands, tried without success to crush a toe.

The Hellhound leaned close to snarl in my ear. "If this black witch enjoys casting spells while we sleep, *forcing* us to fuck *alibat* instead of *kus,* and she *laughs* for days after, pretending nothing happened, then I say her own *alibat* can take a turn with blood as the grease."

Cris-ri-phon protested, "By Gods, you'll *not!*"

"We *must* bind her now, Brom!" Castis declared. "She's too dangerous to our plans."

"She's mine!"

The two tugged me back and forward as Kurn dropped my belt.

"And we'll help," Kurn taunted the sorcerer. "This is what Hellhounds do. Break any resistance to the Empire's approach."

He yanked at my leathers hard enough to lift my feet off the floor as I fought for purchase.

"After we're through, sorcerer," Castis said, "she'll stay with you willingly, and tell us everything you want to know."

*Willingly. Ha.*

As willing as Shyntre was eating Wilsira.

"Hold her still."

From my left side, Castis took hold of my throat, constricting my air as I gasped and began to sweat. "Enough pain blended with the magic of the ruby should be enough to break her will this time."

"I can do that," Kurn sneered, squeezing my buttocks, the heat of our fight and his lust rolling off him.

Their voices were muffled as my ears rang and ached. The soft, bruised organ in my back throbbed as all three had their hands on me, somewhere. I didn't stop trying to reach something, anything, to spring open this trap; I banged my heel on Kurn's shin guard, pitched my skull against his nose, snapping my teeth at Cris-ri-phon's face.

"Stop it, bitch!" Castis squeezed my throat harder until I couldn't breathe, digging in his fingernails.

I fought to stay conscious as my pants loosened and my crotch was exposed to air, my tactics growing ever weaker. Brom tangled his palpable desire with my fear, weakening my body's struggles with one intent, and Kurn began to laugh, grasping my braid and pulling my head back. He bit the tip of my ear, and I flinched as he licked it.

"Let her breathe," ordered the sorcerer.

Castis granted me that full breath as Kurn's hot, bare cock slid threateningly slow along my crack. The friction proved arousing despite the wielder, a sensational defense as the swelling of my netherlips forcing the pain to join with pleasure or recede into the background. That it happened so fast between the three of them, I blamed and blessed my tempering in the Cloister under the Feldeu.

*Goddess damn it.*

"I wager you've not had a *shayf* like mine, *kus*," Kurn sneered.

A mean smile stretched my lips and I laughed. "Does he *last*, Castis? Or were you greased by the river and left with your balls aching?"

"Shut up!" the mage commanded. "Open your eyes! Look at me."

I opened my eyes, black spots obscuring my sight, but fixed on Cris-ri-phon's grey gaze instead. "Where are your 'oaths' of no harm, General? Good only while you decide my mission for me?"

His jaw flexed. "Your Queen betrayed me first. You'll never know. She'll not escape. *You'll* not escape, whatever it takes."

Castis tried to grab my jaw and force my eyes away but I bit his finger, scraping away skin as he wrenched it away with a bark. I refused to look away from the Zauyrian, resolving not to blink the entire time. Cris-ri-phon tried to turn his head but I leaned close, nose-to-nose.

"If I feel this, General, so shall you. *My* oath."

The Ma'ab laughed at this toothless threat. In the shadows behind the ancient man, a high, keening shriek of delight echoed them. Kurn and Castis seemed deaf to it, but the Zauyrian's eyes slid away. For a moment, his resolve wavered.

*What was that?*

I became aware of the Ma'ab pressing his cock to my pucker, seeking the right angle to push in with too much force. I didn't make it easy for Kurn as I struggled, channeling the impending feeling of violation I knew well.

*Jilrina. The Prime. Kerse.*

I was there again, fully conscious. I couldn't hold it in, however; no matter of any pleasure, the fear *had* to flow somewhere. I focused all of it on the sorcerer through the bond he enforced. He who would hold me and let this happen rather than let me go like Osgrid said.

"Do *not* hurt her, Kurn," Cris-ri-phon repeated, holding me locked tight.

*I'll kill you for this.*

The voice behind him whispered eagerly. ★ *Yesss? Yesss, do it…* ★

"Pain is needed for the ruby to work," Castis said imperiously, deaf to this other voice.

"It is *not*," the sorcerer insisted. "Take your revenge for her compelling Kurn to mount you, but we will take this *slow*. I'll make her enjoy it. Pleasure works with this ruby as well as pain."

"Heh. Make her enjoy it?" The Hellhound's chest crushed me between him and the sorcerer, my asshole settled against the leaking head of his prick. "Hm. So, I might feel her quaking on this sword?"

My mouth opened as he pushed.

"Slow!" snarled the Zauyrian. "We can only break her if we focus together."

I chuckled with *that* challenge, and Castis pursed his lips, his nostril curling in contempt. Still, the noble signaled to Kurn, and the larger Ma'ab thumbed one ass cheek open.

"Ready, Sirana?" he taunted, leaning in with his hips.

Enough slickness had smeared around between our skin that we eased into a familiar, inexorable spread of my purple ring. Yet another stiff rod penetrating, seeking pleasure and power in its use. Innumerable memories of my Sisters in the Cloister swept over me, as did the experience of the Sathoet chamber in the Sanctuary.

Three beasts surrounding me, Wilsira watching me with my pants pulled down as those eager sons fondled me. Like these men, the demons could not leave me alone. I'd been here before and survived. I'd done well enough to impress the Conceiver. I surprised her.

*It's up to you, Red Sister.*

My tension relaxed in well-trained reflex as Kurn mounted me; my fear peaked and faded fast in the wake of a stunning spike of pleasure. Cris-ri-phon watched my face, wide-eyed and mouth open, my eyelids half-closed as the big Ma'ab grunted, his cock sliding a finger's length into my ass. There was no cry from me, only a breathy huff of relief. The corner of my mouth twitched.

He was wide but not *that* wide.

Castis panted near my left ear with a squeeze to my throat, whispering encouragement to his rutting Hound, who pulled back and stuffed the ruddy log halfway in again. The mage watched like Wilsira did, undeniably aroused as he clutched the ruby around his neck.

I could feel him testing and nudging my will as an indistinct miasma of pleasure rose around us like a clinging fog. It was weak compared to the Conceiver. Distracted with jealousy. I growled, a feral grin spreading out as I flicked my eyes at the young mage's face, glancing down at his tent pole.

"Wishing you were in my place, aren't you?"

Castis flinched, his expression flickering uncertain, and his breath paused for a moment. A disembodied, shriek joined in as the subtle, red shine of the ruby faltered at the same time the saphgar beneath my armor threatened to sear my skin.

*Yesss… yesss!*

I moaned aloud; in response, Kurn shafted my asshole harder, getting up deeper with each lunge until the man's body hair pressed against my ass and thighs. The coupling was verging on dry and burning now, and I showed this on my face.

"Use your spit, Kurn," Cris-ri-phon ordered with a subtle, magical undertone I recognized. "Slick her up. Now."

In a daze, Kurn pulled his cock all the way out, spitting a glob of his saliva straight down on my cleft, and started over smearing my hole with his glans before working it in again, offering a fresh coat of his own precum as well. I gasped when he bottomed out again, losing my balance as I was forced off my toes.

*"Oh, fuck… my sorcerer,"* I gasped in Davrin. *"Ah! My cunt aches!"*

Cris-ri-phon's face flushed, and there was a hint of that reverence from long ago beneath the waterfall. He freed my right hand as both men caught and lifted me together, my boots leaving the ground.

*"Yes!"* I whispered, leaning forward.

Someone squealed with glee as I dug my fingers into the Za-uyrian's shoulder, cooperating as he pushed my pants down to my calves and quickly freed his own cock, its head soon nudging greedily at my slit. I was unbelievably wet.

His cock sank like a stone in a pond.

*"That's it!"*

I forced a kiss on the ancient sorcerer, and he responded hungrily while the other prick had to work to share the space.

"Fuck her harder, Kurn," Castis muttered, raw and resenting. "Make her scream."

*"Haiye!"* Kurn gasped, elated but exhausted as he fought for breath. "Will…enjoy you like this, black witch."

★*Yesss…*★

"Every night…"

★*Yesss!*★

"On the way to Ennikar…"

The voice laughed in demented derision, and Castis's lip curled as Kurn grunted his true desire out loud. He wasn't making me scream. Cris-ri-phon came much closer to making my holes twitch. I was swept up by the burning possession of his lips as he tried to consume me, filling and pleasuring my swollen, aching sex.

Then the Deathless peaked and spurted inside me, whispering in desperation against my lips. *"Ai! Innathi…!"*

I am **not** your wife.

Another voice cooed, ★*No, you are not. But you could help her if I help you.*★

My vision was lost to flickering, dualling images of swirling red sand and blazing white snow as Cris-ri-phon milked the last of his climax, spreading his semen along my clutching channel.

*Take me with you, Sirana.*

My fingers felt as though they were about to touch lightning. My hand was at a different spot on Cris's back.

*Near his belt.*

Behind me, Kurn's thrusts faltered as I held the Zauyrian tightly, his tongue deep in my mouth as his spent prick slipped out. The Ma'ab's cock seemed to soften as well as he paused, gasping. Castis took his hand from my throat. I filled my chest in a full breath, and another.

"What's wrong?" he asked his brother, the failure of their attempt obvious.

"I... I'm...hot," said the big man with some faltering, half-length thrusts into my raw hole. "Open the door. I need air."

"It is open."

"Suh... summon a breeze, then!"

Castis obeyed and drew in another breeze from the night, and I caught the subtle scent of a witch's hawthorn hut out in the woods. My eyes opened, my lips parting from the sorcerer's as I thought of my stained dagger on the floor.

The poison had fevered Kurn's blood.

*Finally.*

*Hehehe! Oh, yesss!*

That eager laugh was like twin gnats in my ear as Kurn jabbed into me, growling in futile refusal to give up as his scent soured from sickened sweat. His prick softened further; he couldn't climax, and my guts worked naturally to push him out despite the bobble of his hips.

He was done.

"Kurn?"

The Ma'ab stumbled backward with his pants open, leaving my back chilled and my netherhole hot and tingling.

"Kurn!" Castis cried, headed first to him then to my belt tossed aside. He snarled at me as he touched my things. "Which one is the antidote, witch?"

I didn't answer, biting down on a threat as he began looking them over. Cris-ri-phon still held me too tightly to slip loose. We'd finished, but it was temporary. Like a Consort, they and others would continue to fight over me until I broke, as they presented me as a prize and a slave.

And not me alone.

I didn't have D'Shea's potion anymore.

*Escape.*

"Which one is it?" the Ma'ab mage demanded again, surging forward and shaking my tools at me, preparing to strike me back-handed in the Zauyrian's arms.

Cris threatened, "Don't—"

*Now or never.*

I seized that bolt of lightning the sorcerer kept hidden behind him.

Searing, red symbols blinded me, shapes branded in my mind like iron in a forge. My hand cramped up, tightened, and I could not uncurl my fingers to stop from being dragged for eons across broken shards of black light and thorny stars.

I'd grasped the red rune dagger from my first dream terrors.

I discovered something sentient that grasped me back.

# CHAPTER 16

GRAINS OF SAND HISSED FROM A WIND I COULD NOT FEEL, THOUGH I was falling when shadowy hands clasped mine and did not let go.

Underneath me was a waking dream, a blue sand pit collapsing in upon itself at a single, unapproachable point. Deep within the center, someone was screaming. It never ended, wavering and drifting out from the pit like ashes upon a thermal breeze.

Fearfully, I turned away to see the hands of she who pulled me to safety. They belonged to a Davrin, jeweled with rings, bracelets and fine chains of gold and platinum, unbelievably elegant.

*"Thank you, khalithan!"* she cried, sliding her hands up my bare forearms. *"We've escaped their clutches. Thank you for your bravery. You're safe, rest now."*

She had a strange accent, much like Cris-ri-phon, and she wore a fine sleeveless gown, flowing gossamer white in that touchless wind. The rush of sand in my ears changed to the rush of water as the knowledge that I knew this face swept over me.

From Koorul. The waterfall in the Desert.

*"Innathi,"* I whispered, refusing her suggestion to sit.

*"You know of me, khali?"*

She had a beautiful smile, more mature than her General recalled now. I knew nothing beyond that. Not from before the first night her husband mounted me.

*"No, I…where am I?"* I asked. *"Am I in Reverie again?"*

Innathi tilted her head in eager curiosity. *"Again? Are you a Seer? Is this place familiar to your dreams somehow?"*

I swallowed, glancing around me as blue sand shifted into waves of water and changed back again, the shushing pitch shifting with the change. Stars began to peek out from a thick, black sky, blinking at me like spiders' eyes made of prison slime. Anything which once had a solid edge would blur if I focused on it, while the stone platform on which we stood appeared to float atop sandy water.

*"I have never been here before, your grace,"* I admitted. *"Though others seem to dream of similar strange places."*

*"How do you know?"*

I hesitated. How to describe it when "seers" like Auslan and the Valsharess, or ambitious visionaries like D'Shea, competed to influence me?

*"I commune with their minds?"*

*"Hm. Yes, I can see it. Your Vis was not torn apart coming here the first time. That speaks highly of your strength of will, child."*

*"My Vis,"* I repeated slowly.

Gavin's type of Vis? Or the Valsharess, for She had spoken the word first as She interrogated me within a Desert tent. Was I separated from my body? Is that what this long-dead Queen was saying? Is that what Osgrid meant about the relic the Dwarves would see buried?

*'Tis worse than death if the dagger is drawn.*

As I'd just done.

Oh, Goddess, *what* had I done?

*"I unsheathed the red rune dagger,"* I said.

*"Yes. The soul drinker was the most feared relic in my Queendom, once under my command."*

*"A gift from Cris-ri-phon?"*

*"Yes,"* she confirmed again with passion, the bright scarlet of her eyes matching the runes hovering at the rear of my mind. *"When we made our alliance formal, he swore before my court I had the power to undo him if he ever betrayed me and our children."*

*"Undo him?"*

*"Oh, yes. Few blades could kill him in my time, great granddaughter, but he gave me one that could as a wedding gift."*

I frowned. *"Where did he find it?"*

Innathi waved her hand. *"On a quest to be worthy of marriage. He was asking to share my Queendom and my children, warrior. Did you think I would accept him in this unprecedented manner merely for some pleasurable Human cock?"*

*"No, your grace."*

At the mention of children, the cries and calls swelled within the maelstrom behind me.

I swallowed. *"But can I leave here? Or am I forever separated from my body?"*

*"Mm, you are not truly separated,"* said the ancient Queen thoughtfully, appraising me. *"You are aware of here and there, and quite resilient. Your presence here is fluid, you can see it around you, and you have a tether. Follow it back, and you can sheath Soul Drinker to return as you are."*

A tether. As soon as she said it, I knew what it was.

*"In return,"* she added, *"you must help me escape my eternal tomb, so my Queendom's true history may be heard at last."*

That there was more to know was undeniable for the Davrin, now. The Valsharess could have betrayed her sister and him, as Cris-ri-phon maintained, disapproving of the mixed breeding. The "soul drinker" relic was no mere keepsake of his wife and Queen, but the downfall which hadn't gone quiet.

*"Does he see you like this, your grace?"* I asked. *"When he draws the dagger?"*

The matriarch lifted her elegant chin, holding my gaze. The shape of her unblinking eyes reminded me of Jael. *"Not always, but we've spoken of you. He believed you might be strong enough to see me past the gatekeeper. I am pleased he convinced you to draw it this time."*

I arched a sardonic brow—some convincing—and looked to the side, searched for that tether, that bond with my body. I wanted to go back.

To sheath this cursed dagger as she said I could.

*"Take me with you, warrior."* Innathi splayed her glittering hands to me, palms up. *"As a Queen to whom you are not sworn, I must beg you. Take me away from the Deathless."*

*"Why?"* I asked. *"Is he not your husband, still?"*

*"My Sorcerer General from the time of V'Gedra is but one face of the Deathless. He is many now, and you will come to know them all if you do not escape and take me with you."*

In that rush of fear, I found my tether. *"He wants my baby, too."*

Her eyes widened in delight and shock. *"You are pregnant?"*

*"Yes."* And I clutched that tether tightly.

With intensity Innathi asked, *"Have the dreams of your child come? Have you seen her face yet?"*

What? *"Her face?"*

Innathi smiled like a Matron to see my expression. *"Oh, warrior. Your first?"*

Warily I nodded, and Innathi lifted red eyes to the speckled sky.

*"Ah. In time, you will see her. But this answers why the Deathless came to see me, why he wants you to draw Soul Drinker, and why he will try everything to hold on to you now."*

Unfettered chill flooded my heart. Brom had the relic with him in the kitchen, waiting for me. What was he planning to do with it before I touched it?

*"What does he want?"*

Her scarlet eyes glistened with iridescent, blue tears. *"The world eater wants to bring me back to life. Offer me a new body."* Her gaze swept to me with the force of a rockslide. *"You will give birth to his new Queen if you stay."*

No.

Cris-ri-phon could have chosen to be a Deathwalker, but he chose life magic when he met Innathi. Fertility. He held the soul of his dead Queen, searching for her and this dagger when they were lost, collaborating with the Ma'ab Ascended until he succeeded.

*"We must escape the Deathless, my warrior,"* Innathi pressed. *"Please."*

Earnestly, I agreed. *"Yes."*

The Desert Queen's smile was immediate, her teeth straight and white. *"We will help you all we can. The souls within the relic offer our strength to its wielder if you want it."*

*"I-I do."*

*"You have it, my champion. Tell me now, where do you go next?"*

Sorting that out felt like pulling my hand through muck in my head. How had I been planning to get away from Troshin Bend?

*"I ride North. With Gavin, my ally."*

*"Then let it be,"* she intoned, placing her cool, dry hands on my naked shoulders. *"Let that focus be your anchor and tug upon the tether. Do not be afraid. Go. Go back!"*

She pushed me off the platform and toward that small, distant point among the spider-eyed stars. I screamed, chasing that one, stubborn anchor as I clung to what mattered most then.

Go North. With Gavin.

*Set me and my baby free.*

My name echoed in the air.

*Sirana…*

Then the sound of a blade's hilt snapping against its sheath cracked and swept those pieces away. I returned to myself in the kitchen of Brom's Inn. Behind me, someone breathed too quickly, moaned, a big body struggling to roll over.

All else was quiet.

I stared past the relic in my grip and down at my feet.

The Deathless was curled on his left side, grey eyes wide but unfocused, his open mouth mute. His younger Brom persona had vanished, as had the dark-skinned, white-haired Cris-ri-phon. I did not know this face, though it was like the two I had seen. His rough, aged hand clutched a stab wound on his right side, red blood seeping between his fingers. He was alive but stunned.

I waited for him to move or gasp, to glare at me hatefully but he didn't move. He appeared asleep with his eyes open. A trance, maybe.

I glanced at Soul Drinker in my fist, smelled and spotted the blood, and could guess what I'd done.

*I told you to let me go, sorcerer.*

*⋆Indeed, draw me again, warrior. Finish him.⋆*

I froze then distracted myself by pulling up my pants with one hand to cover my sore ass, the leather resting loose on my hips.

"S-Sirana?" someone asked.

To my right toward the open kitchen door, Osgrid stared at me with huge, pale blue eyes. She stood over Castis with a cudgel in her fist. The Ma'ab mage was unconscious, my belt and weapons crumpled and partly scattered next to him. By all appearances, Castis had been threatening me for an antidote for Kurn only moments ago.

"Osgrid," I answered.

The eve witch glanced warily at the red rune dagger. "Ye drew it. An' sheathed it again. Is it you?"

I was wary of her tone and what it meant. "I am Sirana. I came to you in the woods yesterday. I showed you Gavin's grimoire."

She wasn't convinced.

"Rithal called you 'moonlove' before going into the shed," I added, glancing to the other side.

Amelda was still down from the sleep powder, and Kurn complained again of the fever and aches.

"Awright," she accepted tentatively. "Ye gonna keep that?"

"The dagger once belonged to the Dark Elf Queen," I murmured, wrapping two fingers over the crossbar to keep Soul Drinker fully seated in its scabbard. "Though I don't know who made it. The Deathless found it for her on a quest. I'm not leaving it here with him. I cannot."

As I recited this aloud, I felt unsourced pressure upon my gloved hand, like Innathi when she'd been squeezing my hands and pulling me away from the edge. A sense of pleasure and contentment drifted through me.

*Make sure they can't tell others. Use me again… Take their strength and their tongues. Not even a Ma'ab Ascended can summon **my** dead to speak to them.*

Tears filled my eyes. I recognized a voice of the Abyss when I heard it. One of endless hunger. Once the taste was acquired, it never stopped seeking it. I knew it intimately from staring Jilrina in the face, from listening to her for over three decades as I fought to grow up.

Soul Drinker caressed me. *Aww, don't cry, warrior. You're stronger than that. You can't leave them alive, can you?*

Around me, all four were down and helpless: Amelda, her mysterious father, Castis and Kurn. They had all worked together to subjugate me. The wave of anger and humiliation made my knees weak, and my grip tightened on the dark blade.

I reconsidered drawing it.

*Yesss… yesss!*

I shivered, took a slow breath, and let it go. ~None of them could ride me alone, Soul Drinker. Neither can you.~

The demon shrieked with delight at the challenge.

"Sirana," Osgrid said like she could see my struggle. Stowing her cudgel, she showed me empty palms. "If...if ye can, hand me the dagger. I'll see it buried for ye."

*NO!*

I winced at the relic's snapping protest, its mood changing with a coin toss. The eve witch watched me, plainly fearful of what I would do.

*We are for you. Use us!*

My hand gripped the blade so hard it trembled.

*The Queen made the agreement with you. We leave with you and no other, mortal Elf! Lest you dare try us.*

My tears spilled down both cheeks as I trembled. Goddess, Auslan's warning was right! Was this dagger how Braqth had overtaken the Valsharess? Is this why I was born in Sivaraus instead of the Desert? Had she used Soul Drinker in V'Gedra, thinking it would solve the problem of Davrin breeding with the Zauyrian Realms?

Why wasn't it in the Deepearth now? What happened to it that the Deathless needed the Ma'ab to quest for it once again?

Osgrid turned her large, round ear toward the outside, where we heard men calling, and the murder of crows cawing, their wings flapping.

She said, "Th' guests woke up by the Ma'ab a bit ago been linkin' up with Dar an' the other militia."

"Why?" I asked, unlocking my knees to turn toward Castis. "What's happening?"

Osgrid backed up to be halfway out the door as I kneeled, placing Soul Drinker on the ground and stepping on it. She answered as I first secured the ties of my leathers, ignoring the dampness for now, and reached for my belt and the tools around it.

"Yer, um, Deathwalker been makin' Jacob scream too long, methinks. Now ye've stabbed their governor. It ain't gonna get quieter around here."

I replaced what weapons and items could be salvaged. I had room to add Soul Drinker. "I must leave tonight. I can't last another day in this town."

But there remained the reason I'd come here, why I had risked facing Cris-ri-phon in the first place. My spiders. Callitro's ring.

*And the vials that will stop the warp rot for Gaelan.*

I checked over Castis, briefly admiring Osgrid's bump on his head, but knew what to look for and found them quickly: identical vials wrapped in protective cloth. Tucking the wraps in a pouch, I next searched for and filched that damned ruby again.

*The Ma'ab aren't getting it back this time.*

I collected from the floor the poisoned dagger which had ultimately taken down the Hellhound, briefly wiping it and replacing it in my boot before looking around. Amelda and Castis were unconscious, and the ancient sorcerer was perfectly still, bleeding slowly, staring at emptiness. Only the slight, regular breaths he took convinced me he wasn't a wrinkled, empty-eyed corpse.

In contrast to them, Kurn sweated and panted on the floor, having flopped over on his front. He hadn't pulled up his pants; I was staring at his moon-white buttocks, and his belt across his hamstrings. He had a dagger on that belt with an exceptionally large, round pommel.

I smirked.

"Sirana, what are you doing?" Osgrid asked me warily as I stood straddling the Hellhound's naked hips, bending to remove both dagger and sheath from his belt.

"I need you to find my things," I said, indicating the inside hallway. "Brom's office is to the left and two doors down, left side. Break the wards. You said you can."

Osgrid hesitated then asked bluntly, "Dagger tellin' ye tah kill 'im? Or me?"

"Yes, and I refused," I returned in kind. "I will not harm you, Osgrid, nor kill this sludge clot with the relic. But I do have a question I shall ask him before I leave."

*Geas or no geas.*

"Aye," said the Dwarf quietly. After another pause, she nodded acceptance. "M'sorry I couldn't help ye sooner, and Ma'ab have a lotta debts tah pay. I'll break into th' office an' find yer things. Don't take long."

I inclined my head in thanks. "Be careful, don't touch the spiders."

"Oh, don' worry 'bout *that*."

She snickered though it was strained as she left the kitchen, and I stood stiff as a tree above the big man. Ignoring the whispers from the red rune dagger was easier if I wasn't holding it in my hands. The blade was quieter hanging on my belt.

*Good.*

I waited for Osgrid's wide bootsteps to be farther down the hall before grabbing the grease Elana poured into an earthen jar earlier tonight. Removing the lid, I swirled the pommel of Kurn's dagger in the soft animal fat, scooping a generous amount onto the weapon.

*More than you gave me, dog.*

Sitting on the small of his back, facing his legs, and using all my weight, I pried his buttocks open and nestled the large, slippery pommel at his little crinkle and pushed. His hole was quite resistant.

*Am I your first, bua?*

Under steady intervals of pressure, Kurn's netherhole spread while he moaned in fevered confusion. I gave it small reprieves before pressing more, stretching the Hellhound's ass to the widest part of the pommel. His cheeks clenched, and a yelp escaped his lips, but I didn't let up until, abruptly, his backside swallowed the metal plug.

The Hellhound yelled in shock as his dagger firmly lodged inside. I could well imagine the spasming and cramping as a novice and chuckled, pushing the grip of his dagger deeper in and churning the grease around in his shitter. I watched his dark pink ring hugging the invading weapon tightly as he groaned and babbled.

"B-burns!" he finally said.

"Always does the first time," I cooed.

"G-Get o-off!"

"I wager you've not had *shayf* like mine?"

I gave the dagger a twist and fucked him hard as he had me.

"N-No! Stop!"

He bucked like his spirited stallion, trying to throw me off, his arms quivering as he tried to rise to his hands and knees. I held on as I would any steed as he rose and then collapsed again, losing his breath. He rocked to and fro, and I shoved the handle in so far that the cross guard tucked neat and vertical in the crack of his ass. I spun around to grasp his black hair and give it a good yank.

"*Kus f-fagila!*" he roared.

While the Ma'ab fought the hair-pulling, I found that same pain point on him which worked on Amelda. Kurn went rigid, squeezing the hilt between hard cheeks, his mouth open in wordless pain. I twisted his thick neck to one side and stared at one dark eye. He turned further still to look at me, wide eyed.

"Who was at the canyon where you attacked me?" I hissed. "Who made you run like a coward that morning? What did you see?"

I eased off the pressure so he could gain the breath to blurt something out. Anything.

"You s-summoned a yellow-eyed demon to f-follow us, *kus!* You know!"

"Was it the same thing behind me holding a chain, too?"

I pressed down, and his head jerked in a nod until I let up.

"I-It attacks whenever your blood is drawn! The ruby will not work, for you are *already* blood-bound, you trickster!"

I chilled at the thought of being blood-bound and not knowing it. *Not again.*

With both hands, I shoved that fear away. If that was the case, the creature wasn't near to aid me in this conflict.

*This is something else.*

A yellow-eyed demon was following us, like Jacob said followed them.

*It cannot be the same one. It cannot be everywhere at once.*

"Like the creature that turns invisible?" I demanded. "In your training in Ennikar?"

"Cease p-pretending, you manipulative *sogrif!* You lied from the first d-day you arrived to seduce Sarilis, filth-rotting bitch!"

Osgrid called from the door. "Sirana! The townsfolk convergin' on th' shed! I found yer things!"

She held up a bag which looked to hold a sphere of the size which contained my guardians, presenting what I assumed was Callitro's ring in her other hand.

"We gotta move now!" she warned.

Beneath me, Kurn struggled against the pain-point, rolling once to where a metal point caught against the floor, the deep jab making him cry out. A giggle slipped out of me as I pulled one of the last useful capsules from my pouch.

Kurn was familiar with it.

"Here, have another," I said, shoving the compact pellet far up one nostril before leaping up and out of reach.

The string of snorting curses as he scrambled to his knees could make a mata nauseated. I waited until he got one boot under him to kick the dagger jutting out of his ass, forcing him to roll over, howling as I darted after Osgrid outside.

I ignored the Hellhound yelling in Ma'ab, but then suddenly another voice filled my mind clear as the night sky.

*⋆Kill him! Do not leave yet, how dare you?! You are not finished! Kill, kiiillll!⋆*

I snatched my hand away from Soul Drinker's hilt, not recalling when I had set it there. Shame crept in to know I was leaving him alive *again* to chase me.

*Foolish. I should go back.*

No. At least I knew the capsule worked on him, he would be down until I could ride away, and I wouldn't miss his crude remarks. I was out of time, and these men had their weight of flesh.

*We're done. I must reach Gavin.*

The dagger whispered contemptuous and incomprehensible reprimands just beneath my understanding as I ran to the rear of the building. Despite it, I enjoyed those deep breaths of fresh air. It felt like days since I stepped inside.

Behind me, Osgrid tromped as quickly as her own legs would take her, and I slowed to wait at the corner. She closed the distance and held out the swinging bag and a familiar gold ring in both hands. She was shaking as I took them.

"Yer doin' well," she assured us both. "Rithal's got his pony an' Mathias's horse. They'll meetcha North later. Ye an' Gavin gotta get out. Run an' don't stop."

I tugged off one glove to don the gold ring. It was the right one; I knew the moment it settled that it was made for me. Smiling to imagine the young wizard safe in the Tower, I pulled my glove on to look inside the bag.

I reached in to remove the sphere, and my babies leaped anxiously inside, throwing themselves desperately against the magical shield.

~*I'm here, babies, I'm here. Calm, calm, don't injure yourselves.*~

They settled a little, still hopping and sprinting in confused panic for a nonexistent target.

"Osgrid, can you dispel this?"

"Sorry, nae. It's time we ain't got." The Dwarven witch splayed her hands helplessly. "Like as not it'll dissolve with time an' distance from its maker. Nature o' spells like this."

That had to be good enough. Maybe Gavin would have ideas later.

*After we get out of here.*

Osgrid and I peeked around the corner then. The noise and activity had been growing so steadily from all directions to an extent that I hadn't grasped how many crows were in the trees, calling to each other.

With the shed as their epicenter.

"Is yours there?" I muttered to Osgrid.

"Aye. Lost track o' 'im soon as you ran from my place."

"Where did the rest come from?"

"All around. Been buildin' since he woke up."

I wasn't sure what held me back—either the idea of being attacked by that many sharp beaks or splattered with the feces from that many orifices if I wasn't welcome—but I wasn't the only one. Men from town converged too slowly to pretend they weren't afraid of that mass of noisy black feathers. They held torches, swords, axes, and pitchforks. I put up my hood and cursed under my breath.

"*Oi!*" shouted Dar standing out front of the crowd from a good distance away. "Is th' governor in there? *Oi!*"

Without making us wait, the door to the shed opened and Mathias stepped out. I couldn't read the look on his face well, only that he wasn't smiling.

"Master Briar!" Dar acknowledged, nodding his chin toward the darkness behind him. "Is Master Brom in there?"

"Afraid not," Mathias said, raising his voice to be heard above the crows. "He was letting us question the last Witch Hunter."

"Yeah, we heard. We, ah, we want you to go now. Don' understand all th' witchcraft goin' on here the last couple days, but if ye don't go, ye ain't gonna like it."

Mathias grinned weakly. "Ah, but where's that famous hospitality?"

"Where's th' governor?!" Dar shouted back, his patience thin and nerves fraying. "He's not answerin' our summons! D'ye have him in there?"

I watched several in the crowd tighten or adjust their grips on their weapons. I noticed there were no women or children among them.

"Not at all," Mathias denied.

"Then who—?"

The men fell utterly silent when Jacob walked out, bloody and nude, with a carefully cut, gaping hole in his chest. Other magical marks had been created with a fine blade, balanced and aesthetic in design. The Witch Hunter was expressionless and walked with that same inconsistent gait as the undead at Sarilis's tower.

From behind Jacob came Gavin, and the men cried out in fear, their voices overlapping. Much taller and with his hood drawn up, his face was in shadow but for an eerie glow of ice blue when he lifted his chin. He held his spade and was in possession of his pack.

*Ready to run,* I hoped, as I readied the talisman that would call his mare.

"We are finished here," Gavin said dispassionately. "We shall leave Troshin Bend without threat or argument."

The men were shivering, the expressions sweeping them as they looked at Jacob too fast for me to be sure what they would do, but the rising fear was palpable.

*"Where is Brom?!"* Dar bellowed. "I'm not gonna ask again!"

"Help!" cried a woman behind them.

The back half of the crowd spun around, lifting their torches.

"Help, oh by the gods, *help!*"

*Amelda.*

"They've stabbed him! My *Fahdi,* he's trapped in their spell!"

She sprinted from the front door of the inn and up the road. She'd recovered so soon after I left, I wondered if she had been faking unconsciousness at some point.

*Damn it. Too many of them.*

The shift toward accusation among the mob was as swift as any I'd seen in Sivaraus. I loaded my hand crossbow, unsure if it the right was straight after the brawl and fuck in the kitchen.

"Get them!" the pale woman cried, pointing at Gavin and Mathias as she came into my view. "Get that *maknuut!* Cut him up! Look for the black witch and the medicine woman, they've stolen from our sorcerer before stabbing him! He may not live!"

Gavin's shoulders rose and fell again in an actual sigh, either a muscle memory like his mare, or he *did* still need to breathe somewhat. I stayed flat to the wall as Amelda drew breath again and began casting.

*Again indeed, monk. Again indeed.*

I aimed down my arm, trying to sight my slightly damaged weapon. I called on the command word of Callitro's ring, grateful Osgrid recovered it.

*~Help it fly true.~*

Brom's daughter took the bolt in her upper back, destroying her spell. She screamed, arching her back, and fell with multiple men surrounding her, fluttering in some attempt to aid. Some looked in my direction, squinting into the shadows with torches up.

"Get away from here," I whispered to Osgrid, loading another bolt. "Save yourself like Rithal. They'll come to *your* hut next."

Jacob had fearlessly closed distance with the townsmen, and the crows began shifting forward like a screaming, dark wave, frightening many of the men back. The ice blue of Gavin's eyes had disappeared; I could feel the air chilling along the forest floor. Mathias had fled; I spotted him running off toward the river, perhaps to meet Rithal, drawing two of the mob after him.

"What about the relic?" Osgrid murmured, her heart pounding.

"Are you going to try to take it?"

"Nae."

"Then run. There is nothing more you can do."

I shot another man armed with an axe who'd chopped at Jacob's body, taking an arm off at the elbow. The nude Witch Hunter barely bled and kept coming, swinging, grappling, biting. The crows didn't attack or dive but began circling overhead in an enormous cluster. Gavin remained where he was for the moment, his unseen aura strengthening to make these thirty or so individuals loathe to rush him as one.

"All together!" Amelda shrieked, her own aura evidently surging over the men surrounding her. "Attack as one! Don't stop striking until he's carrion!"

That was about the only tactic that might have worked.

Gavin hadn't backed up yet and readied his spade, motioning with it. "Look behind you."

Amelda laughed hoarsely and in pain, shaking her head in refusal, but several of her men looked.

And screamed.

"Oh, sweet goddess, no," Osgrid whispered, sounding prepared to run.

Coming through the trees was a staggered troop of naked, lurching men, some limping or hunched but most walking like Jacob before he lost an arm. They were smeared with dirt, clouds of it falling from their hair if they stumbled. Their bodies were covered with crusted wounds of sword, arrow, and axe packed with black soil. One of them had died from his throat torn open by a shovel.

There were seventeen of them including Bictrius.

"No!" Amelda cried as several of the townsmen fled in a panic.

Gavin spoke above the raucous birds. "You will have to fight them again unless you care to run as well. The Witch Hunters will not chase you, only block you should you keep us from leaving."

*Us.* I clenched the mare's talisman. *~Come, night mare. Come.~*

"He nae gonna massacre 'em?" Osgrid asked as if daring to hope.

I thought he'd been clear. "Only if they attack first."

A handful of men tried. Looking to Amelda, they summoned the lingering rage to rush Gavin, and several naked, dead Witch Hunters sprinted forward and tackled them, unheeding of further damage to their bodies, numb to all pain.

The clopping of hooves sounded as Gavin's mare cantered into sight on the road, and he looked behind him and then peered directly where I hid in shadow, nodding as if to signal me. The Deathwalker turned to make long strides toward our ride.

"I must go," I said.

"Aye," the Dwarf agreed. "Good luck."

"You as well. Don't linger here."

"Nae. Comin' to an end."

I checked the action as Amelda tried one last effort to cast after Gavin, only for the small woman to be snatched by large, undead hands. Her screams from a jostled wound and that naked, dead weight landing on her, pinning her to the ground, made me smile as I sprinted forward to catch up with my ally.

Gavin was in the night mare's saddle, his spade strapped to a pack across her rump when I ran up. Saying nothing, he scooted to give me the front half of the seat, holding out his hand for me. His face was still bone pale, and his eyes solid black. It was so grotesque as to be hypnotizing. I snatched his cold hand, and Gavin lifted me into the driver's seat.

"We'll need your eyes and concentration to guide her," he said. "I will hold back their pursuit as long as I can."

"Check."

My boots and balance secured, reins in hand and talisman beneath my glove against my palm, I smacked my heels into her sides.

"You need not kick her," he said. "She can't feel it."

I grimaced. "Right."

~*Turn around, night mare. Gallop upon the road.*~

The undead horse spun tightly without a whinny or a snort, muscles bunching beneath us before she launched forward into a steady run. The crows did not follow but remained above the conflict between living men and undead, crying in excitement or warning. The mare displayed no distraction or hesitance as she galloped out of Troshin Bend in the black of night.

As we rode together again, I was unaccustomed to Gavin folding himself around me even for stability. He was also *not* the correct temperature for a living man, but we had to get used to this, both of us, as we settled in for a long run toward dawn.

"What is that on your right side?" Gavin asked near my ear.

"Hm?"

"You have several magical items on you, potent ones."

"Yes, both of Sarilis's vials, for the warp rot. The ruby Castis tried to use on me *again*. My spiders are trapped in a bubble. And…"

"And?"

I swallowed. "The red rune dagger that killed the former Queen of the Davrin."

Gavin paused. "You stole it from the Zauyrian sorcerer."

"Yes. He was waiting for me. He had the relic with him."

The horse's hooves continued unabated. There was no harsh breath, only the breeze passing by my ears. Finally Gavin had to ask.

"He offered no insight why he removed it from its chest?"

My heart pounded as I recalled being crushed between two men, both my holes full of cock, forcing their way on me as they held me trapped. Castis coming closer to bind me further, all while threatening whatever was necessary to drag me North.

Was this what happened to the missing Priestess and her Son? Was it better or worse than what Innathi had told me awaited me and my unborn with the Deathless?

*To the Drider Pit with them all.*

"No, the sorcerer did not say," I grumbled. "Kurn and Castis interrupted when they heard something in the shed. I attacked

Amelda to give Osgrid a chance to run. She took it. A fight erupted."

Gavin was quiet for a while, waiting for me to continue. When I didn't, he said, "And you emerged carrying all the spoils."

"There was a cost."

"I do not doubt."

"Don't touch the red rune dagger. It speaks and tries to throttle your will."

"Hm. I shan't. Thank you for the warning."

"I am sorry. It's here because it wants to be."

"Interesting. And concerning."

"As resting your head on a hill of ground stingers," I agreed.

He grunted, and I stopped talking because my voice kept quivering.

Gavin pressed no more as we galloped without pause until dawn. I would discover that Gavin packed a lot of food for me as he planned to see his mare die and rise again. Taking Shyntre's pellets to aid bruises and sores, I also ate and drank atop the horse, not wanting to stop.

The closer dawn came, there rose that familiar but odd, filtered light, changing the depths and arrangements of the forest sweeping by before my eyes. What would have been impossible, inky shadow became nuanced and partially visible as pale mushrooms and bark began to glow and stand out.

At one point, something dark moved against a paler boulder in my periphery, and my gaze snapped to the side to track it. *A bear? A deer?*

Something twisted, the closer we got to the infected forest.

*Nothing.* It was gone.

If it was anything tangible, it was moving South toward Troshin Bend. I swallowed, wondering what it might find.

"I forgot to tell you," I said.

"Yes?"

"That powerful aura which concerned you back at the canyon?"

"Mm-hm."

"And the... other that shot black, dissolving arrows at Witch Hunters the night you died?"

Gavin waited.

"I am almost certain it's the same creature," I said. "It has followed us to Troshin Bend. Kurn confirmed it tormented him in both places. Scaring me away to leave him drugged, then scaring Kurn away from *me,* using that Hellhound chain."

"Interesting. Sounds intelligent." The Deathwalker glanced behind us. "We left Kurn behind. Is he alive to pursue us?"

"Yes."

Though he may have difficulty resting his ass long in his saddle.

"And that 'spell' Amelda claimed trapped the sorcerer?"

I shook my head. "I don't know. The dagger did that. I do not remember stabbing him with the relic, but that's what happened."

Gavin hummed, glancing at the slow brightening of the forest around us. There were no creatures to be seen at all, except the early birds.

"We may find out which prey this creature seeks," he said. "You or Kurn."

Indeed, we would. And should it be what I feared—a half-blood of Davrin origin—then I knew what path I must take.

I would have no choice but to pursue him as he pursued me.

# CHAPTER 17

ELDER RAUSERY APPEARED IN THE JUMP CIRCLE CLOSEST TO home, sitting atop a lizard she chanced to track and bridle on her way down. She believed it was the one which had been carrying Gaelan on the way up.

This far into the Deepearth, the silence and distant, furtive scrapes on stone were eerie after spending spans on the Surface in its constant wind and noise. It always took time to adjust but the Elder let it happen.

Absorbing her surroundings with all her senses, the Davrin found her and her cooperative mount to be alone. The circle was warded and hidden within a comfortably small cave that had three spokes of tunnels: one too small for anything larger than a crawling infant, another enough for individuals going single-file, and the main one large enough for lizard and rider.

The Elder Davrin listened to the pulse rising deep inside her chest and head, pulling her toward the Great Cavern. The two larger tunnels eventually met to lead to one of the main trade routes to and from the Davrin city, but the connection point was located high up on a sheer wall, camouflaged with magic, and required a climbing lizard or some other gear to enter or exit.

The infant-sized tunnel in the hollow of stone was usually ignored or unseen. Rausery dismounted and headed for it, drawing out a message pellet and breaking it. She mouthed words which would be carried beyond what she could shout intelligibly then waited patiently, leaning against the stone.

In time, she heard a response, condensed and meaningful.

*Elder, welcome! No Red Sisters have died. The Sorceress and Right Hand keep balance, but the Left Hand needs support. The Heart has ideas and volunteers. We await the proper time and place.*

Rausery frowned in consideration, deciding there was no need to use a second pellet. She tapped the pommel of her dagger against the stone in a dismissal tattoo then remounted for Sivaraus. Keeping a good pace, she'd reach the Fringe by the end of the cycle, later only depending on how troublesome it was to evade recognition or conflict among the Fringe or with the Valsharess's sentries.

There was an entry into the Great Cavern which was relatively close to High Gate and the Cloister, only used by the Sisterhood. It was the same path on which she'd led Sirana, Gaelan, and Jael out and toward the Surface, and the one place close to the central nerves of the city where the highest ranks could slip in and out without passing sentries or alert wards being set off. Most in the Sisterhood didn't know about the tiny pathway left open without watch or ward, let alone the rest of the Palace-Sanctuary complex, and this made it both a strength and a weakness.

The couple of times the Prime had secretly set some sort of tracker or alarm obtained elsewhere, D'Shea had found and disabled it in an ongoing debate against anything perpetually magical and lasting without a sentry present to maintain it, insisting that the item *would* be found eventually.

"The fields of dissuading wards along the basin and walls in front of it, with *no* magical beacon drawing attention to it, is the best camouflage," Varessa had insisted, going toe-to-toe with the Prime.

Rausery openly agreed with the Sorceress's expertise and pressed the benefit of their own autonomy. The Elder General used it most and encouraged the Prime to do the same, knowing she wouldn't. Fortunately, the way was left open for now.

This was the most expeditious way to present herself and report to the Prime, if that was her intent. As it had been any time she left for the Surface, Rausery returned in no hurry to dive into the political fray. The fewer who witnessed her return, the better for catching those boils which always swelled up unaware, no matter which side of the shadows they stood.

After slinking into the Great Cavern and avoiding notice, Rausery kept to paths high above the rocky basin which required a lizard or climbing equipment. For half the first cycle, she crawled in the opposite direction of the Cloister. Reaching one of the many hidden caches around the city, she removed all the lizard's gear and stashed them before releasing her mount naked to wander where it would. Someone would catch it and make use of their unexpected fortune; maybe the Sisterhood would reclaim it, maybe not.

Rausery trekked further trails above the basin, following the perimeter of the Great Cavern and the border farthest from the Palace and city center. These narrow, dangerous pathways were about as difficult to navigate as some of the mountain goat trails in Surface mountains but had the benefit of keeping her invisible to the best Dark Sight down below. More than a wake cycle after entering the massive cavern, the Elder climbed down and blended into the background on the Fringe, aided by a ring on her finger and centuries of cool practice.

She could see tiny beacons of light in the distance as she got closer to the Fringe Gate, which led in the direction of the Tragar Stronghold. The spots placed some of the small farms feeding the Houses, including the area where Sirana had attacked the healer Consort during her trials. In hindsight, it made sense that the Priestess-healed recruit would have sought a bua—any bua—but also might have been *drawn* by the same type of Sanctuary magic in Auslan.

When Rausery had received those healing pellets from Shyntre to give to Sirana, the Elder had asked him how he knew that Consort could cleanse Kerse's taint from their novice. She'd tentatively accepted his answer.

"I know more about the Consorts than any cait," he'd said. "After what happened to Qivni, the Priestesses always needed buas to help watch them. I was one of them."

After what happened *to* Qivni. It had always seemed a curious way to tilt it, but after the purge, the Elder might understand what Shyntre meant.

*Maybe he'd seen it coming a long way off while the rest of us were blind.*

Rausery had more questions now. Did "Auslan" intend to impregnate Sirana or was it failed control in pushing magic between them, like the first time they met? Given Sirana had told Rausery that the Queen thought Shyntre was the sire for some baffling reason, *and* that the stubborn wizard wasn't going to correct Her...?

*Yet, no matter the sire, the Valsharess knows.*

Rausery still couldn't imagine why the cait would have been allowed to leave for the Surface at all, but so it was. The Queen had touched each of the punished Sisters with Her bare hand before pronouncing sentence.

*She must have seen something bad for us when She touched Sirana.*

No mage in Sivaraus, not even the High Priestess, could read auras and see visions of fates both grand and personal except the Valsharess. It was also a rare and deliberate occurrence; the Queen did not drag every common Davrin before Her to try and wrench their fates from the ether. Rausery had experienced Her searing-cold touch once, when she was younger than Sirana; whatever her ruler knew about the Elder General's fate had not been whispered in over six centuries.

*Maybe what She saw for me already came to pass.*

Likewise, the Queen had not seen fit to inform the Prime or the General of Sirana's condition.

*D'Shea probably knows something.*

Though this royal puzzle made her head ache, Rausery wasn't in a hurry to find the Sorceress or the Prime. Sirana had pleaded with Rausery to help D'Shea protect the Consort, but the Elder shook her head now. That outcome was on the Sorceress.

If Auslan was alive in the Cloister, he was in bad shape and another cycle of reconnoitering the present landscape would make little difference to him. If he was dead, then it was especially pointless to abandon her opportunities to rush her return.

Rausery slipped past Fringe Gate wearing a low commoner's form, the details of her travel wear reduced in both detail and quality. The wall sentries glanced her way but found no reason to approach. Low, filthy streams gave hauling animals a place to sip and shit while creaking wagons, either inbound or outgoing, were surrounded by the poorest traders changing their posture from guardbeast to numb hoarder as she came closer then passed by.

*No fights over the dregs this cycle.*

She stayed on the edge of the Great Cavern and headed deeper into the Fringe, toward the poorest Houses of Sivaraus, keeping an eye out for loitering or crouching groups within the slum, be they Davrin or not. The Valsharess's Army came here regularly to clear out squatters, taking prisoners and slaves or forcing those who received advance warning to either lay low somewhere or leave the Great Cavern entirely. There was no permanence in the faces or makeshift shelters and temporary agreements of the Fringe, yet it always seemed the same.

The roads here could barely be called such and took almost two cycles to reach the army camps from Fringe Gate. They were rough with natural, rocky pits once filled during a more prosperous time to a smooth pathway, with proper drainage when the Cavern's perimeter water springs would occasionally burst and spill into the basin. Now, they were cracked, eroded, and hollowed out; small and numerous craters filling with stagnant moisture and mud releasing dangerous spores and swarms of tiny blood-biters if disturbed.

Rausery stepped lightly, drawing not even their tiny attention.

As she passed glowing fungal markers of the Noble borders, many shelters and pockmark caves, though old structures with a stone foundation continually had repurposed scrap from other ruins added to keep them functional. Some House colors could be seen in a faded banner specifically lit by a lantern from afar, but most places preferred to remain in total darkness. Only the distant string of lanterns from the army's drill fields near House Aurenthin gave Rausery a sense of how many in between snuffed out their lights.

There were fields which grew some food, but they had to be jealously guarded behind crumbling stone walls, and sometimes that did not help if the Valsharess's army trooped through on drills or responded to a threat at Fringe Gate or Low Gate and needed supplies fast. In response, there was a strong black market just outside both Gates with higher risk wilderness food being brought to trade for Elven trinkets and mild potions where they could be stolen or looted.

The small, Dwarvish Ketro and goblinesque Pyte were especially eager to make these regular trades, although Rausery was equally sure both the psionic Tragar and Ornilleth prodded caravans for "suggestions" of what to obtain, as some items in demand over the centuries seemed of little use to the traders asking for them.

There was another aspect of the deep traders that the Prime and the Valsharess less and less wanted to discuss. Worrisome signs of ruined Davrin scripts could be found among the semi-aquatic Yutogul approaching Low Gate, or a recruit like Jael blatantly telling them that the saphgar stone had been seen near Fringe Gate, forged to magically crafted or honed weapons owned by the Grey Dwarves. These weapons were not known to be made in Sivaraus, and the Sisterhood hadn't yet nabbed one to inspect closer.

*Phaelous discovered it turned that bright blue, like the stone around Sirana's neck, in the consistent presence of magic.*

Rausery had once spoken out on the assumption that all the Davrin deep traders on the Fringe originally came from the Great Cavern.

*"They did," said her Queen, bored and dismissive.*

*Not true. It can't be, thought a young and confused Lead.*

It did not go beneath Rausery's notice that certain deep traders disappeared or eventually ended up in the dungeon. With or without this pattern, the answer had seemed clear enough back then, and future insights and evidence would continue to build the image in the darkness around her.

Just as the Sisterhood did not know how many conclaves of Elder Minds there might be in the Deepearth—only clashing with those which crept close enough to become a threat—or as they did not know how many groups may have broken away from the Tragar Stronghold, though the Grey Dwarves loathed to travel far. There *were* Davrin who had broken away from the Valsharess. No one here knew how many.

*Almost no one.*

Rausery would confirm this for herself four centuries ago but would sit on that knowledge as she grew aware of how no one above her spoke much about the possibility. She followed their lead and watched, finding those spots of void silence, letting it lead her gut.

This time, as it had times in the past, the Elder's gut led her to House Aurenthin, the Twenty-Fourth, and the lowest Nobles of Sivaraus.

"Matron," she said, leaning against the hard-to-see doorway of a small, add-on infirmary of a decrepit mansion.

Kennitha displayed annoyance in her posture as she turned around, wiping off her hands with a rough cloth. She looked to have finished setting an arm bone in a splint, and the bua on the cot was sweating and biting down on a hard leather bit, remarkably quiet.

"Oh, it's you," said the Matron of House Aurenthin. "What do you need?"

She offered no honorific, not the least insulting to Rausery given her appearance and circumstance. Instead, this was why the Elder continued to work with Jael's Mother; she was smart enough to be caught by surprise and *not* to announce the disguised arrival of an Elder of the Sisterhood. Rausery also liked how she wasted no effort on unnecessary placation.

The Elder Sister jerked her chin to request a walk together. Kennitha accepted but first called one of her Daughters through the inner hall to sit with the injured one. Rausery watched as the Matron tucked a waterskin next to the bua after removing the bit from his mouth and pulling up a worn blanket to cover him. He nodded in thanks but look bleary-eyed and sleepy now, like a tonic was working on him.

The Third Daughter arrived and was not the least alarmed by the appearance of their visitor. Her Mother made deals often enough that this approach wasn't out of the ordinary, as it would be for a secure and stable House.

"I'll be back," the Matron promised without a hint of doubt, grabbing a hand basket while she was at it.

Rausery smiled wryly as they walked toward an overhang good for mushroom collection. She hadn't chosen the location.

*So, what do you need?* Kennitha repeated.

*Still the primary healer around here, Matron?* Rausery signed, eschewing that for now. *I thought you had a few apprentices now.*

*He's my son,* Kennitha signed tersely, lifting her chin. *I shall tend him myself.*

*Ah. Which one?"

The Matron pursed her lips tight. *Franek. The Second.*

*Yes? I hadn't heard of him being around lately.*

*He hasn't been.* The Matron shrugged. *He was on a trek and was injured. He barely made it home. He was lucky to live.*

*Accident or attack?*

*Both. He was evading pursuit by Tragar when he fell down a slope and broke his arm.*

*Did he happen to steal one of those blue-edge weapons?*

Kennitha shook her head. *And he may not be able to try again. It was not a clean break. He may be crippled despite all I can do.*

Rausery didn't reply, and after a pause where the Matron stooped for mushrooms, she also shifted the topic.

★What happened to Jael a quarter-turn ago?★ Kennitha signed bluntly. ★I can't make sense of the gossip that's been trickling this way following the purge. Tell me something true for whatever you need of me.★

A corner of Rausery's mouth tightened, her hands loose at her sides while she thought, scanning their surroundings. When Kennitha straightened up to face her, glancing expectantly at her hands, the Elder raised them without threat.

★She and several others attacked a rogue Sathoet who tried to sacrifice another Sister in ritual. The Valsharess sentenced her to a Surface mission from which she may not return. I just got back from seeing it done.★

Kennitha absorbed that, various subtle tics in her expression showing Rausery little to no regrets, only that familiar Aurenthin obstinance. ★Attacked a Sathoet. Did she wound it?"

Rausery smirked. ★She helped kill it. Why she was sentenced.★

The Matron considered this, selecting several mushrooms before pulling a trowel from her waist and digging into a drying pile of dung to spread it around.

When her hands were free, she opted to sign, ★Good. I'm glad she had the chance after what those beasts did to her.★

The Elder signed agreement and waited.

Kennitha inhaled slowly and exhaled again. ★Thank you for taking Jael into the Sisterhood when you did, even if she didn't last long. My cait was about to disappear into the Sanctuary. We knew it. She was terrified. I couldn't convince her not to vanish into the Fringe.★

★I can imagine. I trained your Fourth to give her the best chance possible on the Surface, but the Queen's compulsion will probably override it.★

The Matron gripped her trowel and straightened her back. She shook her head. ★Why this slow torment of Aurenthin? It goes for generations, to hear my eldest tell it. What did we do against the Valsharess? What sentence do we serve that we are not aware of the crime? Not the oldest, crumbling notes from past Matrons offer a hint. Why are we not exterminated if we are such vermin to Her?★

This was not the first time Rausery had heard these questions, from Kennitha or others as some of the speculation bled over into the other low Houses who would never climb status again before they disappeared.

The fact that Aurenthin had remained at the bottom for the longest any could remember *without* being expunged or absorbed into another name, combined with the undeniable patterns Rausery had witnessed of their Daughters being abducted by either the Sisterhood or the Sathoet, made Kennitha's questions seem viable and worth looking into.

However, no one Rausery knew except for D'Shea might have had any access to insightful clues at the other end of the Great Cavern: the Palace, Wizard's Tower, and Sanctuary. It was a pity the Sorceress's son, who had potential access to all those same places, couldn't seem to rein in his temper to gain much ground in that regard, and the upper echelons of politics and magic remained beyond Rausery's expertise. Her best eyes, ears, and hands had always been far, far below that, in the nooks and crannies no one bothered to seek or shine light into.

★The Tragar chasing your son,★ Rausery signed instead, pulling the Matron out of her reflection. ★Tell me what he told you about his escape. Every detail.★

The Elder patiently read the story in the Matron's hands, noting what she chose to mention, prodding at those she might have left out. The Matron did not seem to hold anything back intentionally. All the Davrin had learned of the Tragar tongue over the centuries came from the lower Houses forced to do the most trade. Rausery learning that Franek had heard and understood one shout—*blueblind*, like an insult—was most curious.

★I think it's strange for them,★ Kennitha finished. ★Something beyond trade or spats drawing them this close to Sivaraus.★

Rausery nodded thoughtfully. ★Then I need you to keep ears to the ground. Not only Tragar, but for any hint of Ornilleth or psionic threat. I'll send food and healing potions to help you and your family.★ She removed from her belt a healing potion she hadn't used on the Surface and was nearing its potency expiration anyway; she offered it. ★Give that to Franek this cycle. Don't wait, it's not a young potion. It'll heal his arm without lameness. An advance payment for your watch."

The Matron stood still, hesitantly accepting the small bottle. ★Why Ornilleth? Are the mind flayers to return with more thralls?★

★Likely,★ Rausery answered without saying why, ★and a larger force than before. I don't know when.★

★But… what do they want?★

★Don't know yet.★ Rausery tilted her head. ★Don't cause panic, Matron, prepare. However you can.★

Kennitha's eyes were wide, but she looked at the valuable potion meant for her son and signed, ★Always.★

Rausery noted the slide of her eyes, that flexible and resilient mind. The Elder would need regular updates on what the Matron would be up to, particularly as she tended to stick her own hands in the muck alongside everyone else down here. This unwavering trait of a relatively young "slum" Matron had earned and held Rausery's respect these past three centuries. It had been a similar relationship with Kennitha's Mother, as well.

★I need to go,★ the Elder signed. ★Thank you for the whispers.★

Kennitha glanced at her basket of mushrooms, slipping the potion in with them, then touched the Elder's arm before she could leave. ★I know it will be you sent to torture us when the Prime finds out. I know you'll do it and expect nothing else. We'll fight back, Elder.★

Rausery's lips twisted as she looked up from the Matron's hand to the copper color she couldn't see that moment, but she'd always known where Jael got her looks.

She mouthed, "*Good, Matron.*"

Another cycle after leaving the lowest Matron, Rausery crouched unseen above Low Gate, observing the long, repetitive process of letting caravans in and out of Sivaraus. The garrison here seemed to be doing well enough, resisting shortcuts in their inspections, and testing for illusion magic with the help of a hidden piercing they'd be reluctant to reveal for fear of how others might plot to steal it.

Small things would get through, something always would, but any contraband too large or any Davrin or creature too powerful could be dealt with quickly. If insurgents or hostiles couldn't be dragged to the dungeon by the army on the left flank, they would have little time to reach Midwall at the end of the rock funnel before the Driders would be shrieking down upon them from the right flank. If Auranka was sleeping or feeling sadistic enough to wait, any intruders seeking to scale Midwall and reach the first Davrin Houses of Sivaraus would only face trained archers and battlemages high above them.

As each group either readied to exit or were coming in, Rausery watched for anyone she knew, although if one of those was practicing what they should be, she wouldn't be able to spot them. She considered a sound or light signal they might recognize but discarded it. The chances were too slim one would be down there at the right time to be worth the risk of notice. They didn't know she'd returned to the city.

Still, Rausery was in no hurry to move on. She reclined back, feeling the essence this part of the city where she'd come of age. Once a slim cait evading the notice of army and Drider, enforcers, or hidden archers, she survived with the tutoring from another who had managed the same. He'd lived a long time.

It was smelly and dangerous at Low Gate for different reasons, lacking the barren anxiety and eerie quiet of the destitute Fringe, replacing it with sweat, fierce competition, and paranoia. There were resources here, large stockpiles guarded on the other side of the walls and beyond reach of many. This only made the focus on

Low Gate more intense, opening and closing, those who moving through trying to sell or steal.

To spot Jaunda blatantly stroll through the Gate with one caravan brought Rausery quickly to her feet.

"Nope!" said the Lead loudly when one guard came closer for a search. The red uniform became visible beneath the mix of real and heatless torches as her black cloak opened, and she put her hand out and forward in threatening gesture.

The guard put her hands down before falling into a salute. "Red Sister!"

"The fuck back to work," Jaunda replied grumpily and trod through the crowd with a scowl on her face as the way opened before her.

*What in Drider's tits?*

The Elder struggled to recall what the Lead's sentence had been, given she knew little before she left.

*"Do you understand, Lead Jaunda?"*

*"Y-yes, my Queen. I will search for his den."*

His den. His.

Elder D'Shea hadn't had any idea who "he" was and what this could mean, either. If the Prime knew, she said nothing and, sadly, their Lead wouldn't be able to talk about it to anyone except the Valsharess directly. No wonder the normally grinning, swaggering Right Hand was in a sour mood coming in through Low Gate, not for the first time since Rausery had left with her young Sisters.

*She needs support. We have ideas and volunteers.*

Rausery looked forward to hearing more.

The Elder followed as their Lead hooked left to begin the long, pocky road toward the army camps and House Aurenthin. Rausery smirked but was curious. If Jaunda had intended to report straight to D'Shea or the Prime, she'd have gone straight, into the funnel between rock fills to Midwall, where she'd surely be let in and given anything needed to expedite her arrival at the Cloister.

*Headed toward the Fringe, or taking the long way around the Cavern?*

It would take time, and Rausery had to use every shortcut she knew to stay ahead of Jaunda and observe her direction. She did stop in the camps for food and a riding lizard but didn't linger even for sex.

*Odd.* Rausery would have to hustle to keep up.

For the first cycle beyond Low Gate, Jaunda's direction hugged the jagged, stone rise that separated the Fourteenth House from the army, bypassed the ruins of Aurenthin, and led her around the bend to the Eighteenth House and toward the center of the Great Cavern. Jaunda was ostensibly headed in the direction of the Cloister now, but there were *much* easier ways to take that trek and there were many stops between here and there.

The next cycle, resting only when Jaunda did, Rausery skimmed the long edge of the Eighteenth's and the Fifteenth's lands just behind the Lead. She noticed signs the Red Sister might be working against an injury, one that a potion couldn't fully mend if she didn't stop traveling for...

*For however long she's been pushing through the deep routes before entering Low Gate.*

That was the damned things about compulsions.

*Still, where is she headed?*

There were places for Rausery to hide and follow when they got through the center strip frequently contested between Fourteen and Fifteen and into a rolling spread of unfenced pasture, bare rock, rock columns and piles, and small structures housing serfs of one House or another. When they began passing the Twelfth House as well, the Elder was resigned that Jaunda was, indeed, headed for the Cloister taking the longest possible route that wasn't the Fringe.

Then Jaunda turned the lizard into a copse of tall mushrooms on Thalluen land, where she dismounted, loosely tied the lizard to let it feed among the insects of the cover and walked toward the mansion. She was favoring her right side, holding her gut, a deep pain becoming obvious.

*Suck my spinnerets.* If Rausery had realized sooner, she'd have stopped the Lead and put her in a cache to rest while she summoned D'Shea. *We passed three of them!*

Someone exited Thalluen manor as if they were expecting her, and Rausery tried to identify who it was. It didn't take long to recognize the gait and dress of the Matron Rohenvi, herself. Was she expecting her? Or were her early warning eyes and wards that good?

*Not to mention Rohenvi's response time.*

While the Matron did not touch the Lead directly, she followed her closely, leading her inside. Rausery was left outside to wonder what to do next. Then she heard a subtle, complicated mimic making insect noises in the same field with her.

*Son of a netherhole.*

The Elder turned her head and signaled for the shadow to come closer. When he obeyed, kneeling silently on her right, he looked in at Rohenvi welcoming the Red Sisters once again, and Rausery waited until he looked back.

★About time you caught up,★ she signed casually. ★I've been waiting almost a span.★

The Davrin's eyes crinkled at the corners as he smiled, keeping his lips closed. He didn't move his hands, either.

When her blood started to settle, Rausery asked, ★Why here, of all Houses? What changed while I was gone?★

The older male glanced toward the mansion again, their subjects now out of sight. He signed with a small smile, ★House Thalluen has a new healer.★

The Elder's mouth fell open. ★She didn't.★

He affirmed, ★She did.★

★Sorceress?★ she checked.

★Correct.★

Rausery mouthed some breathless curses, and his shoulders shook as he laughed in silence. Double-checking their surroundings, the Elder drew in a slow breath, letting it out without so much as a shush of air.

She signed, *I'm ready. Catch me up on all the shit she's been sifting through.*

# CHAPTER 18

JAUNDA ATTEMPTED TO SLOW HER DESCENT INTO THE WARM BATH but still ended up sloshing water onto the floor. She groaned in pleasure as Auslan rushed to wipe it up.

"Easy, Lead," Rohenvi said, asking no questions at all since Jaunda set off her alert ward intentionally. "We shall help, as always."

The pretty bua laid out the damp towel nice and straight along the back of a chair, smoothed it out, then turned around. He stood with his hands in front of him until the Matron motioned him closer. Jaunda wouldn't complain aloud, but she waited with tense anticipation of his hands on her shoulders.

Her gut had been giving her a worrisome amount of trouble for three cycles now, and this was not the first time she'd given in and used the resource Elder D'Shea insisted she not ignore. As the Sorceress predicted, the Queen's compulsion was rougher on Jaunda's body each time she had to turn around and return to Sivaraus without the answer she sought.

*Fuck. Getting worse each time.*

Delicately, Auslan touched her skin with his fingertips and then slid his palms into place; she heard him breathe in slow as he prepared for that magic touch. Then the Consort firmly massaged her hard shoulders, and Jaunda grinned, relaxing fast as her eyes rolled up. The bua was getting the hang of how she liked her muscles worked. She didn't need to instruct him this time.

When she growled in pleasure, his hands tripped up.

"Don't stop," she demanded, her voice rough in disappointment.

"Do continue, Auslan," the Matron murmured as if trying to soothe. "I'm here. She won't break agreement. She needs you."

Jaunda shrugged. "Yeah. That's right."

It was true, she didn't have to place her Feldeu in a box in the Matron's office first thing, any time she showed up. But she grasped that Sirana's former House and this healer was in jeopardy if she couldn't control her phallus. It was easy enough to agree; no Feldeu inside the Consort's quarters, and Jaunda received Auslan's magic hands in return.

The Consort exhaled and continued, and soon it felt like premium healing ointment without the mess or abrupt plateau; it kept going, making her feel good and strong. There was a calming hum deep in her ears when the Consort finally eased into his healing trance, and she tried to stay conscious to feel each change as he explored her without using his eyes.

Her eyes drooped half-shut, her dark nipples pebbled up tight as they ever had, and her muscles both flexed and softened under his hands. He sought those hotspots in her limbs or joints, those worn and exhausted places needing shoring up, so she could keep going for the Valsharess without exhausting the potion supply her Sisters needed as well. This always left her leaking wet between her legs.

Just as well she was in a small tub of water.

His fingers focused on her abdomen, massaged with both hands as his arms reached over and down like he hugged her from behind.

"What happened here?" he whispered.

Maybe he wasn't expecting an answer, but the question was right next to her ear.

"Gonna heave in your tub, pretty bua," Jaunda complained. "Don't ask."

He sounded worried she might. "Apologies, Lead."

The magic touch continued, the soft hum filling her head, infusing her with vitality and strength. By the time he finished, her crotch ached like a bottom Sister denied the rut after marks of good slapping.

*Holy Drider shit, I need to cum!*

She wanted to grab his hand and put it on her cunt, Feldeu not required.

That was why Rohenvi was here, observing every moment with her infant present in a collapsible hammock. She could tell they were done and stood up, ready with a towel.

*Sigh.*

When the Consort's hands were gone and the water was cool anyway, Jaunda gripped the sides of the freestanding tub and pushed herself to her feet, letting the water drain down her skin as she reached for the towel offered. Auslan had, once again, retreated to sit on his bed with a pillow pulled in front of his bulging crotch.

*At least it's not just me.*

How Sirana got pregnant from his healing while they shared a bed made nothing *but* sense now. Jaunda would much rather bend him over while gripping that long hair instead of clasping his trim hips between her thighs, but given the lack of options, she might reconsider…

*Bah.*

Jaunda stepped out of the tub and finished drying her legs and feet, saving the last wipe for her pouting cunt before tossing it into the laundry pile. Matron Thalluen nodded and stepped back while the Lead shrugged into a waiting robe near her dirty equipment and uniform.

"Your Elder will be here soon," she said. "But you have time to eat."

"Thanks," Jaunda said, taking the other seat in the room.

Soon, the small, garnet-eyed cait whom the Lead had seen hovering around before slipped in through the camouflaged entrance in the corner. She carried a tray of simple fare, heading for the Matron to curtsy before handing her the food first. Rohenvi accepted, inspected it, and set it beside the Red Sister without the child needing to draw closer. It was clear she didn't want to.

"Thank you, Natia."

Nodding to the Matron, the cait watched with wide eyes and big ears as she went to sit on the floor between the infant's hammock and Rohenvi's seat. It was telling that Jaunda's host preferred this little servant bearing witness to a significant secret to a trusted operator of the household.

*Hope she's good at keeping her mouth shut.*

Jaunda chewed her food slowly and in silence. This was her third visit to House Thalluen, seeking Auslan's magic at D'Shea's insistence upon returning from the deep routes. Her early skepticism had melted along with the knots in her back the first time the breeding bua touched her. She was thinking about a fourth dive into those faraway tunnels in as many quad-spans only because of him.

The Lead grasped how valuable he was, no argument. The mage healer could reverse, without potions, most of the mental and physical fatigue any warrior was susceptible to during hard push campaigns. He could do it faster and more thoroughly than any reviving draught Jaunda had quaffed in her time.

It was impressive. Here she was, her body pumped and ready to leave the city the next cycle if necessary.

*As long as I don't think too much.*

Jaunda could not recall a time any Red Sister was under sustained pressure to travel as she was now, and Auslan made it possible, or the geas might have killed her by now. She wasn't sure how long they could keep this quality of the last Consort from the Prime and the Valsharess and *not* be sucked into the funnel web of trouble, taking House Thalluen with them.

*Probably too late at this point.*

The only hint her Elder had given Jaunda, in the brief times they'd seen each other between treks, was holding out until Elder Rausery got back from the Surface. Not because D'Shea expected her peer to come up with a solution to the Consort problem; she must have an idea but couldn't focus on it until the crush of duties operating the Sisterhood lifted again.

Without Rausery and Jaunda, Lead Qivni was critical to D'Shea in this time even if the stern Right hand couldn't take the Elder General's place. Some of the younger Sisters might think Qivni would try. Jaunda knew her peer wouldn't.

*Qiv doesn't want it. She's waiting for Rausery, too.*

Happenings in the Matron's mansion shifted toward the strange for Jaunda. Rohenvi dealt with a fussing infant, Natia helping to tend and clean the babe before her Mother decided to nurse the heir right here and now. She sat comfortably and pulled out both swollen tits.

Jaunda looked elsewhere.

Auslan's stifled erection had gone down when he replaced the pillow at the head of the mattress. His eyes drooping, he lay down fully clothed. Jaunda knew that doing what he did took a lot out of him but watching him relax and ready to slip into Reverie was something she hadn't seen before.

Natia tugged on Rohenvi's gown and signed something Jaunda was too late to catch. The Matron sighed and glanced at Auslan with her mouth tightened, but the cait pled her case until her elder relented. The Lead watched Natia take a wide berth around her and crawl onto the Consort's bed to snuggle down. Auslan smiled on the cusp of consciousness as he made space for her.

*Huh.*

Leaving the empty hammock in the room, Rohenvi finished feeding her Daughter and covered her tits again, preparing to leave. She motioned pleasantly for the Lead to join her. Jaunda collected her dirty leathers, armor, boots, and equipment, following the Matron holding her infant close as they exited through the secret passage, heading to her office.

"Leaving the cait in here with him?" Jaunda whispered, baffled.

The Matron signed with one hand, the only one free. ★Natia lays in Reverie lightly.★

"So she wakes if anyone enters?" the Lead guessed. "Summons you?"

Rohenvi replied, ★That, and he is vulnerable to sleep tortures, especially after healing you. He is weaker then. Natia wakes him if he makes too much noise.★

"Hm," Jaunda grunted as they stepped into the Matron's secure chamber. "I guess with Priestesses raising him, he would have plenty of dream fuel."

The Matron frowned at her. Wards in place, she held her dozing Daughter with both arms and spoke aloud. "Perhaps some, Lead. I regret to add that Natia determined the Consort fears any female attacking him as he tries to sleep. He won't rest with me in the room unless Natia is there as well. He has said he would prefer male guards if needed."

Jaunda huffed. "And you have some in mind who are competent?"

"Several." Without the Red Sister having to ask, Rohenvi motioned her chin toward the box on her desk containing her Feldeu. "However, threats haven't risen yet to need to assign them."

The Lead grinned as she walked up to the box and retrieved her magic cock. She inspected her favorite tool with obvious affection then spotted how the Matron was looking at her. It was suspicious.

"*Heh.* I wasn't one in the pile-up on him, by the way, I was out on mission. I only brought him here after D'Shea pulled him out."

Rohenvi shrugged with indifference. "I understand the uniforms all look the same to survivors."

The Lead smirked. "You criticize, Matron?"

"The intent is clear and effective, Lead Sister. Nothing unusual, nothing has changed. Once he cleans up after you, he'll be better until next time."

Jaunda rolled her eyes. Nobles never grasped what it took to make a Red Sister; most she had taken any time to talk with would crack in the first trial, and this Matron was no exception.

*Sirana made it despite her family.*

They waited in uncomfortable silence for her Elder to arrive. The baby made some grunts but was mostly quiet. Jaunda was offered something to read; she did push-ups and other stationary exercises instead as Rohenvi sat with her Fourth, read some scrolls and made notes. Jaunda could kind of see why D'Shea worked with her.

Finally the Elder Sorceress arrived, and the Matron led her in. The first thing D'Shea did was magically clean and mend Jaunda's uniform and equipment.

"Dress well. We report at the Palace before you may continue."

"What?" Jaunda asked, though she peeled off her borrowed robe, laying it over the back of a chair to begin gearing up.

Her Elder was good at covering any concerns with confidence in front of Rohenvi, but Jaunda couldn't even pretend to be so eager.

"The Valsharess awaits."

*Fuck me stupid.*

The two left the plantation on their lizards without noise or pomp though not with any attempt at secrecy, either. D'Shea smirked, indicating some workers peeking out, anxious as to why Red Sisters kept showing up here recently.

The Elder signed to Jaunda's quirked eyebrow. ★Roh will make use of it to keep them quiet.★

★Roh?★ the Lead signed with a gleaming grin. ★Getting cozy with the Matron while I've been gone, Elder?★

The tease rolled right off the Sorceress's back, as always, and D'Shea glanced backward at the mansion outlined in a few lingering lights. ★With her eldest Daughters gone, her mind is returning to the Matron I once knew. Like her Mother. Sirana takes after Roh and Siranet far more than either of her sisters. She has only never witnessed it.★

Jaunda shrugged. ★Yeah, but Sirana can't ever be a Matron like them.★

D'Shea smiled. ★Better for the Sisterhood.★

In the following pause, the Lead tried to recall anything about the current Matron Thalluen from before that Abyssal-cunt First Daughter was born. It was murky.

Jaunda shook her head. ★I remember the late Matron Thalluen. Never thought Rohenvi was anything *like* Siranet.★

★In focus and tastes, we're agreed,★ the Elder replied. ★But the intangible quality I always seek is there. Siranet, Roh, Sirana all have it. Jilrina and Kaltra did not.★ The Sorceress's body language flowed into a silent chuckle. ★Curious to think how you and Roh are the same age. Your paths could not be more different. The time she was moving about at Court, you were busy rising in the Sisterhood.★

Jaunda's brows lifted. ★Didn't know that.★

★You stopped paying attention after Siranet died and didn't begin again until the First Daughter's accident.★

The Lead grinned readily to recall that cycle. ★Yeah, you're right. Blue Eyes did have that delicious spark. Knew she was meant for us soon as I stood guard in her room.★

D'Shea's smile was both pleasant and proud. ★You spotted sign of what I hoped remained after so long under Jilrina's boot, in her and her Mother.★

Jaunda made a face. ★But how strong is 'Roh' if her own Daughter can crush everyone into slugs until she dies?★

The Sorceress didn't reply at first; she looked in the direction of the Palace and Sanctuary. Her Lead glanced that way curiously but didn't see anything. Then D'Shea explained, but in that abstract way of hers.

*When you are responsible for the governance of many,* she signed, *and yet your closest allies are cut down or kept away while you are isolated from children to whom you give birth, it can be very…draining over decades. Though you continue to live and resist, you are hollower than you were. Seeking a wholeness you dare not forget lest the Abyss consume everything you were.*

Jaunda frowned. Her Elder's cautious skepticism about the city's goddess always sent creeps down her back. She signed something she never had before. *You mean Shyntre? Are you talking about him?*

The Sorceress wasn't feeling ill as far as Jaunda could see; her mouth only twisted with a regret and anger too strong to hide. *Roh saw her most trusted ally killed. I saw mine push me into a trap with his own hands.*

*Shit.*

This caught her blindsided. She hadn't made any connection between D'Shea's two turns held in the Sanctuary to give birth and Rohenvi's decades with Jilrina. But she'd asked, so the Lead scraped out what old memories she had of House Thalluen.

*Most trusted ally killed.*

Jaunda signed, *Rohenvi's brother?*

*Azed,* her Elder confirmed, signing the name with surprising respect. She also seemed pleased with her Left Hand for making the leap. *He held fast for as long as he could against that First Daughter and the hollowness affecting Rohenvi. He wouldn't give ground, wouldn't abandon his sister's interests, so Jilrina likely caught him vulnerable and poisoned him.*

Jaunda remembered that. *But there was no proof.*

*There wasn't enough time granted to find it,* D'Shea replied staunchly. *If not for Wilsira and her politics blocking me, I'd have dragged Jilrina in for interrogation.*

*For a bua?*

★For *that* bua, yes. As intelligent and loyal as they come, Jaunda. Despite what those cunts tried to say, Azed never betrayed Rohenvi.★

*Unlike Phaelous.*

Jaunda heard the unspoken lingering in the air and hesitated to dredge that up before meeting the Queen. The Lead looked at the road ahead. They were headed to the Palace now, where Shyntre was being kept.

*The Valsharess, the Headmaster, the Conceiver, Elder D'Shea… That was a whole other cluster of fucks.*

Now after over two centuries, D'Shea was starting to talk. She never could before. If the Elder recognized some of the old Rohenvi returning after a long, oppressive silence, then maybe the Sisterhood would see the same in their Sorceress.

Following the roads, their mounts reached a large and well-known farm field on one side and the Sixth House plantation on the other. Suddenly, Elder Rausery was there. She had caught up to them on foot. Jaunda had rarely heard such naked exasperation as D'Shea snarled.

"How long have you been back?!"

Rausery grinned at them. "Long enough. Looks like you're headed to the Palace. Can I join you?"

D'Shea leaned down, sniffed, and wrinkled her nose. "You stink, General."

"Ha! And you can fix that with a wave of your hand, Sorceress."

*"Bah!"*

The Sorceress acquiesced, dismounting to helped her black-uniformed peer prepare for the Palace. Despite her grousing, D'Shea was glad Rausery was coming with them. Jaunda was, too; the only part she was sorry for was the abrupt loss of all those subtle smells clinging to the General.

*I remember those scents.*

Within that blip of Surface "stink," Jaunda recalled the scent of sweat on the pale skin of a young, blonde Elf.

And her own punishment for letting her go.

The Lead headed to the Palace, preferring to imagine the slender willow was up there still blooming in Sunlight.

The bua wouldn't go away; he was too frightened of failing his Queen.

"Please, wizard son, eat while I draw the bath."

Shyntre grumbled from under the blankets, "I don't need your help to wash my balls."

The Palace servant hesitated to respond. "Please, hurry. I will get your clean robes."

*Arrgh…*

He hated this.

Throwing back the covers and rolling to sit, he squinted in the candlelight, smelling the warm mushroom soup and both hearing and feeling the steaming water pouring out of his personal cistern into the tub. He scratched his scalp, fingers combing through stiff, short hair, closer-cropped than when he'd arrived.

Auranka's feral face and fangs lingered behind his eyes.

"What's your name?" Shyntre mumbled.

The bua hesitated again. "Gidrae, wizard son. Most call me Gid."

He nodded. "Shyntre."

"I know, wizard son."

"Shyntre."

Gid fell silent and went about his duties, and it only took dredging up a mental image of what would happen to the bua if Shyntre didn't get his ass moving. It had already happened once with a different servant.

He *hated* this.

*Manipulative, greedy, pitiless, violating…*

Standing from the bed nude, the mage slipped into a soft cushioned chair and put his nose down above the soup, letting the scent awaken his empty stomach which clenched in on itself. He picked up the bowl in both hands and slurped to test the temperature, found it tolerable, and guzzled the liquid before impatiently chewing on the chunks without touching the spoon.

Gid turned around. "The bath is— Oh! Uh. Are you ready?"

Shyntre grunted and, with his jaw working the last of the vegetables, got into the tub to start scrubbing himself. He heard Gid exhale softly in relief.

"Any hint at all why I'm being summoned?" he asked sourly.

"Mm, no, wizard son."

Shyntre glanced at him, waited until they met eyes, and cocked a brow expectantly like a Matron would. It worked this time; Gid cleared his throat.

"Her Majesty allowed me to see Red Sisters were present, and She said the Headmaster would arrive soon."

Nodding slowly, Shyntre exhaled and continued cleaning. "Which Red Sisters?"

"I don't know, wizard son, that was the closest I have ever been to one."

*Good point.*

He tended to forget that. He knew their leaders, all their ranks, and most of their faces, though some he might only recognize again if she was naked and had her Feldeu attached.

"Consider yourself lucky," he said, brusquely sudsing up his scalp.

"Oh, I do, wizard son."

With a smirk, Shyntre dunked his head, rinsed off, and stood up to let the water drain down. Gid held a towel open for him; his eyes didn't drop or linger one finger's width on his wet body. The corner of Shyntre's mouth tightened with the wry thought that he wouldn't be so proper with places reversed. It was an impulse that irritated the Valsharess, though he'd learned the hard way.

Shyntre was dressed in new, dark blue wizard's robes with gold trim, soft shoes on his feet, and nothing else. He was at the door, opening it before Gid had a chance to do it for him.

"Return to the servants' quarters," he said. "I'll make it there alone."

The younger male grimaced, caught between true fear of the favored son lying and never showing up and genuine desire to leave as ordered. Fortunately for him, the Headmaster was waiting down the hall and approached. The creases in his dark face showed as he smiled at the servant.

"I will see he arrives," Phaelous said.

"Y-yes, Headmaster!" Gid said in a hush, bowing and escaping now that he could.

Shyntre glared openly at his sire but went along with him, the soft soles of their shoes silent upon the ornate carpet.

"I am glad I did not have to knock on your door," Phaelous said.

"Once was enough," Shyntre replied, his jaw tight.

"Mm. Was it that you had to watch last time?"

Heart pounding, he ground his teeth. "That, and I never asked his name. If I had, it wouldn't have happened. I didn't make that mistake again with Gid."

"How is being responsible for a faceless servant's suffering worse than a named one?"

*"It's not about me!"* Shyntre snapped, his voice echoing down the silent corridor as he rounded on his sire, and they stopped, facing each other. "It's about Her and always will be!"

*"Shhh,"* Phaelous suggested, face expressionless.

Shyntre swallowed his bile and anger, his vision burring until he blinked to clear it. His throat hurt, so he signed his reply.

\*Punishing another in my stead is retribution for disobedience, plain and simple. Using it as a threat which works is coercion, nothing else. It's not. *My*. Doing.\* The young wizard pounded his own chest audibly. \*I am not responsible. I refuse to share Her burden anymore. No more! It is illusion. It never had to be this way!\*

The Headmaster read his hands quietly but slowly tilted his head, brows gently drawing down. He also replied in sign. \*A strange statement to make, Shyntre. Come, let us not be late.\*

*It's not 'strange.' It's true.*

Tremors passed through him as Shyntre walked toward the throne room where Wilsira had finally died and his birth mother had been set free of her compulsion. Phaelous had told him about what happened in the throne room only a few spans ago.

*"That was why Varessa could not be in the same room with you, son. She may have wanted to, but the Priestesses did not want her influence in your upbringing."*

Shyntre shook his head. *Why me? What is all this? What happened when I was born?*

When they entered the round throne room which showed no bare stone, Shyntre stopped and stared at the walls, forgetting his own curiosity about the Red Sister ranks present. He saw instead stylized tapestries of the Surface, a land of red dunes being embraced by the Spider Queen. The horizon and blue sky seemed farther away than ever, and the physical violet and gold throne set upon a staging area loomed larger each time he was brought here.

*Why wasn't it ever this clear before what I was looking at?*

Phaelous touched his shoulder, gently pushing him forward. Shyntre dragged his eyes from the dream-like landscape and blinked, recognizing Elder Rausery and Elder D'Shea standing alone.

Without the Prime. Without anyone else.

He glanced at the empty throne and the platform but felt the oppressive air of the place. There were nearby, the Queen and

Dread Mistress. Then he focused on Rausery, who attempted a smile to reassure.

*Does that mean Sirana is well on the Surface?*

Shyntre looked at D'Shea, as cool and quietly hostile as he'd ever seen her at any distance. If she desired to be in the same room with her son, Shyntre couldn't see it. Nothing had changed there. He wanted to flee to his room and lock the door.

*Why am I brought here?*

The hairs at the young wizard's nape stood up as magic and stone shifted. The Valsharess pulled a tapestry aside and stepped through, clasping Lead Jaunda by the back of the neck. Shyntre's eyes widened and he made room as the Red Sister was pushed forward to rejoin her Elders. The muscular female managed not to fall, catching her breath and her balance next to D'Shea. It had taken effort, and her forehead was dotted with sweat.

"We are not satisfied yet," said Her Majesty without preamble, like She cared not to stay much longer. "Perhaps with the Elder General returned to us, We can make faster progress."

"Yes, Valsharess," D'Shea agreed, her chin up.

"The healer you kept aside for this mission, Elder."

"Yes, my Queen?"

"You and the Confessor shall research his bloodline in the Conceiver's code. Accept the Headmaster's aid. You shall hand off anything to do with Lead Jaunda's task to the General and work in the Palace in all things necessary."

The Sorceress stiffened. "Is not both Sirana and Jaunda's health proof enough he is untainted, your Majesty?"

Numb with disbelief, darkness washed across Shyntre's eyes as he realized who they must mean. They *told* Her a Consort was still alive after the purge!

*No. No. Don't faint.*

The Valsharess straightened, Her long, blonde braid reaching the floor. "It is not taint We wish to know, Varessa. If you would keep him where he is and postpone sanctions on House Thalluen for not making it known sooner, We shall know *how* he was made."

"Yes, Valsharess." His Mother was not eager with this new command, but Shyntre could think only one name then.

*Thalluen.*

His brother wasn't trapped in the Cloister with Red Sisters anymore but at Sirana's House. Was that why the dreams had stopped since Shyntre had left the Tower to live at the Palace again?

Desperately, he tried to mimic his Mother's poise, to match Rausery's calm breathing in the suffocating throne room. He couldn't blame the Elders for talking; there was always a point they couldn't keep things from Her anymore. They were doing it smart, using Jaunda and her mission as the example of his value, borrowing time for his brother, who had little left no matter what happened.

*Don't cry.*

Was he here to listen only to torment? The wizard saw no purpose for his summoning and knew how this usually went. *She* learned *everything* he tried to keep for himself eventually. Yet he kept resisting.

There might be things She did not know about him yet.

The Valsharess turned tawny eyes toward the two males in the room, and they both looked down.

She said, "The Dread Mistress awaits you both outside her Pit. Go, Phaelous. Take him."

*What?!*

"Your Majesty!" Elder D'Shea cried out of turn. "Is my son to be sacrificed? If so, I beg a hearing first."

*My son?*

Elder Rausery and Lead Jaunda looked as stunned as Shyntre felt, but a glance at his sire showed him only resignation.

*Damn this goddess.*

The Valsharess looked at the Elder Sorceress and smiled coolly. "No. Auranka will simply not wait much longer. Phaelous knows what he must do, Varessa. As always."

There was a heavy silence as his birth mother gathered herself.

"Do they need escort, my Queen?" D'Shea asked.

"He never has before. Do you volunteer?"

"If you wish me to change focus to Wilsira's code, I may attend the Headmaster and Your favorite and be sure they return safely."

The Valsharess stood pillar-still, Her eyes boring into the Sorceress. Her lips barely moved. "You may not bear well what you see."

D'Shea stood like she prepared to stop a cave-in by will alone. "A Red Sister bears as she must for the security of Sivaraus and her Queen."

The ancient Davrin chuckled softly.

A pause.

Then the pillar became flesh again.

"We think the Keeper will enjoy seeing you beside them for once," She said. "Go, then. You are all dismissed."

"This isn't wise, Varessa," his sire whispered after they had appeared in a jump circle high above the Seventh House.

D'Shea tucked a red-leather finger beneath her earlobe. "What's that? You're protesting *now*, spineless tutor, when it makes not a cunt-lick of difference?"

Shyntre covered his face with both hands.

"Auranka feeds on a state of mind like yours," the Headmaster replied with more anger than his son had heard until then, though restrained by Shyntre's standard. "You add to our son's danger, you do not lessen it."

The Elder motioned them to follow her down the tunnel steps that would take them through Highwall. "Yet the Valsharess allowed me to escort."

Phaelous followed the Red Sister and, awkwardly, so did Shyntre, keeping his mouth closed.

"She has never seen you challenge any circumstance for the well-being of either of us," said his sire.

Her whisper drifted back to them. "Wilsira took my ability to do so. I am here now."

Shyntre grimaced at that. *As if you care?*

This was grasping for control, like all Matrons trying to claim a sliver of their bua's life.

"It's only curiosity in how you'll behave with your compulsion is gone." Phaelous sounded calmer. "She'll never allow you to place him, you know that."

D'Shea spun around, and they nearly collided. Shyntre was surprised how powerful both her presence and her scent were in the tight tunnel.

"The Conceiver is gone, and *we* shall work on untangling her bloodlines with the Consorts. Do you think we will not find Sisterhood blood in them, Phaelous? I wager you know who quickened which Priestess's essence, and which unfortunate Sister squeezed out that last Consort in the Forming Pit. You could save us both a lot of aggravation speaking it now."

Phaelous put up both his hands in submission at her pointed display of temper. "Varessa, I promise you; I do not know those answers."

"So be it." D'Shea spun around again, her cloak flowing before slapping against the wall. "One way or another, the Sisterhood will unravel that infectious law giving Priestesses the right to pull our children from our wombs and block our involvement. Perhaps my own son wouldn't be tempted to roll his eyes at a simple offer of protecting the one I carried for two turns, most of it in a slightly comfortable prison."

Shyntre felt his face flush, resenting that she somehow made him feel guilty about that. *Apologies, Elder. Would that I could have chosen never to be born.*

They crossed the Highwall in silence, the young wizard attempting to reconcile his growing alarm at D'Shea's pressing involvement with some grudging admiration that she sought change not for herself alone but the Sisterhood as a whole. They were still a venomous nest of ass-fucking humpers who taught each other how to violate those weaker than them, but the greedy Priestesses filling the Third level of the Sanctuary with stolen, parentless Davrin to keep as slaves and livestock in magical experiments was worse, he thought, though not by much.

The Valsharess and entire Sanctuary had systematically *approved* what happened to Auslan and all those like him. At least any conflict Shyntre had with the Red Sisters, no matter how painful, it usually stopped when they lost interest or a cait or bua proved strong enough to withstand it.

*They can break you but don't really consume you if you don't let them.*

Braqth and the Abyss was a whole other matter.

The three Davrin were near the Drider Pit when they appeared within the next jump circle on the far side of a massive rockfill. It was close enough to smell the sickness of the Driders clustered in their lairs. Shyntre had never been here before, yet he felt ill with the dread that he must doubt if that was true.

"*Wellll…*" cooed a hungry, seductive voice above, making his heart skip. "What a surprissse. I so enjoy new sssurprise."

Glimpsing the massive arachnid legs above them, Shyntre jolted in fright, and Phaelous moved in front of him. D'Shea took position in front of the Headmaster as the three looked up at the shape changer, making out what they could of her in pitch blackness.

Auranka was mostly Davrin from the waist up; her wild hair hung down, partly covering her face, and large breasts swung with nipples seeping a magic-laden, milky fluid. Her hips and Elven legs disappeared in transition to the clinging shape of a spider large enough to pounce and pin a Sathoet to the ground. How those eight legs clung to the stone upside-down, Shyntre didn't know, but he dared not look closer.

"Varesssa," Auranka greeted, folding her bristled arms underneath her leaking breasts. "You ssseem out of place."

"I'm their escort," replied the Sorceress. "Phaelous is to conduct a trade, I believe. A quaff of your milk for the same of his purple liquor. I am to witness only the trade and nothing more."

The Drider Keeper began cackling. "Oh? Oh. Ssomething iss left out of that exchange."

"And what is that?"

"Who it's for. Assk him."

Auranka turned her neck, an ordinary tilt of curiosity which went too far, crackling her spine and turning her head right-side-up as she peered at them. She had two large, glowing eyes and six others speckled on her temples. Shyntre shuddered, though D'Shea went still.

"Asssk," the Keeper insisted. "Go on."

Phaelous slowly looked between them, his face conflicted when the Elder Sister glanced at him suspiciously.

"What does a quaff of milk do?" the Sorceress asked instead. "Is it poison?"

Phaelous shook his head. "No. A small amount induces trances."

"Trances?"

"He ssstopped dreaming," Auranka chuckled, pointing at Shyntre and creeping down the wall toward them. "I am not to be given a bua ssacrifice in my Pit while Queen fretss over mind flayerss, under *his* ssuggestion." She flipped dark, clawed fingers toward the Headmaster. "I have fed on this *withered* one long enough. I will take his bua's dreamss for now. Shyntre musst sssuckle my titss and dream for me, by his Queen Mother's command."

Shyntre clutched Phaelous's sleeves. *That's why we're here?*

What was his sire going to do, hold him up while she shoved his mouth onto her nipple? Probably. The Valsharess had commanded the Headmaster, and Shyntre was to take his place.

*I'm going to puke.*

Meanwhile, D'Shea showed her suspicion. "Dreams? I don't understand."

The Keeper shrugged, eight feet clicking on stone as she kept crawling. "You do not rule, Varesssa. Why would you?"

There was movement out of his periphery, and Shyntre dared a glance toward the Drider Pit. He saw the massive spread of web; thick, glossy ropes blocked the entry into the cave. There were lurkers on the other side of it, clicking and hissing inquisitively, no less menacing than their Mistress. Not only was Shyntre near to vomiting, but he had to grab the head of his penis and squeeze to keep from pissing himself.

*Goddess, no. I hate it here, so much.*

Auranka came fully off the wall. Streaks of glimmering, wet fluid decorated her breasts as the dark nipples continued to leak. She swept tangled, blazing white hair back and grinned to show fang, creeping toward Phaelous and Shyntre. The younger heard a high pitch in his ears and wondered if he was about to faint again.

*No. Don't touch me.*

D'Shea stepped in front of her, blocking the way and holding up a bottle. "Fill it up, Auranka."

"Cute, Varesssa," the Keeper leered. "I prefer your sson's lipss ssucking my nippless, as he never did yours."

"Nothing wrong with drinking from a bottle. Shall I do the honors? I'm quite skilled relieving such pressure with no lips willing to help."

A snigger. "Awww, poor Sssisster."

"And not another cait after me. No regrets."

"Hehe! He's a bit old to need your guidance now, is he not?"

"The longer this bottle is empty, Auranka the longer you wait for your dreams."

Shyntre stared with jaw slack as his Mother didn't budge, though the giant shifter should have bowled her over. Auranka knew this as well but seemed curious, distracted, maybe. Phaelous did not speak or interfere, and remained somewhat of a shield as well, though his son detected a slight tremor in his right hand.

Eight eyes narrowed in the blackness. Her smile was gone. "Why aren't you at the Cloisster, Varesssa? Neglecting your dutiess to be sstubborn again?"

"Rausery's back," she said bluntly. "Now the Queen has shifted our focus."

"To what?"

"Dismantling the Forming Pit and decoding Wilsira's blood-lines."

"Oh?" Auranka's neck cracked again as it twisted the other way. "Ohhhh."

The Keeper grinned full again and pulled back her shoulders, presenting her laden breasts. "Very well, Red Ssissster. Take your 'quaff' in your bottle, and I shall take my liquor from the Head-masster."

"The liquor is in a bottle, as well."

"Of coursse."

Shyntre doubted he would forget the sight of his birth mother milking the Drider Mistress's bulbous mounds with a sure, gloved touch. Nor could he dislodge the unnerving giggles nibbling at his ears while D'Shea squeezed and massaged.

At one point, Auranka glanced his way and winked. Shyntre swallowed. The Elder Sorceress did this to delay him drinking straight from the source. He could be glad for a reprieve but knew why he'd been summoned.

"Sire?" Shyntre whispered, unsure what he meant to ask.

The elder wizard clasped at his son's hand where it clung to his sleeve, then let go and wiggled his fingers. Shyntre looked down and read the hidden sign.

*Whoever you wish to protect, remember them when you drink.*

He frowned, touched with doubt. Wouldn't that give Auranka exactly where he was weakest in his dreams? To imagine this creature stalking around House Thalluen right now…

*I can't think of him. There's always Sirana. I'll think of her.*

With a long, shiver-inducing purr, Auranka stretched her arms above her head when D'Shea had finished, and the two traded bottles.

"A pleasssure," said the wild shifter. "Until nexxt."

Their purpose complete, the Sorceress motioned sire and son toward the jump circle, and they obeyed without question. The massive Drider went still and watched them, her gaze making Shyntre's spine itch.

They were near the circle when the Queen's Keeper sprinted toward them with a bone-freezing shriek taken up and amplified by her children trapped in the Pit behind her web. Phaelous cried a warning; D'Shea spun and cast.

Auranka struck Shyntre's shield a tick before a burst of light whited out the tunnel and left everyone blind. The Driders wailed and hissed their displeasure along with their Keeper, though eventually Auranka's laughter rose above them as D'Shea pushed the two males in what Shyntre hoped was the direction of the circle.

"Ahhh, D'Shauranti," the Dread Mistress giggled. "Such fun your House has been, but your magic is almost gone."

Her voice withdrew into the tunnel leading to the Pit.

"Do be careful, Varesssa. Ja'Prohn tends to fail musstering the will to meet your passion the moment you turn your back. You are aware, I think."

*Stop. Stop talking!*

Shyntre felt his Mother take his arm and drag him over the stone. It escaped him how she could tell where the circle was, but he knew it as well once he crossed the border. Blind on all fours with star-spots flashing behind his lids, he closed his useless eyes.

"Get us across, Headmaster," D'Shea said, sounding winded.

His sire's voice burbled a response. "Yes, Elder."

*Did Phaelous just laugh?*

Shyntre turned inward, focused on Sirana and *her* smile as they escaped the Pit with Auranka's milk in a bottle.

Perhaps this slim, united moment was as good as it would get for his family.

# CHAPTER 19

JAEL CROUCHED DEEP IN THE BRUSH, WATCHING TWO MEN dismount and unsaddle their riding beasts for the day. The youngest Red Sister paid special attention to how they removed the tackle on their enviable carriers, imagining how to do the reverse.

*Familiar enough.*

She'd been tracking them for two days, those ridiculously obvious, moon-shaped hoofprints clear through her sun-blind. Twilight was rising, however, and the heat of the day was letting up. Jael stayed downwind of the camp, knowing the animals would smell her sweat even if the men wouldn't unless she was also close enough for them to see.

*The flowers up here must clog their noses.*

The lush collision of colors, scents, noises, and food had grown continually since Rausery's training in the mountains. If Jael had thought it was astonishing then, early summer on the Surface was an experience she could barely ignore long enough to sleep.

For half the distance, she had stubbornly gone on foot, coming down from the ridges to cross an unfathomably wide, flat river flowing along even wider and flatter grassland. It got worse when the river seemed to have babies, splitting and taunting her to ford it yet again.

Then, as Jael reached some real forest hills again, she was caught in the worst storm of her waking imagination. The young Davrin dove into a cave for cover from the battering light and claps of thunder, howling wind, and hard ice balls.

Before the raging weather had moved on, however, her shelter had filled to her thighs with rushing rainwater and forced her back out again, spoiling half her powders as she cowered with her hands over her ears and eyes squeezed shut in a barely adequate copse of trees. The storm had snapped a branch off and tried to hit her with it.

In a blind daze the next morning, Jael continued on with her boots squishing.

*I'll never be dry again.*

Ironically, she had felt her brain withered and burned into a shriveled fruit inside her skull the day after that. She was exhausted yet charged up hills becoming steeper, one after another, each scaled and descended again to leave her face down in the first water source to cool her overheating head.

She couldn't stop for long; she must continue. But once she had reached a high enough point, she had discovered how the mountains spread out in a thick swath of dark green.

All the way to Manalar.

*Fuck!*

Grumbling for several days, Jael had spotted the strange tracks following blatantly obvious paths through the hills and eventually remembered the Trade word she sought.

*I need a 'horse.'*

Now, two Humans were taking a long evening bedding down as Jael itched in the woods in more ways than one. They were larger than her, as Rausery said they'd be, so she didn't spring on them without watching first. Nothing about them seemed memorable except their stink and their light brown skin. They weren't speaking the trading tongue, either, which earned another sneer and wrinkle of her nose.

*All that time practicing, and I still can't make out the gibberish up here.*

This was just as well. She need not speak to claim a horse. Beyond that, just thinking of Sirana and Gaelan practicing with her and wondering what was happening with them only lanced the same festering pain in her chest every morning. She was better off in silence.

At least the Sun was gone after its most reluctant day yet. The hideous day ball seemed to claw its way across the blue expanse ever more grudgingly. She'd been told this would happen, but she hadn't believed it.

Or hadn't wanted to.

*"Your slim chance of success, Aurenthin,"* the Valsharess intoned, sorcerous fangs buried deep and paralyzing, *"rests on a Godblood new to the City of the Sun. You will know him from his followers and can reach him in a brief window at midsummer when the Sun claims the longest day of the seasons.*

*"This male Human will be outside Manalar shoring up defenses, preparing for siege. If he does not possess the shield at that time, you must find it."*

★Shield?!★ the cait cried. ★What shield?★

*"The light bearer,"* the Queen responded. *"A golden circle bearing the Sun and both moons upon its face."*

★But, but how will I—?★

*"Retrieve that shield for the mortal Godblood. Do you understand, Aurenthin?"*

★Yes, but where is it?★

*"In the crypt below. Listen to your blood, faint as it may be. The relic can turn the soul drinker, if not the one wielding it."*

★Soul drinker?★

The Queen ignored her questions then, continued speaking, weaving the geas tightly into her mind as She clutched the youth's throat.

*"We see the Deathless coming to Manalar. If this defending Godblood does not have the golden shield when the world eater arrives, you **will** kill the mortal man and then kill yourself for failing, Aurenthin."*

⋆*No!! Let me go—!*⋆

*"You have no defense against him. Above all, you must not be captured if you fail."*

The tortuous spell completed, Jael had been ripped out of the Queen's trance, her heavy body landing painfully on the stone as she screamed to be set free. The Valsharess's voice had thundered above her throbbing head. She had thought to escape to the Fringe then.

"You *will* find him and kill him, Aurenthin!"

Jael had stayed put, forced to bow to her Queen's demands. She left soon after with her Sisters, like them, unable to speak.

Now her days neared midsummer on the Surface; she felt it.

*I'm running out of time.*

The men in the forest began snoring, their horses' heads down. Jael wiped her damp cheeks with her glove, drew a dagger, and got to her feet.

*Fuck this shit.*

She couldn't leave anyone behind who could chase after their horses.

One man's saddlebag contained a map with a river she'd just passed and the roads pointing to Manalar. Jael couldn't read the script but had learned the basic symbol reading skill from Rausery and stole this along with the sorrel red male horse, who was calmer in the presence of blood than the blonde-brown one.

The map gave her an idea of her bearing and distance, offering her hope that she might travel that far and make it in time.

*Maybe ten days out? Instead of twenty or thirty.*

She couldn't travel at night because the beast couldn't see, but the time saved would make up for it. It had to.

The young Davrin was only three days using her pilfered animal when she first saw sign of being trailed. She wasn't following the easiest roads but the game trails and ravines, so two evenings with the distant scent of a camp fire this far off the nearest road gave her pause.

*Hm. Shit.*

She pushed her horse harder the next day, although never losing the direction of her goal, taking wilder paths across barren stone and up streams where the mount would not leave moon-prints behind.

That evening when she and the horse needed rest, the smoke fire was still there when the wind shifted and, that night, she heard a man yell. She had to accept they could track this horse as easily as she had.

*But how? It is not by using their eyes.*

They were also not gaining much ground while she kept moving, like they were following a vague feeling. Or a beacon.

*Magic, maybe.*

Jael scowled at her various gains, unreasonably angry that she had no way to narrow it down. It could be the map, the saddle or blanket, the bridle, or anything in the bags, though she'd only really kept the food and water. The various trinkets and sunburst symbols had meant nothing to her; she left those behind.

*Get rid of it all. Throw it away.*

But how would she guide the horse?

Jael studied the map in the last of the fading light and again in the weak, grey dawn, then tossed it and everything except the bridle and horse down the next steep hillside.

*Let them track that to a discard pit.*

Staying on the wide back of the horse was difficult without the saddle at first, but Jael clung how she would to a lizard and did not

447

lack the strength or endurance to try. Maybe she was worn after that first day, but she didn't smell a camp fire all night.

*And I'm getting closer.*

The final days were toughest, as more passageways through steep and rocky hills required her to use roads over game paths, and ever-increasing wagons, distant voices, and animals could be heard. There were also hearth and cooking fires in isolated but frequent mountain cabins and huts. Her progress slowed to a crawl as she spent more of her time evading Humans or, as a last resort, silencing those who spotted her and made noise when they did.

In time, it simply became necessary to remove the bridle from her horse and slap him away to run off somewhere else. She simply couldn't hide and travel at the same time with the creature.

*Ridiculous. How will I approach the fringe, much less the Godblood with followers? How will I get over the stone walls of the wealthy if the poorest of them build such things?*

Yet she couldn't stop. Or turn around.

She'd tried.

*Slim chance at success, indeed.*

Jael didn't know how to tell exactly which day was "midsummer" but her first hint was the odd, burgeoning sound rising up from behind a sheer-faced mountain and drifting out through the rustic valley. Some clusters of Humans living in relative isolation seemed to respond to it, playing whistles or beating drums.

When with the sounds came scents of plenty—food, flower, and fire—and Jael realized it must be a crowd. A celebration.

*A festival when a siege is coming?*

Perhaps the common people simply didn't know yet. This "Godblood" hadn't told them though he was preparing.

*Or maybe that's only the Queen dream-jism talking.*

Jael winced at the sharp stab in her head, which sustained an aggravating throb while she waited in hiding. Resigned to spend yet another humid, itchy night in the Paxian mountains, she pondered limited options for finding the Human she sought. Experience told her she wouldn't get excessive rest before she would move forward again, with or without a plan.

Her headache grew, however, her circumstances ill-improved by the time a small troop of armored men on horseback clopped and clanged their way down the mountain valley road.

*Wonderful. Their sound will linger in my ears all night.*

Irritable and exhausted, Jael did not notice at first when the pain in her head suddenly receded. This realization came to her as she spotted the man in front wearing a blue cloak and enough quality trappings to know he was someone of high rank.

*"This male Human will be outside Manalar shoring up defenses, preparing for siege."*

Sneaking to get a better view of the warriors, Jael then noticed how many of them—all but one—had a cloth shirt over his chest piece, brazenly showing a golden circle dead center and two silver curves on each side, upon a blue background.

*"You will know him by his followers. ... A golden circle bearing the Sun and both moons upon its face."*

Did he have the light bearer already? Was her mission complete before she'd set foot here? She didn't know, so she couldn't move away. With a sigh and a quiver, she moved closer, hoping to overhear them speaking in Trade.

No such luck.

*What woofing birdsong is this?*

In uncanny timing, a bird of prey squawked directly above her, grabbing Jael's attention in time to see it squeeze some white goop out from beneath its tail. She leaped to one side, biting off a curse as the spotted raptor's leavings tagged the corner of her cloak.

*You cursed bloat of feathers!*

Blinking impertinently in the dimming day, the bird squawked much louder, its voice echoing in the valley, and the one, round-cheeked rider without any armor at all looked their way. Jael tried to go still, but the creature swooped from its branch and dove toward her head, its talons clipping her hood and pulling it half-down to expose her white hair.

*Fuck!!*

"*Capitan!*" said the beardless one, pointing as Jael attempted to draw back. "*Atapone!*"

"*Ci,*" said the leader in the blue cloak. His first action was to dismount and remove his helmet, handing it to the youth. "*Istea lito, Templari.*"

"*Aye, Capitan,*" replied the troop of men.

Jael groaned, clutching the next tree over from the bird splatter, and kneeled closer to the ground in case she retched. She had tried to run from the men who'd spotted her thanks to that bird.

*I c-can't. Damn you, V-Valsh—*

The Capitan came forward alone, showing both his hands empty. His hair was blond and long enough for the wind to catch it, lifting in his long stride.

"*Paxi!*" he called. "Peace!"

Jael was snarling when she couldn't understand but blinked at the one recognizable word. She didn't believe him, especially when all his men dismounted as well and grabbed either bindings or blades. In thoughtless panic and without advantage, the Dark Elf darted several paces downhill, somehow thinking to outrun them for as long as it took into the night.

"Wait! Don't run!"

The sprint was short-lived regardless. Jael's entire middle seized, strength left her limbs, and she fell upon the sharp rocks, vomiting up her last meal as her head swam and pain streaked up from her knees and arms.

*Oh, goddess! Argh, make it stop!*

"Willven!" someone cried in an oddly hushed voice, light boots running over the stones much quicker than the man in heavy armor. "It's her! It's her!"

"Slowly, Tam. Slowly."

Jael flushed with fever and then deep chill as it took a giant's strength to scramble to her feet. She drew a dagger, didn't trust herself to throw it, and gripped it far too hard as she brandished it; she was shaking.

"Back!" she snarled, spitting the sour taste from her mouth.

"We do not want a fight," said the Capitan, holding his hands where she could see them. He had no ropes or chains or blades on him.

But his men did.

Blackness swarmed her eyes, and she nearly toppled from her feet until she gasped, "Shell! Sh-shell!"

"What?" he asked.

She stuttered, flailing with her hands and her flashing blade. "H-Had y-y-sh-sh-*argh!*" She cursed her Mother's favorite insults until she got her tongue working again. "Had you *shell!*"

The Capitan was only confused, shaking his head, leaving himself open to attack without fear. He had modest dark blond hair growing on his face and deep blue eyes like Sirana; Jael saw them flick to the beardless, pale-skinned male joining them. Jael growled when the young man held out a leather-wrapped arm and called the crying falcon to land there on command.

*Fuckin' magic.*

"Shell?" he asked the other.

The falcon mage shook his head. "Sorry? What shell?"

*"Grrrr,"* Jael rumbled, trying to sign and motion a shield-shape, her dagger flashing, pointing at the symbol on his chest.

He frowned with baffled caution.

*Stupid Godblood.*

*"Capitan!"* called one of the men from the road. *"Dyos Guerrimos ist cheginto!"*

The blond man's jaw tightened as he dared not look away from Jael but slowly lifted a hand to sign acknowledgement instead. Seeing the sheer fright on the bird mage's face, however, hearing him gasp, told her it wasn't good.

Jael looked toward the backside on Mount Sonai, though her ears had already told her what to look for. Another group of men on horses galloping up the road, pushing hard.

"Why are you here?" asked the Capitan, enunciating every word. "Please. Dark Elf, I know what you are. Speak now, for God's Warriors are coming."

Jael shook her head, not sure what that was supposed to mean. "Had you shell?"

His pale, bearded face grew more concerned. He exhaled, glancing to where his men were preparing to block the path and hail the newcomers.

Jael didn't know how she was going to get out of this.

*I'm going to die painfully. Slim chance, as She said.*

Finally, the Capitan removed a dark blue glove to bare his hand to her.

"Willven?"

He murmured reassurance to the falcon's mage and held out his hand to Jael. "May I touch your skin? No harm to you."

Jael stared at him, felt her eyes get big. She couldn't remember the word for *why*.

More shouting at the road as the two groups of men came close enough to interact. The Capitan Willven held his focus on her, his hand out. Jael fidgeted, pointed at her forehead with one finger but kept her blade out, making a jamming motion. He nodded his head, understanding that much.

The Godblood willingly stepped up to her dagger and placed his dry palm on her damp forehead. He watched her face, and she readily looked at those blue eyes again.

*~I am Willven Isboern. What is your name?~*

Jael's body froze stiff, but her thoughts leaped all over the place.

He smiled. "Jael. Well met."

She swallowed. It was a perfect Davrin pronunciation.

*~Why are you here?~*

She thought it and then wanted to scream.

"A shield?" he asked, glancing down at the symbol on his chest. "No, I have not found a shield like that. Why?"

She groaned aloud. *Oh, goddess, no!*

"The Deathless?" He shook his head. "Is that one of the Ma'ab coming here?"

His thoughts had plunged in so easily, drew her answers out from around any magical block, like so many pebbles from silt, that there could be no doubt what he was.

*He's like the Tragar.*

She hadn't imagined it was possible. The Surface had *psionic* Humans!

*~Jael?~*

*Stop!!*

Jael lifted the dagger and brought it down, ramming it above his collarbone. She spotted red but the tip hadn't gone deep before she pushed him away, the Godblood clutching his wound.

"*Willven!*"

The Templari retaliated, and she was struck by several crossbow bolts before she could stab herself with the blade. Jael collapsed as their boots made the ground tremble.

"*Volti!*" the blond man shouted, lifting high a blooded hand. "*Queti atres!*"

The boots slowed, closing with caution. Before Jael could pass out from shock or pain or failing her geas, the Godblood gathered her close to him, his touch light when he took her jaw. They met eyes again.

*~I'm sorry,~* he said. *~I will help. Please, trust me. It doesn't have to be this hard.~*

Jael understood him perfectly. She chuckled as the shock spread much like it had after fighting the Tragar for her life. Soon it would pull her under into darkness, and Sirana wasn't here to make her drink a potion.

"I-It... *do*," she replied before going limp in the Human's arms.

# Acknowledgements

Many thanks to my readers and spot-checkers. Reading your renewed delight for these characters breathes life into these typing fingers!

*Eris Adderly, Leonard, Gerrit, Ile Depak, Dark Pulse, NecrosisBob, Axelotl, & Pastor of Muppets.*

Much love to my Hubs, for hug breaks during long days.

Deepest gratitude to *Doc Kangey*, for his work and encouragement through this year as we build a **new series archive** for www.Etaski.com

My recognition and sincere appreciation for my top patrons!

*Sir Cumference, Baelus, Lesley P.L.A.Y., Does, John K., Roy & Stacy Meyer, Julie S., Jesse C., Paul B., Carla H., Briana R., Josanna, RainbowNight, Kalculyszero, Daolord, Raymond T., Lexanii, Zeroharas, Elan, NotSoWeird, Neil M., & Fingon.*

# ABOUT THE AUTHOR

Etaski has entertained herself with fantasy stories since the first day she sat on a school bus looking out the window. When hand-written letters were disappearing, she scribbled no less than five pages to be worth the postage. Her early stories were written by hand, and she had a writer's callus and three embarrassing novels before graduating high school.

She studied science, archaeology, history, and theater. Frank discussion of sexuality was rare growing up, so she wrote fantasies, theories, and observations within stories for deeper contemplation or just be entertained.

History speaks little on sexuality, yet biology demonstrates how it sways basic choices. Drama reveals our strongest bonds but may fade to black at its most intimate. In the Sister Seekers, the sex and the story are inseparable, and their discoveries will change the journey of Miurag without cutting away.

Please consider leaving a review of this book. It truly helps!
smarturl.it/etaskiamazon
www.goodreads.com/etaski
www.bookbub.com/authors/a-s-etaski

Sign up to Etaski's newsletter for Sister Seekers releases at:
www.etaski.com